Tunnel Vision

Book One of the

Eyes to See Trilogy

by

Darrell McGowan

Enlightened Publishing Company

Tunnel Vision

Book One of the Eyes To See Trilogy

Enlightened Publishing Company paperback edition published in 2016

ISBN 978-0-9975870-0-5 (pbk)

Acknowledgements:

I am as dependent on gifted storytellers as any who've ever ventured forth to tell a story of their own. I'm grateful for my grandmothers who read to me while I sat on their laps. I'm grateful for my mother who only occasionally threw me outside after I'd spent most of the day in my room reading. I'm grateful for my many devoted teachers who introduced us to truly great stories, and nurtured our imaginations.

When anyone undertakes something as time-consuming and as maddening as writing a novel, he or she needs at least a few folks who will consistently encourage and affirm. I owe tremendous thanks to Liz DiTomaso, Lynda and Rick Hamilton, Jerome Santos, Mary Bright, and Ann Bray for reading my first draft, offering constructive advice, and telling me it was wonderful, even when it was very, very rough. Special thanks to Lynda for all the editorial help!

I am especially grateful that, as the years rolled by, those closest to me loved me whether I was writing or not, cheered me on every time I sat down with my manuscript, and never tired of me talking about one day finishing what I had started. In addition to those I named above, I am grateful for Dominique McGowan, Jonathan McGowan, Susan Britton, Hunter Britton, Myrna McGowan, and Frank McGowan.

Writing is a lonely endeavor, but the loneliness is bearable if the writer has a community to which he can return when he stumbles away from the keyboard. I love all of you for being that community to me!

Dedication:

To my beloved children, Dominique and Jonathan, for all the love you wrung from my heart and the subsequent lesson that there is no limit to the love that can pass through us. Thank you for so consistently and generously returning my affection!

To my beloved partner, friend, confidant, and fiancé, Susan, for loving me through the completion of this project, proofreading the final draft, and reminding me by your very presence and your consistent, supportive words that dreams do come true.

Contact Info:

Darrell McGowan can be reached at

darrellmac@mac.com

or on Facebook through the Tunnel Vision page:

https://www.facebook.com/eyestoseetrilogy/

or through the Eyes To See Trilogy website:

https://eyestoseetrilogy.com

Table of Contents

Chapter 1

The chief night shift guardian was in a rage long before she turned the corner and saw the intermittent blue light indicative of her nemesis. The telltale light flickered from a solitary station of the otherwise dormant study, and she felt her blood pressure rise with her pace as she raced to the door.

Adele Cuff was charged with keeping order and maintaining discipline in the nursery and she took personally any action that made her job more challenging. She knew who she'd find sitting in front of the computer monitor in the study, and she knew what he'd be doing. She'd seen the little outcast there so many times she'd lost count. He was always staring at a screen flashing text and images so fast it was mind-numbing.

On several previous occasions, she'd taken time to watch him. He never moved, never reacted in any way to the flashing screen. He just stared. He'd blink occasionally, but the only other discernible movement was the opening and closing of his fingers as his right hand floated above the control pad for the computer.

As near as she could tell, the boy was looking at or looking for something academic. She never saw any images she'd suspect a 12 year-old, curfew-violating, stiff-necked kid to be viewing. She only caught pages of text, interspersed with diagrams, charts, and the occasional small photo. But he must hear her coming, thought Adele. It didn't matter what he thought he was doing, she reminded herself; he was, in fact, violating the rules—and that made his intentions irrelevant.

Slink just saw images racing by in breath-taking ascent like steam escaping a boiler, yet he effortlessly absorbed every idea, equation, and image they contained. On and on they came: mathematics, chemistry, physics, engineering. Each appeared for no more than a second before being supplanted by the next. He glanced, he captured, and he retained the information they bore. It was as effortless and natural as breathing, only far more satisfying.

He didn't really feel the first strike; everything just disappeared in a blinding flash. Then his ears started ringing like a firecracker had exploded too close to his head. Had he been struck by lightning?

With the second strike came darkness. He felt the third strike in his aching bones, then his burning muscles, and finally his paralyzed lungs.

Slink was vaguely aware of his body crashing to the ground. Surely something had hit him, he thought, as he fought desperately to open his eyes and find shelter from the storm. When he finally managed to crack his eyelids, Slink was startled to see cold metal posts rising from a tiled floor. Then he registered a dozen or more lights bathing him in their sterile glow, and suddenly--sensation--the cold floor against his backside, searing pain along the right side of his face and neck, down through his shoulders and along his side. The ringing in his ears subsided enough to hear--something. What was it?

He dimly registered movement to his left just before he felt the back of a hand make contact with the side of his face followed closely by the back of his head cracking the tile floor. His ears rang anew, their complaint reaching the back of his eyes. His vision clouded again, shrouding his assailant. He couldn't fight through the swirling fog quickly enough to avoid a fifth blow, a foot striking his solar plexus. He instinctively rolled onto his side and brought his knees up to his chest. His panic rose as his lungs begged for air, overcoming his aching body's desire for unconsciousness.

"What the hell are you doin' here?" a deep female voice demanded.

"How many times do we have to go through this?" she continued.

"If you think I'm going to get tired of kicking your little butt and leave you to do whatever you please, you have another thing comin', Mr. Macdonald," she bellowed.

This time he saw the kick coming, but he was powerless to do anything about it. His shoulder took the brunt of the impact just as the first breath finally seeped into his lungs. The sound of air across his vocal cords gave the impression Slink was trying to say something.

"Eeeee," he squeaked.

"Pleeeeease?" Mrs Cuff mimicked.

Suddenly she wasn't bellowing anymore, her words rolling off her tongue with a sickening sweetness between wheezes. Her piercing black eyes, peered from under her equally black bangs and over her puffy red cheeks. "It's too late for favors, my little friend. Ya knew the risk when ya chose to leave yur bed durin' curfew. Actions lead to consequences. Ya know that better than most, don't ya now?"

She grabbed Slink by the back of the neck and pulled him to his feet. The exertion made her reach back to steady herself against a post. Three or four at a time amid her asthmatic gasps, her words barely churned over her lips.

"I don't know...why yur comin'...down here to stare...at a monitor all night...instead of sleepin'...in a nice warm bed...but I don't really care."

Mrs. Cuff hacked and spat and her words came in bigger chunks,

"We must be makin' yur life too comfortable. We'll fix that. Evenin' kitchen duty outta do the trick. For the next several weeks...when ya finally make it back to the dorm...you'll be too stinkin' tired to leave your bed."

Mrs. Cuff half carried, half dragged Slink through the room. He was tall for his age, but he was rail thin. None of the outcasts had a chance to get fat, but they were wiry and limber where Slink was skinny and frail. Slink hadn't yet started his final growth spurt, and he was already well over five feet tall. Mrs. Cuff was a full six feet and she outweighed him by a hundred pounds.

3

She tightened her grip around his neck and shoved him out the door. The pressure of her grip cleared his head, though, and Slink recognized the entrance to the study as she dragged him through it out into the hall.

"I have to hand ya one thing, boy," she barked. "Every time I find ya here, you got some uppity science, math, or some other hoo-ha on the screen. Don't know how ya switch screens so fast, but ya ain't foolin' me. Think Mrs. Cuff don't know what a 12 year-old boy is sneakin' a peek of? Ya may fool the teachers, but I'm too smart for ya, Mr. Macdonald!"

By the time she finished belittling him, Mrs. Cuff had hauled Slink down the hall to the discipline chamber. She selected her favorite tool of the trade, a long, bright red paddle with holes drilled into it.

"Ya know the routine, Slinky. Bend over and grab yur ankles," she commanded.

The first swat knocked Slink against the wall. He'd learned he was going to end up there eventually, so he now stationed himself a few inches from the wall so he wouldn't have to crumple to the ground, pull himself up, and resume the position so Mrs. Cuff could hit him again. The second and third swats spread the stinging down his thighs and into his knees. The fourth and fifth ones froze his trembling legs in place. When Mrs. Cuff reached down and pulled him upright, Slink gasped. He never intended to hold his breath, but he found the first swat always took his breath and he never managed to inhale again until the beating was over. Five swats was the most allowed at any one disciplinary session, and Slink had been receiving the maximum as long as he could remember. It seemed odd to Slink that Mrs. Cuff thought nothing of violating the limits of corporal punishment, slugging and kicking him elsewhere in the giant nursery complex, but she always followed the rules inside the discipline chamber.

"Third time this week, Slinky! Think I'm enjoyin' this more than usual," Mrs Cuff chortled. "Ya do keep my blood flowin', I'll give ya that. Now get yur aching butt back to bed before I haul ya out of here and hit ya some more!"

4

Slink shuffled out of the room and hustled down the hall, around the corner, and into the outcasts' dorm. He knew the pain was going to get a lot worse, and he wanted to be coiled on his side in bed with his pillow between his teeth before it hit.

The hardest thing about these beatings, as far as Slink was concerned, was that he could never remember leaving his bed and going to the study in the first place. As far as he was ever aware, he was just having very vivid, bizarre dreams--always with the endless parade of images--never the kind of dreams his friends reported. Every image bore complex information, but Slink never had a problem remembering each one in vivid detail. Why, then, couldn't he remember leaving his bed? He was always mystified when Mrs. Cuff started hitting him and he awoke to find himself at a desk again. She said she wanted to know why Slink was so stubborn. Heck, he wanted to know what drove him to the study night after night.

Slink tried to puzzle out his late night wanderings as the stinging in his butt gave way to burning pain and the tears started trickling down his cheeks. The skin on his buttocks and the back of his legs felt like it was on fire. He forced himself to think back, to try to remember waking up, getting out of bed, walking down the hall, sitting at the desk, turning on the monitor--anything. He couldn't remember one step of the journey he'd obviously taken.

Slink sometimes thought maybe his wanderings were caused by the surgeries to correct a rare pituitary disorder. After all, the surgeons had stuck instruments into his brain. Maybe they'd nicked something, damaged his ability to regain consciousness once he fell asleep. The pain running down his backside overwhelmed his thoughts, and Slink started to whimper. He curled his body as tight as he could and wished the mother he'd never known were here now, wished he could escape the nurseries and Mrs. Cuff, wished his life was a nightmare from which he would awaken to find a loving family gathered around his bed soothing his discomfort and wiping his tears.

Jonathan and Adela Lansing's great grandson never heard a robin sing, never saw a sunrise, never felt the rain softly pelt his skin or the wind blow dust in his eyes. Stanis Web Macdonald lived his first twelve years in a bubble, or to be precise, he lived his first twelve years under a dome, one of three giant domes he shared with Garsow's three thousand other inhabitants of the Ideal Society. Stanis grew up thinking his name was Slink. He knew neither the source nor the meaning of his nickname. He left the Garson nurseries, the only home he'd ever known, just after his twelfth birthday. His was not a grand rite of passage as was common for children coming of age, but a quiet disappearance noted only by a few nursery guardians, his dorm mates, a small surgical team, and a handful of people who knew of his notorious heritage.

Every child on their solar-edge outpost grew up in a nursery, and nearly every child left that nursery between the ages of ten and thirteen. In respect to his nursery upbringing, Slink was much like any other Garson child. In most other respects, he couldn't have been more different.

Slink cared for the citizen children two years younger than he and helped them prepare to take their places in the society from which he was forever excluded. One night, as he was performing his nursery duties, Slink's life took an unexpected turn.

He'd heard of the Technoids, but he never expected to encounter one of the notorious terrorists. The Technoids knew all about Slink long before he ever heard mention of them. Though they spent nearly all their time in the tunnels just beneath the Garson surface, the Technoids had better access to information than the average citizen of the Model Society. They knew more about Slink than he knew about himself: descended from Garsow's first family, separated from his famous family when they were imprisoned for treason. In addition to information the Technoids gleaned from the Supernet, the many outcasts who escaped the nurseries ahead of Slink had told their Tunnel Rat and Technoid rescuers of the bizarre boy so fascinated with learning that he endured countless beatings to pursue forbidden knowledge. They reported overhearing the guardians' whispered references to the Lansing family whenever Mrs. Cuff hauled Slink off and punished him for overstepping his bounds.

The Technoids were the only organized resistance to the Model Society. Desperate to avoid the mandatory surgical implant of a commlink, a dozen women and men had gone underground and formed the Technoids, swearing to bring down the Supernet, the wireless network at the heart of the commlink technology.

By the time Slink came to the Technoids' attention, nearly three generations after they'd forsaken the surface, the Technoids recruited most of their members from the Tunnel Rats--nursery escapees living a marginal existence as scavengers in the service tunnels beneath Garsow. When the Technoids learned Slink was the great-grandson of Jonathan and Adela Lansing who'd become symbolic of the resistance movement, they set out to add Slink to their ranks. They turned to a beautiful, young Tunnel Rat named Neoko who had refused the coveted invitation to join the Technoids so she could apply herself to freeing as many children as possible from the servitude of the nurseries.

Garson society's mandated commlink couldn't be tolerated by a small percentage of its members, and if those "unfortunates" survived a failed attempt to implant the commlink, they became nursery attendants. Within a generation, Garson had more nursery attendants than it needed.

The Tunnel Rats were the subject of halfwitted social commentary and halfhearted legislation. Politicians depicted the Tunnel Rats as a drain on the Garson economy, though in reality every would-be nursery attendant who joined the Tunnel Rats relieved their society of the burden of supporting them.

Beyond the economic relief the Tunnel Rats provided, they filled other essential roles for the Model Society. Every society needs scavengers, and every body politic needs scapegoats.

Neoko regularly visited the nurseries in search of the free spirits who could not abide a life of servitude. Those who never resisted their relegation to nursery duty could not imagine enduring the hardships of tunnel living. Neoko drew from amongst the unfortunates those who would choose a life of freedom even when it meant harsh living and further marginalization. Recruiting for the Tunnel Rats or Technoids was a capital offense. Hers was dangerous work, and she relished it!

On the fateful night of his departure as he entered the pantry for yet another clandestine meeting with Neoko, Slink couldn't be certain he'd spent his last day in the nurseries, but the goose bumps running down the back of his neck betrayed his hope. He couldn't place a finger on any one reason he thought this might be the night. She'd said nothing to tip him off or asked him to make any particular preparations. Of course, he knew Neoko would not and could not. He'd seen some of his fellows disappear. Their few belongings were always in order the morning their absence was discovered. Though they'd almost certainly cooperated in their disappearance, (there was never any sign of struggle) they'd clearly made no plans in anticipation of their departure.

Slink yearned to escape the ever more frequent beatings he was enduring. He'd made no progress understanding what compelled him to leave his bed two or three nights a week. He still couldn't once remember waking and walking to the citizen's study. His fellow outcasts avoided conversing with him for fear of being thought guilty by association. Slink ached to be free.

From early morning to late evening, the pantry was filled with outcasts working at a feverish pace, so naturally it was deserted after dinner as everyone scrambled for a few hours of rest for their weary bones. During the day, the kitchen was filled with the pleasant aroma of baking bread, fresh fruits and vegetables, simmering soups, and hearty stews, but the scents elicited no joy amongst the outcasts. For them, the kitchen meant seemingly endless days of hard work and food became little more than a requisite for survival.

Most of the outcasts kept their heads down, did their jobs exactly as they were trained, and stayed out of the way. No matter how many times he resolved to go along so he could get along, Slink couldn't resist the impulse to improve on recipes and regimens. He had to fine-tune the soup with some fresh oregano or polish off the french bread with a little egg-white glaze. He was always asking why "this" and why not "that," to the point that the head chef, who had a soft spot for Slink, took to calling him "Mr. Why." Slink was never satisfied knowing what he was expected to do, he always wanted, no, he needed to know why he was supposed to do it, and if he thought he had a better approach Slink seldom asked anyone for permission to try it out.

By the time he was eleven, he knew every recipe the kitchen offered and could prepare any dish requested. None of his fellows ever taught him anything, shunning the lanky kid who had a way of attracting trouble. Still Slink watched, he learned, and he mastered everything around him.

Now as he stole through the deserted pantry, Slink thought about the first time he'd met Neoko. He'd been in the company of his fellow outcast, Dante, who along with Slink, had been assigned the punitive evening duty of laundering the soiled aprons, towels, and dish rags in the basement rooms beneath the kitchen. Dante was about a foot taller than Slink and hadn't yet grown into his feet. Though his final growth spurt had spread his weight more evenly over his frame, he was anything but athletic and his face still looked like it belonged to the pudgy kid who'd worn it for the first sixteen years. Dante was serving evening kitchen duty because his upper body had yet again set a pace his lower body could not keep while he was conveying the midday soup to the serving table.

Slink and Dante had shared this duty many times before. Slink felt bad for Dante, thinking it unfair that Dante was being punished for the effects of a growth spurt he did not choose. Dante felt for the younger Slink who seemed incapable of escaping the wrath of Mrs. Cuff for more than a couple days at a time.

In each other's company they found an unspoken camaraderie forged in misery.

Images of Dante gave way in Slink's mind to the tantalizing image of Neoko as he stopped along the back wall of the pantry and slumped down on his haunches. Slink smiled to himself, transforming his habitually gloomy countenance. If anyone else had wandered into the pantry at that moment, they might not have recognized the young man crouched down and staring wistfully across the kitchen through sparkling blue eyes. Early for what he hoped would be his last rendezvous, Slink now waited in the shadows of the quiet pantry and reveled in some of the sweetest memories he had.

On the night of their first fateful encounter, as he and Dante entered the pantry, the odor of cleaning compounds was already giving way to the pleasantly sour smell of rising bread dough. Slink had drawn the moist, tangy air into his nostrils and known without looking the cooks had doubled the usual amount of dough. The citizen children were in for a pleasant surprise!

Dante and Slink had gathered the aprons and other laundry, and just as they had turned to leave, Slink had seen her. She'd been squatting in the corner near the rear entrance to the pantry. She'd held a slab of bread leftover from the loaves Slink had helped bake earlier that morning.

Dante had threatened to call for security before being silenced by a wave of Neoko's hand. Later that night, Slink would think back and realize Dante had only feigned surprise at Neoko's presence.

She'd been dressed to look like a man, but with the hood of her cloak pulled back and her shoulder-length jet-black hair pulled outside the cloak, her masculine attire couldn't hide her gender. And those eyes...Slink had been transfixed by the young woman's gaze; he hadn't even seen her subtle hand signal to Dante, hadn't made the connection that Dante knew her.

Neoko had looked to be Dante's age, about six or seven years older than Slink, but it hadn't taken long for Slink to realize she was a thousand times more worldly wise than either boy.

She'd held herself alert to every movement, every sound, every nonverbal cue of the boys in front of her, yet her voice had been relaxed and steady when she'd spoken. Her eyes had darted from Dante to Slink, from Slink's eyes, to hands, to just over his right shoulder while her almost lyrical voice had broken the silence between them.

"Well, ya goin' to stare at me all day or offer me somethin' to go with my measly crust of bread, boys? You can tell by lookin' at me that it's a bit long since my last meal, eh? How's about gettin' me a plate of whate'er it was you had for supper, boy?" She'd stared at Dante as she spoke the last few words.

"No problem, miss. We're always ready to help someone in need. Back in a flash."

She'd showed her teeth in what might have been a smile if it had ever reached her eyes. Her lips had closed over her teeth as she'd waved Dante away, and he'd disappeared before Slink could take his eyes from Neoko.

"Never seen a visorless outsida', have ya?" she'd asked.

While Slink had stood speechless, she'd chuckled and said, "no, the only visorless folks ya'r used to seein' live with ya here, they do. You'd not be used to seein' anybody come through a door from beyond yar little world without a damned visor."

It had finally dawned on him then. That was why her gaze had held him mesmerized—her dark eyes were easy enough to get lost in, but his mental alarms sounded because those beautiful eyes should have been hidden behind a visor! When she'd gazed at him through those dark brown eyes, Slink had felt like Neoko could see right through him. Then she'd shocked him even more by pulling a visor from her long, black cloak and slipping it onto her face, deftly tucking the lead wires under a braid of her hair and hooking them there so they seemed to emerge from her scalp as they would any Garson's.

"How's that do ya, honey?"

Slink's knees had buckled and he'd dropped to the floor. It was strange to see an outsider without a visor, but it was impossible for anyone to attach or detach lead wires from his or her skull.

Slink had seen the visor demonstrations offered the citizen children while he completed his housekeeping duties or set supplies out for a class. He knew the visors could be removed to sleep, but the lead wires were disconnected at the visor, not at the person's scalp. Neoko's visor was a fake! She'd jerked the visor off her face and bent down over the trembling boy. Her countenance had hardened, her eyes had narrowed, and her Alpha Sector drawl had disappeared.

"I'm sorry to hit you with this so quickly, Slink, but I don't have time to go through the song and dance I usually do when I meet a new potential. We need you to join us. I grew up in these nurseries and I knew, just as you know now, there was no way I could be a servant all my life. The taunting and teasing of the citizens (she spat the word more than spoke it) got to me because I knew they were no better than me. If I couldn't be one of them, and I couldn't remember ever wanting to be, I needed to get away from them completely. Tell me you want more than anything else to be forever free of them. Tell me that, and I'll make your wish come true. Tell me!"

Her eyes blazed brighter then, black pupils swallowing their brown irises. Her high cheekbones and sharp, pointed chin had seemed sculpted from Garson stone. Slink had felt lost in her gaze, and Neoko had seemed ready to pounce on him and shake the answer she wanted out of him, but his momentary shock had been no equal to his seething hatred of this place. He had been in constant pain from the relentless discipline he'd received for what was characterized as his stubborn, uncooperative attitude. The ruthless beatings had neither softened his bearing nor broken his spirit. He wasn't meant for the servile life of a nursery attendant, and he'd known it long before Neoko asked him to articulate it.

"I hate this place!" he'd croaked. Then he'd raised his face and locked eyes with Neoko. His voice had steadied, then grown hard. "The citizens...the guardians...and most of all, Mrs. Cuff! I hate everything about her!"

Slink had drawn a long, deep breath.

"I want out...and I'll do anything to get out," he'd hissed.

Questions had poured over his trembling lips before Slink took another breath.

"How are we going to get out of here? When do we leave? Will I need to bring anything? Where will we go? Will anyone else be with us? Will you stay with me?"

Neoko had stopped him with a gentle finger across his lips when he'd finally paused to inhale.

"We'll leave without warning one night when I come to meet you. Be ready each time you hear my signal."

He'd opened his mouth to question her, but had stopped when she raised her hand in front of him.

"Dante will teach you how to know I'm coming. You know nothing of the Model Society, and I can teach you little. I've been away from the surface too long to teach you much about its ways. I live with others who've rejected the society that would reject us. We live beneath the surface in the tunnels your great-grandparents designed and developed."

Slink had again opened his mouth to speak, and just as quickly Neoko had raised her hand to stop him.

"We'll speak of your family only when we're safely away from here. When I've brought you to the tunnels and shown you to safety, I'll tell you the story of the Lansing family, and you'll better understand why I've come for you. For now, know I'll come several more times before I take you. Each time we meet be prepared to listen and learn. I must do all I can to prepare you before I try to bring you out. Life in the tunnels is hard, and you must know more of the trials that await you before you walk away from the comforts of the nursery."

Dante had returned and Slink had listened as Neoko spoke of dark underground passages, hard sleeping pads, long dangerous days, and endless chores. In her words, Slink had heard only hope. Slink's response to Neoko's tales of danger and hardship in the tunnels had revealed his destiny.

After Neoko's second visit with Slink, Dante had disappeared. She'd said nothing when Slink asked about Dante the next time he'd seen her. Her slight pause and half smile upon hearing

13

the question had told Slink all he'd needed to know. He'd yearned every day since then for the day he'd join his friend.

Neoko had used her subsequent meetings with Slink to school him on the nature of the Model Society. Outcasts usually identified the commlink with the visors that covered every Garson citizen's eyes. In reality, the visor was the least intrusive piece of the commlink hardware. Three chips were implanted into the recipient's brain. Transmitters and receptors were fused to the inside of the skull. Of the three chips, one monitored, interpreted, and broadcast information on its host's identity and vital functions. This information was commonly used to bypass the need for introductions, communicate changes in emotional states, and alert others to rising tensions before they erupted into conflicts. Subtlety was impossible with the commlink, but so was dishonesty. Before long, Garsons prided themselves on their open, honest society, where conflict was rare and mutual understanding was nearly universal.

A second chip translated data from the Supernet servers into text or images for viewing on the lenses of the host's visor. It also relayed information from the host's cognitive centers to the Supernet computers. Colleagues could collaborate on projects with stunning efficiency, since every contribution was cross-checked and either stored in data banks for retrieval or bounced back to its contributor for error correction. News and information on any vital subject was instantly accessible.

The third chip translated information into auditory signals that were transmitted through a jewel implanted in the ear of the host. "Linked" individuals, then, received supplementary information through their ears as well as their eyes. A more visual person, because he was more responsive to visual information, would soon find his commlink feed favoring the visor, and consequently, would see most of the information as text or images. A more auditory person, given her heightened response to auditory information, would automatically receive more data via the jewel, and as a result would hear most of the information as a pleasant synthesized voice.

The additional information was, at first, disconcerting to the uninitiated, but given time, the average Garson quickly adapted, then became dependent on the constant images flashing in front of his eyes and/or the promptings in her ear. There was no need to respond to the subtle visual cues of body language or interpret the occasional unspoken gesture. All such non-verbal information was translated by the individual's commlink and broadcast to any appropriate recipient.

If outsiders had come to Garsow without first undergoing a commlink implant and orienting to its use, they would have been stunned by relative stillness of Garson society. The dome-covered, barren landscape provided far less stimulation than Earthlings expected and Garson citizens fit into their surroundings to a degree that would have been unnerving to the most introverted Earthling. Fortunately for Earthlings and Garsons, they seldom met.

Garsons did not have leisure time. They spent about half of every standard day working, where they were kept on task with constant feedback from the commlink. Most of their remaining time was spent in the modest confines of an apartment limited to 300 square feet plus 150 square feet for each additional person in the same household. Upon coming home from work they first followed a uniform fitness regimen, then ate an evening meal, before enjoying an hour of organized recreation or relaxation carefully designed to meet their needs as identified from their commlink's biofeedback. Finally, they prepared for the following day's work before retiring to their sleeping pad for sex with their partner if the desire was mutual, or sleep if not. These activities were guided and reinforced through the commlink. Single adults were scheduled for two nights out each standard week where they would gather in one of six social clubs. Married couples spent one night each week in the clubs. Teenagers also had one night a week out.

No accommodations were needed for children or their parents, since children were raised in the communal nurseries until age twelve.

The commlink made communication with "unlinked" adults or children uncomfortable, even baffling. Subtlety, manipulation, humor, outright lying, and other indirect or non-verbal communication was lost on the "linked." Fortunately for the children and their hapless parents, Garson had a natural supply of "unlinked" adults to raise their children.

These rejects of Garson society though publicly referred to as "unfortunates," were seen by citizens as unfit for their society. From the time he was born, Slink and the children of the other unfortunates had been the last babies fed, the last to have their diapers changed, and always the last to receive any attention. The first unfortunates were people whose neurological structure would not tolerate the commlink. By the time Slink joined their ranks, most of his fellow unfortunates were offspring of these neurological misfits. Their sin was genetic; Slink's was genealogical. None of Slink's peers knew there was any difference. The paths by which they came to be outcasts didn't matter. Slink and others like him shared the fate their grand society visited on those who could not or would not conform.

Shortly after he learned to walk and talk, the nursery attendants (whom most referred to as guardians) began preparing Slink to join their ranks as they trained him to care for the children who would one day be respectable members of Garson society. Even without their close-cropped hair, no one within the nurseries would have mistaken any of the outcasts for citizens. The outcasts were never allowed to mix with the citizens. They were given different dress, met in separate classrooms for instruction, and ate in separate dining rooms. The outcasts waited tables for citizen's meals, cleaned the citizens rooms, and held the gaze of their naked, unworthy eyes at the floor, lest they look into the eyes of a citizen. Gazing into the uncovered eyes of a minor citizen brought shame to that child, and any outcast who dared to shame a citizen quickly regretted it.

Slink would never have the status or the recognition automatically granted all the children for whom he cared. Before he could even string two or three words together, he knew he was different from the citizen children, and they knew it too. He was a victim of prejudice in a society that prided itself on its openness and acceptance. Had his parents been members of a racial minority, a religious sect, or even a radical political party, he would have been afforded the same privilege any other Garson citizen enjoyed. Unfortunately, he was an outcast before he was ever born because his forebears had refused to be fitted with a commlink or after being fitted for it, had taken their visor and crushed it underfoot at the now infamous final episode of the Garson Awards.

He had no way of knowing he was descended from those who led the early resistance to biotechnology. Most who shared his fate had parents who seized or stroked when the leads for the commlink were implanted. They were born into their misfortune, had done nothing to deserve their fate as outcasts, and were afforded a modicum of pity blended in their daily draft of disdain that poured from the visored eyes of Garsow's citizens. By the time Slink approached the age of passage, three generations had come of age since the commlink technology had become pervasive on Garsow. In 60 short years, to be seen in public without a visor went from the norm to an exception that labeled one a pariah. Those who once opposed the commlinks and the visors that marked their hosts quietly dropped their opposition or were forcefully silenced.

For almost three standard months, Slink had met with Neoko about once a week, knowing to meet her in the pantry whenever he heard the syncopated rhythms of the Alley Cats echoing through the dormitory sound system. Neoko could hack the system without raising suspicion, since no one paid much attention to the endless white noise of the looping music. Purely by coincidence, the music he and Neoko used as their signal would occasionally pop up on the evening playlist and Slink would venture to the pantry for a rendezvous that never materialized. On those occasions, he could only hope nothing had happened to Neoko, since he had no way of knowing whether she had met with interference or he had heard the music by virtue of the random playlist.

On the night of his departure, however, Slink entered the pantry without any doubt Neoko would be waiting for him. The telltale tingling down the back of his neck had started half an hour before he heard the Alley Cats.

The moment he saw her, any lingering doubt disappeared! He felt weak in the knees and ready to jump for joy, so of course he stumbled over his own feet and nearly knocked her over. She had a dark blue cloak for him, identical to the ones worn by residents of Garsow's Alpha Sector. Slink had no idea what Sector might normally wear the cloak; he just knew Neoko wouldn't have brought it unless she was taking him with her!

If the cloak wasn't enough to get his heart racing, Neoko pulled from beneath her cloak a shiny new black visor! To be sure, it was not fully functional, but no one glancing at the pair would ever be able to distinguish them from any other couple out for a walk. Even if they were attentive to the feedback of their visors, any observers would simply receive a signal from a jamming device Neoko wore under her cloak saying:

Neoko Aguilera
18 Circle E
Alpha Sector
<PRIVATE>
or
Stanis Macflory
26 Circle B
Beta Sector
<PRIVATE>

Slink was tall for his age, so Neoko was only a couple inches taller than him. Neoko had chosen a night designated for teenage socialization so they could pass as a young couple out for a date, and a young couple's privacy setting wouldn't raise an eyebrow. If the two should encounter someone who had clearance for a deeper scan, their limited broadcast would raise suspicion. Fortunately for Slink, Neoko was especially adept at avoiding those encounters.

Slink fitted the visor to his face and found that, though its lenses appeared tinted from the outside, they did little to change the view of the wearer. The visor pinched the bridge of his nose a bit, but it'd be tolerable. All that mattered was the he'd pass for a newly initiated citizen of the Model Society.

Neoko was not concerned about Slink's appearance. She was determined to avoid any close encounters during which any- one might notice something out of sorts. Neoko knew Slink's movements and manner, not his dress, were far more likely to draw attention. She was bent over him, whispering rather harshly, a few inches from his face when he regained awareness of her.

"Snap out of it," she hissed. "This may all seem fascinating to you, but if you don't stay focused, we could both be arrested. When we leave here, you're goin' to see things that make you want to stop and stand with your chin on your chest. If you do that, we're doomed! Keep your head down and the hood of your cloak pulled over your head, see?"

She yanked his hood roughly over bristly scalp and kept pulling the hood until Slink was staring at his shoe tops.

"Someday, you'll have time to see the wonders of our little rock, but not tonight. Don't look further than your next step. Life in the nursery has left you ill prepared for this little jaunt, but we can't help that now."

Neoko cuffed Slink lightly across the side of his hooded head.

"Listen to me!"

Slink had started marveling at the many pockets of his cloak before Neoko had even finished her first sentence. This was the most excitement he had ever known. Now he was supposed to set aside emotion and concentrate? Right!

19

Neoko knew she was asking a lot of Slink; no, she knew she was asking the impossible. On top of overcoming the excitement he felt, she wanted him to shut his inquisitive mind away and concentrate on her words and on taking one step after another. She knew the boy couldn't comply, but she could no more refrain from making her demands than he could conform to them.

Neoko encountered challenge with every outcast she freed from the nursery, but Slink was younger than most and more distractible than any she'd freed. She'd known before setting out that evening that freeing Slink was going to be dangerous!

After taking a few deep breaths and repeating her instructions more slowly, Neoko knew she had little time to get Slink out of the nursery, across the transway, into Alpha Sector, and to the remote alley where her friends waited for them. They slipped out the door from the service porch to the narrow pedway running between the nursery and the next building. Neoko grabbed Slink's arm, pointing him down the pedway toward the transway that ran in front of the nursery. Slink did fine as he and Neoko walked the length of the narrow nursery pedway and turned to their right onto the broader pedway that ran alongside the transway.

As they emerged from the nursery pedway, and the view from the broader pedway opened before them through a break in the heavy pedestrian traffic, Slink noticed the evening sky of Garsow for the first time. During the evening hours, the charge passing through the biodome that formed the artificial sky was reduced by about seventy percent from daytime hours. It gave the sky an eerie green tint set off by yellowish waves that passed from one side of the dome to the other. The evening domed sky was remarkable, unlike the daytime hours when the dome took on a dull white glow like an overcast day on earth or the nighttime hours when the dome looked almost black.

They hadn't taken a dozen steps amongst the first group of pedestrians before Slink stopped dead in his steps. He'd never been more than a couple steps down the little pedway that ran alongside the nursery. In fact, he'd only been outside the nursery and a step or so onto the little pedway twice--both times for very brief periods, loading staples into the pantry when the autoloaders had failed.

Slink's eyes flew up to the cascading waves of yellow light, then to his right where the homogenous, round structures that looked like miniature clones of the nursery stretched as far as he could see like a perfect arrangement of giant cereal bowls turned over to dry. Streaming all around him was a sea of visored pedestrians, and to his left sat idle transbots showered in the bright ambient lights of the transway. It all overloaded Slinks senses, and he froze.

Freezing up so close to the nursery would raise suspicion in all but the most disinterested passersby. Inspired by the urgency of the moment, Neoko recognized his paralysis and reacted instinctively; she leaned into Slinks wiry frame and purred,

"You're so right...this view totally reminds me of the first time we ever went private! You're so romantic."

Even while she looked dreamily down the transway in the same general direction Slink stared unblinking, she pulled herself close to him and leaned down to whisper in his ear. Two busy transworkers, grumbling about stupid kids standing right in the way of everything, turned to avoid them as Neoko hissed in Slink's ear:

"Wake up, Slink, or I'm dumping you back into the nursery pedway to fend for yourself!"

He started and stopped, then after another interminable pause, his gaze fell to his feet and he took a step with his right foot.

"Sorry," he croaked, "I never...."

His voice trailed off, but his feet kept moving, first the left, then the right, now the left again. She coaxed him along with gentle whispers in between the loud giggles and mindless comments she bellowed for anyone within earshot. DAN agents were few and far between, but the pedway was far too crowded with people for Neoko's liking. Slink was moving now, but Neoko knew that he hadn't seen anything yet, and she feared he'd be incapacitated if he ventured another glance above his shoe tops.

For the next few minutes, Slink's fear kept him focused. He'd seen the duties assigned the outcasts who'd disappeared only to reappear days or weeks later. He knew if he wanted to live outside the nurseries, he'd only receive one chance to do so. He listened to Neoko's voice, stared at his shoe tops, and counted steps. Still, he was only twelve years old, and he couldn't hold onto any emotion, even terror, for very long.

When he was tempted to lift his head, Slink considered all the terrible things that might happen if he were caught, hoping this would help him ignore the wonders of the surface. Had he been a little older and more experienced, he'd have foreseen that engaging his imagination would inevitably draw his attention away from his shoe tops. Before long, his mind eased away from his catalogue of fears, he raised his head, and his eyes locked onto a gleaming object as big as the nursery hovering perfectly still above the transway as if it were weightless.

The transbot was awesome! It was huge! Even in the dimmer evening light, it shone as if someone had polished it; no, as if a hundred people had polished it all day. It hummed with a low whine Slink could only compare to the sound of the big nursery washing machines on their spin cycle. His body followed his gaze and he turned and stood staring at the gleaming, whining cylindrical object. He realized it was floating at least four feet off the ground!

Suddenly, someone appeared in a doorway that seemed to magically materialize in the side of the transbot. Then a staircase emerged from somewhere beneath the floating floor and provided a graduated path from the doorway to the ground! The person in the doorway descended the stairs in Slink's direction while he stood immobilized, staring open-mouthed.

"You're going to get us both killed...or worse!"

Neoko's words would've escaped him had her hand not closed around his left shoulder, fingers biting into the soft tissue just beneath the bony curve of his shoulder. Her arm was wrapped around him behind his back and she spun him back to his right. She was wheezing as she fought back the panic that rose swiftly in her throat again.

"Listen to me, Slink. We have to cross this transway a little way up from here, and you can't falter."

"NO, SILLY, THAT'S NOT SAMMY. SAMMY WORKS DAYS!" she bellowed and followed it with raucous laughter.

"Any hesitation will call attention to us, and the crossing is under constant surveillance. Do you know what that means? Someone is always watching."

Slink took a deep breath and nodded, then dropped his eyes to his shoes.

"COME ON, WE'VE GOT TO GET HOME SO YOU CAN SEE ME AGAIN NEXT WEEK."

"They'll snatch anyone who stops moving while we're crossing, afraid some fool will try to stow away on a transbot. Keep your eyes down and keep moving. Do...you...understand?"

He was embarrassed to recognize how easily his attention had been drawn from Neoko and the task before them.

"I'm sorry," he rasped, breathlessly. "I won't do it again. I promise!"

Once again, his fear served him well, and he watched his feet and started counting. He could only hope his focus lasted longer this time.

As they approached the crossing, out of the corner of his eye Slink saw a sudden flash of reflected light illuminating the translucent barrier that separated them from the expansive transway. He hadn't noticed the barrier before because it was nearly invisible. Constructed from some sort of transparent material, it was as tall as any of the smaller buildings on the other side of the pedway, and was made up of long panels connected at points Slink had taken for light poles. Now he saw these poles were the connecting points for the great panels as well as the structures for the light sources lighting their way as they walked alongside the great transway.

"Slink!"

He snapped his attention back to his shoes and resumed counting his steps. He'd never realized staring at his shoes could be so hard!

Neoko knew crossing the transway was the biggest challenge they faced. The crossings were always bottlenecks where life slowed to a crawl. As such, they served perfectly the purpose of those paid to be suspicious; DAN agents could silently survey the good citizens in search of individuals who merited closer inspection. The agents were easy to spot even when they wore plain clothes. They always stood in one place too long, looking like they were peering right through people.

Neoko had brought more than a dozen escapees from the nursery through this crossing and into Alpha. The oldest of the surface settlements, Alpha provided the easiest, most discreet entry into the tunnels. In Alpha sector, most of the entries to the tunnels were in remote alleys away from residential domes.

The previous day's article decrying the despicable Tunnel Rats had been written to pressure DAN to arrest more of the subterranean exiles. Neoko knew from experience that DAN would increase the number of agents on duty for a few days to appease the public. The article's appearance on the daily vid broadcast had nearly scrapped Neoko's plan to bring Slink out, but in the end, the many factors that favored this night as the one for his escape overcame the concern over the article and any reaction it might cause.

Neoko didn't know all the reasons the Technoids were so interested in this kid, but she was beginning to regret her promise to bring him out. She'd managed to maintain a professional distance from the previous escapees, but Slink had broken through her defenses almost immediately. The others she'd brought had been at least five years older than Slink, and though none of them was as bright as the precocious kid, they were more mature, more passive, and more desperate. Their age and their demeanor made it much easier to sneak them by any watchful eyes. They followed directions, kept their heads down, and stayed focused. Slink was too innocent, still too hopeful to bring out safely. Neoko knew he'd have suffered untold abuse every day he remained in the nursery, so she wanted to bring him out, but if they were apprehended--Slink's life would be far worse than he'd ever imagined.

She liked the kid--and that personalized her concern. She didn't want to end up in a detention center--the worst fate for a Tunnel Rat, let alone one caught smuggling nursery attendants. Still, she found herself trying to figure out how she could give herself up to give Slink a chance if they were stopped. He and his heartbreaking stories of the ruthless Mrs. Cuff had cracked, then shattered, any semblance of professional boundaries. His story called forth protective maternal instincts Neoko didn't even know she had. He'd become like a little brother to her, and she was starting to hate the Technoids for asking her to do this. If he was so important, why not leave him in the nursery until he could make this run without giving himself away so easily?

"HOLD!"

The command came while Neoko was still lost in her recriminations. She'd been so worried about Slink giving them away

25

she'd tipped the DAN agent off when she had walked through the entry point without waiting to be waved on.

"Access, please."

Neoko's pulse instantly doubled, her breath caught, but she managed to stifle a groan. The command called for everyone waiting at the crossing to activate public access to his or her commlink.

When Neoko failed to comply with the sharp order, Slink and she would be pulled out of line and questioned. She needed to explain why she and her companion would not go public. She'd never heard anyone else refuse the order when given. She gathered her wits, smiled without looking into the face of the DAN officer barking orders, and hoped her gift of gab would serve her now.

"I'd love to, sir. This long walk bein' private the whole time is creepy, you know? But my brothers commlink has been acting up. He just received it, you know?"

Her voice steadied and she let the words tumble from her lips so fast they blurred together.

"My Daddy--he asked me to take 'im to Urgent Care to have it checked out. It comforts 'im so for me to stay private with 'im, you know, so he can hear my voice over the interference he's gettin'. Please let me stay private for his sake, sir! He's only been out a couple days now and everythin' is still so confusin'--you 'member how that is, right? Well, on top of all the normal shit of gettin' used to 'is commlink, now he's got this screamin' in his head, and its scarin' him to death, you know? The doctor says it's just a minor adjustment, but it don't feel too minor to 'im, you know?"

By the time she finished talking, Neoko's words were coming so fast the agent was squinting like he was in serious pain. Neoko snatched a quick breath, but before she could say anything else, the man waved her forward.

"Get going, get going. Both of you--get goin'! We're not interested in your life story."

Neoko grabbed Slink and shoved him through the entry-way. They were half way across the transway before she took her next breath.

Slink had no problem staying focused for a good while af-ter the encounter with the DAN officer. The pain shooting up his arm from his wrist, where Neoko held him in her powerful grip demanded his attention. Twice, he whimpered for her to let him go, but her icy glance silenced him on both occasions. He had to race to keep up with her or be dragged across the transway and onto one of the pedways that led from the gate on the far side of the crossing. His legs were longer than hers, but he'd never used them for walking any distance. His calves were cramping, and his knees felt unsteady.

Neoko was not angry with Slink, but she was willing to let him think otherwise; she was determined to get him across the transway and into the relative safety of the pedways surrounding the apartments of Alpha. She'd nearly blown it once, and she was not taking any more chances. Once they reached the far side of the crossing, she glanced up at the female guard avoiding visor con-tact, and squeezed through the gates. Neoko didn't shove her way through the gate on the far side, but she held her ground amidst the jostling pedestrians squeezing through the opening in the bar-rier. She and Slink barely fit side-by-side as they jammed through the narrow opening of the transway barrier. They could've passed through more easily if Neoko would've allowed Slink go in front of her or after, but she never considered it. Slink was going to re-main under her protective right arm, his right wrist held firmly in her left hand until they made it to safety or someone pried them apart.

The DAN agents on the Alpha side were unconcerned about people passing into their quarter. Who would come here to cause trouble? Alphas prided themselves on being tougher than their counterparts, and they wouldn't tolerate some Beta kid coming to Alpha to sow wild oats. The occasional Beta and Gamma kids who thought they could cross the transway and take on a new identity as one of the tough Alpha dwellers learned otherwise very quickly. Most Alphas quietly looked for an opportunity to pack up and move across the transway, but while they lived here, they fiercely defended their turf. The Alphas were the Garsons with whom the Tunnel Rats and Technoids had the most in common, since the former lived just a couple rungs up the social ladder from their outcast counterparts. And so, of course, the Alphas were the strongest persecutors of the Tunnel Rats and the Technoids.

Neoko brought Slink here for several reasons. Tunnel access in Beta sector and Gamma sector was almost nonexistent since the tunnels beneath those sectors had been built to serve only as service corridors. Unlike the Alpha Sector tunnels that originally served as underground communities, the Beta and Gamma tunnels were never built to accommodate human settlement. In Beta and Gamma sectors, nearly all the access shafts were built beneath surface structures that stored equipment in the tunnels. In addition, dressed in her best clothes, even without any stains, tears, or other telltale signs of tunnel dwelling, Neoko still would never have passed for a Beta or Gamma. When she was groomed and dressed her best, she could only hope to pass for an Alpha, most of whom were laborers. So her forays to the nursery were always brief and they always started and ended in Alpha sector.

Once she and Slink had walked some distance down one of the pedways and stood in the shadows surrounded by apartments that looked like clumps of interlinked, stemless mushrooms, Neoko pulled Slink into a dark passageway between two clumps of buildings.

"We're going to lay low here for a few hours, so we're not trying to cross the sector during curfew. We'll start moving again just before curfew ends and the morning chimes signal the start of the day. We'll have a short walk ahead of us, through some more apartment buildings like these. When the morning chimes go off, the pedway will fill with people, and you need to make sure you keep your cloak pulled up around your neck, like you're really cold. Your clothes underneath the cloak will give you away as someone who doesn't live here. You're too young to be here on any kind of business, and we'll be heading away from the Urgent Care center, so the story I gave the security agent won't do us any good. You just need to stay close to me, keep your head down, and let me do the talking, if there's any talking to be done. When we get closer to the vent shaft we'll be entering, a few friends are going to join us. When the time comes to enter the vent, they'll give us the cover we need to lift the grate and drop into the shaft without notice. We'll have only a few seconds, so you'll need to stick close and follow my lead. I'll go over all this again before we take off. For now, get some rest--you're probably more tired than you think."

Slink was convinced he was too wired to fall asleep. Nonetheless, when Neoko pointed toward the side of one of the dome shaped buildings and motioned for him to sit down, he did as she wanted. He looked around for a while, but they were tucked back in-between two clusters of buildings and there wasn't much to look at. Before long, he laid his head back, and a few minutes later, he was sound asleep.

He awoke with a start as he became aware of someone gripping his shoulder and shaking him. Neoko reassured him and reiterated the instructions she'd laid out earlier. Slink nodded mutely to Neoko's instructions. He was glad to be told to keep the cloak pulled up tight to his neck. He felt really cold, even though he knew the temperature was the same as it would be on any "night" on Garsow. "Day" and "night" were artificial constructs on Garsow, designed to maintain earthside rhythms of a 24-hour day, known across all the Solar colonies as a "standard day." The daytime temperatures were slightly warmer than the nights, only because some exhaustive government study had suggested people living in controlled environments functioned better when the daytime temperatures exceeded the nighttime temperatures, if only by a few degrees. This night was as warm as any other night. Slink knew it was surely a comfortable night, like every Garson night, but he'd felt chills running down his spine since they left the nursery and he now felt chilled to the bone.

They moved deliberately but not frantically, and Slink sensed that Neoko was no longer as apprehensive. She was looking in the entryways of the buildings they passed and even nodding at the occasional passerby. She seemed much more comfortable with this part of Garsow, and that helped Slink relax. He began to look around and noticed immediately how much different the structures looked. He struggled for a word that described their difference from Beta structures.

They didn't look older, though he knew from his clandestine studies that they were. Even to his inexperienced eye, the Beta structures looked softer and more appealing. His late nights at the citizens learning centers had taught him the buildings in Beta Sector were built as much for aesthetic as functional appeal with small differences in elevation giving them a sense of individuality. Alpha Sector buildings were never intended to be beautiful. Most still had airlocks left from the days before the domes were built over Garsow. The airlocks extended like long archways from the entrances to the bubble-like buildings. Slink couldn't tell by looking at a building if it served as a dwelling, a business, or something altogether different. Each one sat within inches of the buildings around it. They all looked like giant half-buried soccer balls made from a burnished orange-brown metal of some sort. It was as if Neoko and he had wandered into some great nesting place of a strange alien race that laid geodesic eggs.

Slink was shocked out of his reverie when the pedways suddenly filled with residents of Alpha Sector. It was as if they'd responded en masse to some imperceptible alarm signaling the beginning of the new day. In fact, that's exactly what had happened.

One minute he and Neoko were walking quietly amongst the domes in near solitude. The next minute, the doors burst open all around them and the pedways were jammed with pedestrians, most of whom were heading in the opposite direction of the two small cloaked figures who held close to each other and doggedly made their way against the stream of humanity.

At first, no one even seemed to notice the two weary pedestrians swimming against the stream of people heading for another day's work. Neoko knew it was not entirely out of character for young people to be out and walking the pedways early in the morning. She only hoped their direction wouldn't raise suspicion. She'd hoped to reach the ventilation shaft before the morning signal. She was familiar with the amazing way in which Garsow mornings began. Occasionally, maintenance work needed to be done during the night on the giant dome over one of the three sectors comprising Garsow. Though these maintenance projects posed little risk to the inhabitants, people had become accustomed to waiting for the morning signal on their visor before leaving their dwellings.

Neoko was only a couple of minutes from the ventilation shaft where she and Slink were to enter the tunnels when she heard Slink let out a cry, followed by cursing in a voice Neoko didn't recognize. Slink had been captivated by his first sight of a dog, and while he stood motionless staring at the animal, a man with his arms full of books had bowled him over and went tumbling onto the pedway following the same path of his precious books.

"Watch where you're goin'!" screamed the man. "These are valuable antiques, and now look at 'em!"

Slink looked down and saw the books strewn across the pedway with several clumps of pages separated from their bindings. He'd never seen books up close, but it was obvious even to his untrained eye the man had a legitimate complaint. Slink wanted to apologize, but he had a bigger problem. He dared not raise his head and reveal the nature of his dilemma, but the man was demanding he do just that.

"Look me in the face when I speak to you, young man!" the man bellowed.

Fortunately for Slink, Neoko intervened.

"Beggin' your pardon, sir!" said Neoko, adopting an Alpha drawl. She stacked the man's books on the pedway as words tumbled out of her mouth as quickly as they came to mind.

"We're rushin' to meet my uncle who's takin' my little brother under his care. I just can't manage for the both of us any longer, ya' know? Since Dad died, we can't make ends meet."

As the crowd of people walking along the pedway slammed to a stop, more than one hurled a sharp word at the three people blocking the path. Neoko wanted to grab Slink and bolt for the next intersecting pedway, around the corner, and down the narrow alley to the ventilation shaft her friends would be encircling. She drew a deep breath and released it. Neoko knew she needed to maintain a sense of normalcy for a few more minutes to get down the last stretch of the pedway without raising suspicion.

The bookman was calming down, although his voice still betrayed his irritation, even as it assumed a more erudite air. He no longer sounded like an Alpha worker but a man of letters.

"I'm sorry to hear about your troubles, young lady, but I haven't time for your troubles to become mine. I've enough troubles of my own. Life is no picnic for any of us, now is it? With the supply ship delayed again, we're going to have rations tightened once more, and I'm wasting away on the meager supplies we now receive."

In truth, the man did not look like he was in danger of wasting away regardless of any reduction in rations.

"Now, missy," he said, "would you care to explain to me why you and your brother have gone private? I'm a bit suspicious of anyone these days who is afraid to let others scan them. So I'd like to hear your explanation, if you don't mind."

Neoko responded without hesitation, bowing over Slink protectively.

"My little brother just received his link, don't you know? It comforts 'im for me to go private with 'im when we're in public. We don't mean no offense to you or any other."

The bookman raised an eyebrow and frowned.

"He'll never grow up if you protect him so. Now, I want both of you to go public, and I'll have a word with your brother. I want him linked while I give him a piece of my mind, so he can revisit my words when he stops blubbering. Come on...I don't have all day."

"I won't be doin' that to 'im!" cried Neoko. "He's havin' a tough enough time goin' to live with our uncle--a man a lot like you who'll insist he grow up and be quick about it. He'll have no choice in the matter soon enough, but for the short time we're still together, he's stayin' private, and so am I!"

"That's no way to talk to your elders, Missy!"

The bookman started looking around at the faces of people passing by on the pedway. Neoko was afraid the man was going to flag down a DAN officer and their charade would come to a screeching halt. Just as Neoko was trying to concoct the means to draw the man's attention, he stopped cold, then turned back to Slink and her as suddenly as he had turned away.

"I'm late already, young lady, or I'd stay right here and see your petulance punished. I suppose you'll have your way today, but your brother will be doing well to be rid of you. Perhaps he'll learn some manners living with your uncle."

He began to create one tall stack from the many small stacks of books Neoko had created on the pedway. He turned back to Neoko and waved she and Slink away.

"Well then, be off with you before I report the both of you for truancy and see how your story plays to the DAN officers."

Neoko took a deep breath, still bowed over Slink.

"Beggin' your pardon again, sir. And you may be right about my brother, but I'll have my way today and be glad of it. Good day!"

With that, Neoko grabbed Slink by the arm, pulled him up on his feet, and steered him away from the red-faced man as the pudgy fellow bent laboriously and stacked his books on the pedway. They'd nearly turned the last corner leading to the ventilation shaft when the bookman started yelling at the top of his lungs. Neoko couldn't make out the bookman's words above the

33

sounds of bustling pedway walkers, but the object Slink thrust in front of her face made the bookman's meaning easy to guess. Slink was holding half his visor, and the missing half was the one with the lead wire attached!

It took Neoko a second to catch her breath, but when she did, she just grabbed Slink and started running. They were sure to attract attention now, but she had to turn the corner and get down the alley before someone saw Slink's visorless face and put the sight together with the bellowing bookman, who was probably waving the other half of Slink's visor as he shouted. Neoko didn't need to see the sight behind her to know the urgency of reaching and rounding the next corner.

Slink kept replaying in his mind the encounter with the bookman.

He hadn't seen the man coming. When his face had struck the bookman's forearm and sent him flying across the pedway, he felt sick to his stomach before he felt any physical pain from the impact. He knew he was in big trouble and he knew he'd drawn Neoko into that trouble. Then, when he hit the ground and his visor fell from his face in two pieces, he knew they were doomed. He grabbed the broken visor, head bowed with his cloak hood pulled up around his face, crouched on his knees, and succumbed to the growing nausea.

He threw up twice in the time it took Neoko to spin another cover story. As he caught his breath, and his head started to clear, he felt Neoko's hand pull him to his feet by his arm and snap him around to face in the direction they were heading. He was vaguely aware of the visor piece falling from his hand as Neoko plowed through the crowd that had gathered at the bottleneck they'd created.

Now, as they rushed for the corner, Slink feared his mistakes were finally going to catch up with them. He couldn't look up for fear one of the people on the street would notice he wore no visor, yet he was desperate to know if anyone was trying to intercept them as they ran for the corner. When the cries of "Stop!" and "Grab them!" started from behind them, he had his answer.

34

Neoko removed her grip from his arm long enough to hook her arm around his back and under his armpit. She pulled him in tight to her even as she broke into a hard run. He couldn't keep pace with her, but he didn't have to. She was much stronger than her short stature indicated, and she half carried and half dragged Slink to the corner, twice slapping away hands that grabbed at Slink's cloak. They reached the corner, and just as Slink thought they would continue in the same direction, Neoko lunged to their right and darted into the alley. A moment later, they lunged to their left and into the tiny space between two of the dome-shaped structures. Neoko scrambled between the structures, dragging Slink behind her, then lunged back to their right into another alley.

Ahead Slink could hear voices yelling "Quickly!" and "Hurry up, before they catch sight of you!" As soon as they reached the people whose voices had urged Neoko and him on, and passed into the midst of anxious but friendly faces, Slink saw it. A hole no more than three feet across gaped right in front of him. Neoko released her grip on him and he fell to one side of the ventilation shaft. She dropped into it deftly, then popped her head

out and said, "Follow me, feet first. There are rungs along one side of the shaft." Before he could react, Neoko disappeared, then someone picked him up by the shoulders and dropped him into the shaft. "Catch one of the rungs with your feet, little man," said a disembodied voice. Slink threw his feet forward and his right toe caught a rung. As he was lowered into the tunnel he stepped down the rungs. Slink looked up and saw four brightly dressed people with long sticks pass between the shaft and the entrance to the alleyway. One dropped a ball onto the alley surface and they began to slap the ball back and forth. As he found the first rung with his hands, the arms holding him withdrew. "Stay close to Neoko, little man, and you'll be fine," said the voice. Then stripes of shadow moved across his face as the lights of Alpha Sector were filtered through the ventilation grate being slid back across the shaft. Above him, he could hear the cries of their pursuers and the feigned surprise of their protectors as he followed Neoko's persistent tugging on his pant legs and descended into the darkness.

Chapter 2

Dr. Henry White wanted to be remembered. Well, hell, he wanted more than that--he wanted to be famous. He didn't really care if his kids remembered him, which was fortunate, since he rarely spent any time with them and any remembrance they offered would surely have been unflattering.

He started working with the Solar Alliance Space Administration, SASA, when it was still a national entity of the former United States and thus known as the National Aeronautics and Space Administration or NASA. Truth be told, he never really "worked" for NASA, since he was an unpaid intern, but that was only a technicality as far as he was concerned. He gave thirty-four years to the bloody organization and he wanted his name to be synonymous with the expansion of SASA beyond the solar system. One day, when people referred to the Inter-Stellar Space Agency, ISSA, or some other such successor to SASA, he wanted them to know that it was Henry Malcolm White who made the dream of interstellar travel a reality.

Unfortunately for Henry, he never passed inorganic chemistry, let alone theoretical physics. If Henry was going to be famous, he was going to have to ride someone else's coattails to fame. The good news was that Henry knew how to spot talent and exploit it. He hated kissing butt, but he was very, very good at it! His talents in this area had already brought him two honorary doctorates, and with the passage of time, most people didn't even know that Henry had only a Bachelor's degree in Business Administration from the University of Phoenix.

Henry especially hated relying on the Lansings. He hated the fact that Jonathan and Adela Lansing had each earned Ph.D.'s at one of the most prestigious universities on the planet. He hated the fact that the Lansings were always two steps ahead of any other scientist working on the Light Speed Travel project. He hated the fact that they were filling the role that he had coveted for his own-- that they were making the actual breakthroughs that would likely lead to the illusive goal of interstellar travel. Most of all, he hated needing them so much. But need them, he did.

When the grate slid closed far above her head, Neoko's eyes filled with tears. She'd never before come so close to losing one of the kids she freed. Her straight black hair stuck to her face and neck as sweat beaded on her forehead and ran into her eyes. Her breath came in hard, sharp little gasps, accentuated by the lump forming in her throat. She was determined not to let Slink know how badly their run had frightened her, so she said nothing, took two steps down the rungs of the vent shaft ladder, tugged on his pants to get him to follow, and took two more steps. After three minutes that felt like thirty, they reached the floor of the service tunnel nearly 40 meters beneath the Garsow surface.

Neoko helped Slink off the ladder and activated the lumawand she pulled from her cloak. She pressed his hood back and looked down into his face for the first time since they left the street. He was chewing on his lip, and from the crimson color of his teeth, he had been at it a while. His eyes were red and swollen; his cheeks stained with tunnel dust following the tracks of his tears. His hair was matted to his head, and his nostrils shone in the dim light of the lumawand, the source of their sheen continuing down the cleft of his top lip, before he wiped his face clumsily with his sleeve. His chin told the real story, though. His jaw was set, and his chin jutted forward in defiance of the message the rest of his face might otherwise have conveyed. He drew his lower lip between his teeth so tightly his chin shown bone-white in the dim light of the lumawand. He was scared half to death, and absolutely determined to overcome his fear.

Neoko took him in her arms, and despite her resolve, her chest began to heave; she drew her next breath in a quick gasp, and then a series of little coughs gave way to a deep shudder, and she fought back her own tears. Slink held her close and his little body shook like a leaf, but he never uttered a sound. Neoko dropped into a sitting position and deftly pulled Slink into her lap where he stayed until they were both breathing steadily again. It might have been two minutes or twenty--neither could tell. When she could trust her feet again, Neoko lifted Slink from her lap and rose without words. Slink stood and brushed himself off more to occupy himself than to rid his clothes of any dust. Neoko reached for Slink's hand, and they started on their way down the foreboding tunnel.

From the first night Slink met Neoko and heard Neoko speak of the tunnels, he'd suffered from terrifying nightmares where his fear of the dark seeded his imagination. His dreams gave birth to lumawands that always failed at critical moments, dark shapes that emerged from tunnel walls to snarl and snap at him, and countless occasions where Neoko disappeared and left him to cry in the impenetrable darkness.

"I'm not afraid!" Slink exclaimed, not even aware he was talking out loud.

"Are you talking to me?" asked Neoko. She'd heard his words, but Slink's tone suggested he was speaking for his own benefit more than hers.

"Not really," replied Slink. He took her inquiry as an invitation, though, and gave voice to his thoughts.

"In the nurseries, I did everything I could to avoid having to turn out the lights. I hated being in the dark. I can't remember anything else that scared me, but I've always been afraid of the dark."

Neoko opened her mouth to say something then thought better of it and just squeezed Slink's hand.

"During one of my secret late-night study sessions, I learned there was a name for my problem: nyctophobia. There's even medicine that helps make it better. I tried to tell Mrs. Cuff what I had, so she could give me permission to see the doctor. She laughed at me, then she led me back to the dormitory, where she stood me in front of the other kids and told them to be nice to me because I was a nyctophobe. She never told them what "nyctophobe" meant, so she might as well have just told them I was a bed-wetting crybaby. The other kids just saw one more reason to tease me."

Neoko could picture the scene and imagine Slink standing in front of the other outcasts with Mrs. Cuff doing her best to make Slink the target of their ire. The thought turned her stomach! She knew the citizen children shared semiprivate rooms with up to five of their peers, but the outcast kids lived in one of two dormitories separated by sex.

"I put up with the other kids teasing me all the time. Their words didn't bother me much--I was more worried about what they might do than anything they might say. The other kids constantly looked for ways to trap me alone in the dark. I got to where I'd stop at any doorway and make sure the room I was going into already had other people in it."

"Kids can be cruel and kids who suffer great cruelty can be crueler than any others," thought Neoko.

"I'm sorry, Slink," Neoko said in a low voice, almost a whisper. "I can see why you might be afraid down here...."

Slink cut her off.

"But that's just it--I'm not afraid! I thought I'd be terrified, but it's not so bad."

Neoko gave his hand another squeeze and picked up the pace. Slink returned her hand-squeeze and lengthened his steps to match hers.

After talking to Neoko, Slink found his remaining discomfort had evaporated. They walked in silence for a while. When his imagination threatened to conjure demons from the shadows, Slink took comfort in the dusky orange luminescence of the widely staggered emergency lumatorches along the walls of the tunnel. He never saw one suddenly blink out, and they were spaced close enough that the darkness never had a chance to envelope Neoko and him.

"This tunnel is wide enough for more than twenty people to walk side-by-side without touching shoulders!" thought Slink.

Neoko pulled him along at a steady pace, but the tunnel floor was smooth, so he could look around without being afraid of tripping.

He imagined seven or eight people standing on each other's shoulders to reach the ceiling. There was no dampness, and the walls all looked like Mrs. Cuff had overseen their polishing with the same demanding eye she lent to cleaning the dining commons after every nursery meal. Everything on Garsow seemed like it'd been poured into the desired shape. Slink knew this wasn't far from the truth.

Neoko and he walked silently in the tunnel for what seemed like days--Slink guessed it was actually closer to an hour-- before they heard any noise other than their footfalls and the gentle buzzing of the lumatorches. When another sound came to his ears, it brought tingles up his spine. He'd never heard anything like it before. At first, he thought it was just the low growling hum of the lumatorches, fading in and out as they passed. When they paused so Neoko could adjust her cloak, Slink realized the sound

41

still faded and rose as if coming from a long distance. Gradually, the humming grew louder and it was joined by a brushing sound, along with irregular clicking noises.

Neoko was too lost in thought for Slink's or her own good. By the time Slink began to pick up the clicking noises and felt the tingles running up his spine turn to chills, Neoko emerged from her reflections with a start.

"We've got to get out of this tunnel--and quick!" she said, grabbing Slink under the arm and breaking into a run.

"Where are we going?" asked Slink.

"There's another vent shaft up a ways, and we have to get to it before the beetle spots us."

Neoko felt Slink's shoulders tighten when she said the word "beetle," so she explained as best she could while they ran.

"They're not really beetles, Slink. They're robotic ships with long arms that sweep the tunnels to keep them clean. They maintain all the pipes and conduit that run along the ceilings of the tunnels. You can't see them too well, but above us are the water, sewer, electrical, and Supernet lines for Alpha Sector. In Beta Sector, if anyone ever mentioned beetles in the nursery, they probably called them "maintenance drones.""

Slink's grip on her wrist loosened slightly as she spoke, but he still held her tightly enough for her fingers to grow numb. Neoko realized her explanation probably did little more than feed his imagination's image of the "beetles."

"That's fine," she thought. It wouldn't hurt him a bit to be good and scared of the beetles. If the drones found a human being in the tunnels, they made no distinction between human flesh and any other organic material. The maintenance drones were programmed to eliminate organics, and they were very, very efficient.

"Right up here," Neoko shouted.

She was almost screaming to be heard over the growing hum and rhythmic "shhhhh, shhhhhh" of the drone relentlessly crawling toward them. Slink could see the bottom rungs of a ladder extending from what had to be a ventilation shaft as Neoko pointed her lumawand just ahead of them and toward the right side of the tunnel.

"Hurry," screamed Neoko.

"That's stupid," chided a little voice in the back of Neoko's head. "You've got your arm wrapped around Slink and he can't help but keep up!"

Slink didn't need any urging. His pulse pounded so loud in his ears, it sounded more ominous than the approaching beetle.

"Drone," he exclaimed, even though his voice was drowned out by the sound sweeper. "It's not a beetle, it is not a beetle, it is NOT a beetle," he huffed as he ran.

He could see the lights from the drone and realized the tunnel turned upward and to their right about a hundred meters beyond the ladder protruding from the vent shaft toward which they ran. The turn in the tunnel seemed to slow the drone, because its humming changed pitch and the sweeping sound assumed a much slower rhythm.

As they reached the vent shaft, Neoko spun Slink around in front of her, reached down with one hand and grabbed Slink just above his knee, then grabbed his other thigh with her free hand, pressed him above her head, and finally lowered him until he was seated on her shoulders.

"Climb up until you are standing on my shoulders and see if you can grab the bottom rung of the ladder," she screamed.

She reached up and grabbed his hands in hers and steadied him while he brought up his left foot, slid his butt backwards to make room for his foot on her shoulder, then stood up on his left leg, bent at the waist to maintain his grip on Neoko's hands. He moved his right foot to her right shoulder, then slowly straightened up until, in one smooth movement, he released her hands and raised them above his head to grasp the ladder. Once he had ahold of the ladder, he jerked his knees upward and grabbed the second rung. Then, with another quick jerk of his knees, he reached for and grabbed the third rung. After that, he swung back and forth to get some momentum going, then swung his legs up and caught the bottom rung with is feet. From there, he

43

had no problem getting up the ladder and out of Neoko's way. After all that, it dawned on him: how was Neoko going to reach the ladder and get out of the tunnel?

As he looked down, Slink saw Neoko crouching, and then he saw her spring up and reach for the ladder. She missed it by a foot or more. She crouched again, then slowly stood up, looked into the vent shaft where Slink watched, waved to him and shouted something he couldn't hear, then stepped back out of his line of sight.

Slink was frantic. Was she leaving him in this vent shaft to fend for himself? And what about Neoko? She'd said they needed to get out of the way of the drone or they'd be killed. Was she giving up?

Just as the panic was closing his throat, he saw Neoko flash by the opening below him. Then, he saw her hands appear from the opposite direction, reaching for the ladder. She caught the bottom rung and managed to hold on as her momentum threatened to tear her hands loose. She may have only been a couple of inches taller than Slink, but she was growing to legendary heights in his mind! She had taken a running start, ran up the tunnel wall as far as she could and flung herself backward at the ladder. Slink didn't know it, but Neoko had been running the tunnel walls for so long it was second nature to her.

She shouted up the ventilation shaft, "Get out of the way! Move further up so I can get clear of the tunnel."

He was more than happy to oblige.

After the drone passed uneventfully beneath them and continued on its way, Neoko and Slink descended the ladder and walked down the big turn Slink had noticed in the tunnel. They were definitely climbing--Slink could feel it in his legs--and since Garsow had no hills or mountains, they had to be moving closer to the surface. Since the Alpha tunnels followed the path of the natural caverns from which they were developed, they had no uniform depth in comparison to the surface.

After a minute or so of gradual and steady ascent, the tunnel seemed to level out again, and they continued their relentless march. Slink was beginning to wonder if Neoko had a specific purpose to their wandering or if she was just trying to put some distance between them and the ventilation shaft they had entered.

The tunnel began to take another long, gradual turn, this time to their left. As Slink reached the point where he could see down the tunnel again, he stopped. Where before they had been able to see some distance down the tunnel with the light from the evenly spaced lumatorches, they now looked into a foreboding dark space. After they walked a few more steps, Neoko shined the light from her lumawand in a sweeping motion from one side of her body, over her head, to the other side. Slink gasped. They were in a gigantic room whose walls were at the edge of the lumawand's reach.

Neoko sat down and motioned for Slink to sit with her.

"We wait here," she said. "We need to be still, though. This cavern is particularly close to the surface, and I don't want to raise the suspicion of the people working in the offices above us by making some sharp noise if one of us drops something or smacks into one of the walls."

"Why wait here, then?" Slink asked.

"Once the work day is over, this will be one of the safest places," said Neoko. "We can hack the lights in the building above us to make it look like there is a late meeting going on. That'll give us the cover we need, should anyone hear some noise coming from near the building. The reality is, the tunnel is still several feet underground, and no one is likely to hear us no matter how loud we get. The walls of all the buildings are made from molded slabs of the planetoid's natural materials, and you know what a great sound barrier they make. One thing you'll learn about Tunnel Rats, though, is we don't take chances if we don't have to. None of us wants to end up in detention or back in the nurseries!"

Slink knew that if a nursery door was shut tight, no one standing outside a room could hear sounds coming from inside. He never got quite used to the way silence could be shattered by people bursting out of a room to a cacophony of sound. Nonetheless, he understood Neoko's caution. He knew he had no ener-

45

gy left for any sudden crisis, and he understood why Neoko wouldn't want it even if she had the energy.

The next thing Slink knew, he was jolting awake. He had no memory of laying down or going to sleep. He remembered Neoko talking about offices and tunnels and quiet, but...Neoko! Where was she?

He stood up quickly and tried to focus his eyes on something. It was pitch black--he couldn't see so much as his hand in front of his face.

"I'm right here," said a disembodied voice a few feet away.

"Neoko?" Slink asked.

"Who else do you think it could be, stupid?" said a voice in his head. It was the voice of Mrs. Cuff. Already, he was renting space in his head to people who couldn't bother him in person anymore. Slink was vaguely aware there was nothing unusual about carrying critical voices around in his head and, at the same time, aware his recognition of what he was doing was more than just a little unusual, especially for a twelve year-old. It was another of those times he felt like an old man living in a boy's body. He regained awareness of Neoko while she was in mid-sentence.

"...and you'll continue from here with them." she was saying.

"Did she say I'm leaving her and being passed on to someone else?" he thought.

"Wh..wh..why?" he stammered.

"Slink, you don't want to stay with me and my crew," Neoko said with a sigh. "We're always on the run, scrambling to stay one step ahead of the beetles...."

"How would you know what I want?"

It came out a lot harsher than he'd intended. He was practically spitting his words now.

"We've known each other for a few weeks; spent a few hours together over that time; and now, you know me well enough to tell me what I want? You're a lot more like Mrs. Cuff than you think!"

He could see the last remark stung. They had a number of conversations about Mrs. Cuff and the other nursery guardians. "Good," thought Slink. "I want it to. Stupid girl thinks she knows me--let's see what she thinks of me now!"

"Slink, listen! It's just that..." her voice trailed off. She looked into his eyes for a long time before she spoke again.

"You're right," she whispered. Her voice cracking, she continued, "You're right! I'm sorry. I don't know what's best for you, what you want, or what you ought to do. I don't want to let you go either, and I'm just trying to make us both feel better about something that sucks."

Now that was not like Mrs. Cuff! She'd never apologized for anything so far as Slink knew. Neoko's response made Slink realize how unfair his accusation had been.

"Neoko--I can't leave you. Not yet." A long pause followed the last phrase. Then, "Why are you in such a hurry to hand me off, anyway?"

Neoko felt a little hurt when Slink compared her to the ruthless Mrs. Cuff. His last question, though, struck deeper than any accusation or angry comparison. She knew it was time to come clean. Slink deserved to know she'd come to the nurseries looking specifically for him, and he deserved to know why. He also deserved to know why he had not escaped the nursery to live with her and the other Tunnel Rats. His destiny lay with the Technoids. She didn't know how to tell him he was going to be living inside one of the beetles!

"Slink, you need to know a little more about your future, and that means you need to know a little more about your past. Are you in a mood to listen?"

"What else am I going to do?" he said with an air of resignation.

She reached into her cloak and pulled out a pocket vid. When she looked up and saw Slink's curious expression, she explained, "it's an antique, but it's fine for storing and displaying text files. Some of us have gone to great pains to collect Garsow's history as told by those who have no voice in our, " she cleared her throat and attempted a deeper, dignified voice as she said "model society."

"You are more important to Garsow than you could ever know, Slink. You weren't in the nurseries because you were some kind of misfit. I know that's what you've been told all along, but in your case, it couldn't be further from the truth."

Neoko looked down at the display of the handheld and started reading. At first she read to herself and gave Slink a loose interpretation of the text. Before long, she simply read to Slink.

"Your great-grandparents, the Lansings, founded this colony, Slink. They were both great scientists and great people. They had a vision of Garsow serving the people of our Solar System as a jumping-off point for interstellar missions when we finally managed near light-speed travel. They were hailed as heroes and their statues were erected in front of the SASA embassy while they were still young."

"While they supplied the initial vision for our society, that vision had little in common with the vision of the Earthsider who developed the commlink technology. When the commlinks were first introduced on Garsow, they were a novelty, and they were used only by government officials , SASA representatives, and other technicians, and the visors were only worn at work. Little by little, they were introduced in most workplaces, and a few people started to wear their visors all the time. Before long, no one felt comfortable being visorless around other people."

"Jonathan and Adela Lansing were outspoken about their opposition to the commlink's integration into Garson society. Still, within a couple years of its development, the commlinks were introduced into all work places, but they weren't forced on anyone. It didn't take long, of course, before anyone with ambition underwent the procedure to have the commlink implanted. The rejection rate of implants was kept strictly confidential, although as the commlink grew in popularity almost everyone knew someone who could not tolerate the implant. Many of these "unfortunates," as they were called, returned to productive lives after the failure. Still, a sizable number never returned after going in for the procedure."

"When Garsow Council announced that every Garson would be required to have a commlink, your great-grandparents weren't the only ones who protested. They were just the most famous protesters. They didn't have much access to the public, though, and their opposition hardly slowed the 'March to a Model Society,' as the Council called it. Before long, the early adopters easily out-produced their coworkers. It wasn't long before most people were clamoring for a commlink; those who received the implant quickly became dependent upon it. Those who couldn't tolerate it included a sizable percentage of adults and all children up to the age of eight or so. To be safe, the Council set the age of ten as the minimum age when children could receive their implant."

"The commlink gives its wearer access to far more information than he or she could gather through the five senses alone. A crystal in the ear gives verbal information--translated from files in the data base of the Supernet. Anything that would occupy the eyes too long if read is instead transmitted as a voice file. The visor is used to transmit short text messages and visual cues. For example, if you are conversing with someone and the sensors embedded in her body indicate changes in heart rate, blood pressure, and perspiration consistent with lying, you know instantly because the view through your visor tints red. If you're walking, the path to your destination is highlighted. If you're cooking, you see measurements for ingredients and prompts for timely actions. If you're watching the vid, you control what you're watching with a glance at a menu. Everything you do is supplemented with information to guide your decisions and actions."

"The commlink also monitors your bodily functions continuously. It translates those readings into interpretations broadcast to others when you interact. They know when you're uneasy, frightened, excited, confused, or tense. The Supernet mainframes keep profiles of every person with a commlink and fine-tune interpretation of the biofeedback from the commlink continuously."

"The Council promoted the commlink as the path to a more open, honest family and neighborhood as well as a more productive workplace. They presented the commlink as the means for our society to progress beyond misunderstandings and conflicts. They spoke of a society without room for deception--everyone would learn to be honest or be ostracized."

"Of course, the commlink brought some unexpected side effects, the most significant of which led to the formation of the nurseries. Because people quickly attuned to and relied upon their commlink, they were less aware, and eventually, virtually oblivious to the subtle visual and verbal cues they'd once picked up without conscious awareness. Consequently, they couldn't interact with confidence with anyone who didn't have a commlink including their own children. Interacting with others in their "linked" world, they were almost never misunderstood and just as seldom confronted with someone who suggested they didn't understand. At home, with their children, the frustration level was intolerable for children and adults alike."

"The formation of the nurseries served two purposes. It provided a means of raising children with the patience and understanding they deserved. It also gave Garsow the means to deal with those adults who couldn't tolerate the commlink implant. Instead of having a small, but significant group of unvisored adults mingling in a society that found their presence discomforting at best and downright disturbing at worst, they could be confined to the nurseries. Publicly, they were honored for their contribution to the "Model Society." Privately, they were regarded as outcasts and second-class citizens."

"Your great-grandparents and others of their generation outspoken in their opposition to biotechnology were few in number by this time. Most of the original settlers returned to earth as heroes. There might have been twenty 'old-timers' who remained on Garsow, so they were allowed to live out their days without

50

submitting to the commlink implant. They were, however, required to move into a 'retirement villa' built especially for their occupancy. When they arrived there, your great-grandfather's suspicions were confirmed. Their new home functioned more like a prison than a residence."

"When they were tucked safely out of the way, their son, Garrett Lansing, was quietly given an ultimatum: he and his wife could receive commlinks or return to earth. All four of his siblings had undergone the procedure over time. Garrett was the oldest son and was extremely loyal to his parents, whether he thought their views were a bit antiquated or not. With his parents under a sort of "house arrest," he knew his priorities. He decided to undergo the implant, since it was the only way he could remain on Garsow with his parents. He didn't want to disrupt their lives or the lives of his wife and two daughters. He'd taken over your great-grandmother's work, inheriting her love and her aptitude for biochemistry. He'd recognized early on how the commlink could speed his research."

"He thought he'd be able to complete his mother's research before she died. He hoped his parents would see their son fulfill their vision."

"Two days later, in a most unusual move, his death was announced on the evening vid report. He was honored as a great scientist and his death was mourned as a great loss to all of Garsow. The cause of death was even reported as a cerebral hemorrhage, though there was no mention of a failed commlink implant."

"His wife. Lela, and their two teenage daughters, Denae and Renae, announced their intentions to return to earth. The Council then scheduled a ceremony to honor the contributions of the entire Lansing family. Jonathan and Adela would be the first recipients of the 'Lifetime Achievement Award,' and the whole thing would be shown on the evening vid report."

"On the appointed night, the entire Council gathered to present the awards. Jonathan Lansing was said to be too ill to offer an acceptance speech. When the award was presented, Adela

51

pushed Jonathan before her in his wheel chair. Everyone was smiling so graciously, each of the Council members rising and processing by the Lansings to shake both Adela's and Jonathan's hands. As the applause died down and Adela turned Jonathan's chair around to return to the front row where they had been seated, Jonathan sprang out of his wheel chair. Before anyone could react, he was at the podium, before the live microphone, his image and words being broadcast to every household on Garsow and a good many on Earth, the Moon, and Mars."

"'Garsons, let me start by saying thank you,' he began. 'We must never forget the many good men and women who gave their lives to make this settlement, this society possible. Many others dedicated their lives to making everything we enjoy possible. Adela and I receive this award on behalf of all those who worked beside us over the years. Let me also take this moment to thank the members of the Garson Council for arranging for this award ceremony.'"

"He turned and bowed to all the Council members who, much to their consternation, were caught in the camera's eye still standing around, waving furiously to unseen people just off stage and gesticulating wildly to each other. They immediately began making their way back to their seats with their best politician's smiles glued to their faces. Still, it would have taken a lot more than their visors and artificial expressions to hide their discomfort."

"They had little choice but to resume their charade of honoring this great man, woman, and family. They had only enough time to take a deep breath and hope Jonathan didn't do too much damage. They'd returned to their seats at the places of honor behind the head table, a couple of meters behind the podium where Jonathan now stood. A few had to be quietly encouraged to sit down and face the studio audience. There was no point in whispering commands to staff people or each other. After all, they couldn't very well have security come in and hustle off Dr. Lansing on this auspicious occasion, now could they? And, of course, what politicians want an expression of consternation and powerlessness broadcast to the people they serve? Jonathan had them right where he wanted them. They knew it; he knew it; and there wasn't a thing anyone could do to alter the course Jonathan steered."

"'Even with your visors on and your senses deadened, I'm sure most of you can see how uncomfortable our gracious leaders are. If you didn't notice it, let me assure you, the other guests in this room could cut the tension with a knife. You might wonder why your great leaders would be uncomfortable at a moment like this. I think I can help you. They are afraid, and politicians do not ever want their fears broadcast. They are afraid of a 62-year-old man whose face you can read like a book--if you can still read faces. They are afraid you will see in my face and in their empty visored visages the reality of the life you've chosen. They'd be even more afraid if they realized my family members gathered for this great event have now taken up the company of those charged with bringing this broadcast to you. Unlike your illustrious Council members, you, my fellow Garsons, can relax; no one will interrupt our little chat.'"

"'You are blind and deaf, my dear friends. If you've not gone completely blind yet, see what I show you. If you've not grown completely deaf, hear me. Do you remember when you were a child the horror you felt at the sound of the word, 'cyborg?' It's always chilled people to think of a man or woman reduced to a biological shell for a robot, controlled by the programming written by another. You've been told no one controls you, no one programs you. You've been told you are simply given more information, more accurate information, more instantaneous information to make your own decisions. You've been assured you are more productive, less combative, more cooperative, and less conflicted. Your life has been made easier, or so…you've…been…told.'"

"'In reality, your every emotion is monitored and displayed. You're conditioned to express only those emotions that will benefit the organization you serve. Your every bodily function is monitored and interpreted by a computer. You have no control over who sees this information, how they interpret it or where it is stored. If one of you displays instability threatening your effectiveness, you're quietly replaced with someone who more closely meets the expectations of the Council. Of course, this isn't terribly disturbing to you, because those of you hearing my voice have, for the most part, been found worthy of this 'model society.' You've noticed neighbors have left without a word, purportedly returning to earth. You've witnessed new employees replacing colleagues who never even said 'goodbye.' You've tolerated each loss, even learned to welcome it. The ones who were replaced were always the ones who were too outspoken anyway--the ones who might make a scene at work, or be heard arguing with a spouse late in the evening. Your life has grown more comfortable as Garsow has been filled with people just like you.'"

"'Oh, you can argue that our population is diverse. We come from every quadrant of earth, moon settlements, even Mars. Our skin's pigmentation is widely varied. We are women and men, young and old...well, at least we are older. People who are really old would never fit into a 'model society.' Even at 88, I live in a guarded compound euphemistically called a 'retirement villa.' Nonetheless, Garsow is diverse...if you only scratch skin deep.'"

"'But there is no one here who does not toe the Council line. Everyone here has been chosen for his or her predisposition to cooperate with a life whose path has been predetermined. You may think you chose to come here, but you had no choice in the matter. If you came with the original colonists, you came because you had the skills needed to build this colony. After it was built, if you fit the profile, you stayed. If you did not fit the profile of a citizen of the 'model society,' unless your skills were extraordinary, (he gestured with a flourish towards himself), you were sent back to Earth or one of the other colonies.'"

"'If you immigrated here, you saw a nice vid about our 'model society,' submitted to a battery of physical, emotional, and cognitive tests, and waited to get the good news that you were one in ten thousand invited to be part of this 'model society.'"

"'Even with all these grand schemes to screen out the fly before he lands in the ointment, a few more independent types still made it to Garsow. Some were extraordinary minds, whose expertise was needed more than their compliance. Some were less than forthcoming on their tests and in their interviews. Most of these have been dispatched from whence they came. A few, though, have gone underground and formed the resistance known as the Technoids. We are told to fear them above all others and to be vigilant, lest they destroy our 'model society.'"

"'I have done everything I can to live in this model society, make my contribution, and stand against those aspects I could not support. I have sought to engage in meaningful debate those with whom I disagree. They have given me no meaningful way of expressing my views, let alone discussing them with any of our leaders. I have not been arrested or deported because I am famous. I have simply been shut away. So this is my last hurrah.'"

"'I stand before you tonight to challenge you to remember what you were. Some of you have had a commlink since you came of age, but most of you had the commlink implanted as adults. Do you remember the thrill of wondering how someone to whom you were attracted felt about you? Do you remember working through painful conflict with your spouse, and the way it spiced up your love life afterward? Do you remember when the best ideas came from gatherings of people who didn't agree--who often didn't even like each other? Do you remember what a joy it was to see your baby go from crying hysterically to giggling uncontrollably because of the way you clowned with her? How long has it been since you heard someone tell you they love you? They miss you? They need you?'"

"'We're not building a model society, we're building a 'zombie society.' And before long, if we continue on this path, we'll be the very thing we fear most: cyborgs!'"

"At that point, Jonathan Lansing stepped back from the microphone. There was no applause, no chorus of 'boos', no scattered catcalls. The room was completely silent. Quietly, ever so steadily, the stage upon which he stood was filled with people. They came from both sides of the stage, walking solemnly from the audience up the steps on each side of the stage to stand at

Jonathan's and Adela's sides. When all who were coming forward had taken their places, they numbered over twenty. Jonathan stepped forward to the microphone again."

"'You must decide where you will stand. As for me and my family, we will stand with each other.'"

"Having received their cue, each of the people standing on the stage reached up and withdrew his or her visor. They carefully disconnected the lead wires and gently placed the visor on the ground in front of them. Then each family member raised a foot and brought it down on his or her visor."

"'We will not be anyone's cyborg!' shouted your great-grandfather."

Neoko looked up from the handheld.

"We still don't really know what happened next. We know the broadcast ended without a word from any of the Council. We later heard the Lansings had all been arrested. As time went by, rumors flew that some family members had been executed. Little by little, it became clear many of the Lansing family had been placed in the nurseries as caregivers. These were reported to have been subjected to various procedures designed to assure their compliance. One or two, we know for a fact, came to live with the Technoids, but that is a story for another time."

"Slink, what you need to know is you're more than an extraordinarily bright kid who had the misfortune of being born to an outcast family. You are Jonathan and Adela Lansing's great-grandson, Garrett and Lela Lansing's grandson, and Renae Lansing's son, born to her in the nurseries, and taken from her upon your birth. I was sent to retrieve you from the nurseries and bring you here. You and I are waiting here to meet your Great Aunt Dorothea, daughter of Adela and Jonathan Lansing, sister to your late grandfather, Garrett. She is known as Dot to everyone down here and is universally respected. She is the leader of the Technoids, and…she's late."

Chapter 3

Dr. Jonathan Francis Lansing was dedicated to his work and driven to succeed--at least those were the public impressions his peers and superiors offered. In private, they characterized him as obsessed, stubborn, and egotistical. Whatever their vocabulary, no one doubted Jonathan's desire or his ability to overcome the obstacles of space colonization.

From the time he was a small boy, he was fascinated with space exploration. He spent every summer night of his childhood sleeping on the hard synthetic boards of the deck outside his family's fourth floor apartment so he could catch a glimpse of the stars through the haze and reflected light of the city. In high school he earned pocket money selling greeting cards to his neighbors and spent most of it on the premium satellite television package that gave him the opportunity to watch the Space channel twenty-four hours a day. His sister characterized his fascination with space as the weirdest obsession a person could possibly have, and she constantly lamented the way he was ruining her reputation by preceding her in school and doing nothing to hide his nerdiness.

He thrilled at the establishment of the early space stations and the first moon colony. When he came of age, he eschewed far more lucrative opportunities in the private sector to work for the Solar Aeronautics and Space Administration. While his SASA colleagues chased the noble but elusive goal of near light-speed travel, Jonathan was driven to give humanity the means to colonize the rest of the solar system. His obsession with his work made his relatively sudden marriage a shock to friends and family alike. Most had long assumed he would be a lifelong bachelor. But then, no one could imagine he would find a woman so like him in aptitude, outlook, and obsession.

Adela Coella Jentana's family and friends had given up on her ever dating, let alone marrying. After all, eligible bachelors don't usually hang out at corporate science labs late at night on the chance they might find a beautiful scientist bent over a microscope with a half-eaten instant burrito laying forgotten next to the slides smeared with deadly bacteria.

When Adela presented her doctoral thesis, "Developing Self-Repairing Bio-shields for Sustaining Extraterrestrial Settlements," she had only one member of her audience glued to her every word. Jonathan was so excited about applying her discoveries to space colonization that he nearly knocked Adela down rushing to her as she descended the stage. The two talked late into the night, and by the time an opening at SASA made it possible for Adela and Jonathan to work side-by-side, their marriage was a foregone conclusion.

After overseeing the development of two moon colonies and a Mars colony, the Solar Council knew that humanity was tiring of expensive forays into space that seemed to have little benefit for anyone but the employees of SASA. Every time another colony was established, precious resources had to be diverted from Earth and the existing colonies. They desperately needed a project that could stimulate the imaginations and galvanize the desire of the planet for further space exploration.

They had hoped by now to announce a grand plan to travel to a nearby star and establish the first human colony beyond the reaches of their solar system. Practicality had intervened, though, and near light-speed travel was still decades away, at best. So they had determined that any outpost beyond the lunar and Martian settlements was going to have to be established closer to home, but far enough away to stir the spirit of adventure amongst a skeptical public.

Garsow was a dense, though relatively small, planetoid orbiting the sun on an elliptical path whose average radius was twice that of Pluto's. Scientists had known of its existence for nearly a century, but no one had considered trying to settle or colonize the formidable rock. When Jonathan and Adela Lansing first suggested that Garsow, not Mars, was the logical environment for the next settlement, their colleagues scoffed. But the skepticism didn't last long.

The Drs. Lansing had done their homework, and before they made their proposal public, they'd drawn up detailed plans for establishing not just a colony, but a society on Garsow! The idea of a few more oversized tin cans linked together by air locks on Mars or anywhere else was not going to fly this time--and the Lansings knew that. They proposed an entire community--two hundred people initially, then growing to five thousand, living in a city sheltered in an artificial atmosphere underneath giant bubbles! The initial drawings looked like something from the cover art of a twentieth-century science fiction novel, and the public ate it up!

Dot stood in front of the command chair and stared at the vid. The screen covered an eight foot square in the center of the front-most bulwark of the first sweeper the Technoids had ever converted for human occupancy. Home, as they had named the little robotic drone, had served as the command center for the Technoids ever since the need became obvious. The Technoids had disabled and converted four other drones over the ten years since Home was commandeered.

The others were all smaller than Home, having been built in more recent years during which Beta Sector and Gamma Sector were developed with their smaller underground passages. Since the tunnels beneath Alpha Sector had once been used as permanent dwellings, they'd been enlarged beyond the natural size of the caverns from which they were formed. The tunnels beneath Beta and Gamma Sectors were much smaller than those beneath Alpha. The sweepers built after Beta and Gamma Sector were developed had to be smaller, so they were designed to reach the walls of the larger tunnels in Alpha Sector with long "arms" extending from the body of the drone. They retracted those arms and used the brushes extending over the surface of the drone only when they were below Beta and Gamma Sector. Home was the only larger early generation drone the Technoids had acquired.

Dot's erect stance and commanding presence in the center of the deck made her seem even bigger than her six-foot frame. Her light brown hair curling around the base of her neck and onto her back did little to soften the sharp angles of her broad shoulders. Her thick eye brows above piercing green eyes that looked out over sharp cheek bones and an even sharper nose gave her the appearance of an eagle looking over its domain. A stranger stepping onto the deck would have needed no one to point her out as the commanding officer.

The command module took up about half the top floor of the drone. The top-floor was evenly divided between the command module and the Cave, where the Technoid brainiacs worked together to bring down the Supernet. The middle floor was carved into sleeping quarters for the crew. There were cabins built in the center of the middle floor, one private cabin that Dot called home and two semiprivate cabins shared by the other four officers. Two large sleeping compartments, one on each side of the officer's cabins, divided into curtained cubicles stacked three high and two abreast on each side of a narrow hallway provided the bare necessities for sleeping for the remainder of the crew of 48. Each crew member had access to a cubicle for 12 hours of each 24. Crew members were required to get a minimum of six hours sleep unless called to duty. Some chose to sleep as soon as their shift ended, others needed to unwind before they slept. Consequently, someone was almost always asleep in the compartment, so everyone moved quietly in the sleeping compartments out of courtesy to their fellows.

The bottom floor of the drone was equally divided between a mess hall on one side and the galley, showers, laundry, and engineering center on the other. The mess was further divided into a large mess for crew and a smaller one for officers.

At any given time, at least half the crew was on the top floor, serving duty in the command center or the tech room, often referred to as the "Cave." On this particular occasion, all but a handful of the crew were topside. Dot had asked all available hands to join her for a conference. She'd opened the compartment doors between the command center and the tech room, and every available space was occupied by the time she rose from her command chair and addressed the crew.

"The Data Acquisition Network has decided that its agents must demonstrate their competence by arresting known Technoid operatives in large number. They have identified some of our members by name and posted on the daily vid report those person's faces and descriptions. Some of you are amongst those named."

The reaction to her revelation was muted. Most of the crew had heard rumors to this affect and were prepared for the announcement. Everyone present was far more interested in Dot's proposed response to the DAN initiative.

"For the first time since we began operating in unity beneath the surface, DAN will take the offensive. They've been tipped off that we are using drones as bases of operation."

The room exploded with groans of dismay. A few epithets were hurled at DAN. A single voice rose above the others from the back of the adjoining rooms.

"Who betrayed us?"

"We have no reason to believe we were betrayed!"

Dot spoke quickly and forcefully before the idea behind the question could take hold.

"Since we commandeered Home, we've been hacking the maintenance records and giving the appearance our drones were not due for maintenance. Likewise, we hacked the guidance system and charted courses for our drones that suited our needs. Both hacks were relatively easy to accomplish and easy to hide, since both systems are low security and open to all of the utility contractors."

"Up to this point, we must assume no one examined the maintenance records or guidance charts to detect any anomalies. After all, in addition to being low security, the reports are low priority. We can only deduce someone finally took a closer look at one of those systems or the reports it generates. We hope that is the basis of their suspicion."

"Our deductions seem to be born out in that the guidance commands Home is now receiving are coded differently. They seem to be designed to aid in detecting any changes we might make if we tried to hack their system. In addition, the Tunnel Rats tell us they are seeing fewer sweepers in the tunnels, except for the tunnel leading to the maintenance corridor."

"DAN is trying to identify us through a process of elimination and isolate our drones for the purpose of arresting us. Fortunately, Garsons have no stomach for murder, even if it is sanctioned by the state. We can be relatively certain we are not in mortal danger, though the prospect of being incarcerated on the surface may seem a fate worse than death for most of us. We must not allow DAN to discover Home or any of our other drones."

"I've established a relationship with one of the operators at the remanufacturing plant where outdated drones are disassembled and melted down to create new drones. We'll stash all five of our drones there, where he'll do his best to see they are kept out of sight and out of mind. We're relatively confident we could escape detection by switching the electronic identity of our drones with others that have already been examined. We've successfully tested our ability to swap drone identities, but we can't risk being discovered in this systemwide crackdown. Therefore, for the next several weeks, most of us will return to the tunnels and join the Tunnel Rats."

Dot held unquestioning command over the Technoids, and especially, over the denizens of Home. Still, her revelation was met with a buzz of muttering, some of it clearly discernible as grumbling. She expected this. Many of her crew hadn't endured the hardships of tunnel life for years. They'd become accustomed to their rudimentary comforts. Carrying the necessities of life on their backs, scavenging for food, and living on the run were not conditions they relished. Dot sympathized. She lifted her hand, palm outward, fingers spread wide, in a gesture of command. The room grew still.

"I know this course seems drastic to some of you and its consequences are unwelcome to all of us. Nonetheless, after reviewing all our options, I'm certain this solution offers us the best chance of escaping the DAN security sweeps and maintaining the progress we've made over the long run. We can't lose a large number of our people or our drones. We've worked for ten years to reach the point where we can dare to imagine a bloodless revolution. We need more time to make that dream a reality. A few weeks of roughing it is a small price to pay for our continued freedom and the cause we serve."

"Prepare yourselves for disembarking. We'll exit the drone in our pre-assigned companies. Alpha Company will be dropped in one hour."

More mumbling--the protestations more discernible this time.

"Beta Company will be dropped in two and a half hours. Gamma Company, we'll exit the drone shortly before it reaches the remanufacturing plant. The extra time we have on board will be used to download all our data and rig the data room for self-destruction if the hull is breached. Two of you will be selected confidentially to join me in carrying a complete copy of all the data. If any one of us is captured, we'll destroy the data disks before they can be confiscated, even if this means sacrificing ourselves. Gamma Company--Understood?"

"Yes, commander!" came the sharp reply.

"Company commanders--check the drop zones in your area every day. We will pass information, with the help of the Tunnel Rats, by leaving memory coins at the drop zone. All messages are to be encoded and overlaid with dummy information. Report each day on your whereabouts, any encounters with DAN, and any ventures onto the surface."

"People--we've made it through challenges before, and we'll make it through this one. Keep your heads down and move with extreme caution. We expect this operation will last two or three weeks. I look forward to seeing you all back on Home when the crackdown is over. Dismissed."

The nine hours that passed before disembarking Home was barely long enough for Dot and Gamma Company to accomplish everything they'd set out to do. When they stepped off the drone loaded with packs, bedrolls, and the data disks, they could only hope they'd not forgotten anything critical as they watched Home drift down the tunnel governed by the guidance instructions it was receiving from Central Command. Their stop shouldn't have raised any suspicions since they'd masked it with a small series of communication failures designed to make the drone look like it was suffering a simple component disfunction.

Dot was extremely disappointed with the timing of their departure from Home. She was supposed to be on the other side of the Garson settlements, receiving the most precious cargo her crew would ever carry. When Home's guidance system had started receiving instructions in new code, her crew knew better than to modify any of those instructions, and yet, Dot was extremely unhappy to see Home was being directed away from the rendezvous. In the time it took to develop and implement a response to the DAN initiative, Home traveled far from where the crew had hoped to go. Now instead of meeting her grand nephew for the first time, Dot was trying to direct her company down a service tunnel to a hollow used by a band of Tunnel Rats. She hadn't seen this particular hollow since she'd been brought here in the dead of night many years earlier.

On that fateful night the bold leader of that Tunnel Rat band, Rhant, had led his Tunnel Rat enclave on a surface scavenging mission knowing the Garson Awards would capture the attention of nearly all the surface dwellers. Their visors and cloaks couldn't pass close inspection, but they'd given them easy passage that night. He and his band had stood before an outdoor monitor in stunned disbelief while Dot's parents made their notorious last stand. He'd known the family would be arrested and held in detention, and he anticipated their transfer to the detention center might present the only opportunity the Tunnel Rats would have for freeing some or all of them.

Rhant had signaled for the members of his band to retreat from the plaza where they'd been watching the outdoor monitor and had gathered them in a nearby alley. He'd crouched down spreading a crude map on the ground. His long, straight black hair had shrouded his face as he leaned over the map devising a route for his band. When he'd stood and flicked his hair back with a snap of his neck his band had stood ready around him. He'd pursed his thin lips for a moment, making the whiskers of his mustache and soul patch stand on point. His band had recognized this meant they were about to be asked to do something dangerous.

Rhant never took lightly putting his band in harms way, but he'd realized they were less than a five minute walk from the detention site where the family would likely be held. He'd proposed the rescue to his band offering any of them a chance to step away, but they'd all assented immediately. Rhant and two others had gone back into the tunnels for guard uniforms. When they'd emerged, they'd looked like everyday security guards walking to work. They'd known they could never get into the detention center without functioning commlinks, so they'd formed a plan that wouldn't require their admittance.

By the time the transports carrying the detainees came to a stop in front of the detention center, it was well into the night. Curfew had long since passed, and the pedways were deserted, or so it appeared. The two guards transporting the detainees had their defenses down, and they weren't suspicious as the impostor guards approached them. In a matter of seconds, the guards were disabled and the detainees were whisked off to the tunnels. Unfortunately for the Lansing family, Dot and her sister-in-law, Lela were the only members of the family on that transport. The others were a few minutes behind in two other transports. By the time they arrived at the detention center, security was heightened tenfold. Dot and Lela had escaped imprisonment at the probable cost of ever seeing another member of their family.

It was with this bitter memory in mind that Dot now wondered how her grand nephew was doing. Had he escaped the nurseries? Was he waiting to rendezvous with her or did he know by now that she wouldn't be coming? Had Alpha Company reached the rendezvous point in time to reassure his escort and him? Or was he sitting in the dark with someone he barely knew wondering what'd gone wrong with a plan he had no hand in preparing?

When they reached the narrow, camouflaged entry to the hollow, Dot was disturbed to see it was deserted. Where she expected to find the crude furnishings of a Tunnel Rat enclave, she saw only bare, translucent walls like those of the tunnels, though here, Dot could see patches of impenetrable black scattered across the dome shape of the enclosure. The walls of the tunnels normally looked like poorly refined glass, with hues of yellow and black beneath and along the surface, seeming to move as the one peering into them moved. These black smudges on the walls of the hollow were clearly on the surface. Dot realized they were mold spores multiplying out of control in one of the few subterranean spaces the sweeper drones couldn't reach. The mold told Dot the Tunnel Rats had deserted the hollow within the last week.

"Either Central Command has begun to sweep the tunnels in earnest and caught our friends in their dragnet, or Rhant and his band have relocated to avoid being snared. Either way, we will not have the help of our allies. We'll have to break into three patrols and rotate watches. Each patrol will spend one shift on the surface scavenging for food and supplies and listening for information. They'll spend a second shift on lookout and the third on R&R."

"Sendra, you have red patrol and will be first on the surface. Ivonyov, you take blue patrol on guard duty. As the senior officer, in more ways than one, I am getting some rest, and I'd advise the other members of yellow patrol to do the same."

Sendra and Ivonyov nodded, stepped forward, and turned to the others in the company.

"You heard Dot," Sendra hollered in her characteristic baritone that belied her diminutive stature. "Red patrol, you have one hour to rest and get something to eat. Be in cloaks and visors outside the hollow in one hour."

"Blue patrol outside," commanded Ivonyov.

The broad-shouldered man of few words stepped out, looked over his patrol from the vantage point of his superior height, pointed at each person in turn, and assigned a guard post with a word. He then distributed rations to each person in his patrol and dispatched them with the same two words,

"Stay alert!"

By the time Ivonyov checked in on each post and returned to the hollow, Red Patrol had left for the surface. Yellow patrol had set camp and Dot was nowhere to be seen, but her telltale snore could already be heard rising from within the makeshift enclosure at the rear of the hollow.

Chapter 4

The Lansings proposed an ambitious ten-year program for reaching their goal to establish a self-sustaining society on a planetoid at the outer reaches of the solar system. The initial step involved building another space station in orbit around Garsow, smaller than the ones orbiting Earth and Mars. The modules for the new space station would be delivered to Garsow orbit first, using a series of unmanned missions. They would leave two months in advance of the first Garsow Station crews.

Those first two crews of six would shuttle from Mars Station and would be transported to the life support module of Garsow station already orbiting the planetoid. They would spend the next six months assembling the remainder of Garsow station. Six months after those two crews had departed Mars Station, another series of unmanned rockets would depart from Earth and deliver a life support module and building materials to the surface of Garsow. A few weeks after that, two more shuttles would depart from Mars Station, each carrying crews of six, with one also carrying a station-to-surface lander. The shuttles would dock with Garsow

Station, and the lander would make two trips to the surface, delivering the fresh crew of 12, who would then begin construction on underground facilities to accommodate two hundred settlers.

The Lansings had determined that Garsow was dense, stable, and riddled with natural caverns. It was more like an asteroid than a planet, in that it was little more than a giant rock in orbit around the sun. Yet, it was much larger than any asteroid. It had an atmosphere, though it was thinner than earth's, no oceans, and very little variation in its topography. Most fascinating was its surface. Though it had to have been impacted by asteroids in its many millennia of existence, it showed no craters or other signs of such impacts. Its surface was smooth, almost polished. The Lansings made all these geological determinations despite the fact that Garsow was covered in ice! They had scanned the planetoid's surface from Earth and Mars, and mapped the underlying topography of Garsow.

Robotic explorers later determined that the planet's surface was nearly impermeable, but susceptible to heat. When the robots used torches on the surface, it melted, becoming semitransparent. Then, when the heat was removed, it hardened again, growing cloudy, dark, and smooth.

The caverns beneath the polished surface were filled with gas under such pressure that it exploded violently when one of the robotic explorers inadvertently melted through the surface material into a cavern. The gas had to be coming from the planetoid's core, though its source and composition were not certain. It was first feared to be flammable or explosive, but was later determined to be mostly nitrogen. The Lansings were confident that some of the caverns could be sealed off and the pressure stabilized at a level suitable for human habitation. They hoped a relatively small ground crew living in surface life support modules could prepare a system

70

of interconnected caverns for human inhabitation over a period of several months. The infrastructure for sustaining a community within the cavern dwellings would have to be developed over a longer period of time, with the supplies for their construction being shipped from earth in advance of the colonists.

Given that it took a year to travel from Earth to Garsow, each mission would leave Earth or Mars Station long before the previous mission's outcome could be determined. There was risk to such a plan, but what great adventure did not carry risk?

Like the Mars missions four decades earlier and the Lunar missions before them, the Garsow mission was conceived at a time when society needed a dream. The mission caught the public imagination and desire for exploration. It took the scientific community only a year from the time it was introduced to the United Assembly to fine-tune the Lansing Plan, as it came to be called, develop a budget, and go back before the Assembly to lobby for funding. Even the scientists were surprised when the request was granted--in full--without any significant modification. A few more skeptical souls suggested that perhaps members of the Assembly had their own agenda for approving the project so quickly. The vast majority of the project's scientists and engineers, along with most gum-chewing citizens were too busy indulging their imaginations to ask a silly question like, "Why?"

Slink was full of questions when Neoko finished telling him the story of his great-grandparents. Were they still alive? Did they know of their daughter's involvement with the Technoids? Was there any chance he would ever meet them?

He only had enough time to ask his first question and was disappointed when Neoko didn't even answer that one.

"I am not the one to tell you any more. I've told you every-thing I know, and it was probably obvious I was just repeating stories I've been told."

"Slink, our rendezvous time has come and gone. We can't stay here anymore. I have to be back to my enclave within a cou-ple hours or a search party will waste a lot of time and energy looking for me. If we leave now, we can reach the enclave as the morning meal is served and before a search party is formed."

Slink squinted, head cocked to the side.

"Why would anyone living down here care whether it was eight in the morning or six at night?" he asked. "What difference would it make if they ate dinner in the morning and breakfast at night?"

"Most tunnel enclaves keep the same rituals as the people on the surface. Day and night are artificial constructs up top too, remember? Human beings just do better if their lives have a rhythm. There are some of us who work from sundown to sunrise, and we tend to change things up a bit, but we still maintain meals with the band. It helps us to trust each other, learn from each oth-er, and work with each other when we gather together twice a day, and there's no better way to gather than over a meal!"

"Come on, Slink," Neoko prodded. "We can talk as we walk."

All the talk about food finally awoke Slink's appetite. He'd been trained well, though, and he'd never ask for food. From the time he could express his desires the guardians had either ignored him or punished him for speaking up. Asking for food as an out-cast in the nurseries guaranteed going without.

"You hungry, Slink?"

Slink lowered his eyes and hunched his shoulders. He was still sitting with his back up against the smooth, curved wall of the hollow with his legs folded in front of him. His posture now made him look so small he could have been half his age.

"You gotta break that habit," said Neoko.

"What?" said Slink.

"In the tunnels, you get what you ask for unless it can't be had. No one will punish you for letting us know you're hungry. We may not have anything to eat, but we aren't going to withhold what we have."

Slink took Neoko's last sentence to suggest she had nothing to offer him. He raised his head enough to see Neoko's feet.

"That's OK," he said. "I'm all right."

"What do you mean, 'That's OK?' I'm not tellin' you I don't have anything. I'm tellin' you to speak up and let me know how you're feelin'."

Slink stuttered, "I'm hungry, Ma'am."

"Slink! Who are you talkin' to?" Neoko's tone was playfully indignant, not harsh. "Don't ever call me 'Ma'am.' Now come on over here and let me share my food with you. It isn't much, but you're welcome to it."

Neoko pulled out her food. It looked strange to Slink, but it would have been familiar to most working Garsons. The first thing Neoko pulled out looked like a long, narrow bar, and it was soft and dense. It was made from soy flour and various dried fruits cultivated in the Gamma Sector green houses and fortified with all the daily nutrients a person needed. Though it wasn't made for taste, it was palatable, and after going without any food for a day, Slink thought it was one of the best things he'd ever tasted. He devoured his bar in a few mouth-stuffing bites.

"Hungry?" Neoko chuckled. "I have one more we can share on the way, but for now--drink the water you have left. The bar will expand in your stomach, and your hunger pangs will go away in a few minutes."

Now that his most urgent need had been met, Slink felt rising anxiety.

"If I was supposed to be handed off to the Technoids, what're we going to do? Your band isn't expecting to support another person." His voice rose in pitch until it cracked. "And how're you going to get hold of the people we were supposed to meet tonight? What if something happened to them, and they can't take me in?"

73

"Slink, we won't let you down." She paused. "I won't let you down."

Neoko stared into his eyes silently for several seconds, then lowered her head. She couldn't be sure she could keep any promises she made. Tunnel Rats lived one day at a time. She wanted to protect Slink, but she knew his fate was not hers to decide.

"I can't answer all your questions right now, but I want you to know—I'll take care of you as long as we're together." She saw in his frown he recognized the message she was not verbalizing, and she winced at his recognition. "When the time comes, we'll worry about gettin' you to the Technoids. For now let's just enjoy the fact we made it out of the nursery and you never have to go back there again. Think about it, Slink. You're free. No one's ever going to abuse you again. We may be facing a little uncertainty, but you're really free!"

Nook's words rolled over Slink. Like a helpless swimmer caught in heavy surf, Slink couldn't stop the wave of emotion that broke over him now. His earlier anxiety over his immediate circumstances was swept away by a tidal wave of relief as he realized he was never going back to the nurseries. His fear of the unknown was washed away as he realized he was with someone who genuinely cared about him. His earlier questions were swept away by wave after gentle wave of dawning awareness grounded him in this new reality: he was free! Though the tunnels presented their own challenges, the nurseries and every other structure of control conceived by the Mrs. Cuffs of the world were gone. Tunnel life might be hard, but he would not live the rest of his days being controlled like a puppet at the end of a string. The words echoed in his mind several times before they rose to his lips as a barely audible whisper.

"I'm free!"

Finally, the tears came.

They walked back the way they'd come for a while, then off in a new direction down a tunnel Slink had never seen. Neoko filled the time by telling her story--backward. She started with her time in the tunnels, went to the story of her escape from the nurseries, and finished with a few tales of her childhood. Slink took great delight in hearing Neoko had her share of run-ins with Mrs. Cuff. He especially enjoyed hearing about the night Neoko and one of the other guardians short-sheeted Mrs. Cuff's bed. Neoko had to explain short sheeting to Slink, and he was disappointed to hear the Tunnel Rats didn't sleep in beds, let alone use sheets, when he expressed his desire to try short sheeting someone else. Neoko's stories and their shared laughter made the time pass quickly and it brought the two even closer.

Almost two hours later, Slink had almost forgotten about their immediate goal when Neoko suddenly announced, "We're here."

They stood before a small elliptical opening in the tunnel wall. Slink assumed it opened on another of the hollows that branched off the tunnels every few hundred feet. He'd looked into several openings along the way while Neoko hung back, allowing him to explore a bit on his own. He could see why the little hollows existed. The natural caverns from which the tunnels were formed had branched in every direction. When the settlers mapped the tunnels, they chose their routes with two things in mind--the natural formation of the caverns and the needs of the human settlers. The tunnels under Alpha Sector more closely followed the natural caverns. They'd been built for permanent or semi-permanent occupancy. They didn't serve surface settlements at the time they were fashioned from the caverns, so they meandered wherever the caverns dictated they must. The settlers melted the surface of the cavern walls and smoothed them as they hardened. Where there were little fissures, they sealed them. Where the opening was larger, they left it, and sealed a hollow instead, making a semiprivate dwelling or workplace off the main tunnel. Years later, many of the tunnels under Alpha Sector whose meanderings made them of little use to the surface settlements were sealed off completely as the settlers moved above ground. Those tunnels that could be retrofitted with sewer lines and utility conduit and cables were maintained while the others were abandoned. It was into one of those long-abandoned tunnels that Slink now entered with Neoko.

At first, Slink didn't notice anything unusual about the hollow. As they moved into it, though, he realized it was narrower and deeper than most. It was more like a small tunnel than a hollow, barely wide enough for Neoko and him to stand side-by-side, though it was very deep, continuing far beyond the point light from the outside tunnel could reach. He also realized the ceiling was dropping, quickly reaching the point where it was half the height of most of the hollows he'd seen. Slink couldn't quite touch the ceiling, but he thought most adults probably could. Neoko left his side and advanced with her lumawand until she stood in front of a wall that appeared at the end of the little tunnel. She dropped the lumawand on the floor of the tunnel, extended her arms forward and placed her hands side-by-side about waist high,with her palms out, then moved them slowly upward, then apart, fanning outward in a large arc until her arms were outstretched like she was anticipating an embrace.

When she reached forward, the wall suddenly slid aside, and Slink gasped as Neoko slipped forward and disappeared in the darkness. Slink's knees almost buckled when he saw her suddenly vanish, even as he reminded himself they were here to meet her friends. He barely stifled the cry that rose to his lips. Several long seconds passed and Slink didn't hear a thing. Just as he was going to call out to her, Neoko reappeared and motioned for Slink to follow.

"Come on," she said. "This passage is narrow and dark, but there's nothin' to run into. Just walk straight ahead with your left hand on the wall. When you feel the tunnel turning to your left, wait for me. I'll be right behind you--I have to close this entryway."

Slink couldn't figure out why Neoko would send him into the tunnel without her, but he assumed there was a reason. He knew Neoko didn't give instructions without one.

When he entered the tunnel, he knew right away why she'd sent him ahead. The tunnel was so narrow they'd have been tripping over each other if they'd tried to pass through it side-by-side. He walked about fifteen or twenty steps before he felt the tunnel begin to turn.

"Are you there yet?" Neoko's voice boomed.

It sounded to Slink like she was yelling, but he realized almost as soon as he jerked his head toward her voice she was only speaking in a loud whisper. The narrow tunnel directed her voice and seemed to amplify it.

"I'm waiting...."

His voice came out sounding much louder than he expected. He paused and lowered his voice to a whisper.

"I'm waiting for you," he rasped.

"Good," she whispered, making him jump.

She was a lot closer than he expected.

"I'm right behind you. Now squeeze to your left, and I'll pass on your right. I'll reach my left hand back to you so you can hold it while we go the rest of the way."

A few seconds later, Neoko squeezed by Slink, reached back and took his hand and guided him another thirty steps or so before they stopped again. This time, she just knocked on the surface in front of them. Slink couldn't see anything, but her knocks resounded in the tunnel as though she were beating a drum. She pounded on the door until Slink wanted to cry out for her to stop for the sake of his aching ears. Then he noticed the rhythm--Neoko was pounding out the rhythm from one of the Alley Cats tunes she'd used to signal a rendezvous with Slink while he was still in the nurseries. All of a sudden, a door was thrown open flooding the tunnel with light and blinding Slink completely.

Neoko reached back and pulled Slink forward. He was trying to open his eyes, but they stubbornly refused to open.

"Relax little man, your eyes will open when they're ready," said a vaguely familiar voice. "Welcome to Kansas! Sit down over here." Two hands grasped his arms just above the elbows and guided him to one side and down into a chair.

"Neoko!"

Whoever owned that voice knew her and knew her well, thought Slink. He almost breathed her name instead of saying it. It rolled out of his throat like a heavy sigh.

"Neoko, we were so worried about you!"

Slink could hear the two of them embrace and kiss. Slink wished he could disappear.

"There's been lots of activity in the tunnels since we met you in the alley," the man continued. "We thought maybe you were caught up in some of the commotion. We thought you'd be back last night. Jesus, Neoko--you scared me!"

Slink heard them kiss again and he tried to open his eyes.

"Somethin' must have gone wrong, or he wouldn't be with you."

Slink was holding his hands in front of his face and peering through his fingers in an attempt to control the light hitting his eyes. He could see the man's hand gesture toward him. He opened his fingers wider and let a little more light in.

"They didn't show," said Neoko, turning away from the man and dropping her pack. "We got to the rendezvous OK, but the Technoids never showed up."

She turned back.

"The kid's hungry, and so am I. I'm sure he could do with a little rest after we eat, too."

"Sure, sure, Neoko. I'll get somethin' together for you and we'll talk while you eat."

He was gone.

"Slink--what's wrong?" asked Neoko. "You look like you're not too happy to be here. Cheer up--we're in good hands now!"

Slink wanted to shout at her.

"You know what's wrong!" he wanted to say. "Now that we're back on your turf, I'm just 'the kid.' I'm...nobody."

Instead he just shook his head.

"You'll feel better when you get used to the light and have something to eat. Your eyes aren't used to such a long stretch in darkness or near-darkness. Don't worry, they'll adjust in a few more minutes. You're in for a treat--Gen is a good cook. He'll fix up a breakfast that'll have you feelin' good as new!"

Slink hadn't known Neoko that long, and their most recent time together had lasted what--a day, a day and a half? Still, Slink felt hurt suddenly having to share her. He'd never been the intense object of another person's attention until Neoko led him out of the nursery. She'd taken care of him--mothered him. He'd never been mothered. He missed her already, wanted to grab her and say let's go back out into the tunnels--let's get away from here, from HIM. At the same time, he felt embarrassed to even be entertaining those desires. In the end, he resorted to the familiar, stuffed his feelings, and just nodded at Neoko when she finished speaking. Then he got up from the chair and followed her into the next room.

As soon as the fragrance of cooking food hit his nostrils he almost fainted. Any residual anger or hurt gave way to the more urgent sensation of hunger. He felt weak and light-headed as he took a place on the floor in front of the low-lying table where Gen was setting plates with steaming food.

Gen's cooking lived up to Neoko's billing. Gen served Slink an omelet filled with wonderful flavors Slink had never tasted. Slink devoured the omelet and a couple biscuits before Gen even had a chance to sit down. In the nurseries, he'd never tasted anything fresh from an oven. He and the other servants ate long after the food was served to the citizen children.

"No need to eat so fast, little man!" exclaimed Gen. "We'll make sure you get plenty to eat."

Slink looked up sheepishly, but before he could say anything, Gen continued,

"No problem little man! I'll take it as a compliment that you devoured my food so quickly."

"Thanks," said Slink awkwardly, even as he reached for another of the biscuits. The way Gen referred to him as "little man" rattled Slink. Slink could swear he'd heard Gen's distinctive voice calling him little man before, but he couldn't quite grasp the memory. He gave up trying when Gen slid the biscuits back in front of him again.

As soon as he pushed himself back from the table, Neoko spoke up.

"Slink, let me show you where you're gonna sleep, then I'll come back and finish my breakfast. You may be here a while, so you'll have your own space. We call the place "Kansas," because there's no place we'd rather be."

Slink knew enough to recognize the name of a U.S. state, but any analogy was lost on him. Neoko didn't notice his puzzled expression and continued with her description of the enclave.

"You can't get in too much trouble if you want to look around a bit. There's only a couple of other people here right now, so it's pretty quiet. You might want to take advantage of the quiet, though, and catch some shut eye."

Neoko got up and walked through one of the archways connecting the dining room to a large hallway. As Slink got up, she disappeared on the other side of the arch. He passed through the arch and saw Neoko halfway down a long tunnel walking away from him. This wasn't the way he was used to her treating him. She hadn't allowed herself to get more than a couple feet away from him since they'd left the nursery. Now she was taking off in front of him as if he was an afterthought. Resentment rose in his throat.

"Why'd I ever let myself believe Neoko cared about me?" Slink asked himself. "If the nurseries taught me anything, they taught me not to expect anything from anybody."

His inner dialogue continued as he trailed after Neoko.

"Getting a job done is all that really matters. Neoko's finished her job--I'm out of the nursery and safe in the tunnels. She's moving on, and I can either follow her around and beg for attention or get busy doing what I gotta' do. Well--I'm no beggar!"

Neoko stopped and turned to Slink.

"What'd you say?" Neoko asked.

Slink shook his head. He hadn't realized he'd started talking out loud.

"Nothing." he mumbled.

Neoko looked at Slink for several seconds with her head tilted to the side and eyebrows raised. She opened her mouth to speak, then shook her head. She turned and continued down the tunnel.

"You'll feel better after you get some rest," she said over her shoulder a couple seconds later.

Neoko showed Slink to a small hollow off the long narrow tunnel. It was furnished with a small sleeping pad, a latched box for belongings, and a bar for hanging clothes. The bar had been melted into the dome-shaped wall of the hollow. The pad was longer than Slink's boyhood frame required, obviously intended for the average adult. Slink wondered if he was the only young person here. His hopes rose for a moment, then he remembered he was far younger than most the nursery workers who'd disappeared. Neoko had explained his family heritage had spurred them to come for him years earlier than usual. They were afraid his family background would make it nearly impossible to free him if they waited until he was older. Slink sighed as he realized he was almost certainly the youngest person who'd ever seen this hollow.

"Get some sleep, Slink. I'll see you in a few hours."

Before Slink could reply, she was gone.

Slink fell asleep quickly, but he didn't sleep well. His sleep was interrupted by dreams of giant hands chasing him through tunnels he'd never seen. Each time he awoke he'd shake off the nightmare as best he could, only to find himself immersed in another one the moment he fell back asleep. Each time, the dream quickly reached the same painful climax. He always turned down a tunnel only to discover a dead-end. Just as the giant hand was going to squeeze around him, he awoke with a start and realized he was still in the little hollow in the Tunnel Rat enclave. After three hours of fitful sleep he pushed the little cover down off his body and sat up on the sleeping pad. There was no use trying to go back to sleep. Every time he closed his eyes he could see the giant hand coming down a dark tunnel. Exasperated, he got up and set out to take a look around.

The enclave was bigger than Slink might have guessed. He walked down several long tunnels and saw dozens of hollows, most of them with makeshift curtains across their entrances. The few that opened onto the tunnel unobstructed were larger and rudely furnished or without any furnishings at all. Slink assumed they served as gathering places. Slink figured the enclave was home to more people than the nursery. He'd once been told over sixty people lived in the nursery, so he assumed there were more than that living in this little enclave.

He wondered how many other enclaves like this one were hidden in the long-abandoned passages beneath Alpha Sector. He'd learned in his history lessons the underground tunnels were once home to nearly a thousand people before the settlers moved to the surface. It looked to Slink like the Tunnel Rats were living in much tighter quarters than the early settlers, so he imagined there might be several hundred Tunnel Rats, considering they only used a portion of the abandoned tunnels. He'd never have guessed so many people could squeeze out a living beneath the surface.

As he paused to take stock of what he'd seen, a hidden entryway suddenly opened and a stream of people poured through, nearly knocking Slink off his feet as they entered the enclave. One particularly stout woman grabbed him under his arms and swung him up into her arms. He instinctively wrapped his arms around her neck as she made her way down the hall and into the dining room where he'd eaten breakfast.

Only after she'd stepped into the dining room did Slink realize he was clinging to a complete stranger. He abruptly released her neck.

"Whoa...better warn me if you're gonna turn loose all of a sudden, little man."

She was grinning as she caught him under the arms and lifted him up before setting him down.

"You've gotta be the one Neoko pulled outta the nurseries night before last. I thought you were goin' straight to the Technoids. What you doin' here, little man?"

"Well, we were going...."

"Sorry," she interrupted as she pulled a scarf off her head releasing red curls that framed her freckled face. "I'm so rude. I'm Janie. Been down here for nine years now. Just a surface grunt. I heard about ya, but I don't remember ever hearin' your name."

"My name's Slink, ma'am, and there's no need to apologize."

"Oh, you are a little gentleman, aren't you?" she said, breaking into laughter. "Been trained in Beta Sector manners and speech, too, I see! Don't worry, you'll learn to speak Kansan soon enough, I 'magine."

She stepped back and waved to him as she turned to leave. "I'll prob'ly see ya at dinner, Slink. If I was you, I'd be stayin' out of the tunnels for the next hour or so. The dinner bell will ring when it's time to come back here. Otherwise, you might be stayin' in your hollow, so's not to get run over, ya hear?"

"Yes, ma'am," came his automatic response.

He could hear her laughing as she went down the tunnel. "Little man's a charmer, I'll give him that," he heard her say to an unseen comrade. Their conversation blended into the other voices of those streaming into the enclave and walking down the tunnel to their respective hollows.

When Slink ventured out of the dining room to make his way down the tunnel to his hollow, he heard something that made him feel another longing--running water splashing on a shower floor! He stopped and listened for a moment, thinking his imagination may have gotten the better of him. When he realized it was, indeed, a shower, he rushed for his hollow paying close attention to his route so he could retrace his steps to the showers before dinner. Having gone three days without so much as a spit bath for the first time in his limited memory, he wanted that shower as bad as he'd ever wanted a meal.

He made it to his little hollow without incident by walking with the flow of people heading down the tunnel. On the way back, he took advantage of his size as he made the return trip to the showers. He could wedge himself against the curved wall of the tunnel and walk by all the oncoming pedestrians without concern for his safety.

His shower was invigorating! He'd been so intent on it he'd felt no discomfort standing in line, undressing in one of the dozen stalls, and showering amidst the constant banter of the other men and boys sharing the shower room. In his previous life, he'd have been so self-conscious he might have foregone the shower altogether. He was a little startled when the water shut off abruptly and a face peeked over the stall and laughed, hands resting atop the door of the stall just above the hook holding his clothes. Slink couldn't make out the man's face, but Gen's voice and manner gave him away.

"Don't just stand there, little man, dry off! We've all got to shower before the bell, and that means no messin' around. Towel off and throw your pants on so I can come in behind ya. Hurry up!"

Slink jumped when he spoke those last two words more like a command than a request. He toweled off quickly and slipped his pants on. Before he could do anything else, a big hand thrust his shirt, socks, and shoes toward him. When he wrapped his arms around the clothes, the hand moved to his back and ushered him unceremoniously from one side of the stall while he stepped through from the other. The bare-chested, muscular man would have intimidated most anyone as his thin lips parted into a broad smile from beneath a thick, black mustache, his mirth showing in his sparkling brown eyes peering from beneath raised eyebrows. His teeth, offset by his dark, pockmarked skin, gleamed in the ambient light of the lumatorches.

As he moved inside the stall, he shut the little door and leaned over it to look down on Slink who now stood on the other side with his clothes piled in his arms. He bowed his head in mock respect, and said,

"Thank you for making room for me, young prince!"

Then he laughed and disappeared from Slink's sight. Slink still felt indebted to this man for cooking his breakfast earlier that day, but he liked Gen less with each encounter. The sarcastic reference to royalty only made Slink feel deeper animosity for the man.

As soon as Slink stepped into the dining room, he felt an arm wrap around his back. As she pulled him out of the entrance and over to a table, Neoko asked, "did you get some rest?"

Slink didn't respond. He wanted to push her away and yell at her for leaving him. At the same time, he wanted to curl into her shoulder and stay perfectly still in the hope she would leave her arm around him for a long, long time. He wanted to cry in outrage, "Neoko!" He wanted to shout for joy, "Neoko!" He wanted to call out to her from the broken places in his heart, "Neoko!" Instead, he said nothing.

She led him over to an empty table, removed her arm from around his back, and motioned for him to sit down. She sat down opposite him and leaned in close.

"Slink, I'm sorry I left you alone all day. I checked in on you and you were sleeping, so I tended to some things I had to do."

"I'll bet!" he thought. He had a hard time believing she'd managed to check on him during one of those brief stretches when he was actually sleeping. No, more than likely, she hadn't checked on him at all, just moved on to the next job on her list.

His silence was getting to her. She was talking about showing him around and introducing him to some of the Tunnel Rats closest to his age. She had her hands over his and was rubbing the tops of his fingers. He made no motion to remove his hands, and said nothing. He didn't look away from her, or right at her--he looked right through her. He wasn't going to let her in again. She'd gotten inside too easily, gotten past all his defenses, and when she was suddenly gone, he'd ached like he'd been punched in the stomach, and he wasn't going to hurt like that again--not now, not ever! He noticed when she stopped talking, but he'd heard little, listened to even less. He knew how to live inside. He knew how to shut everyone out and survive, and he was good at it, or at least he told himself he was.

Neoko stared at him. How did this kid get so far under her skin? She felt like she was the younger one, begging for approval from her older sibling or parent. He needed to learn she had a life, most of which had nothing to do with their relationship. She'd carve out a place for him, make time for him, help him get through his time with the Tunnel Rats, but she couldn't just drop everything and be his personal servant or surrogate mother.

She knew she'd done nothing wrong. She'd only been away from him for a few hours, and he'd slept most of that time, or so she thought. So why did she feel so bad?

She loved him. It was really that simple. She knew that seemed silly, given how little time she'd spent with him, but she also knew her heart. Whether it was logical or not, she loved this kid.

He was a supposed genius, and he was descended from the most famous family on Garsow...and he was twelve! You could talk to him like he was an adult and he could understand you and reply in kind...but he was a kid. He hadn't acted like a kid when she met him, and even through their harrowing escape from the nursery and trek through the tunnels he'd held up as well as she could have expected from anyone her age. But there were times when he couldn't hold up the facade and he became twelve again, and allowed himself to need her, to rely on her, to trust her. Those were the times that'd done her in. She could keep the "little man" at arms length, but the little boy had already made a home in her heart, and she couldn't bear to have him shut her out.

"Slink, I didn't," Her voice trailed off. "Slink, I'm sorry I hurt you. I should've stuck closer to you after we got here."

He stood silently while she searched for words.

"I could tell you I just fell into my familiar routine, or I was just relieved to get back here, or even that I was just really hungry, and I'd be telling you the truth, but I don't want to start making excuses."

He never even changed expression, although she thought his eyes looked a little glossier for just a second.

"Please, Slink, I need to hear your voice. I need to know we're OK."

"Of course, we're OK, Neoko."

He sounded almost clinical. His voice wasn't flat like someone hiding his emotions--it was soft and steady, as if he was unaffected by any of this.

"You've done nothing wrong, and I'm not angry with you."

It was a lie, but Slink didn't even know it. He was gone. He'd retreated into the safety of his head, and his heart was completely inaccessible.

Her eyes filled with tears as she said, "Good...that's good, Slink."

She fell silent now, confounded by his complete withdrawal.

The table filled with people.

As soon as dinner was served the table was crowded with people. Slink withdrew a little further, taking up space at the table without attracting attention from anyone. When he bumped elbows with the person on his left, he apologized with impeccable nursery manners. He disappeared into the banter of table mates, deflecting any inquiries with a one or two word answer.

Within a few minutes, he'd detached completely from the group and its lively exchanges, and if anyone noticed, they made no indication. When Neoko was called away from the table for a moment, Slink took the opportunity to feign fatigue and excuse himself from the table. He was alone in his hollow within a couple minutes, indulging his long-standing preference for his own company over the company of others. When sleep engulfed him, there was no giant hand waiting, and he slept well and long.

―――――――

     Slink was assigned to the kitchen for his duties. At first, he was disturbed to think he'd be working alongside Gen all day long. His fears were unjustified. Gen was the head cook of the enclave and Slink was assigned to washing utensils and dishes. If he finished his duties in the kitchen, he helped clean the dining area. Slink's coworkers approached his first days with typically low expectations of a new kitchen mate. They raised those expectations quickly. By his fifth day working alongside them, his kitchen mates were soon encouraging Slink to relax and work at a slower pace. He seldom took their advice. Slink was civil to everyone he encountered, but he seemed determined to complete his work and return to his hollow as quickly as possible.

     Within his first week in Kansas, word came that DAN was mounting an all-out offensive against the Technoids. The sweeper drones converted by the Technoids had all been destroyed, according to one of the smaller Tunnel Rat enclaves closer to the maintenance center. The enclave itself had endured having their home destroyed when they refused to give the DAN officers any information on the Technoids. The leaders of the enclave, pointed out by a former member of the enclave who'd been captured a week earlier, were all arrested. Everyone else was left to fend for themselves in the tunnels. They split up into small groups and headed for other enclaves. With their defenses high, they made sure no one could follow their movements, traveling mostly during late night hours and using abandoned tunnels whenever possible.

     A small group made it to Kansas and passed on the news of the DAN offensive. It seemed most of DAN's efforts were focused below Beta Sector, but Slink's enclave leaders weren't about to take chances. Surface excursions left the enclave earlier and returned later to coincide with surface darkness. Water and electricity usage was cut to the bone. The Tunnel Rats had to get used to an abundance of natural odors, since showers were restricted to once-a-week. The grumbling was minimal; everyone understood the seriousness of the threat.

The second week of Slink's new life brought more devastating news. In two separate offensives, DAN had hunted down the Technoids and arrested them. Those who mounted resistance were killed. It marked the first time in Garsow's history lethal force had been used on a dissident group. Occasionally, the security police had used deadly force on an individual who posed a threat to self or others, but nothing close to a war had ever occurred on Garsow. Of course, the surface dwellers would never have thought of the DAN offensive as a war. It was simply a security operation designed to mitigate a threat mounted by a bunch of radical anti-technology terrorists. It was unfortunate, in the average surface dweller's opinion, that some of the terrorists were killed, but it had to be expected when the decision was made to neutralize the threat of the Technoid resistance.

To those living in the tunnels having long characterized their lives in the context of resistance and struggle, the DAN offensive could only be understood as all-out war. The operation struck mortal fear in the heart of every Tunnel Rat. The Tunnel Rats were even less prepared than the Technoids to meet any such offensive with meaningful resistance. Fortunately, no such offensive ever came. When DAN had satisfied itself it had eliminated the Technoid threat, it retreated, and left the Tunnel Rats to continue their marginal existence in the tunnels. After all, the Tunnel Rats were ignorant, helpless misfits who'd fled from the nurseries in a misguided attempt to be free, or so went the ideal society's official reasoning. The Tunnel Rats provided helpful assistance with recycling unwanted or surplus goods. They even recycled about a third of the refuse Garsow would have otherwise jettisoned into space. The Technoids were a threat, but the Tunnel Rats were no worse than a nuisance in the eyes of those who shaped policy on Garsow.

Slink's only solid link with his family disappeared in the chaos of the DAN offensive. That is to say, Dot was unaccounted for after her company was caught up in the offensive. One of her company soldiers had escaped the ambush in which half a dozen were wounded or killed trying to hold DAN off long enough to enable Dot to escape. He couldn't be sure she'd escaped, although he hadn't seen her amongst the Technoids he witnessed being led off by DAN agents. He'd fled when he had the chance and was discovered in the tunnels by one of the Tunnel Rat enclaves. He was spirited away to safety before the DAN patrol swept back through the tunnels. His report, along with other similar stories, was circulated throughout the tunnels amongst the Tunnel Rat enclaves. All told, it was estimated no more than a couple dozen Technoids escaped capture during the two-week offensive. When it was over, the Technoid resistance was, for all intents and purposes, dead.

Through it all, Slink labored, ate, and slept. As far as most of his fellows were concerned, that was all he did. Eventually, a couple noticed Slink in the rudimentary library of the enclave. The enclave didn't dare establish a permanent link to the Supernet or one of the subnets, but they did manage to copy files when they were on their surface excursions. They had wireless handhelds that could masquerade as a visor link for short intervals without raising alarm. It only took seconds to access and download educational, news, and entertainment files, since they weren't protected or encrypted. The memory coins with files suitable for the library were catalogued and downloaded to one of a half dozen antique terminals in Kansas. Slink thrived in this chaotic system.

He wasn't well-suited for formal education, since formal instruction was always designed at a pace dictated by the slowest student. Slink preferred to move quickly from one topic to another. He concentrated on one subject until he'd mastered it, then moved on to another. He'd always been advanced. Now, his education accelerated beyond anything any of the other Tunnel Rats had ever seen or imagined.

On one occasion, Gen found Slink in the library and decided to pull him away from his studies. Gen was wondering if Neoko had let slip with Slink how she felt about Gen.

"Slinkie, my boy, what say you push back from the monitor for a few minutes and join the real world?"

Gen pulled up a chair next to Slink who sat with his back facing the entrance to the hollow that housed the library. Slink didn't so much as twitch with Gen's entrance into the Library or the sudden sound of Gen's voice.

"Don't ignore me!" Gen roared in mock indignation.

Slink still didn't move. Gen stooped and peered into Slink's eyes. Gen could see Slink's eyes scanning top to bottom as he absorbed the contents of the screen. He was conscious--just totally oblivious!

"Slee-ink," Gen called, with his face right next to Slink's ear.

Nothing.

Gen reached out and grabbed Slink by the shoulder as he barked his name.

"Slink!"

Still nothing.

Gen pinched Slink's shoulder. Slink still didn't respond. Finally, Gen turned Slink's chair on its axis until Slink was facing him.

"What is up with you, little man?" he asked as he reached up and pinched Slink's cheek with his free hand.

Slink's eyelids fluttered, then he blinked deliberately a couple of times.

"Gen!" Slink slurred. "What're you doing here?"

Slink seemed to struggle for each word like he was pulling apart a honey sandwich.

"What are you doing here?" Gen mimicked in a slow drawl. "Come on, Slink! I'm not an idiot. I know you heard me and felt me pinching your shoulder. Why were you ignoring me?"

Slink's forehead wrinkled in confusion. He started to say something, then stopped, then opened his mouth again, and thought better of it again.

It was Gen's turn to be speechless. With his head cocked to the side, Gen stared at Slink for several seconds before he found words.

"You really had no idea I was here, did you?" Gen asked.

Slink's confusion was too obvious. Gen knew the kid couldn't be faking. He was genuinely dumbstruck when he finally realized Gen was stooped over him.

"Sometimes you scare me kid," Gen almost whispered. He shook his head and turned to leave. He mumbled to himself as he escaped the library.

Long days stretched into weeks and the weeks into months. Slink grew in stature and wisdom. He saw the passing of his thirteenth birthday and the beginning of his fourteenth year bring the most accelerated growth spurt since his infancy. Half way through his fourteenth year of life, he was well over five feet tall. He no longer could be easily picked out as a youngster in the dining room crowd. He came to know many of the other Tunnel Rats, though none could have said they knew him. He was always polite, even solicitous with others, but they seldom came away from the lengthiest conversation with any sense they knew Slink.

Neoko was no more able to penetrate his defenses than were any of her comrades. One night, after a particularly harrowing surface excursion, Neoko dropped by the library to bring Slink some bad news.

"Slink. Slink. Slee-ink."

Neoko knelt next to her prodigy and shook him gently. His trance-like states neither surprised her nor alarmed her by then. She knew what to expect when she walked in and saw him sitting motionless in front of the monitor.

"Slink!"

She rubbed his arms and slowly rotated his chair to face her.

"Neoko!"

He named her before his eyes fluttered, he blinked, and focused on her.

"Hey little man. How ya' doin?" Neoko asked.

"I'm OK" Slink responded. "You look tired, though" he asserted.

"It was a long one," Neoko acknowledged. "Slink..."

Her voice trailed off. Neoko lowered her eyes, then looked up again to make eye contact.

"I've got some bad news."

Slink's eyes narrowed. Neoko knew he was following her.

"Your great aunt, Dot, has been captured," Neoko blurted.

Slink's facial expression didn't change. Neoko might have wondered if he'd even heard her if she hadn't seen his eyes narrow slightly. Anyone else might have been compelled to repeat herself. Neoko just waited.

"I'm sorry to hear that." Slink finally said. "Thank you for taking the time to bring me the news. You need sleep. We can talk tomorrow night."

Neoko wanted to shake him. The closest family member he had was in DAN custody and he didn't seem moved at all by the news. She stood and opened her mouth to lash out at him. Then she just turned and walked out. She stood outside the Library entrance for two or three minutes to regain her composure. When she looked back into the library, Slink sat motionless in front of the monitor again. Neoko turned and headed for her hollow.

Despite the frustration she felt with Slink, Neoko consistently made it a point to seek him out in the evening and tear him away from the library. She engaged him in short conversations most of the time and occasionally got him to play one of the many card games he'd learned from other Tunnel Rats or in his studies. At times, they reached a level of camaraderie that allowed for teasing and easy banter, and when these brief interludes occurred, Slink seemed comfortable enough.

Whenever Neoko tried to entice Slink into a more personal exchange though, she immediately ran up against Slink's impenetrable emotional barriers. He would deftly turn the conversation back to the game they were playing or otherwise redirect to issues affecting Kansas. If he felt anything deeper than curiosity, no one around him, including Neoko, ever knew it.

Nonetheless, Neoko found she enjoyed her time with Slink to the point that most of her discomfort over his emotional isolation disappeared when they were together. The fact that Slink had abandoned his antagonistic attitude toward Gen allowed Neoko to spend more time with Slink, since the three of them could share the time together. Neoko, Gen, and Slink spent hours playing card games. Slink also made numerous alterations of the games, and many of his renditions of the card games were more fun than any of the traditional approaches.

Slink occasionally applied his newfound knowledge to the work he did in the enclave, but most of his studies didn't have an immediate application to the very constrained life of tunnel living. He recognized, though, how easily he could help his fellow Kansans improve their academic abilities, and he set about finding subtle ways to do just that. He'd engage one man in a game of cribbage or dice quietly teaching him basic math skills. He'd get to know a woman's interests and feed her articles on subjects he knew she'd enjoy just to help her improve her subpar reading abilities. Sometimes he would tutor small groups with history lessons cleverly disguised as grand adventure stories. He was a natural teacher.

Like Neoko, Gen was troubled by Slink's ability to conceal his inner life so completely. He stopped by Slink's hollow unannounced on many occasions and observed him closely in the kitchen, but he never saw any sign Slink was expressing any discomfort or pain. He never found him crying quietly on his sleeping pad or saw him throw a utensil or speak tersely to one of his coworkers. Either Slink was the most emotionally secure person Gen had ever met or he was going down a path bound to end in turmoil. Gen knew something of that path, and he didn't want to see the kid suffer the way he'd suffered when his emotional dam broke after years of holding back his feelings. He was impotent to act on his concern, however, since he was no better than anyone else at reaching behind Slink's defenses. After Slink's first full day with the enclave, Gen had never been able to get a reaction out of Slink despite his numerous attempts to bait him. It was scary... and oddly fascinating.

At first, Slink had worked hard to keep his emotions from rising to the surface. The first time Neoko had openly wept over the emotional chasm between them, Slink had nearly thrown himself into her arms and released a flood of his own tears. He'd nearly opened up, but in the end his defenses held, then hardened to the point he never again came so close to catharsis. As time went by his emotional isolation became less and less a matter of will and more a matter of fact. He was now seldom aware of any sense of isolation or loneliness. He laughed when something was funny, listened attentively to his fellows' stories and attendant feelings, and even offered words of support or condolence as appropriate. It all came naturally to Slink and never seemed forced or contrived. Most of the time, he really felt as though all was well with Stanis Web Macdonald. On occasion, though, he couldn't ignore the growing uneasiness deep beneath the surface.

The lessons Slink absorbed were mostly academic and practical. By the time he approached his fourteenth birthday, he'd far surpassed the knowledge of any of his fellow Tunnel Rats. Consequently, his voracious appetite for knowledge was well known throughout the enclave. He started making lists of the subjects and specific areas of study he needed the surface units to download for him. Gen had quietly directed the surface units to do their best to fulfill Slink's requests.

Slink wasn't allowed to join their incursions out of fear he'd be recognized. The coincidence of his disappearance and the largest DAN crackdown the tunnels had even known wasn't lost on the Tunnel Rats. Surface reports indicated every interrogation of a Tunnel Rat captured by DAN officers included questions as to Slink's whereabouts.

The enclave had also come to recognize Slink's extraordinary intelligence would one day be an asset to all of them, so they did their best to satisfy his appetite for information and protect him from detection. Their enclave never spoke of Slink to other Tunnel Rat enclaves. As far as the other enclaves knew, Slink had been captured in the DAN sweeps for Technoids. Now, their best ongoing defense against his detection consisted of measures to prevent any of their enclave from being captured and interrogated, and in this endeavor, they were extraordinarily successful.

Slink made notes of those areas where the enclave's electronic files lacked information on subjects of interest and gave his requests for any such files to Neoko. Sooner or later, she always came to him with memory coins containing data on the subjects he'd requested. He never seemed to tire of pouring over files and committing to memory every useful tidbit of information. The days passed quickly into weeks then months, and before it seemed possible, Slink was approaching his fifteenth birthday. His days were nearly indistinguishable, but Slink never seemed restless or bored. If he ever felt any desire to reestablish a deeper connection with Neoko or any of the other Tunnel Rats, he never voiced that desire.

Slink never allowed his studies to interfere with his commitment to the kitchen crew and never grumbled about his duties. He had no problem with his assignment, but the enclave leaders knew his talents were being wasted. Slink had belonged on the Leadership Council for a long time, but members of the Leadership Council weren't quite ready to welcome a teenager, though they couldn't help but recognize their need for his insight and knowledge as they planned for the future. Their enclave was at capacity for the area it occupied, and if they were to continue providing a home for the outcasts they freed from the nurseries, it would soon be necessary for them to establish another enclave. Slink's knowledge of Garson geology and, specifically, the maps of the caverns and developed tunnels would be invaluable. Though he was three years short of meeting the age requirement for the leadership council, the members of the Council calling for an exception were gaining ground.

Slink was invited to attend the leadership council two days in advance of its regularly scheduled meeting. This was the lengthiest notice he'd ever received for any event taking place in the enclave. He had two days to ponder the many issues brought up by the invitation. The fact that he'd been given a personal invitation by Neoko on the occasion of his fifteenth birthday didn't strike him as significant at first.

He was more caught up with the underlying revelation of the leadership council's existence. He'd recognized some time earlier the enclave functioned far too efficiently to be without centralized leadership. Nonetheless, he'd never heard anyone talking about the council or a meeting of any such group.

He wondered what would prompt them to invite him to attend one of their meetings. Perhaps they hoped he could share some tidbit of information that might help them solve some dilemma facing the enclave. He was aware, as was each member of the enclave, they were at or above the comfortable capacity of the tunnels they'd reclaimed as their home. Perhaps they needed to know if he had any knowledge of nearby abandoned tunnels likely to be in good enough condition to be reclaimed for the planting of a new enclave. This was almost certain to be one of the reasons they wanted to talk to him. He'd made it known he'd done a detailed study of the old tunnel structures and mapped them in comparison to the modern tunnels serving the surface dwellers.

They had to want more than information, though, thought Slink. In the past, one or more of his fellows had approached him for facts or figures pertinent to some project. They'd listen well, occasionally taking notes on a handheld, and when they'd heard everything he had to offer, or at least, everything they'd come to hear, they'd thank him and leave him to his studies. If all they wanted was more information, why'd they need to invite him to attend the council this time? No--there was more to this summons than a need for information. They needed him.

The exact nature of their need escaped him, since he had no concept of his rising importance to those who shared his existence in the tunnels. Nor did he have any knowledge of the scope of the challenge before the enclave. In his mind, he was no more than a bright kid who tried to stay out of the way and work hard when given a chance. He was happy to be sheltered from the bigger picture of their existence, and he might have resisted answering their invitation had he known it would mean the end to his naiveté.

When Slink entered the hollow where he'd been directed for the council meeting, he was surprised to find only one person standing near the back of the hollow. Upon seeing Slink, the regal figure moved to her right, turned toward the back wall, and extended her graceful arms making hand gestures facing the wall. Slink wasn't surprised when the wall suddenly shuttered, the outline of a door appeared, and a portion of the wall slid back and away to one side to reveal another small tunnel. Slink didn't need to be ushered through the tunnel. He moved forward, bowed beneath the penetrating gaze of the woman who'd opened the door for him, and moved into the tunnel. It was very dark, and to his consternation, seemed to stretch on without end.

He pulled the lumatorch from a stand just inside the doorway, and wound his way down the tunnel. After he'd walked a hundred meters or more, he puzzled over the absence of any connecting passages. He'd never been in a tunnel so thoroughly isolated. It had obviously been formed with the sole purpose of reaching his destination. It was not part of any network of tunnels or maze of natural caverns he'd mapped. It curved slightly now and then, but for the most part, it headed ever onward in the same general direction, with a lingering sensation of descent.

After what seemed like an hour, but was probably closer to five minutes, as near as Slink could tell, he reached an apparent barricade. He couldn't see any way to open it, so he knocked tentatively on it. It echoed like knocking on the side of an empty supply barrel. Within a few seconds a previously indiscernible door opened a crack and someone asked for his name. He gave it and the door opened wide so he could enter. By his accounting he was early, but all the places except two were filled around a circular table so large it left only a few feet between the hollow's walls and the table's edge. One place had personal belongings laid on the table in front of it, so Slink went to the other empty place and, upon making eye contact with Gen and seeing his slight bow, took his seat. The man who'd opened the door for his entry had already closed the door and returned to his place.

"Now that we are all here, I would ask Gen to offer an opening prayer."

The voice came from a woman, large in stature, though soft in voice. Her voice conveyed authority in its precision and tenor.

"Look within your own heart and the hearts of those who surround this table and see the Source that binds us together. Open your hearts to one another and to that Source now," said Gen as he stood, bowed his head, and closed his eyes.

Everyone around the table closed his or her eyes and bowed their heads in unison with Gen.

"We seek harmony with that creative energy that casts out fear and binds us together in a singular purpose. We seek to set aside our fears and concerns and see through our deliberations the path prepared for the healing of our world. We lay ourselves at one another's service and seek peace--in the tunnels, on the surface, and beyond. We surrender our desires and our efforts accordingly."

After a prolonged silence, Gen reassumed a seated posture and the woman who'd invited the prayer motioned outward with her arms fixing her gaze on Slink. She smiled softly and spoke.

"Welcome my young apprentice. We've waited as long as we could before bringing you here. Entrance into this circle means you shall now live with awareness of events whose reality you may otherwise have chosen to ignore. The burdens of this council are heavy for one many years older than you, and, I fear, may seem unfair to you. Please know--if we could choose the time of your entry based only on your well-being, you would not be here. The urgency and profundity of our need dictates our timing, and we must trust in powers much greater than ours to keep you whole. Let me introduce you to the other members of this inner circle of inner circles."

Slink's head was swimming with too many sudden revelations to catch or retain many of the names he heard. Gen was the first she introduced, but it seemed to Slink she referred to Gen as "Moderator" or some such title. How could the head cook of his enclave be some high leader of this group? And what was that speech Gen had made? The woman had called upon him to offer a specific type of speech--a "prair-er," or something like that. It was so strange to Slink's ears, but its content stuck to him the same way mathematical formulas did. He could repeat every word Gen had said without much effort at all! But those words--who or what was this "Source" of whom Gen spoke and to whom he addressed his speech? Was there an invisible leader in the room who'd yet to reveal himself or herself?

His eyes must have stopped tracking the faces of the people being introduced, because the woman was calling his name again and again. Slink snapped his eyes around to meet hers.

"Don't worry, Slink, we shall all introduce ourselves each time we speak. You needn't try to remember everything you are hearing. But I do want you to hear this:

I am Jonathan and Adela Lansing's daughter, Lela Lansing's sister, Renae Lansing's aunt, and your great-aunt. My name is Dorothea Lansing, but like you, I have never been known by that name. I am called Dot, and I am three standard years late for our appointment. Please forgive my tardiness, it could not be helped."

His mind was swimming now and he could feel a cold coming over him, sweeping around his shoulders, and ascending the back of his neck. He fought back the blackness that threatened his vision and concentrated on her voice over the ringing in his ears.

"Slink--there is one more introduction I wanted to make this evening."

"Here it comes," thought Slink. She's going to identify this "One" at the heart of Gen's prair-er.

"The place where you sit is intended for two. The one who should occupy the seat next to you would have done her best to make this easier on you, but it was not to be. Slink--Neoko was detained along with her entire surface detail by DAN officers in a tunnel sweep yesterday. Even as we speak, DAN interrogators are surely working to gain information as to your whereabouts. Their ways are not gentle, and though she is strong, your enclave must evacuate in the certain event that DAN will know in days, if not hours, everything Neoko knew about the enclave and about you. Your way now lies with me, with this small circle of comrades, and with the Source. May we find that way together!"

Chapter 5

"We're going."

No one ever spoke to the Director of the Solar Aeronautics and Space Administration in the imperative. Queries and compliant responses were more the order of his office, but Jonathan Lansing held all the cards and he knew it. No complicated presentation, no written proposal in triplicate, just two simple words.

Dr. Lansing had all the justification he needed for demanding he and his wife be two of the first to land on Garsow. He had personally overseen the development and construction of the proton booster system that would provide the necessary acceleration the shuttle crew needed to reach the planetoid before they exhausted their fuel. He alone knew how to safely recharge that system so the shuttle could return to earth and be outfitted for subsequent trips to Garsow. Adela was the foremost expert on developing life support systems for large-scale extra-planetary settlements. Jonathan knew SASA and its mercurial director couldn't say "no." He didn't know the director was happy to say "yes."

When Jonathan Lansing came into his office and demanded to oversee the establishment of the first Solar-edge base on Garsow, Henry had almost missed seeing the golden opportunity Dr. Lansing gave him. His first impulse was to reassert his authority and put the good doctor in his place. Then, in the back of his head, a rare flicker of insight saved him. Garsow was half again the distance of Pluto from the Earth! Even with the recent advances in propulsion, that meant any breakthroughs on Garsow would be very old news if and when the Lansings returned to Earth. Henry would be front and center with the media for every advancement made, and he would graciously give credit to the Lansings and the rest of the team on Garsow, along with the many teams working on Earth, Mars, and the moon. At the end of the day, though, no one would mistake any of the circus performers for the ringmaster, and that was the only thing Henry Malcolm White cared about!

Over a year and a half passed from the morning the first rockets blasted from Earth with the space station modules to the day the first colonist stepped onto Garsow's surface. In that time, only two people died working on the project. One had a heart attack en-route to Garsow orbit, and another's space suit failed during a space walk building Garsow station in orbit around the planetoid. No one had dared hope the mission could go so well. Their good fortune was short-lived. Once they stepped foot on the planetoid's surface, they suffered their most serious setback.

Two weeks after the first crew landed, a failed electrical breaker claimed the lives of everyone in the life support module-- half the crew. The exhausted Station crew orbiting the planetoid drew lots and half their number, instead of boarding a ship for Earth, boarded the lander, descended to Garsow, and assumed the jobs of the deceased surface crew.

Jonathan might have been amongst the casualties of the first crew had he been well enough to make the first landing on Garsow. Instead, he was struck with space sickness after arriving at Garsow Station. Space sickness, with its accompanying seizures, was thought to be associated with prolonged zero gravity, but Dr. Lansing had not suffered any ill affects until reaching the artificial gravity of Garsow Station. His case was unique and resolving it proved to be beyond the scope of the medical staff. When he did not respond to any of the medications on board the station, and half the colonizing crew perished on the surface, Jonathan had little difficulty convincing the Solar Council to let him join the replacement crew on Garsow. They needed him, and he could not be any worse off on Garsow, with its near-Earth gravity. As it turned out, Jonathan never had another seizure once he touched the surface of the barren planetoid.

The last thing Slink remembered of the council meeting was the gasps of the others at the table at the sound of his head cracking the floor. When he woke, he was back in a hollow, lying on a sleeping mat surrounded by unfamiliar instruments, and he couldn't help but notice the area around his head was soaking wet.

He had no way of knowing how long he was out. He knew he'd passed out, but he didn't know how much time had passed since. A quick look around convinced him he was not in Kansas anymore. Whatever this place was, it was nothing like anything he'd ever seen. If this was a tunnel hollow, someone had gone to a great deal of trouble to conceal that. The walls were not the smooth stone of a Garson tunnel, but rough metal. They didn't bow outward like a tunnel wall, but were flat and at right angles to one another.

"Glad to see you're still with us!"

The voice was familiar. Gen put a hand on Slink's shoulder and squeezed it affectionately. Then he sat down next to Slink and looked into his eyes. Slink looked away.

"I can't say I faired much better when I heard the news about Neoko, Slink. I always knew something like this could happen, but somehow I'd completely denied that possibility. When I heard they had her--well, let's just say my reaction required much stronger intervention than yours."

He paused for a while, then let out a long sigh. Slink fought to keep his head down and his tongue still.

"I wish I could give you some time to mourn--I can't. I wish I could give you some time to get used to your new surroundings--I can't. I wish I could assure you we won't meet the same fate Neoko met. I can't do that either. About all I can do is promise to answer your questions, or introduce you to someone with the answers. For now, let me say, 'welcome Home.' This (he motioned with his arms in a grand sweep) is the mother ship of the Technoids. It seems the news of her demise was as premature as was the news of her mistress's capture."

"I'm on a ship?" thought Slink. Without any conscious forethought, he directed his attention away from the subject matter Gen wanted to address and toward his newfound object of fascination. Since he'd first learned of the Technoid's adaptation of the drones, he'd wanted to see the inside of one. He never dreamed he'd be able to live aboard the first one! If Home survived, Slink wondered, how many of the other converted drones survived? If Dot escaped the DAN sweep, despite an eye witness report of her capture, how many of the other Technoids likewise escaped capture?

"Uh, Slink, did you hear anything I just said?" asked Gen.

Slink raised an eyebrow toward Gen, then smiled.

"I didn't think so," said Gen with mock disgust written all over his face. "I should've known better. Well, let me show you around a bit. Dot wants to meet with you after you have a quick tour, a bite to eat, and a ship shower."

Now it was Slink's turn to look at Gen with mock disgust.

"Well, you are a little ripe, dude! You can't be meeting the high commander of the resistance smelling like that, even if you are her nephew!"

There was more room in the drone than Slink would have thought. From Slink's typical tunnel vantage point, always at a safe distance from any moving drone, the drones had looked much smaller. Now that he was touring one, he quickly understood how it could be home to some fifty people when it was fully staffed. Gen told him the ship was short of its normal crew by at least a dozen people, and given the fact that another fifteen of those on board were members of the council, most of whom had no more knowledge of the ship than he, Slink imagined Home was running very short-handed.

"This completes our grand tour of Home," Gen said a few minutes later. "You can grab a bite to eat here in the galley, then head back up to middle deck and take a shower. Dot will be expecting you at 2:00 standard. That's an hour from now, so if you don't go off exploring, you should have no problem being on time. She's very, very busy Slink. Honor her schedule by being on time. And Slink...we still need to talk about the events of the last few days, and I'm not going to let you off the hook, so I'll catch up with you soon."

He turned and left Slink in the galley. Slink noticed the smell of the food for the first time since they'd entered the galley, and his awareness quickly moved from the wafting odors to his rumbling stomach. Five minutes later, he'd wolfed down a plate full of food and was returning for more. The food was as good as any he'd had in the tunnels or the nursery. After he ate his fill, he went back up to the room where he'd awoken and found his few belongings folded in an open footlocker. He grabbed a clean pair of pants and a pullover and headed for the shower. He was surprised to find the shower room had six showers and the water pressure and volume was more than adequate for a satisfying shower.

Life on Home was proving to be a step up from his experiences in Kansas. So why did he feel so desolate? It'd been too long since Slink asked why he felt anything, let alone acknowledged such a deep, disturbing emotion as the one now lapping the boundaries of his emotional dam, threatening to burst over the rigid construct of his psychological flatlands. The question arose like a distant, though compelling S.O.S. in an otherwise blissful sea of ignorance, and he pushed away its plaintive appeal as he dressed and turned his attention to finding the commander.

Slink stepped into the commander's private quarters after her voice over the intercom bid him enter and the automatic door slid into the bulwark. Dot's quarters served as both a private office and personal quarters. As he stepped in, Slink saw her sitting at her desk built into the wall on the right side of her room. She had three different monitors built into the wall above her desk, and she appeared to be dictating instructions to someone. As she spoke, the text of her message appeared on one of the screens a word at a time, then disappeared completely when she finished the message and gave the command, "send."

Slink saw that the room was about twice the size of his. The furniture wasn't any fancier, and though it was not crowded, no space was wasted. Next to the desk and turned outward facing the room was a large, overstuffed chair like Slink had seen in the nursery library. On the other side of the chair were shelves filled with books. There were more books on those shelves than Slink had ever seen! Books were an extraordinary luxury on a remote outpost like Garsow. He wondered if they had belonged to his great-grandfather and great-grandmother. The titles he could read seemed to support that idea. They were all scientific volumes devoted to obscure areas of physics, geology, and chemistry. Dot interrupted his musings.

"Stanis!"

Slink turned to look at the door expecting someone had come in behind him before it dawned on him that Dot was calling him by his given name. He looked back to her, eyes slightly lowered in embarrassment over his misunderstanding.

"Yes, Commander; Stanis Web Macdonald reporting for duty."

"You may call me Commander when we are in public, but when we're alone, please call me Dot. I don't expect you to call me Aunt or Auntie. I suppose you're too old for such intimacies, and I won't burden you with my hunger for family endearments, nephew."

She spoke this last sentence with a widening smile on her face and drew out the word "nephew" playfully. Slink relaxed and returned her smile.

"Let me show you around." She pushed back from the desk and rose from the chair where she'd been sitting. She motioned to the desk with a broad sweep of her hands. "You saw my messy desk. It gives me the means to stay abreast of everything on Home without having to be on the bridge 24-7. Truth be told, I prefer as much time alone as I can find, and under the circumstances, that amounts to far less time than I'd prefer."

He noticed how gracefully she moved away from the desk and over to the shelves. She had to be fifty years old, thought Slink. She looked much younger. She was slender and muscular. Her face was smooth with the exception of the crow's feet at the edges of her eyes. She was two or three inches taller than Slink, which made her better than six feet by about the same margin. She also smelled good thought Slink, becoming self-conscious that he'd noticed anything so personal.

"I caught you eyeing my books. They're all I have left of my parents, your great-grandparents. Though all the information they contain was long since committed to the Garson data banks, I cannot bear to part with them. I still hope to give them back to Mom and Dad someday. They both loved books and preferred them over digital images. Until I know for certain I will not see my parents again, I'll hold on to these books and to the hope they represent."

As she spoke she ran her fingers across the spines of the books as though they were a living extension of Jonathan and Adela Lansing. Slink felt an odd sensation coming over him. If he weren't so detached from his feelings, he might've identified a sense of connection. As it was, the feeling dissipated as quickly as it had arisen.

"This is my sitting area," Dot continued, pointing to the corner of her room on the other side of her raised sleeping platform. She passed over her sleeping platform assuming Slink had seen enough of them in the nursery to forego any explanation. The sitting area was little more than a pile of pillows and a solitary shelf filled with candles. Slink had known one guardian in the nurseries who had a candle. He loved to watch that candle burn, and he now imagined the atmosphere created by Dot's candles when they were all lit.

Dot motioned to the pillows.

"Sit."

She folded her legs and positioned herself to face him.

"My parents were fascinated with science, and though they passed to me an appreciation of the field, my passion is in a field they never understood or valued. This little corner filled with pillows is where I engage an ancient practice known in various times or places as sitting, contemplation, meditation, or prayer.

I'm convinced some power greater than ourselves is at work in us, and I devote a significant amount of energy to maintaining conscious contact with that power. Some who have maintained similar devotion have called the object of their devotion 'God,' 'the universe,' or as you heard in Gen's prayer before the Council, 'the One.' Some early practitioners focused on the practice itself, calling it 'mindfulness' or 'higher consciousness;' and still others have focused on the end result of the practice, referring to 'shared consciousness' or 'oneness.' All of them refer to these practices as 'spiritual.'

I care less for names or labels. I'm interested in the effect of the practice. I'm better able to direct my conscious attention, manage my emotions, measure my responses, make better decisions, treat people better, and lead more effectively when I'm faithful to this practice.

Gen told me of your penchant for sitting in front of the vid monitor and losing yourself so completely you don't have any awareness of what's going on around you--even when people are screaming for your attention. He says you lose all sense of time and seem surprised to realize how long you were sitting at a work station. He also tells me you have a near-perfect photographic memory. I think these ancient practices can help you balance your extraordinary intellect with a more expansive awareness.

I can teach many of these ancient practices. Though I have been trained in many of them, I engage those practices that work for me. If you are willing, I can help you identify practices that can work for you. I most often refer to my practice as 'sitting,' borrowing from the ancient practice of Zen Buddhism. Would you be willing to try it with me sometime?"

"Can I ask a few questions?" inquired Slink.

"Of course," replied Dot.

"So this 'One' Gen addressed at the council meeting is not a real person?" Slink asked.

Not a person...but no less a reality, in my humble opinion." answered Dot.

"So you sit quietly and--what--talk to this reality in your mind?" Slink probed.

"I do not talk, silently or out loud," Dot offered.

She continued before Slink could pose his next question.

"I sit and consciously release all questions, all answers, all concerns, all ideas. I sit and watch, without judging or manipulating. As I observe the landscape of my inner world, fresh thoughts arise that are often far more helpful than the ones I released when I first sat. Mindfulness opens me to seeing my circumstances, my challenges, even my relationships in a new light. Over the years, I've seen I make much better decisions after I sit. As my daily practice has extended over years of sitting, I find I am more able to carry mindfulness beyond this room and into all my affairs."

Slink listened intently to Dot, holding silence long after her words ended. Finally, he broke his silence to ask one more question.

"I think...I think I'd like to explore these practices," he finally said. "What kind of a commitment would you expect from me?"

Part of him thought Dot's practice bizarre, but another part of him hungered to know more, to share her experience. He sensed he might learn something he could not learn from any computer program, and the prospect of acquiring knowledge in a new field, as always, lifted his spirits. This time, though, Slink felt a sudden chill come over him when the question arose unbidden in his mind: if his spirits had been lifted, where were they before their sudden rise? It was nothing really, just a small unsolicited tidbit of awareness, but it was another crack in the dam, and it felt foreboding to Slink. He breathed deeply and swallowed the rising tension in his throat.

"No need to be nervous," said Dot, misinterpreting the deep sigh that Slink unconsciously released. "You are welcome to sit with me any morning. I am here from 5:00 to 6:00 every morning."

Slink raised his eyebrows.

"I like rising before things get busy around here. I take an hour to sit, forty-five minutes to read, and 30 minutes to shower and dress. The crew works standard 12 hour shifts, from 8:00 to 8:00. I cherish my quiet time before I join the officers in the mess at 7:15. The only other time I get to myself is after 10:00 or so in the evening, depending on how many hands of cards I play with the crew before I come back here. The card play is important for the morale of the crew, and it gives me a chance to interact with them on a social basis. Besides that, I'm the best card player on Home!"

This last statement came with a hard stare, then a widening smile that eventually showed off Dot's perfectly straight, bright white teeth. Her grin seemed alternately comforting and disarming to Slink. As he stepped back from her emotionally, he felt a bit threatened by her deliberate self-revelation. She wanted to connect with Slink as family, and he wasn't sure he wanted to connect with her on any level deeper than he would share with a superior officer.

She again misinterpreted his withdrawal and said, "I'm not trying to intimidate you, Stanis. I thought a brain like you would thrive on a challenge! Besides, I heard you play cards--I also heard you're not bad!"

Her smile returned to her lips, but it never reached her eyes. She was challenging him!

"I wasn't intimidated, and I'd be happy to accept your challenge. Name the night...Dot."

Slink held her gaze for several long seconds. Then he remembered why he'd hesitated in the first place. Her challenge to engage on a more personal level was the threat he feared. He'd play cards, and he'd beat her, but right now he just needed to escape!

Dot recognized his discomfort, and though she wanted to question him, she thought better of it and turned her efforts to creating gracious closure to their conversation. She stood and motioned for him to follow.

"I am pleased to have you with us on Home, Stanis. You'll be a valuable addition to the crew, and in time, I hope you'll come to feel more comfortable living on a ship. Before you leave, I'm determined to help you grow comfortable with your heritage and those who share it."

She caught his eyes again and held them with the same cold stare she'd used when she spoke of card games. Slink just lowered his eyes and said, "I'm grateful for your hospitality and the opportunity to serve aboard this vessel."

"Then enjoy the rest of your day off. You've been assigned to the day crew, Company A. You'll have every seventh day off with the rest of our Company. Tomorrow, report to the bridge at 8:00 standard, and I'll introduce you to the members of the strategic team. I want you to observe them for the first week, then we'll see how you feel about joining their efforts. Welcome aboard, nephew."

Slink backed toward the door, eyes down and replied, "Tomorrow at 8:00 on the bridge. I'll be there...."

He paused, confused as to how he should address her. Before he could decide, he remembered her offer.

"If I want to join you at 5:00 to...."

He didn't know what to call her early morning practice.

"Meditate?" offered Dot.

Slink nodded self-consciously.

"Just come to my quarters and buzz me. Should I expect you tomorrow?" asked Dot.

"Yes, Ma'am, I mean...Dot," replied Slink.

Dot smiled in reply.

Slink turned awkwardly and headed for the door. He never noticed Dot's hand extended toward him.

Dot so wanted to gather Slink in her arms and hold him, and she was pained by his chilly countenance. She resolved in that moment to forge a connection with her nephew no matter how long it took. This new resolution steeled her as it evoked her long-standing vow to bring down the social system that robbed children of their childhood and turned them into automatons.

———————

His encounter with Dot left Slink feeling uneasy. It reminded him of the mornings in Kansas when one of the cooks, mistaking his reclusive behavior for fatigue, would pour him a cup of coffee. His stomach hurt, his head ached, and his mind wouldn't stop racing. He tried to convince himself he just needed some food in his stomach, but the smell of food only made it worse when he reached the galley. Then he thought exercise might do the trick, so he went back to his hollow on the top deck only to find that his sleeping mat and his few belongings had been removed. Luckily, one of the crew saw him looking over the area and hollered,

"Hey, Macdonald, you're one of us now!"

"No one calls me Macdonald," thought Slink.

"Let me show you to your bunk," the young woman said. "This is the guest quarters, and you've graduated!"

She pronounced the last word, "grad-gee-ated." She must have thought her odd pronunciation or her entire sentence was pretty funny, because she erupted into laughter. "Follow me," she said, still chuckling softly. She flipped her long, braided, jet black hair over one shoulder as she turned and looked back over the other. As her dark brown eyes met his, she met his gaze and held it for several seconds before she turned her head down and away from him, took a couple steps, then looked back again and motioned for him to follow.

She walked him back to the tight spiral stairs in the center of the ship, down to the second deck where they turned left at the bottom of the stairs. There his escort stopped short and stepped aside. He turned to her. She smiled and motioned to the doorway before him,

"You'll walk in, turn left down the aisle...." Her words grew distant as Slink watched her dancing hands while she spoke. Her slender brown forearm rose from her side until it was parallel to the floor and across her body; then she turned her hand 90° out from her body as her long, slender fingers pointed directly in front of her and her hand swam at the end of her arm like a swan cutting a graceful path through a maze of clumsy waterfowl. "...and your bunk will be half way down on your right. It'll be a lower bunk; all your stuff 'll be piled on it." Her hand swept down and to her side to punctuate the end of her directions.

When Slink looked at her and cocked his head as if to say, "how do you know that?" she pointed to a chart on the wall next to the doorway where they'd stopped. He immediately picked his name out on the bunk chart because his name, "Macdonald," was written in a different hand than the others. Another name, "Montoya," was written above the bed icon, and his was below it. He blushed as he realized the chart had been right in front of him the entire time she spoke.

"Oh," he stammered; "Thanks."

"No problem," she replied with another look down and a small giggle. She looked back up at him, cleared her throat, and in a more business-like manner said, "My name's Jenna. I'm part of Alpha Company. We'll be working the same shift. I look forward to getting to know you. All the bunks are shared, Slink. The bunk is yours from 20:00 to 8:00 standard. Take all your stuff and put it in the lower locker on the left hand side of the bunk. Any questions?"

When he shook his head, she smiled again, then turned on her heals and left him standing in the doorway to the men's quarters. He watched her go until she disappeared up the stairs. His attention swung back to his uneasiness, and now he was beginning to wonder if he was sick. He walked into the room to find most of the bunks occupied by sleeping men. He made his way down the aisle, with bunks on both sides of him until he saw his small pile of belongings on one of the beds.

"Why had his exchange with Jenna stilled his discomfort?" he wondered. His mind seemed to have lost all ability to approach such a question with its usual orderliness and coherence. Instead, it insisted on returning to the image of Jenna's smiling face. His queasy stomach grew still and his cheeks warmed. He could see every detail, from her dark brown eyes framed by her jet black bangs covering her forehead, to her smooth, dark-skinned cheeks, her small button nose with its flaring nostrils, her full, bright red lips and her sharp chin. He could even see in his mind's eye the hint of downy hair that framed her jaw and accented the curve of her upper lip. As he allowed himself to mull over her image in his mind, his heart rose into his throat.

One thing for sure--he didn't need any exercise--he was exhausted. He cleared his bunk, put his things away, and laid down for a nap. The next thing he knew, he was staring down a long, hazy tunnel that seemed to slope upward just enough to prevent him from making any progress as he struggled to escape the giant hand that chased him.

―――――――――――――――

He awoke to the harassment of one of his fellow bunk-mates. He hadn't heard the alarm. Though it was designed to awaken a drunkard with a mind-numbing blood-alcohol level, Slink never heard a sound. He couldn't sleep through his bunk-mate's efforts to toss him and his mattress off the bed frame, though.

"Hey, Sleeping Beauty," said a loud, deep, disembodied voice. "You plannin' on waitin' until Montoya comes in here and finds you in HIS bunk? You must not've met Montoya yet, huh kid?"

He didn't know who spoke to him or whether the foot kicking the side of his bunk was attached to the same person. He only knew his head was swimming, his eyes burned when he opened them even a little, and his mouth was so dry he couldn't even coax saliva by running his tongue over his teeth. None-theless, he'd heard enough to know it was in his best interest to meet his bunkmate on better terms.

He rolled onto his side, slid his arm up alongside his body and lifted himself onto one elbow. He forced his eyes to open, though they welled with tears as he forced his eyelids apart.

"What time is it?"

"7:30," came the reply in the same voice that had stirred him from slumber. "If you want somethin' to eat before you work half your shift, you betta' get a move on!"

"Sure, sure. Thanks. I'm movin'. Thanks."

The words came from between his lips like maple syrup left drying on a long-forgotten breakfast dish. Slink didn't look up to see who spoke to him. He didn't introduce himself. It took all the energy he could muster to sit, face down, on the side of the bunk. He heard his antagonist utter an epithet and saw the feet in front of him turn and walk out of his limited line of sight.

116

After another couple minutes, he managed to lift himself up onto his feet. He took a couple steps to his left, lurched to his right and banged into one of the bunks. He caught himself, took a deep breath, then made his way to the head without incident. After he relieved himself into the low-slung urinal with his forearm resting on the wall above and his head resting on his forearm, he made his way back to the bunk. He was the only one in the bunk house, so he knew he needed to get a move on. He pulled off the clothes he'd worn the previous day and slept in all night. He cupped a hand under each armpit in turn and sniffed. Not bad enough to demand a shower. A quick smear of deodorant would get him through another day. He walked back to the head, found the deodorant dispenser on the wall next to the sink, pressed his hand against the bottom valve to dispense a dab, rubbed it between his hands, and slapped it under his arms, wiping the excess across his hairless chest.

He was coming to life now. He didn't want to be the last one arriving on the command deck for his first day of work, so he started moving with a purpose. He slapped some water in his face, thought for a moment about his tooth brush in his locker, then smeared his finger with some tooth gel from another dispenser on the wall, and used his finger to rub his teeth with the gel for a few seconds. He rinsed his mouth, looked in the mirror above the sink at his hair, still cropped close enough to forego any care, and called it good.

He went back to his locker, found his only other fresh set of clothes and put them on. He stuffed his bedding and other belongings into the locker and, after a quick glance to make sure he hadn't forgotten anything, he headed for the door leading to the landing that separated the men's and women's quarters and at its center, the spiral stairs leading to the top deck and his first day of work aboard Home.

Slink arrived on deck before many of his coworkers, but he was by no means the first of the day shift. Dot had been on deck for at least an hour, as was her custom, and most of her officers had been there nearly as long. Several of the crew members had already set up the strategic command center for the day's work. The bridge covered the forward half of the deck and the forward facing walls were covered with screens showing multiple views of the outside environment and an array of other information vital for coordinating the internal operations of Home. The strategic command center was an enclosed room that took up the rear half of the deck. Two large metal doors leading into the command center were swung open when Slink arrived on the deck. Dot acknowledged him with a quick nod and motioned for him to go right into the command center.

Once inside, Slink saw it was really little more than a conference room with a large table running the length of the room and covering a full third of the floor space, down the middle of the room. Around the walls work stations were jammed side-by-side, and each one had enough personal items on the desk or tacked to the walls to recognize that it was the exclusive domain of one crew member.

As he looked around, Slink saw one of the stations was empty except for a brightly lettered sign taped to the monitor that said, "Welcome Home Stanis Macdonald." He made his way over to the work station and noticed that it had been modified with some of the antiquated equipment he'd become accustomed to using in the Kansan library. Instead of the clear plexi input boards the other stations had installed on the pull out trays below the desk, Slink found his old keyboard and mouse. On his desk he spotted the memory coin reader he'd used to access the files surface excursion crews had gathered for him. When he opened the single drawer to the right of his pull out tray, he found his precious memory coins all carefully organized in a slotted tray. Somebody had put a lot of work into trying to make him feel comfortable.

When he finally turned around to investigate a noise, he found most of his fellow command center colleagues standing in the doorway, looking his direction, and smiling. One of them, a shorter, rounded man with reddish cheeks, oversized glasses, and very little hair stepped around the conference table and extended his hand.

"Welcome to the Cave, Slink," he said. "Name's Chris. Chris Detera, Chief Strategist. The people in this room are known as Consultants. Some of us are braniacs like you, but most are specialists: coders, analysts, or engineers. We usually work at our stations, but occasionally we collaborate around the conference table. We all came here from the nurseries, just like you, although most of us spent a lot more time in the tunnels and working other posts on Home before we got here. You don't volunteer for this duty— you're chosen. Everyone here earned his or her station, one way or another. You're in good company, and we're delighted to add you to the team. So, once again, 'welcome!'"

Slink shook Chris's hand silently, then extended it to each of the others as they streamed in front of and by him. Each of them offered a name, but Slink didn't pay much attention. He hardly noticed the people passing in front of him. When the others had taken their posts in front of their respective cubicles, they all turned so they were facing inward toward the center of the room and, on some unrecognizable cue, bowed their heads together. They spoke no words, made no audible sounds, and remained completely motionless for what must have been two or three minutes, but seemed like a quarter of an hour to Slink. Then, in unison again, they turned and sat at their stations each diving into the work waiting there.

Slink was not entirely sure he liked the idea of being "chosen" for this work. There had been no mention of any choice on his part, and clearly the assumption was that he would never exercise any choice to countermand the decision they'd made on his behalf. They assumed, thought Slink, no one would ever contest their decision and choose other duty on Home. And while they evidently had yet to meet with any evidence to the contrary, their assumption bothered him. He'd become very independent after almost four years in the tunnels. He'd been allowed complete freedom outside of meeting his duties in the kitchen, and even there, he was sure he could have asked to be relieved. His place in

Kansas was to be the dedicated student of the Model Society and all that led to its development. He was the resident philosopher, scientist, historian, and engineer. He studied, tested his knowledge in the little computer lab they'd built for him and waited for his day to arrive. He had no doubt that day had come, and he was 99% sure the course this group had prepared for him was the one he wanted to travel. Nonetheless, he was uncomfortable knowing they'd led him to this moment without his knowledge or consent. It felt too much like the nurseries.

He kept these thoughts to himself.

He found he'd instinctively readied his work station while he was lost in thought and was ready to browse Home's files when he returned his attention to the images flashing on the screen. Most of the files fell into two categories he mentally characterized as ship files or surface files. The former group had to do with the functioning of Home. The second were files addressing Garson society. Most of the first group were, of course, unfamiliar to him. Most of the second dealt with subjects over which Slink had developed an impressive mastery. Neither of these larger groups had a significant interest for Slink. He could take a closer look at them later.

The files Slink had instinctively zeroed in on were a smaller group of the surface files. The surface files dealt with human society at large and most with Garson society in particular, but the ones that caught Slink's attention dealt with a subject matter Slink hadn't seen before! Slink forgot any misgivings he had about being chosen for this group and dived into the new files with enthusiasm he'd previously reserved for one of Gen's cheesecakes. It was the first time since he woke up on Home that he didn't feel the strange uneasiness churning in his gut.

By the time Chris tapped Slink on the shoulder and pointed out that they were the only two people in the room, Slink was so absorbed in his work he brushed Chris's hand aside. He would have gone on staring at the monitor until he lost consciousness. In fact, he was a lot closer to that point than he realized. His head was already pounding and his eyes were having a tough time focusing.

"Come on, Slink, lunch time. We enter this room together and we leave it together. We tried to rouse you several times, but you were so focused you didn't hear a word. I told the group to head down without us after assuring them I'd talk to you about our customs. Let's get a bite--you gotta be hungry!"

Slink slowly unfolded his legs and slipped off his chair. However, as he stood to follow Chris he discovered his right leg was numb from his foot halfway up his thigh. He started to fall and grabbed the back of his chair. A minute later his foot was tingling so bad he was alternately giggling, apologizing, and wincing in pain. The corners of Chris's mouth turned with the beginning of a smile, but he offered no assistance where none was requested. Instead, Chris waited patiently for Slink to regain his feet.

"Sorry," said Slink when he could stand again. "I lost all track of time. There's more new information on Home's files than I have seen in a long, long time. I feel like a termite in a rain forest during a drought."

Chris laughed.

"Where in the world did you ever hear a phrase like that? Have you ever even seen a picture of a forest, let alone a termite?"

Slink realized what he'd said and laughed. "One of the old guardians in the nursery used to say it all the time. He told lots of stories about growing up on Earth and used a lot of strange phrases we'd pick up without really knowing what we were saying. He explained that one to me, and I guess I just liked the sound of it."

"There's worse reasons to pick up a turn of phrase, I guess," said Chris.

They made their way down to the mess and went through the chow line to get their food. When they made their way back to the tables, Chris took them to the back of the dining hall where they found the rest of the consultants seated around three closely grouped tables.

Slink found a seat at the table where Gen was already sitting with four of their colleagues. They all ignored Slink as he sat down. They were all fixed on Gen as he finished a story about life in Kansas. When he was done, Slink interjected.

"I'm sorry I didn't hear you calling when it was time for lunch," he said. "Chris told me we enter the room together and leave together, and I guess I violated both of those customs. I meant no offense."

His simple, humble apology won everyone over right away. They each accepted his apology in turn and assured him there was no offense taken.

"So, Stanis," started a young woman sitting at the table, breaking the uncomfortable silence that had settled over the group, "what'd you think of Home's data files?"

"Call me Slink---and I never dreamed you could have so many files I'd never seen before," he replied.

"A lot of people combined their efforts to collect those files," she said.

"Sandra's being humble," said another woman. She smiled at Sandra, while Sandra blushed, obviously uncomfortable with the attention the second woman was directing her way.

"Sandra was the one who managed to find a way to hack some of the more sensitive data banks of the Grid. Anything that you haven't seen before likely came from one of the more sensitive data banks to which Sandra opened the door."

"Then I owe you a special debt of gratitude," said Slink, looking directly at Sandra, who returned his gaze from over the oval lenses of her antique eye glasses, while she kept her head bowed. "I live to learn new things, and it's been a while since I've felt the excitement I felt this morning."

"Oh really?" said the second woman. "That's too bad, Slink," she continued. "You really need to widen your horizons a bit. I could help you out if you like."

"Leave him alone, Dimitra," said a third woman who looked to be quite a bit older than the other two. "He hasn't been aboard Home three days yet. Let him get his bearings before you start hitting on him. Besides, I have a feeling that your efforts are lost on the young man anyway, aren't they Slink?"

"I'm afraid you've all lost me," said Slink. "We aren't talking about database files anymore, are we?"

The table erupted in laughter. It was Slink's turn to blush.

Gen wrapped an arm around Slink and said, "We'll have a man-to-man a little later, bud. You're going to have to get used to being the center of attention. There's more to life than computer files, little man, and there's more to you than that oversized brain of yours. I almost hate to break the little bubble you been living in, but it's going to happen sooner or later anyway, and I'll be a lot more gentle than these feisty females."

Gen's words combined with Slink's blank stare and drew another burst of laughter from the table.

"Eat your lunch little man or you're going to break your group's customs for the third time."

Slink did as Gen suggested, more than happy to escape the center of attention. A few minutes later, he was again standing as part of the human circle around the conference table in the Cave, head bowed, doing his best to endure the interminable silence. When the group raised their heads and turned to resume work Slink sighed so deep he was sure everyone else could hear him. He didn't really care--he was already absorbed in the treasure trove of files from Home's mainframe.

The remainder of that first week in the Cave passed quickly for Slink. He poured through the database files and organized them according to subject matter, then according to his degree of mastery over the information they contained. He found about a third of the ship's reference files were completely new to him, and most of those files had to do with biotechnology--the field that produced the commlink. Slink was especially happy to make this discovery because he'd wanted to explore the commlink's near universal acceptance on Garsow. He'd long wondered why people seemed to become so passive after the brain chips for the commlink were implanted. Why did so few recognize the way their field of perception narrowed even though they clearly recognized the

123

flip side of the coin--namely, the way their powers of concentration were enhanced? Would not an objective, rational person see the tradeoffs associated with such a significant change in perception? The commlink seemed to dramatically enhance rational analysis in most people receiving the implants, yet none of these recipients ever seemed to apply these higher cognitive abilities to an objective analysis of the commlink and its affects on Garson society. There were no studies Slink could find on the long-term affects of commlink implants on individuals or the society to which they belonged.

The Technoids had long considered themselves crusaders who had a moral duty to ask the questions their society didn't seem to have any interest in asking. They were largely convinced the commlink had done more harm than good. Of course, their perspective was predictable in that they were cut off from any of the benefits of being linked. The Technoids were virtually all outcasts from the Model Society. They were shaped by the experience of being excluded from mainstream society and labeled as "unfit." Many had come to feel so oppressed by their exclusion they saw themselves as revolutionaries. Some part of Slink wanted to embrace this viewpoint and do his part to further the revolution. Another part of him felt certain that like most things in life, the issue was not as simple as some would like to believe.

Could some form of biotechnology be integrated into a society without forming such dramatic divisions between those who embraced the technology and those who did not or could not? From the time they first formed in his mind, he'd known instinctively that he didn't want to ask these questions openly. Revolutionaries never took well to having their motives questioned, especially in cases like his where the questioner was not assuming the daily risks of surface excursions, including arrest and imprisonment or enslavement.

Nonetheless, Slink couldn't quell the questions. They rose in his mind like air bubbles rising to the surface of a pond, and once they made the surface of his consciousness, they demanded answers. The new files held the first promise of the answers he'd quietly sought since he knew enough to start asking questions.

Chapter 6

Jonathan and Adela were pleasantly surprised when the first crews discovered the caverns could easily be made habitable if they could devise a means of entering them without setting off a deadly explosion. The first crews struck something more valuable than gold--water! They determined the most common element filling the caverns was not the nitrogen the robots had discovered but hydrogen and oxygen in the form of ice! Garsow had an abundant supply of water, hydrogen, oxygen, and nitrogen. Once a hydrogen-powered electrical generator was completed and the reactor's core was activated, the crews had electricity, heat, and water in abundant supply!

Jonathan Lansing asked Adela to help them address the challenge of the caverns' explosive pressure. His brilliant wife had stayed on the orbiting Garsow Station, though she'd made the trip from Earth expecting to accompany her husband and work alongside him on the Garsow surface. The long trip to the planetoid had seen them welcome twins, a daughter and a son, and Adela had little real choice but to stay behind with the children when Jonathan joined the replacement crew.

When she received Jonathan's report, she was delighted to have a scientific focus to which she could put her time. She developed a means of drilling small holes into a cavern using a heat drill enclosed in a pressurized chamber clamped to the surface of the planet. The chamber was pressurized to approximate the cavern pressure so the gas would not explode from the cavern when the drill bit broke the surface. Instead, a release valve could be employed on the pressurized chamber once the drilling was complete and the gas could be slowly siphoned from the cavern.

Building settlements in natural underground catacombs avoided a lot of the costly provisions necessary for surface settlements, but as shuttle traffic increased, and building materials became more plentiful, establishing surface settlements became more plausible. Underground living had a nasty effect on the mental health of most settlers, so the last of the tunnel settlements was abandoned for the surface after only 5 years--less than half the time originally intended!

While they were living underground, the original colonists oversaw the building of two surface ports and three additional shuttles, which they used to bring all of the materials necessary for building and enclosing the surface settlements in three giant organic shells. Since Garsow was extraordinarily dense, the planetoid generated its own gravity roughly two-third's of Earth's and provided a stable surface to serve as a foundation for man-made structures. Once they were enclosed with organic self-repairing shells, the three interconnected settlements provided an ideal habitat for one of humanity's great experiments.

On the afternoon of his sixth day of work, Slink received a communique from Dot. It appeared on his monitor amongst the many messages that scrolled across his message window. Slink had become accustomed to scanning the window once or twice every minute to monitor the messages he received. Most of them were auto-generated messages from his colleagues in the cave summarizing the work they currently engaged. If Slink was intrigued by any of these messages, all he had to do was reply with a question mark and they would copy the files related to the original summary message so Slink could take a closer look at them. Slink absorbed information faster than any other human being his colleagues had ever known, and his memory was near-photographic. His fellow consultants quickly recognized the value of passing any useful discoveries on to Slink so he could catalogue them. He was their walking encyclopedia, and he often drew out connections between the various isolated efforts of his coworkers.

Dot's message stood out from these other summary messages. For one thing, hers had an animated little smiley face attached to it that winked at Slink every couple of seconds. For another, her message consisted of one word: "dinner?"

Slink was thrown off guard by the extremely informal tone of the message. He'd never seen an animated smiley face, and he certainly didn't expect to see it next to a message from his commander. His heart rose in his throat for a moment, but he swallowed, took a deep breath, and wrote a simple, though more formal response.

"I would be honored, commander. Where and when shall I meet you?"

"Officers' Mess, 18:00," came the quick response, this time lacking any unusual adornment.

"I look forward to seeing you," he wrote.

He forced himself to return to his work. He'd been sifting through files on the anterior commlink chip, implanted in the occipital lobe of recipients. The information was vital to his understanding and complex enough to demand his close attention, but

128

to his consternation, Slink found he couldn't focus on the files anymore.

Did Dot just want to catch up with her grand nephew as he completed his first week of work, kind of an "atta boy" dinner? Or did she want to hear what he was working on, maybe get a feel for how he could help their mission? Or, as he feared, did she want to try to get him to open up to her a little more, try to get inside his head? He'd thought that was what she was trying to do when he'd met her in her quarters a week earlier and in the early mornings since. Even when they just sat in meditation together, Dot giving and Slink following instruction, she had a way of coaxing him out of his shell and threatening his carefully constructed barriers. She frightened him.

Still, Slink knew he couldn't refuse her invitation. So he sat immobilized in front of his screen, shuffling through electronic files he'd dismissed earlier and biding the time before he joined his fellows packing up his belongings, shutting down his work station, and swinging out of his chair to face the center of the room and stand in ritual silence, head bowed trying to ignore the gnawing discomfort in his stomach while he counted the seconds before he could break for the door.

―――――――――――――――――――――

The officers' mess was right next to the main mess, separated by a bulwark with a door at its center that hung open when Slink arrived. Dot must have been watching for him, because as soon as he approached, she stepped into the doorway and invited him in. The chairs in the officers mess were the same swing-out variety as in the main mess, bolted to the floor by a single center support. Dot motioned to a table near the back where no one else was seated. She slid into the seat in the corner and motioned for him to have a seat.

"The officers eat the same food as the rest of the crew, so I'm afraid I can't offer you any culinary delights," she said after they'd both settled into their seats.

"The food on board Home is better than anything we had in Kansas," replied Slink. "I can hardly remember the food in the nurseries, probably since it was usually cold by the time I got to eat. I'm sure our meal will be more than satisfying, Comman..." he caught himself and, after a moment's hesitation, finishing his sentence, "...Dot."

She smiled at him with her sincere, disarming smile that probably calmed most people's nerves and, instead, set Slink's on edge.

"Thanks for keeping this more informal Slink. It would seem a little weird to have my nephew be the only person on Home who insists on calling me 'Commander' whether we're on duty or not."

"I'm happy to call you whatever you wish...Dot," he said. His nerves were singing already, and try as he might he couldn't do anything to steady himself.

He couldn't wait for Dot to bring up her reason for their meeting, so he asked, "Dot, am I disappointing you or Chris? I know I've spent this entire week pouring over files without producing anything useful."

He was speaking quickly now.

"I'll be up to speed soon, and hopefully, I'll be contributing to the collective efforts of The Cave."

She laughed--really laughed--from deep in her gut. It took her a while to regain her composure.

"Slink--you don't really think I asked you here to dress you down, do you? Come on--you already know me better than that. When have you ever seen me dress someone down?"

She waited, though he doubted she expected a response.

"And you won't," she continued. "I asked you to meet me here for what I hope will become a habit for both of us. I want to spend my night off with the only family I have. Like it or not, you're all I have left of my family, and that's likely to remain true for some time yet."

She dropped her head and dropped her voice so only Slink could hear what she said next.

"We certainly haven't figured out a way to free any of the other family members from the nurseries where they're locked down. As near as we can tell, they're all tattooed with surveillance chips, so every DAN officer within the sector would come running the moment they left the nursery grounds. They might as well be dead..."

Her voice trailed off and she was quiet for several long seconds. She looked up again, and Slink saw her eyes were filled with tears.

"In some ways it would be easier if they were dead. I can hardly stand to think of them being forced to work in the nurseries. Every day, they get up and work to solidify the hold the hated commlink has over our society. Every child they're raising looks down on them with disdain. Every day, they wake up knowing the precocious babies they'll hold in their arms are going to become little cyborgs just like their parents and grandparents before them. They'd do anything to be sitting here looking into your unvisored eyes. They'd die happy if they could see what I see, and I want to look across this table at the end of every work week and remember why we're doing what we are doing."

"Maybe my motivation for these dinners is selfish. I don't think it's asking too much, though. It's probably just as important for you to look across the table at me and realize how damn lucky you and I are. It's probably just as important for you to realize whatever pain you're carrying around that has you so shut down isn't anything compared to the pain your mother carries with her everyday. She would gladly trade the rest of her days to be sitting in my place for just one night. I think maybe we both need to remember that, and so I want you to have dinner with me every week, remember with me every week, and give thanks with me...every week. OK?"

Her voice was barely audible at the end, but it had an edge to it that could have cut the air between them with a knife. She wasn't mad at him--Slink knew that much. She loved him even though she hardly knew him.

It was this unconditional, unearned, and Slink thought, undeserved love that disarmed him he finally realized. His carefully constructed emotional wall had been undermined more than he would admit by the news of Neoko's arrest. It was further shaken by the sudden demise of the Tunnel Rat enclave he'd called home for close to four years. Now this powerful woman was knocking huge chunks from it with her challenge to...remember. If there was one thing he dared not do over these past few years, it was remember. Now she asked and before he could deny her request, his heart complied. He didn't give his assent but it didn't matter. He could feel his pain rising to the surface too fast to shove back down, feel his eyes growing at first hot, then wet, feel his breath catching in his throat, and he knew--this time he'd drown.

All of a sudden, it was not Dot sitting across the table from him, but Neoko. In his mind's eye, she looked malnourished, hollows of her cheeks looking like dark pools bordered by protruding white cheek bones. Her hair was matted to her head, but her beautiful brown eyes shown fiercely and cut him to the bone. She spoke, and her words flayed open the cuts her eyes had made.

"All those times I tried to reach you--for what? You were too determined not to feel any pain--hiding in your precious books and electronic files. So now you may be the smartest person on Garsow--so what? All that knowledge and insight is wasted on someone who's never going to stick his neck out. How often have you thought of me, rotting in this cell, always refusing to return to the nurseries? How much sleep have you lost wondering about the people trapped in the nurseries without any hope of ever knowing the freedom you now take for granted? You might as well stop trying to understand anything if you aren't going to do anything with that knowledge. Just find a nice safe little hollow where you can retreat from the rest of us and protect your fragile little heart. God damn it, Slink, you're my best hope. I can't wait forever--I need you to remember."

"Remember," the word crushed his defenses. From the foundations he'd poured while still too young to speak to the walls he'd fashioned to keep Neoko out night after night--the barriers came tumbling down. Dot watched as first the tears began to flow then the racking sobs started, then the loud pleading with a woman whose name she'd heard on Gen's lips but whose face she'd never seen. Over and over he called to her,

"Neoko...Neoko...NEOKO!"

The hand on her shoulder brought Dot to the realization everyone in the officer's mess was transfixed on her and her nephew. Slink had collapsed on the floor, and she'd followed him without thinking, sitting next to him and pulling his head up and cradling it in her lap. She was doing everything in her power to soothe him, though nothing she did seemed to even slow the escalation of his cries or stem the flow of his tears. She'd seen this before--some who broke so suddenly and completely recovered with enough time and support. Many never did. She started to cry. The hand tightened its grip. One of her officers spoke.

"Clear the mess now! All officers will eat in the main mess tonight. This room is off limits until further notice. GO!"

She couldn't hear much of anything over Slink's cries of Neoko's name, his sobs, or her own sobs, and she couldn't see much out of her blurry eyes, but she sensed the room emptying. The hand on her shoulder never left, never tried to move her, never wavered. It held her, anchored her, and thus secured, she let go and cried for the only family member she'd seen in almost twenty years as he slipped into his own oblivion, cried for the family members still removed by immovable circumstances, cried for Neoko and the others who'd given themselves to the cause, and cried for herself. She had no idea how long she and Slink were there crumpled together on the floor, and she had no idea how she got back to her quarters where she awoke nearly four hours later. She sat bolt upright as she became fully conscious.

"Where is he?" she asked.

133

"He's in my quarters, resting, and he'll stay there for some time I think. I'll take his bunk when I'm not keeping vigil with him or working. Right now, I've posted a watch to see he stays calm, but I think it'll be days, if not longer, before he regains awareness. I'll see him through this. I've worked toward this day, albeit awkwardly and fruitlessly. I've prayed for this as you prayed for me--and I'd nearly given up hope he could be reached. I should've known you'd reach him. Once again, I'm grateful!"

Gen stood up from the chair where he'd been sitting in the shadows and crossed to Dot's elevated sleeping pad where he sat next to her. She reached out and embraced him. He received her into his arms and returned her embrace. After a minute or so, she withdrew and grasped his upper arms firmly.

"You're the one who deserves thanks, my steadfast friend. I know his calls for your dear Neoko must've broken your heart, and yet you steadied me throughout so I could hold him. You have the healing touch, and I drew from you to stay with him in his grief and pain. Perhaps you enabled me to walk far enough with him into his darkness that he can find his way back to us. I'll devote my practice to the fulfillment of this hope—here in my quarters and later with him if the circumstances permit."

"Our ways can heal many wounds that would otherwise be devastating or even fatal. I hope Slink's will be such a case. Together we can devote ourselves to this end."

She released his arms and he stood. He bowed to her and she bowed in return. It was more than custom. It was the wordless way of those who know the path.

As Slink sunk into the rising sea of emotion that overwhelmed him upon hearing Dot's words in the officers' mess and hearing Neoko's in his mind, he saw Neoko recede from him as if into a thick fog on a moonless night. He called to her, but she drifted away from him and disappeared. He called out to her again, and again, and again.

In the mist that had swallowed her he began to see images of others who had tried to reach him at one time or another. Many of them had been residents in Kansas. They would appear and stare at him for a moment, silently asking why he'd forgotten them and by their very presence commanding him to remember.

His mind wove them together by threads that wrapped amongst and between them like a giant spider web. This web wove all the people from his past together into a visual collage compelling him to remember. The strands of this web reached out from Slink's memory, then entangled him becoming anchor lines dragging him ever downward into the soup of swirling emotion he had held behind his once impenetrable walls.

Now as those walls crumbled, he was drowning in this sea of guilt, anger, outrage, betrayal, abandonment, loneliness, and so many other feelings he'd never realized were locked away. He felt surprise, then relief, then hope, attachment, belonging, forgiveness, acceptance, and love, yes there was love swirling in this... this...soup.

And through it all, there was complete loss of control. His tears flowed, his moans and cries poured across his lips, and at first, he fought. He fought to identify, quantify, and clarify his thoughts and emotions. His fight was intense, but it was short-lived. He let go and gave into the tears, gave into the cries, gave into what he feared would be his annihilation.

Slink slept for almost two days, and when he awoke he was only marginally responsive. For the most part he didn't respond to impulses beyond his digestive tract. Even those responses were muted. He chewed and swallowed when food was placed in his mouth and ambulated to the head when he needed to void his bladder or bowels. Beyond that, he seemed to be lost in a sort of waking dream. Gen fed him, showered him, and got him dressed each day. He made sure Slink spent several hours sitting up each day and went for a couple of short walks as well. He cared for him as well as any medical attendant could have. Slink suffered deterioration as the days stretched into weeks, though far less than might have been expected.

Each day, Gen spent time morning and night praying over the motionless frame of his friend. He'd sit down next to him and find a position he could hold comfortably for a half hour or so. Then, he'd reach out with his mind to hold in consciousness his connection to Source and his connection to Slink. He'd long since given up any need to name that to which he was eternally bound. He'd grown to appreciate the power inherent in consciously holding an awareness of this intrinsic connection. He'd also come to appreciate the beneficial nature of holding a connection to someone in need as he held a deep connection to Source.

Each time he sat with Slink, he'd first establish conscious awareness of Source, deepening his awareness with each breath, before turning his awareness to Slink. He offered no words, simply stretched his hands out over Slink and reached out to him with his mind. He would draw connection points between himself and Slink, between Slink and all else. He would keep company with him this way, giving support to anything he felt coming from his friend and passing strength and hope through himself to the motionless form under his outstretched hands. He'd speak to his unresponsive friend of every life-giving connection Slink had ever known. Day after day, though Gen could never be certain anything he did was reaching Slink, he faithfully sat with his friend morning and night.

Dot engaged a similar practice, first from her quarters, then as the weeks passed she, too, took time with Slink everyday. By the fourth week, she and Gen took to praying over their friend together every morning, as much to support each other as to affect healing in Slink.

All of the crew on Home respected the spiritual practices of their commander. A sizable number engaged those practices to the best of their abilities and according to their own understanding. Everyone kept Slink in their thoughts and many set aside a part of their day to hold him in focused concentration.

One morning, as they concluded their time with Slink, Gen caught Dot's eye and nodded toward the door of his quarters. The two stepped out together, and when the door slid closed, Gen asked Dot to give her take on what was happening to Slink.

"You're more familiar than any of us on Home with Slink's powers of concentration," she said. "You've told me stories from your times together in Kansas when you approached him sitting in front of a monitor and had to physically shake him to get his attention."

"OK," replied Gen. "And you think his unique abilities have something to do with what is happening now?"

"We all have the capacity to push aside things we don't want to think about. We suppress different feelings or experiences that cause us discomfort. We compartmentalize so we can continue to function after a trauma or in difficult circumstances."

"And you think Slink's compartments collapsed." Gen concluded.

"Only I don't think he had compartments like any of us have," added Dot. "I'd guess he just had a vast reservoir behind an impermeable dam. I think Slink's extraordinary powers of concentration allowed him to escape completely from any feeling or thought he wanted to shove aside. He somehow developed the ability to tune out anything but the object of his focus. And while he consciously focused on one thing, his unconscious mind acted like a sweeper drone and swept away any thought outside that focus. Whenever he was uncomfortable, he learned to concentrate on one thing to the exclusion of all else, and by the time he broke that concentration, all his discomfort was gone—swept away as if it never existed."

"So when his dam broke, he was literally carried off by the tsunami," Gen offered.

"You and I slowly developed all kinds of coping mechanisms over the years," continued Dot. "Slink didn't do that. He

137

doesn't experience denial, projection, rationalization, or other defense mechanisms the way you and I do. When we utilize those defenses, we don't completely lose touch with the experience that triggered our defenses. We employ coping mechanisms that may give us some distance from painful experiences, but they usually don't divorce us from those experiences altogether. When Slink hyperfocuses, everything else disappears. When he experienced something that evoked strong emotions, he may have had a vague recollection of the incident that caused discomfort, but the feelings associated with that incident may as well have never existed."

Dot leaned forward, grimacing.

"It's one thing to have painful memories resurface, but imagine if all the pain you've ever experienced suddenly burst into awareness. Not memories rising to the surface, but multi-dimensional experiences bursting into consciousness as if they were happening in that moment."

She sighed deeply and Gen held the silence with her. A few seconds later, she reached out and grasped Gen's shoulder as she continued.

"Slink has an extraordinary intellect, and he harnessed that intellect by developing equally extraordinary powers of concentration. And while those attributes have given him the ability to absorb information faster than anyone we've ever known, they were also the brick and mortar of the dams that are no more. When those dams broke, the one thing he could rely on became untrustworthy. His intellect failed him!"

"Then we've been giving him exactly what he needs," exclaimed Gen. "He needs something, someone, to rely on. He needs to know he has people in his life who'll stand by him when his internal resources fail. It seems almost inevitable that he put too much trust in himself because he couldn't trust the people around him. Now he's learned the painful lesson that he, too, is prone to failure."

"Dot, we're showing him people can be trustworthy. When he comes around, he's going to know he doesn't have to go it alone anymore. With our support, and all of Home's support, he can learn to rely on his innate gifts and rely on his family and friends. He can learn to endure the shortcomings of others and his own failings by creating a support system that draws from many wells."

"If we can do that," replied Dot, "there's no telling what Slink could do. If he learns to trust others when his own resources are inadequate, he can mine the depths of his understanding without fear of getting lost. When he comes around, we need to gently guide him into a more balanced, sustainable life."

"That's a tall order, Dot, but I think it's one we have to fulfill. We need Slink, and he needs us. I don't know that he's ever trusted anyone enough to admit he needed them. How do you build trust with someone who's never relied on another person?"

"We start, Gen, by making sure my nephew and your friend Stanis Web McDonald knows we love him!"

Gen pulled Dot into an embrace.

"Then, like I said, we're doing exactly what needs to be done."

_____

Slink's awakening came without drama. One morning as Gen and Dot sat on each side of him extending their hands above him, eyes closed, passing to him whatever strength they could share, he reached out and took their hands in his. They opened their eyes to see him still laying motionless, but with tears streaming down his cheeks, eyes moving slowly from one of them to the other. He opened his mouth as if to speak then released their hands, reached up their arms, and pulled them down next to him. He wept softly with them. His body shook in rhythm with his weeping. Gen and Dot held him so tightly they shook with him.

Slink had awoken and instead of recoiling or withdrawing, he'd extended himself, inviting them in. They'd not have to earn his trust; he was freely offering it. In his weeping, they sensed his openness, his vulnerability, and his decision to welcome them into his experience. As Slink's weeping slowly subsided, the three clung tighter and tighter to hold onto each other as his tears baptized them with healing and bound their hearts together.

Slink saw the clear choice before him and did not withdraw; he chose to open himself, welcome the binding, and draw in all the ghosts of his past. He was too weak to make peace with his demons alone, but bound to family and friends, through Dot and Gen, he could make room for them in his conscious awareness. No longer did they need to be banished along with any emotion they evoked to some dungeon he created deep in his subconscious mind. They no longer threatened to drown him, but bore promises of purpose, ongoing meaning, and lasting motivation. He would live now, not for himself alone, but for all of them. The lines that bound him to others no longer seemed like they were tied to an anchor that drew him into a dark, foreboding sea, but more like they were the lifelines that held him secure through any storm life might bring.

"Welcome back, Stanis Web McDonald," Dot exclaimed as she pulled back from their embrace and stared down at Slink.

Gen just tousled Slink's hair and grinned at him.

"You'll need some time to regain your strength and get your bearings," continued Dot.

Slink opened his mouth to protest and thought better of it. He couldn't even raise his head without feeling dizzy.

"I'll be coming by twice a day for the next few days, Slink. I want to give you some new tools to help you cope and to help you forge a healthy course from here. I think you'll master those tools and regain your bearings far more quickly than anyone else could, but we're not going to rush this. I need you to trust Gen's and my judgment. We'll tell you when we think you're ready to reenter life on Home. Until then, I'm asking you as my nephew to follow our lead. And if that's not compelling enough, I'll order you as your commanding officer to remain in these quarters until you receive further orders."

"Do I need to give that order?" Dot asked.

Slink shook his head. He held Dot's gaze for several seconds, then turned and stared at Gen for several more.

"Why?" he croaked.

He cleared his throat.

"Why have you stayed so close to me over the last..."

His voice trailed off and he cleared his throat again.

"I don't know how long I've been out, but it has to have been a long time. Every foggy memory I have of the recent past includes at least one of you, though. Why?"

"Why do you think, Slink? Use that big brain of yours," chided Gen. "And before you start working out some complex scenario to explain why we made so much effort to see you through this, remember Occam's razor. The simplest explanation is usually the best explanation."

"I don't need my big brain to answer that question," Slink said softly. "I think I knew the answer when I opened my eyes and saw you two leaning over me with your eyes closed and your hands outstretched—you really care about me."

"It's even simpler than that, little man," replied Gen. "You don't need five words, just three. We love you!"

At Dot's and Gen's insistence, Slink stayed sequestered in Gen's quarters. Gen brought his meals and news of events on board and outside of Home. Gen told Slink about the outpouring of support he'd received while he was incoherent. Gen minimized his own role, but Dot made sure Slink heard of all that Gen had done for him. After a couple days, Slink thought he was ready to resume his duties. Dot insisted otherwise.

―――――――――――――――――――

After Slink had a couple days to regain some strength and reorient himself, Dot decided it was time to provide the training she'd promised.

"How you feeling this morning?" she asked when she entered Gen's quarters and found Slink pacing in front of Gen's sleeping pad.

"I'm fine," replied Slink.

He looked at Dot, caught her raised eyebrows, and sighed.

"Really, Dot, I'm fine. I'm a little weak, but my mind isn't near as foggy anymore. I'm a little uneasy and antsy, but I'm sure that'll pass when I get back to work. Can't I please return to the Cave?"

Dot smiled, and motioned for Slink to sit on one of the cushions along the wall opposite Gen's sleeping pad. When they'd taken seats facing each other, Dot spoke.

"I promised to give you some tools, and though I'm confident you'll master in days the practices I mastered over years, we'll need several days, not hours."

Slink sighed again. When he saw Dot's quizzical expression, he hurried to assure her.

"I trust you, Dot. I'll give you my full attention and devote myself to mastering the lessons you offer. I'm just anxious. I wish I could push that aside, but I can't. I used to be so good at dismissing my feelings, but they seem so much more...solid...now."

"That's actually a good thing, Slink," Dot replied. "I want to teach you how to carry a much broader awareness into each moment. Most of us have a tendency to focus on one thing to the exclusion of everything else. You developed an extraordinary ability to do that. I think your extraordinary ability contributed strongly to your recent experience. I want to encourage you to consider another approach."

"I'll follow your lead, Dot. Even if I wanted to, I don't think I could go back to my old ways. I just hope you can help me get used to all the emotion I'm feeling. One minute, I'm feeling overwhelming gratitude and babbling to anyone who will listen and the next I'm paralyzed with fear. I feel like I'm on a roller coaster!"

"Slink, time will help calm the flood of emotions more than anything I can teach you. Your emotions have been shut down so

142

long they're going to be overactive for a while. I can help you live with them, though. The task is to step back from them and observe them from a distance. I can give you a few tools to help you do that."

"Let's get going, then," responded Slink. "How do we start?"

Dot chuckled.

"It's all about slowing down, Slink. First, take your shoes off. Then, you want to find a comfortable position you can maintain without fidgeting."

"If you want to stay on that cushion, just cross your legs in front of you, then move your left foot up against the inside of your right thigh. After that, lift your right foot over your left leg and place your right foot against your left thigh. Sit up straight, and slightly forward until your weight is balanced between your butt and your knees. How's that feel?"

"Not bad," replied Slink. "I sit like this a lot on chairs."

"Good," said Dot. "Now just close your eyes and breathe. You don't have to take deep breaths or alter your breathing at all. Just breath and try to focus on your breath."

Dot waited in silence for a couple minutes that seemed to stretch much longer to Slink. He tried to keep his mind on his breath, but he kept wondering what came next and kept anticipating Dot's voice giving him further instruction. When that didn't happen, his mind wandered to other questions until he'd forgotten his breath completely. When he realized what was happening, he'd start paying attention to his breath again, but it wasn't long before he'd start wondering when Dot was going to break the silence and soon he'd be distracted again.

Finally Dot said, "pay attention to the sensation of air cooling your throat as your breathe in."

Slink noticed that his throat felt cooler with each inhale and warmer with each exhale. Then he started wondering what Gen was doing and whether he might intrude on his meditation training. He snapped his attention back to the sensations in his throat, angry with himself for becoming so easily distracted again.

143

"Feel your chest expanding and contracting with each breath. Listen to the sound of your breath and notice the difference in the tone of your inhale versus your exhale."

Slink paid attention to the sensation of his chest expanding against the fabric of his shirt then contracting inward. The sensation was more familiar and strange at the same time. He was noticing qualities of the experience he'd never given attention before. He became aware of the tightness in his lower abdomen and that led to recognizing the anxiety behind that physical tension. He became aware of an itch between his shoulder blades and tried to ignore it, which just gave it a deeper quality of urgency. Then he remembered Dot's instruction and forced his attention back to his expanding and contracting chest.

"Now open your eyes, Slink. What was that like?"

"Exhausting!" Slink exclaimed, chuckling in embarrassment. "That was a lot harder than I'd expected. I couldn't keep my attention on the simple thing you asked me to focus on. I kept getting distracted by thoughts or sensations outside my focus. I'm going to have to work on this for a while!"

"If the object of this exercise was to develop focus, I'm sure you'd master it in no time," replied Dot. "You'll be surprised to hear you've fulfilled the intention of the exercise rather well."

Slink was baffled, and he shook his head in disbelief.

"Slink, what I wanted you to notice is the constant chatter in your mind, the boundless sensations in your body, and the emotions that roil just beneath the surface. We are complex creatures, and we always have a lot going on inside of us."

"So I was supposed to get distracted?" Slink asked.

"It's not a question of what you were 'supposed' to do. It was simply a matter of noticing what you're always doing. Well, what most people are always doing."

Dot smiled and winked at Slink.

"You have an ability to laser focus, to drill down to the most minute detail and shut out everything else. Others can do this too, but they can't maintain that focus for long. Their mind, their body, and/or their emotions will draw their attention outward before long. They have to force those other stimuli aside and refocus their attention. You seem to effortlessly shut down all other awareness until you've finished whatever you started."

Dot's expression grew more serious.

"I think that unique ability to hyperfocus comes at a price, Slink. And I'm not talking about the embarrassment of realizing someone's been shaking you for several minutes or your body's been convulsing with muscle spasms while you were lost in your own little world. I mean losing touch with yourself to the point that you become disconnected from everything and everyone around you. I mean having repressed emotions undermine your mental health."

"Ignoring bodily sensations and mental observations can cause problems, Slink, but you know now the greater danger comes from repressing emotions. Emotions always find expression."

Dot paused and looked deeply into Slink's eyes. He nodded and smiled sheepishly.

"I want to help you develop a wider awareness you can carry into all your experiences. I want to help you discover and develop your inner eye."

"Inner eye?" asked Slink.

"Think about the phrase, 'I was angry with myself.' Who is angry at whom? We all have a part of ourselves that experiences things directly and another part that observes our experiences from a distance. We get angry with ourselves when we react to a situation without thinking about it and our inner observer takes issue with our immediate reaction."

"OK, I can see that," offered Slink.

"We can learn to be patient and give more weight to the observer so we don't react, we thoughtfully respond. I call that developing your inner eye. I have found that some people have more capacity for patient observation than others, but everyone can get better at developing his or her inner eye."

"Well, I can see where my inner observer could be a lot stronger. I'm pretty good at observing others, but I've ignored most of my feelings for a long time. Since my…time away…my feelings have been a lot stronger. I can't push them away as easily and part of me really doesn't want to. I feel like a yo-yo, though. My feelings seem to swing from one extreme to the other. When I try to understand why I'm feeling what I'm feeling, I just get confused. It was a lot easier when I could just shove aside my feelings and focus on one thing."

"And that's probably why you got so good at doing just that," replied Dot. "Feelings aren't easy to break down and quantify the way you can with information. Sometimes they make sense, and sometimes they don't. They can always tell you something about yourself, but first you have to resist the assumption they tell you something about someone else."

Slink tilted his head to the side and frowned. Dot laughed.

"It's really not as confusing as I make it sound," Dot said. "When you feel fear, your natural tendency is to look for something frightening outside yourself. You look for some external cause. You are conditioned to identify threats and react without conscious thought. The challenge is to give more power to the inner observer and recognize the fear before you react instinctively. You learn to report to yourself, 'I am feeling afraid.' That report allows you to own your feeling before your unconscious mind projects that feeling at some perceived threat, you react, and your attention is focused on the perceived threat and your corresponding reaction."

"That makes a lot of sense," responded Slink. "So how do I shift my focus from my reaction to my underlying feelings?"

"The part of your mind that projects your feelings and reacts instinctively to perceived threats is hard-wired into the oldest part of your brain, Slink. It will do what it is there to do. You won't ever be able to 'shift your focus' from the older, more primitive part of your mind to your inner observer. You must learn to have great compassion for the older mind, to accept it as it is, and to observe it without trying to alter it or shut it down."

"Why?" interrupted Slink. "Why accept it? That just seems like giving up."

"If you want to go from one point in the tunnels to another point some distance away, how important is it that you correctly identify your starting point?" asked Dot.

"It's important," snapped Slink. "But..."

"It is equally important in developing your inner eye," interjected Dot. "You must accept where you are, who you are, what you are. Being human has its limitations. We are biological beings who respond to stimulation unconsciously."

"But..."

"We are also highly intelligent beings," insisted Dot. "We can learn to observe our more primitive responses and choose behavior more consistent with our intelligent intentions. We can only do this, though, if we are determined to observe our unconscious responses, including our feelings, without insisting they be something they are not. Our primitive responses arise unbidden and insisting they should be different only creates self-hatred. We can learn to observe our unbidden responses without losing our ability to observe our surroundings and consciously reflect on our intentions. You don't shift focus, Slink, you expand awareness. You step back from yourself so you can see your inner world, the outer world, and consciously carry your intelligent intentions. You must learn to be more objective, more impassive, more non-judgmental. Judgment will always push you toward instinctive reaction. Instead, learn to watch, reflect, and watch some more."

"Great," sighed Slink. "And while I'm watching someone will act and I'll be powerless to do anything about it."

"I'm making this sound like a complex, drawn-out process," replied Dot. "It's not. It's a subtle shift in consciousness that doesn't slow down your response to genuine threat or need. Once trained, you'll respond when necessary as quickly or quicker than you ever have. You'll just be far less likely to react mindlessly and cause harm to yourself or to others."

"Wow," Slink exclaimed. "I think I understand why you said we couldn't do this in a couple days. This sounds like it could take years."

"Mastery will take a while," replied Dot. "With your aptitude and determination, competence will come quickly. I'm certain you'll be able to use the tools I'll give you by the time you're ready to reassume your duties."

Slink raised his eyebrows inquisitively.

"Jerome, the Senior Medtech, says if it was up to him, he'd clear you to return to work in two weeks. That's good enough for me. So let's make good use of the next couple of weeks."

Slink inhaled, then exhaled loudly.

"All right," he replied. "I'd rather be working, but I can see how this is going to help me, so I'll give it my best."

Dot smiled, then pulled her nephew into a sideways embrace and squeezed.

"Thank you, Slink," she said softly.

Slink just wrapped his arm behind Dot's back and returned her squeeze.

Over the next few days, Dot met with Slink every morning and evening and instructed him on different practices for developing mindfulness. Slink was not one to embrace anything without knowing everything he could about it, but Dot knew all she had to do was tell Slink where and when the practice originated, and Slink would research the practice on his own time to satisfy his curiosity.

Dot taught Slink breathing techniques from Hinduism and Yoga. She taught him meditation techniques from Hinduism, Buddhism, Christianity, and Transcendentalism. She also introduced him to studies on mindfulness practices and neuroscience.

Slink was fascinated by studies on the elasticity of the brain and the ways meditation practices could dramatically alter the way the brain responded to stimuli. He was even more amazed at the dramatic changes he experienced as he engaged the practices Dot taught.

On one occasion, as Dot was teaching Slink a deep-breathing technique, Slink was acutely aware of the breadth of ideas passing through his mind simultaneously. He followed Dot's instruction and even as his breath deepened and his heart slowed, he watched and catalogued his thoughts.

When they finished their session, Dot asked Slink what he had experienced. He told her about observing his thoughts and noting them in detail.

Dot asked him, "Can you still recall what you were thinking about?"

Slink rattled off twenty distinct subjects before Dot stopped him.

"You're kidding, right?"

"You interrupted me," Slink responded. "I can recall 47 different ideas that passed through my mind as we breathed."

"First of all," said Dot, "most people could never identify more than four or five different thoughts passing through their mind at any given moment. Secondly, they'd never be able to recall those ideas after several minutes had passed. You are amazing, Slink! Your brain does things most of us just can't do."

Slink shrugged, a little embarrassed at Dot's words and more uncertain how to respond.

"The thing that really amazes me, though," continued Dot, "is that you have already developed the ability to observe this chaos of swirling thought, catalogue it, commit it to memory, and not get swept away by it. You maintained mindfulness while you recorded the details of your thoughts?" she asked.

"I think so," said Slink sheepishly.

"Well, you must have maintained it to some degree," said Dot, "or you would've been swept up in one of those ideas."

The two of them sat in the silence for a while before Dot asked, "What were you feeling while we were doing the exercise?"

"That's harder for me to pay attention to," Slink replied. "I really have to remind myself to watch my emotions or they just run in the background."

Dot nodded but didn't say anything.

"I was feeling some anxiety, like I always do when we sit together," Slink offered.

Dot nodded again, still not breaking the silence.

"I was also feeling kind of confused," Slink said.

"About what?" Dot asked.

Slink smiled sheepishly.

"About Jenna," he replied. "She's a girl...a woman...here. She showed me around a bit when I first got here. She seems... nice."

Dot smiled.

"I know Jenna," said Dot. "She is nice...and she's pretty."

Slink blushed and looked down at his lap.

"You feel attracted to her, don't you Slink?"

Dot didn't wait for Slink to answer.

"That's a good thing," she asserted. "Have you considered why you found her attractive? There were plenty of attractive young women in Kansas, but none of them ever caught your eye."

Dot waited, but Slink didn't respond.

"Interesting isn't it?" Dot asked.

They sat together in the silence for a while before Dot continued. Slink kept his face down.

"I think your boundaries were breaking down long before you met me in the mess, Slink. From the first time we spent any time together we connected with each other, and that made you uncomfortable, but you couldn't shut it down, could you?"

Slink looked up and met Dot's eyes, then his eyes rose to the ceiling as he recalled their first meeting, he shook his head, and the corners of his mouth rose into a soft smile.

"Jenna got under your skin, too, but in a much more pleasant way. Still, that must have made you uneasy."

Slink nodded his head without returning Dot's gaze.

"No one can be an island forever, Slink. Sooner or later, someone breaches our barriers and reawakens our need for connection. By the time I breached yours, they were already failing. Jenna broke them down further. When you met me in the mess it was inevitable your barriers, like a failing dam holding back a giant reservoir, were going to burst."

Slink returned his gaze to Dot. His eyes were glassy and tears streaked his face.

"Emotions always find expression, Slink. They can feel overwhelming and even dangerous when they explode over us. The solution isn't to banish them but to embrace them. When they're acknowledged as they ebb and flow, they aren't near as threatening. You can learn to watch them, give them room, and choose how you're going to express them. Even though you quickly mastered observing your thoughts, you'll probably find it considerably more challenging to observe your emotions without being drawn into them. I can help you, though. I can teach you a practice designed just for that purpose. Are you willing to try now, or would you rather wait for our next session?"

Slink swallowed and wiped his face with a tissue.

"I'm OK," he said.

Then he laughed.

"I'm not OK," he corrected. "I'm sad, I'm scared, and I'm uneasy."

He paused, chuckled again, and wiped his eyes again.

"I'd like to learn this new practice, though," he finally said. "If you have time, I'd like to try it now."

Dot held Slink's gaze and smiled warmly.

"It's not hard," replied Dot. "It won't take long, and I think it will really help."

Dot stretched for a minute before she sat in half-lotus. Slink followed her lead and sat in the same position facing her.

"The key to watching your emotions is releasing all judgment," Dot began. "If you measure your emotions in any way - how understandable they seem, how socially acceptable they are, or any other standard you might apply - you'll have a tough time keeping your inner eye open. You'll naturally ignore or even sublimate those emotions you judge as unacceptable."

"Think of emotions like waves on an ocean. Waves crest and fall. Like waves, your emotions rise in intensity then wane. So

151

you always want to remember emotions, by their nature, are transitory. One of the first things you need to learn is let your emotions do what they do - rise and fall."

"It can also aid your ability to watch non-judgmentally if you look at your emotions as if they were happening to a younger version of you. We all tend to be more compassionate toward children, and while we may have a tough time cutting ourselves slack, we'll cut the little girl or little boy version of us the slack they deserve."

Slink nodded slowly.

"I can see why that would be helpful," he said.

Dot tilted her head and raised her eyebrows, inviting Slink to elaborate.

"The limbic brain, that's the more primitive part of our brain," explained Slink, "is where most of our emotions originate. We don't have much control over our limbic brain, and when that part of our brain sends a message, that message is usually designed to get immediate response. It bypasses the more reflective, thoughtful part of our brain so we will act to respond to a perceived threat. Seeing emotions as happening to our inner child could help us appreciate that we can't control the emotions any more than most children can control what happens to them."

Dot smiled.

"It's helpful to understand why things work, isn't it, Slink? I'm the same way; I don't just want to know how something works, I always need to ask 'why.' We have that in common. What is unique about you, though, is your ability to answer your own 'why' questions before you've even articulated them. I don't think I've ever seen anyone make connections as quickly as you!"

Dot caught Slink's eye and her smile broadened. Slink returned her smile. After a moment, Dot continued her instruction.

"After we've sat in silence and watched our breath for a few minutes, I will begin to guide you. At first I'm just going to invite you to survey the landscape of your feelings. Just follow my lead as best you can. If you start to feel overwhelmed at any point, just open your eyes until the feelings wane, start your breathing again, and close your eyes when you're ready to proceed."

"After a few minutes of watching your emotions, I'll invite you to imagine those emotions happening in a much younger you. If you're able to make that shift, see if it changes anything about the way you're watching your emotions. Try not to figure out what any shift in perspective means. Just watch. We'll talk about your experience afterwards."

"You ready?" asked Dot.

Slink nodded.

"So let's relax and breathe for a few minutes," she said in reply.

Dot arched her back and turned her head from side to side to stretch for a minute, then she assumed her erect, but relaxed sitting position. She lowered her eyes and started to breathe more deeply. Slink followed her lead, mimicking closely Dot's every move.

Now you can close your eyes whenever you feel ready and just pay attention to your breathing. After we've sat in the silence for a while, I'll offer a few words to guide our meditation and help you anchor this practice."

Slink kept an eye on Dot until she closed her eyes; then he closed his.

They sat in silence for several minutes. Slink tried to just focus on his breathing and relax. He couldn't help but notice, though, that his emotions were exploding in different directions. He felt anxious and uneasy. He felt uncertain. He felt frustrated. Why was this so hard?

"Slink, your frustration is written all over your face," interjected Dot.

Her voice was soft and compassionate.

"Focus on your breathing. You don't need to catalogue your emotions or calm them. Just breathe in and breathe out. Watch each breath and slowly deepen your respiration."

He followed her direction, and he felt himself relaxing. He breathed. He watched as he inhaled and exhaled. Slowly his respiration deepened and a calm settled over him.

Dot's voice entered the silence gracefully like a dancer stepping slowly and gracefully to a simple, repetitive tune.

"As you breathe in and breathe out, imagine you sit on a very small, sandy island. The water surrounding your island is relatively calm. Occasionally, an air bubble rises from the depths of the waters surrounding your island and bursts onto the surface. As the bubble bursts, disrupting the surface, and sending waves outward in every direction, some of those waves climb a little ways up the sides of your island. The bubbles are small enough and infrequent enough, though, that your island is not threatened. You breathe in and breathe out, watching your breath even as you take in the occasional bubble bursting above the surface of the surrounding waters."

Dot remained quiet for the span of several breaths. When her voice gently returned, she spoke one sentence at a time, inhaling slowly but audibly in between each sentence, giving Slink time to form the images in his mind.

"As you breathe in and breathe out, you become aware of a large bubble breaking the surface of the water far off in the distance. It disrupts the surface calm dramatically and sends much larger waves rolling outward from where it burst. You can see the waves rising steadily and moving relentlessly toward you. As you breathe in, you feel your anxiety rising with the approaching wave. You breathe out slowly, and you imagine anchoring yourself to your island, like a great palm tree sending a tap root deep into the earth beneath you. You have time to breathe in and breathe out several times before the wave reaches you. Your anxiety is still there, but it is joined by a deep trust that all will be well. Each time you exhale, you anchor yourself more deeply in the earth and your trust grows accordingly. The wave breaks over your island, over you, and for a moment you are immersed. Because you have been breathing deeply, though, holding your breath for a few seconds is effortless. In a moment the wave has

154

passed, and with it your anxiety; though you are wet, you have not been moved. You sit on your island safe and sound, watch your breath, and welcome a rising sense of gratitude."

Dot kept the silence even longer now than she had at the previous interlude. Slink found it much easier to focus on his breath this time without trying to anticipate Dot's voice breaking the silence. With each breath he took, he felt an ever-deepening sense of calm. When her voice came, it was soft and slow, keeping the same rhythm as before, each sentence separated from the next by a slow, deliberate inhale.

"Your breathing is steady and deep now. You are rooted firmly to your island, safe and secure. You feel peaceful, relaxed, and confident—all is well. Suddenly two very large bubbles burst very near you on each side of your island. The water engulfs you mid-breath, and you start to fight with your arms to swim upward. You are anchored to the island, though, and swimming is not an option. Your anxiety skyrockets and you feel the beginnings of panic. Then, you remember you were breathing deeply for a while before the water engulfed you. Surely you can hold your breath long enough for the water to recede. You look above and see you're not nearly as deep as you feared. You feel the water rushing by you and your head breaks the surface. You suck in cool, refreshing air, even as the water continues to recede. You can still feel the adrenaline rush that came with the panic. Your natural tendency is to gasp quick breaths, but you resist this impulse and breathe slowly and deeply. Your anchor is secure; your island is intact. You straighten your back, lower your chin, and breathe in and out. You are safe; you are secure; you have weathered the unexpected and unpredictable. Gratitude rises again as you breathe deeply and slowly."

After a few minutes of silence, Dot began to stretch, then rose and moved to a chair. Slink heard her movement and soon opened his eyes and stretched his legs in front of him. After one last stretch forward, he rose and took the chair across from Dot.

"That was different from what I expected," he said.

"What did you expect?" asked Dot.

155

"Well, I thought you were going to invite me to survey my emotions and watch them from a distance the way you taught me to do with my thoughts. I was a bit surprised by the fantasy landscape you described and the events you narrated from within that landscape."

Dot smiled.

"Don't get me wrong," urged Slink. "It was...well...it was surprisingly captivating. I was really shocked at how quickly I became immersed in the mental images that arose in my mind in response to your descriptions. I didn't think I had much of an imagination."

Dot's smile widened to a grin.

"Well, I know I can imagine things, but I'm more used to building what I think of as logic puzzles. I take pieces of information and put those pieces together in a logical whole, filling in the missing pieces from the surrounding ones. Somehow that seems a lot different than having someone describe a landscape and seeing myself immersed in it. That kind of shocked me!"

Dot sighed.

"Nothing shocks me anymore with you, Slink. You're not just smarter than anyone I've ever met, you're more advanced in every way. I've known a lot of smart people, many of whom were my parents' friends and colleagues. Some of them could barely function outside the narrow context of their work. They were brilliant, but really limited. You're truly unique. You just get it, no matter what 'it' is. I suppose it would scare a lot of people, but I find it fascinating."

Dot looked Slink in the eye.

"But I think you missed a connection with this exercise, and I'm going to enjoy helping you make it."

Slink furrowed his brow and tilted his head slightly to the side.

"What do the body of water and the rising bubbles represent?" Dot asked. "Your mind embraced the images and fleshed them out for you because they're familiar."

Slink's eyes widened and he broke into a smile.

"The water is my subconscious mind and the bubbles are emotions breaking the surface of awareness," Slink exclaimed.

Dot chuckled and nodded her head.

"So when the emotion bubbles burst," Slink continued, "they charge the surface of awareness causing waves, so I feel like I'm threatened by emotions rising to consciousness."

Slink stood up and paced as the words tumbled from his lips.

"But I'm not threatened by my emotions; I'm securely grounded to a deeper reality, whether I think of that as my mind, life in general, or some abstraction of collective consciousness. And to take it even further, if I'm not trying to stifle my emotions, I'm simply allowing them to rise to the surface, I'll have far fewer of the big eruptions that feel so threatening. Most importantly, your exercise showed me that I can weather those eruptions I can't prevent, whether they come from within or from someone close to me!"

Dot just smiled and shook her head.

"You are amazing, Slink. All you need is one small thread, and you can make a cloak!"

Slink's eyes suddenly widened.

"You never led me through the experience of seeing my emotions as if they were happening to a much younger me," he exclaimed.

"I didn't think we needed to go there together," she replied. "You can explore weaving that dynamic into your practice. I'm sure you can already see how that might change the experience."

Slink nodded his head absentmindedly.

"I'm sure I'd find it much easier to empathize with a younger me experiencing emotion, and I'd help anchor him to withstand the stronger eruptions," said Slink quietly.

He was talking to himself more than answering Dot.

She replied just as quietly.

"This practice can help you resist the urge to shut yourself away from your emotions. That temptation will come as you

157

move back into your role here in Home and start interacting with people again. I want you to practice mindfulness twice a day, using all the tools I have given you and a few more I have yet to share. I'll meet with you each morning until you return to work, but I'm going to let you practice on your own in the evening. I think you are ready to take your practice in directions that suit you as well or better than mimicking my practice."

Slink started to interject, but Dot held up a hand to quiet him.

"Don't let your anxiety get the best of you, Slink," she said. "I know your're itching to get back to work, but I want you to focus your practice on sitting with the discomfort you're feeling and finding calm in the midst of your feelings. Your body needs time to heal completely, and this is an opportunity you are not likely to get again. Take advantage of this respite and train yourself so you can return to work more capable than ever."

Slink looked at the floor and sighed, then looked up and nodded.

"Thank you, Dot. I don't know that I can ever express how much your love and support means to me."

Dot held her hand up before Slink again.

"You have thanked me repeatedly, and I know you are sincere. You are welcome. You'll just have to trust that I am getting as much out of this as I am giving, nephew. You have filled a place in my heart that has only known pain for a very long time."

Ten days later, Slink returned to his bunk on what would have been his normal night off anyway. No one was in the sleeping quarters when he walked in. He placed his things back in his locker and looked around. It felt good to be back--he felt like he belonged here with the other crew members. He was not ready to be an officer--he wanted to blend in and feel "normal" for a while.

He had never really felt like he belonged, and now he was really looking forward to being one of the crew.

Fortunately, he was received more graciously than he could have hoped. No one made a big deal about his return, but no one avoided him either. Those who saw him in the sleeping quarters made some remark like, "nice to have you back," or "glad you're feelin' better little man." He joined in the card game that night and even managed to come away as the big winner at his table. He had joined the loudest table and quickly became one of the liveliest players. By the time they broke up and headed for the sleeping quarters, Slink had made a couple new friends. He went to sleep that night looking forward to his return to The Cave.

The next morning, he was up before anyone in the men's sleeping quarters, showered, and even ate some breakfast in the Mess, although he was so early all they could offer him was some warmed Garsow mush. Gamma Sector, where most of the food was grown for the colony, had been restricted to growing a form of oats and a hybrid soy, which when combined and ground into cereal made a mush that most Garsons grew to hate by the time they left the nurseries. Slink didn't mind. Nothing could dampen his spirits. He hadn't felt so happy to be alive in all his days!

He arrived on the bridge almost an hour before his shift was to start. Dot was already sitting at the command console. She saw him come in out of the corner of her eye and turned to face him. She smiled and waved him over.

"I'm sure you want to wait for the rest of your colleagues to join them in opening the Cave," she said. "So, why don't you hang with me. You can watch me ready the Bridge and set up command operations for the day."

He had forgotten about the ritual opening of the Cave. He was grateful that Dot had saved him the embarrassment of violating the ritual on his first day back.

"That'd be cool!" he said. Then, realizing they were surrounded by members of the night command, he added, "I'm sorry. Thank you for the invitation, Dot. I would be privileged to join you."

She laughed. "I'm glad you think it'd be cool," she said. "I hoped you'd find interest in what we do."

First she punched her command code into her console. The main screen came to life. A map materialized on the screen after a few seconds. Slink determined that it was a schematic of the tunnels. He saw tiny blue squares appear at different points along the tunnels. After a few minutes, he realized they were moving. They had to be sweeper drones, thought Slink. This had to be a condensed recording of the movements of the drones over some past period of time. They were covering far too much ground for the image to represent real time.

"What do you make of that, Slink?" Dot asked.

"It's a schematic of the tunnels, with the blue squares depicting the movements of the sweeper drones over some period of time. I can't tell how long a period is represented by the recording."

"I thought you'd figure that out pretty easily. The recording shows the movement of the drones over the past 12 hours. I have been off the bridge for 36 hours, since I had yesterday off, so I have three such recordings to review. I'm going to move through the other two a little faster. Don't worry if you can't track the images."

He had no problem recognizing and tracking the images. He recognized that the drones below Alpha Sector moved more quickly than those below Beta and Gamma Sectors. That made sense, since the tunnels underneath Alpha Sector were significantly larger. One drone caught his attention, though.

"Stop!" he barked. Then he immediately apologized. "Oh, sorry, Dot, I just meant to give the computer a voice command."

"It's OK, Slink. What did you see?"

"The drone under Alpha Sector, at the far lower left corner of the screen. It jumped from one point to another. One second it was here," he pointed with a laser pointer to a point just a few millimeters away, "then it was here," he pointed to the corner. "It couldn't move that fast. Is it just an anomaly in the recording?"

Dot was smiling broadly. Several of the night crew had stopped attending to their own screens or consoles and turned to watch and listen to the exchange between Dot and Slink.

"Are you sure it jumped?" she asked.

"I'm sure," he said without hesitation.

"There are over 30 drones on the screen, Slink, and we're watching a 12 hour recording condensed into 1 minute. All the drones skip when we condense it that much. I can't even follow the movements of a single drone unless I am concentrating on it to the exclusion of all else."

"No offense, Dot, but I can follow them. That one jumped a distance well beyond anything that could be accounted for with the time lapse of the recording."

"Let me play it back again at the same speed, and you command the computer to display the image as you like," she said.

"OK," said Slink. The image blurred for a second, then came back into focus, and the little blue lights started their dance through the tunnels, seeming to flash several times a second as they moved through the contours of the tunnels.

"Slow," said Slink. "Slow," he called again, then "Play." A few seconds later, he called, "Pause." He turned to Dot. "This one," he pointed to one of the little motionless blue squares. "Watch it closely now."

"Play," he commanded.

A few seconds later, the blue square jumped--not much, but about three times as far as any previous skip the image had made. The jump was no more than a few millimeters--barely noticeable in real time--unless someone stopped the recording and pointed it out in advance. When they saw it, the crew all gasped in unison.

"Thank God DAN doesn't have anyone with your powers of observation," she said. Then she broke out laughing. "At least we have to pray they don't have anybody like you!"

"Why...why do you say that?" Slink asked.

161

"That little blue square represents Home," said Dot. "We cloak our actual movements from the system most of the time. Occasionally we can't avoid coming into visual contact with another drone, so we have to make sure our computer representation shows us to be where we are actually sighted, or we would set off an alarm. We do our best to anticipate those encounters and bring our virtual image into alignment with our physical location over a longer period. Occasionally, we have to "jump" the virtual image to bring it into alignment before the visual contact. It is supposed to be undetectable, and so far as we know, it has been...until now!"

"OK, everyone, back to your stations, We still need to have the bridge ready for the morning crew in a half hour," Dot said.

She returned to her routine. She brought up reports of the last thirty-six hours' activities on Home. After she didn't find anything out of the ordinary or hear any objection from Slink, she closed down the video feed to the screen and it went dark again.

She got up from her station, motioning Slink to follow, and went from station to station on the bridge. Each person gave a report of the areas he or she oversaw. One reported on communiques with other Technoid drones. Another reported on any unusual surface activity as reported to them by the Tunnel Rat enclaves. Still another gave a report on Home's supply of food stores, water, and power. Each of the eight stations on the bridge had specific areas of oversight, and one by one they all reported to their commander. She did not look to Slink for comment and he did not offer any.

When they had finished their rounds, Dot motioned to the Cave. "Your team is waiting for you," she said.

Slink glanced up at the clock above the bulwark that separated the Bridge from the Cave and saw that it was already 7:58. After he thanked Dot for the provocative tour, he entered the Cave, took his place in front of his station and turned to face his colleagues. They were all in their places.

Chris spoke for the group. "Welcome back, Slink. We're glad to have you at your station again. We haven't altered your files or their arrangement since you left. We have, however, taken the liberty of summarizing the data we've collected in your absence and placing it in a folder labeled 'new' on your desktop."

He turned to the others. "Our circle is whole once again," he said as he looked around the room at each one in turn. "Let us begin."

They bowed and held silence together. It was still uncomfortable for Slink but it wasn't as difficult as he remembered. His mind still wanted to wander, but there were moments where he was able to be still, listen to his breath passing into and out of his lungs, and take in the silent presence of his colleagues and the common purpose that bound them together. He could not define that purpose yet, but he was sure it existed and was at the center of their shared silence as they began and ended each shift.

The contribution he was to make in the Cave began to take shape that morning as he reviewed the work of his colleagues in the files they had compiled for him. He began to recognize patterns in their independent work. Although each person was working within a relatively small field, they were each pulling information from the files they scanned that had to do with the functioning of the Supernet.

His colleagues had become extraordinarily clever at gleaning information about the Supernet from ordinary reports and the code that shaped them. The composers of the reports they collected, for the most part, made no overt reference to the Supernet. In fact, most of them undoubtedly took the existence and function of the Supernet for granted.

The Supernet was originally the name given the network through which all communications on Garsow were conducted.

The servers at the heart of the Supernet were kept deep beneath the tunnels in secure vaults. In those early days, the data network was designed primarily to maintain the life support systems and monitor the structural integrity of the tunnels.

As the colony established surface settlements, the network was used more and more for communication between working parties on the surface and support crews in the tunnels or on the Garsow space station. When the commlink was introduced, the Supernet became the backbone of the commlink system. Every bit of data originating as a chemical signal in someone's brain and translated into an electrical impulse by his or her commlink was transmitted via the Supernet. Eventually, the servers that supported the commlink were isolated from the servers that supported the other planetoid systems. Over the years, the Supernet came to refer to the commlink network, including the servers that formed the backbone of that network. The network that relayed information on the planetoid's life support systems and other utilities was usually referred to as the Grid. Occasionally, someone regressed by lumping all the systems together under the name "Supernet," but as time passed, the two networks were seen as being more and more distinct from each other.

Slink recognized this distinction in his own mind, and he could see that while his colleagues were gathering a lot of information from the Grid, which was much easier to hack, even that information gave some indirect insight into the operation of the Supernet. Those files they had forwarded to him from the Supernet itself were usually chosen because something in their headers or coding gave clues as to how information was routed or packaged for transmission on the Supernet.

"What's so funny?"

Slink was startled by Chris standing behind him and asking his sudden question.

"You're not going to believe this, but I'm just catching on to what we're studying here. Before my...," his voice trailed off. He cleared his throat. "Before, I was just so happy to have new information to absorb, new subjects to study, I didn't pay much attention to any commonalities amongst the files. Now, all of a sudden, I see we're performing some pretty focused research. We're not just a bunch of smart people here to learn anything and everything we can."

Slink laughed out loud. It felt so good! Everything was truly different now. It was as if he'd gone to sleep in one world and awoken in another. Where once he'd seen only information to be absorbed, he now saw connections. Where previously he'd seen only passing individuals who occasionally shared his company, he now saw relationships. Where he had unconsciously protected himself from any vulnerability, now he unselfconsciously opened himself to every new feeling and experience that came his way. On one level, he knew he'd swung from one extreme to the other, and he'd one day soon begin to swing back toward the middle, developing some boundaries and barriers, but for the moment he relished taking the world in like a newborn baby fascinated with every new discovery!

"We're zeroing in on the Supernet--trying to learn everything we can about it. We must be looking at how we might alter it, disrupt it, or even destroy it, eh Chris?"

Now it was Chris' turn to smile. He brought his hand up and rubbed Slink's scalp through the short bristles of his hair.

"We're glad you came back ready to work, little man! We're counting on you to help us put the pieces together. That's why you're going to see new files in that desktop folder every morning. We want you to look at the files we're finding, figure out which ones show us anything valuable, and help us draw conclusions about our target. Once we have those conclusions, we'll discuss what we might do with that information. Until then, we'll keep our speculations to ourselves, OK?"

Slink saw the smile on Chris' face and took his meaning.

"Sure, skip," he said. "I study, find puzzle pieces that fit together, and report to you what I find. No problem!"

"Just so you don't start feeling too burdened by your responsibility, Slink, I want you to know that two of your colleagues are getting the same information for the same purpose. I'm responsible for taking the reports from you three and bringing them together to make some kind of sense. Just grab the stuff that jumps out at you and let your mind work with it. When patterns emerge, let me know. Otherwise, let it go."

"You've got it," said Slink, and turned back to his screen.

This was going to be fun!

Chapter 7

The material used for the organic shells encasing the plane-toid's settlements, like the pressurized drill enclosures, was developed by Dr. Adela Lansing. Before she and Jonathan met, she had been commissioned to develop a coating for interplanetary space ships that could withstand the rigors of high-speed space travel. Until she entered the field, the entire focus of the scientists working to protect the space fleet had been on developing a material that would be nearly impermeable. Dr. Lansing recognized the futility of this effort, and she instead sought to develop a material that could repair itself from any damage it sustained.

During one of her Mars expeditions she discovered Carbon Cnidus 6, a bacteria that lay dormant for millennia. Human discovery of the bacteria, like so many discoveries, began tragically. An unknowing grad student had come into contact with the bacteria and by the time he was found his body was encased in a material that looked and felt like plastic, but was several times stronger than any plastic human beings had ever developed, and immediate-

ly repaired any damage inflicted upon it by those trying to extract the poor young man's body from its bacterial tomb.

The moment Adela studied the bacteria, she knew she had found the material she was looking for. It took her only six months to determine how to grow the bacteria apart from a host by creating a synthetic web from micro fibers and soaking that web material in a nutrient rich liquid before introducing the bacteria. When she developed the ability to supply a continuous infusion of the nutrient to the material supporting the bacteria she found she had a nearly impermeable shell that could repair itself with remarkable ease.

Jonathan found the only hardship that tested his endurance in those first two years on Garsow was the long periods of separation from Adela and his children. He shuttled to Garsow Station for three months out of each year, as did each of the crew members. For the other nine months, he had to content himself with video-conferencing, first from the surface where he engineered the construction of the underground settlements and the permanent landing bay for the shuttle, then from the underground settlements, where he engineered the surface settlements.

After five years of working on his own, Jonathan was happy to have Adela at his side. The surface crews were also happy to have her working amongst them. Jonathan was the one who designed and oversaw the building. Adela was the one who solved the problems that baffled everyone else. When she was not developing the drill enclosure or the settlement enclosures, Adela was working diligently to develop new chemical compounds with which they might treat their tools to withstand the corrosive effects of space dust. When she stepped off the shuttle she came armed with these new tools to make life easier for all Garsons, and a warm embrace that made life much easier for one particular Garson.

After he finished his shift, Slink headed for the men's quarters to make a few notes in the digital journal he'd started when he emerged from his...he still hadn't figured out how to characterize the event that had changed his life. Referring to his "breakdown" seemed too negative--it was already beginning to feel like the best thing that ever happened to him! If he referred to his "time away" that seemed just plain weird. After all, he hadn't gone anywhere! The word that came to mind when he thought of that time was "retreat." So, he wrote about his first day at work since his retreat, the lightness he felt in his mind and his heart, and the quickness of his insight and wit. As to the former, he'd been as startled as anyone at the way he immediately recognized the "jump" of the little blue square that was Home on the recording of the mapped drone movements. As to the latter, he'd never seen much use for humor before his retreat, and now he seemed to find the humor in every thought, every conversation, and every word out of someone else's mouth. It was all rather amazing!

He made his entry as fast as he could, using the virtual keyboard on the little handheld Gen had given him. It would have been much faster for him to use the voice recorder, but he'd quickly discovered using the keyboard accessed a different part of his mind than dictating; the keyboard seemed to give him more access to the newly awakened reflective part of his mind.

When he ran out of the sleeping quarters toward the Mess he was so intent on making his way down the stairs he almost tripped over the back of the woman sitting on the top stair. He'd hardly noticed her sitting there. It was a strange place for someone to be sitting--unless she was waiting for someone to come down those stairs!

Jenna had begun to wonder if Slink was ever coming out of the men's sleeping quarters. She'd snuck a peek a couple of times and seen him sitting on his bunk intently looking down into the screen of his handheld, so she knew he wasn't taking a nap, but she was beginning to wonder if they were going to miss dinner because of some obsession Slink needed to pacify.

When he came flying out of the sleeping quarters, Slink nearly ran Jenna over. He jumped to the side and stumbled down the first stair. Jenna grabbed his arm to slow his momentum sending a jolt down her spine. She blushed furiously. It wasn't the first time she was grateful for her dark complexion.

"Hi, Slink. I saw you leave the deck, and I thought, I thought..." she stammered.

"Get ahold of yourself, girl," she silently chided.

"I thought we could sit together at dinner," she finished.

When Slink recognized Jenna, he realized not everything had changed since his retreat. This girl had made him feel uncomfortable when she'd shown him to the sleeping quarters, and here he was again--feeling his throat tighten, his face grow hot, and his heart race.

"Uh, well, I, uh," he started.

"It's OK, I know I'm being really presumptuous," she said, "maybe some other time." She turned and started down the stairs.

"Wait!" Slink shouted. He startled them both with his forcefulness. She turned.

He laughed, and then she was laughing with him. His legs grew solid underneath him and his tongue grew limber.

"I'd love to share dinner with you," he said. "We're so late, I thought I was going to have to eat alone. It'll be nice to have your company."

"Well, come on then," she said. "If we wait any longer, we're going to be out of luck!"

He fell in behind her down the stairs, then came alongside her as they reached the landing at the bottom of the stairs. The exit from the Mess was near the landing, so they had to make their way through a stream of crew members who'd already finished dinner in order to get to the entrance. Slink fell back behind Jenna to make it easier to pass through the crowded passageway. As he did, she reached back and took his hand. Slink felt heat rush up his neck and into his face. He looked down to hide his discomfort,

170

so he didn't notice the many stares they got as they made their way through the crowd.

He and Jenna might have been more deeply disappointed with the meager remains of dinner. They might have--if they'd been paying any attention. Instead, they scooped the last spoonful of one dish, scraped the remainder of another, and loaded up on the fried Garsow mush that had hardly been touched. It didn't matter much what they had on their plates. The little they ate passed across their taste buds without causing a synapse to fire. The Mess workers ran them out after they'd finished their nightly cleaning duties and shut off half the lights without the couple even taking notice.

Jenna had grown up in an Alpha Sector nursery, not far from where Slink had first descended into the tunnels. Her escape from the tunnels was relatively uneventful. She hung on every word as Slink related the harrowing escape he'd endured. She laughed as he recalled the way he stood transfixed in the middle of the pedway, while Neoko coaxed him, then threatened him to keep him moving. She was shocked when he casually mentioned that he'd been only ten years old when Neoko led him across the transway, through Alpha Sector, and into the tunnels.

Like Slink, Jenna had spent a number of years with the Tunnel Rats, before she was brought onto Home. She thought it was three or four years, but she couldn't be sure. It had to be close, she said, because she'd been almost fourteen when she left the nursery and she'd soon turn eighteen. Slink felt self-conscious acknowledging that he'd just turned sixteen. Jenna assured him their age difference meant little to her. She pointed out they were two of the youngest people on Home. She kept to herself that women outnumbered men two to one. She didn't want to seem desperate! If he hadn't figured out that men were in short supply, she wasn't going to point it out.

Slink was a little shocked to hear that Jenna served as the personal assistant for Gen. Jenna explained that Gen had become the Tunnel Rat ambassador, maintaining contact and strengthening relationships with the Tunnel Rat enclaves. Occasionally, he'd disembark Home, according to Jenna, and she'd oversee communications in his absence. When he was on board, she helped Gen stay organized and keep track of all the information he received from the enclaves. She was adept at creating and overseeing the database Gen needed, and she had the experience to tie everything he did into the existing databases on Home.

Jenna told Slink that Gen had left Home that morning. She mentioned in passing that Gen had neglected his work while Slink was sick, so he had some catching up to do. When she saw a pained expression cross Slink's face, she reached out and ran her hand back and forth across his forearm that rested on the table between them.

"He wouldn't have had it any other way, Slink. He loves you like a brother. He was determined to bring you through your crisis..."

"I prefer to think of it as a "retreat," Slink interrupted.

"He was determined to bring you through your retreat, then," Jenna corrected. "Now that you're doing better, he asked me to make sure you were OK."

Slink recoiled from her.

"Is that what you're doing? Keeping an eye on me for Gen?"

"No, Slink!" she exclaimed. "Come on...you're too smart to believe that. I understand your cautiousness--after what you told me about your, uh, retreat—I can see how you might question my motives. But come on, Slink. I could've checked up on you in five minutes. Do you think I'd spend the entire evening with you and go to work exhausted out of some over-developed sense of obligation? I'm here because I've wanted to be here--right here beside you--since we first met."

Jenna leaned across the table and squeezed Slink's arm in both her hands.

"Slink...I like you."

His face split ear to ear with a spontaneous grin then clouded with confusion. What the heck did that mean? She liked him?

Jenna read Slink's face instantly and decided to clarify matters; she stood and leaned across the table. Slink's apprehension gave way to an instinctual response as he leaned forward in his chair to meet her. She leaned over the table and closed her eyes. His head was a few inches above hers, so he had to scoot back against his chair, and lean forward, before tilting his head upward to receive her. Their lips met. Slink closed his eyes and was swept away by the exquisite sensation. They came together, not with the awkwardness and urgency typical of a first kiss, but with the tenderness and patience of more practiced lovers.

Slink felt his lips press Jenna's softly, felt her turn upward into the kiss, felt her lips part ever so slightly, then press back against his. His entire body tingled. His muscles tensed and his pulse thumped in his ears. He swelled with anticipation, though he had only the vaguest notion of where this encounter might lead. His extraordinary ability to hyper-focus, for the first time, served his heart rather than his head.

She gently pulled away, turned her head from one side to the other and re-engaged with him. Again their lips came together. This time her full lips parted long enough for him to feel her teeth pressing ever so softly against his lips before her lips closed on his again in an all-encompassing embrace. The back of his head felt like it could explode. He couldn't breath because his nose was sealed against her soft, warm cheek--and he didn't care. He just wanted to preserve this feeling as long as he could.

When she pulled away, she fell back in her swing-out chair and sighed.

"Wow!"

With her eyes still closed, Jenna broke into a broad smile. Slink realized then how wide he was grinning. He reached across the table and took her hands in his. Jenna opened her eyes.

"I like you, too, Jenna."

They both broke out laughing. It was at that point that one of the Mess workers said,

"Hey, you two, we're calling it a night. You two lovebirds can stay, but we're shutting off the rest of the lights."

"Come on," said Jenna. "We shouldn't be seen here without anyone else around. Dot frowns on crew members meeting in private, and I don't want to violate that rule with her nephew!"

She laughed again, swung her chair out, and stood. Slink swung his chair out and started to stand, before he fell back. His lower legs were asleep because he'd been pressing the back of his thighs so hard against the edge of the chair as their conversation had grown more intense.

"I can't stand up," he said. "My legs are asleep."

They both started laughing and in no time they were giggling uncontrollably. Slink couldn't have stopped if he wanted to because the tingling in his legs was almost unbearable, and the more he laughed, the harder Jenna laughed with him. The Mess worker gave them a disgusted look and walked away. A few seconds later the lights went out. A couple minutes after that, the two of them walked out of the Mess, up the stairs, and onto the landing that separated the men's and women's sleeping quarters.

Slink took Jenna in his arms and embraced her. He loved the feel of her hair against his face as he held her close. After a minute, she pulled back, gave him a quick peck on the lips and said,

"Good night."

She turned and walked into the darkened doorway, leaving him standing on the landing.

"Yes it was," he said to himself. "Yes it was!"

The first day after his encounter with Jenna, Chris met him at the door of the Cave.

"Use the time of silence to let go of all thought of her."

Slink looked at him in shock. He could tell by looking at Chris that he meant what Slink thought he meant, but how? How could he know that Slink and Jenna had come together, and how could he know she'd taken up residence in Slink's mind?

"Never mind how I know."

"Now you're freaking me out," Slink replied under his breath.

"The important thing," Chris continued," is that I can help you do what you must while you're here. If you allow yourself to become distracted or pre-occupied by her, I'll need to report your disposition to Dot, who will, in turn, feel compelled to restrict your access to Jenna."

Slink shot Chris a menacing look to say, "you wouldn't do that!"

"On the other hand," Chris continued, "if you can let go of her while you're in the Cave, why should I care what you do when you're not here?"

Chris leaned into Slink then, lowered his voice, and repeated the sentence with which he had opened their conversation, "use the time of silence to let go of all thought of her. First, bring her into your mind, then consciously release her into the care of the silence. She'll wait there for you until you return at the end of your shift."

Slink was really quite amazed at how well this little technique worked. Sometimes he had to release his thoughts of her more than once in their opening time of silence, but usually, by the time he turned to his work station, Jenna was safely tucked away in the benevolent silence.

At those times when the ritual silence might not have cleared his mind, his uncanny ability to focus served him well. Once he sat down at his work station and began to open files and scan data, his mind locked in on the task at hand. It was as if a door opened in his mind, and as it did, every other door and window slammed shut.

By the end of his first week back at work in the Cave, he'd gone from recognizing their collective focus was concentrated on the Supernet to forming a number of tentative hypotheses about the network that governed the commlink. He laid these out in notes intended for his eyes only. He wanted to gain more clarity before he shared his thoughts with Chris.

He surmised the Supernet had to be hard wired throughout the tunnels and linked wirelessly to the commlinks through a series of transmitters on the surface. He assumed the information on the network was broken into "packets" for transmission, then reassembled into decipherable data at either end of the transmission. He also recognized the raw data transmitted from one commlink appeared to another person through their commlink as an interpretation of that data and surmised that the Supernet was more than a communications relay system. It performed complex interpretations of data and transmitted these interpretations in a span of milliseconds. Thus, if one person experienced a rise in pulse rate, looked downward, and broke out in a sweat while they were talking, someone listening to that person would see through his visor a red overlay on the upper right quadrant of his vision indicating the speaker was likely lying.

These were relatively basic hypotheses formed from cursory observations, but since the Technoids had no schematic of the Supernet, all their knowledge came in this manner. The Cave was designed to expose the brightest of the Technoids to the data their company could gather, and from their observations form theses, test those theses, and draw conclusions that could be assembled into a coherent understanding of the Supernet.

"You cannot defeat an opponent you do not understand," Dot would often say when someone asked her why they spent all their time gathering information.

She was convinced they would have only one opportunity to disrupt or disable the Supernet. If they failed, their intention would nonetheless be obvious, and their inherent threat to Garson society would be equally as obvious. At that point, DAN would go to any lengths required to root them out and destroy them. Dot made clear they would not act until they'd developed a plan upon which they were willing to stake their entire future.

Slink worked tirelessly to form theses from the observations of his colleagues, then in turn to test those theses against the raw data from which they had formed their observations. When he was confident that a thesis passed his scrutiny, he would pass it on to Chris. Chris often reassured Slink he was doing good work, though he never came back to Slink and reported on whether or not one of his theses had helped him reach a useful conclusion.

Slink didn't need to hear Chris had reached any useful conclusions as a result of reading Slink's theses. He couldn't help forming his own conclusions from the theses he developed. His mind automatically took every thesis like a piece to a puzzle and tried to fit it to an emerging picture of the Supernet. Slink's mind grasped the general shape of the commlink's central nervous system and, just as effortlessly, saw its specific attributes along with its consequent vulnerabilities. Slink formulated strategies for hacking the network without being detected, for altering data on the network as it passed from one point to another, for corrupting streams of data that passed through a specific branch of the network, and of course, he slowly formulated a strategy for destroying the network altogether.

Slink didn't formulate all these strategies deliberately; his mind did all this while he scanned hundreds and thousands of files, while he drew out their commonalities, while he formulated thesis after thesis from those commonalities. It took no conscious effort really. His mind detected connections and drew conclusions like a fish swimming to get where it wanted to go.

When he left the Cave, thoughts of Jenna quickly became an overriding obsession. He hadn't been infatuated with anything or anyone since he was ten years old and Neoko stole his heart. Prior to that, the only attachment he'd ever formed was destroyed by a thoughtless nursery guardian. Tubby the stuffed rabbit kept Slink's secrets and gave expression to thoughts and feelings too dangerous for a little outcast to express. Slink would lay in his bunk at night and carry on long, whispered conversations with Tubby. Slink would parrot the commands of the guardians and Tubby would express every resistant or contrary attitude. Tubby was "bad," but every morning Tubby stayed behind tucked underneath Slink's pillow, while Slink, the compliant little guardian-to-be, would attend to his chores. One night Slink returned to his bunk and found his freshly laundered pillow no longer sheltered Tubby, and he was furious. He started screaming threats aimed at the unidentified culprit who had taken his precious Tubby. The older kids teased him, and he struck out.

Mrs. Cuff had probably been standing in the dormitory doorway for some time before one of the boys noticed her and pointed. Most of the boys stopped scuffling immediately. Slink was oblivious to the sudden calm. The storm that roiled within him was reaching hurricane proportions. The boys' teasing and scuffling just reinforced his suspicions that one of them had taken his little stuffed rabbit. He screamed at them and swung his fists wildly at the biggest of the boys who held him at a safe distance with a straight-arm to the forehead. Mrs. Cuff yelled.

"This will stop...now!"

Slink did not hear her. He was beyond hearing anything. The winds of emotion blew so violently in his head he might as well been deaf.

She grabbed him and lifted him off the ground by one arm. She turned and slammed him into one of the walls, still holding him a foot or more off the ground. The shock jolted him enough to allow her voice to cut through the storm.

"I said...stop!"

"What the devil has gotten into you, young man? I have a mind to send you downstairs to cool off for a few nights."

Slink did not want to go downstairs. The cellar was little more than a warehouse for the nursery's many supplies. There were two tiny rooms in the furthest corner of the expansive cellar, though, and they each had a cot, a toilet, no windows, and a door that locked from the outside. Every guardian child knew about the

178

rooms. They were at the center of many a frightening story the kids heard from their older peers.

"What is this about?" Mrs. Cuff demanded.

"My rabbit...Tubby...gone," Slink managed to blurt out between gasps for breath.

"You mean this?"

She pulled Tubby from one of her apron pockets.

"Surely, this turmoil is not about this stupid, worn, little germ magnet. We have rules about keeping these dirty little things in the dorm. Where'd you find this, anyway? You must've stolen it from the refuse bin, where one of the future citizens quite rightfully dumped it. I'm in a very generous mood tonight, young Slink. I'll throw it out for you and overlook this disturbance if you'll apologize to your dorm mates. What do you think of my generosity?"

She asked her last question with an ear-to-ear grin on her face as she surveyed the eyes of the boys all watching her every move and hanging on her words. She didn't see Slink purse his lips, didn't hear him clear his throat, and was utterly unprepared when he spit in her face. Slink spent a week downstairs in what turned out to be the first of many stretches in the basement.

He never forgot Tubby. Whenever he developed the slightest attraction to any object or person, his mind brought forth the image of Tubby squeezed in Mrs. Cuff's fat hand, limbs flapping helplessly around her stubby fingers, and in response, he squelched any attachment germinating in his mind. Over a ten year period, Neoko was the only person who got close to Slink without bringing forth the specter of the little stuffed rabbit. Slink became deeply attached to Neoko before he even realizing what was happening. While he grew closer and closer to Neoko, Tubby remained curiously absent. In Tubby's place, Slink found a grasping, relentless hand, Mrs' Cuff's awful hand, gloved in white and determined to chase him down and carry him away like it'd carried away Tubby. The dreadful giant hand first appeared in his dreams just after Neoko abandoned him in Kansas and it stayed just behind his conscious awareness always a threat to jump into his dreams whenever he laid down to rest.

When dreaming, he swore that awful hand would never catch him. When awake, he swore he'd never again lose himself in another person. And as a consequence, he'd nearly lost his soul.

Now he was in deep, and he didn't care. He was head-over-heals. Jenna had entered his life at the only point where she could possibly have found an opening. And when she found that opening, she thrust herself into his life and staked claim to his heart. He was in no position to deny her. He'd awoken from his retreat completely defenseless. He was more vulnerable than he'd ever been since he first learned to bite the hand that brought medicine he didn't want to take.

Gen had returned from his visits to the Tunnel Rat enclaves and found an administrative assistant who was almost completely immobilized. Usually a picture of efficiency, Jenna hadn't completed any of the work he'd left her. She was moving fast enough to accomplish three people's jobs, but her perpetual motion had no underlying purpose. She was a picture of a syncaff addict who'd been on a week-long binge without any sleep. Gen knew Jenna's problem couldn't possibly be drug addiction if for no other reason than Technoids simply didn't have access to the stuff.

He sat down with her and tried to talk to her. He didn't get far. She was so confused by the state of affairs that she couldn't begin to explain why she'd not finished her work. She'd start in about one subject, then move to another, then still another, never saying anything coherent on a single one. She was aware she wasn't functioning well, but she felt powerless to do anything about it. She never spoke Slink's name; never even made reference to a budding relationship. She saw no connection.

Fifteen minutes of listening to her had Gen nearly as confused as Jenna. He told her to take the rest of the day off and go by the med unit to have them run a scan just to make sure there was nothing physically wrong. He probably would've remained in the dark for some time if he hadn't tracked Slink down later that day to check in with him regarding his first week back at work.

While Slink had become adept at maintaining focus on his work while he was in the Cave, he practiced no such discipline outside that realm, and probably couldn't have if he tried. Gen found Slink in the Mess, picking at a tray of food that looked like it had already spent far too much time on that tray. When Slink saw Gen, he jumped up from the table.

"What'd you do to her?" he snapped. "I've been waiting almost an hour for her--something's wrong. She was really worried about your return--said she couldn't get her work done, said you'd be really upset with her. I told her you'd understand, you'd give her a break. But I guess that was too much to expect of the Tunnel Rat ambassador, huh? What'd you do to her?" Slink yelled as he asked his question a second time.

Gen really felt for the kid, but when he made the connection, he couldn't help himself--it was just too funny! He started to laugh and once he started, he couldn't stop. He dropped into one of the swing out chairs, put his head down on the table, and laughed himself silly.

Slink wanted to pull his head up and punch him. Gen's reaction only confirmed for Slink Gen had something to do with Jenna's tardiness. She'd never been more than five minutes late for their dinner rendezvous, and now he'd endured an hour of waiting, wondering, and imagining. He'd nearly convinced himself that Gen had learned of their budding relationship and forbid her from seeing him. Now he was all but certain his suspicions were confirmed.

Just as he was about to make a further scene, screaming his accusations at the slumping figure across the table, Slink looked up. Jenna stood five or six feet away, tray of food in hand, worry lines etched across her forehead, gaze jumping from Slink to Gen and back to Slink.

Slink jumped up from the table and over to her.

"What did you do to him?" she blurted. "You made him cry?" she asked, completely baffled by Gen's shaking, slumped over figure in the chair.

At her first words, Gen raised his head off the table and looked up at them. His face was streaked with tears, and he was still convulsing involuntarily with spasms that rose from his aching abdomen. Jenna's second question set him off again and he threw his arms down on the table, with his head clutched between them; his knees jerked upward and hit the underside of the table as he doubled over, gasping for breath between hoots of laughter.

"I didn't do anything to him," Slink insisted. "I was afraid he'd done something to you. I asked him what he did to you, and I guess he put two and two together and found our relationship to be one of the funniest things he's ever imagined. Part of me wants to make him suffer while he's so helpless with his stupid laughing fit!"

"He was really worried about me, Slink. He made me go down to the Med unit and get a scan. I couldn't tell him why I wasn't getting any work done, so he thought maybe something really bad was happening to me. No wonder it seemed so funny to him, when he realized that you and I..." she didn't finish her sentence. This was not going to be the context where she used the word "love" for the first time in reference to their relationship.

Slink admitted the situation could be kind of funny if you were in Gen's shoes, but he wasn't ready to laugh.

"You're OK?" he asked her.

"Well, I'm as good as could be expected. I feel a lot better now that I'm here with you," she said.

He wrapped his arm around her waist, pulled her in next to him, and kissed her on the forehead.

Gen finally looked up from his chair and croaked, "give me another minute."

Once he regained his composure, he sat up and faced them across the table. Slink had helped Jenna put her tray down and they'd sat down next to each other and across from Gen.

"I guess it's too late to tell you that you don't want to be starting any new relationships for a few months after your, uh, retreat, huh Slink?" He turned to Jenna. "And you--why didn't you tell me you were dating someone? Of course, it's who you're dating that's makes this a little more complicated, now isn't it? Oh well--life's what happens when we're making other plans."

He looked off into the distance and said this last phrase as much for himself as for them. Their relationship scrambled too many roles for him. He wasn't sure whether he should be talking to them as Slink's friend and caregiver, or as Jenna's boss, or as an officer of Home. He decided at last to approach their relationship from each of his various roles in turn.

"As your boss, Jenna, and an officer on this ship, I can tell you that you'll find a sense of rhythm at work again soon. Talking with me today will probably go a long way in helping you both settle down. I'm not going to intervene to cut off your relationship. We didn't work that way in the tunnels when people formed an attraction, and I don't think Dot wants to approach it that way either."

"As your friend, Slink, I must say this isn't the best timing for you to hook up. You're a lot more fragile than you'd like to believe. At the very least, you need to take this slowly. You've probably already told each other your life story, including all those parts you thought you'd never tell anyone."

They looked at each other and smiled sheepishly before turning back to Gen.

"If one of you decided to stop this thing today, it'd be tough on the other person for a while. If you keep building this relationship with the momentum you've developed over the last week, one or both of you will end up feeling completely crushed if this doesn't work out. Of course all the warnings in the world aren't going to get you to stop building what you've started. Infatuation is far more powerful than the sum of wills of any two people. You'll only be able to decide where you are going to draw some limits in your relationship for now. Draw them close! Hell, contain the relationship to being close friends who kiss each other if you can. The slower you take this, the stronger it'll be, and the stronger you'll each be."

"Stay in the present or the past when you talk with each other. Don't get caught up talking about the future too much. None of us on this ship or anywhere in the tunnels has much of an idea what tomorrow'll bring. You two've even less of an idea than most of us. Let tomorrow bring what it will, and enjoy today."

"Finally, find at least one other person you can talk to about this relationship. You need to have someone else you can trust to help you work things out by talking them through. No one is good at working a relationship out in his or her head. You need to have a confidant who will listen to you without judgment and help you figure out what's right for you."

"I care about both of you very much. Right now, you can hardly imagine saying a harsh word to each other. One day, you'll have the power, if you don't already, to cause great harm to each other with your words. And one day, you'll be more inclined to let some of those words go when you're really hurting and you see the other as the source of your pain. Promise each other now to do everything you can to refrain from being unkind to each other. Give each other room to make mistakes and the assurance you'll forgive those mistakes. If you can do some of these things, you'll have a much better chance of getting through this whole. If you can do most of them, you may end up having something really special. At the very least, you'll end up with a solid friendship, and all of us could use another friend, huh?"

Gen must have found the right words for the moment, because without so much as looking at each other, Slink and Jenna responded simultaneously.

"Thank you, Gen."

It wasn't the words so much. It was the way they looked at him through tear-filled eyes, it was the way the words caught in their throats, it was the way they burst out laughing afterwards. And most of all, it was the way they looked at each other after they stopped laughing. Gen could see these two had already learned how to be tender with each other. Only time would tell if they could carry that lesson through the days ahead, whether they ended up together or not.

Gen was happy for Slink and he was terrified for him at the same time. He'd seen how bad Jenna had it for Slink, and looking at them together, he could see that Slink had fallen just as hard for her. The kid was in way too deep for any sixteen year-old, let alone one who'd just come through an emotional breakdown. One thing was sure--Gen was going to be working a bit harder to cement his friendship with Slink. No matter how things went with Jenna, the kid was going to need a friend!

"What's it like when you stand in the circle and open or close the Cave with your colleagues, Slink?"

Dot was trying to keep Slink engaged. She knew he was probably wishing he could be with Jenna instead of her. She'd wondered whether or not he'd even keep their weekly appointment for dinner in the officer's Mess, though to his credit, he'd not missed his early morning meditation time with her since he went back to work. She was pleasantly surprised when Slink was as faithful to his social commitment with her as he was with his meditation commitment.

The two of them were really starting to make a connection, and though it probably was good for Slink, it was great for Dot. She'd known what it was like to have family in her life, to feel connected to others who loved you whether you were at your best or not. Slink was family, and though they were only beginning to build trust with each other, his presence brought back memories of those days when she shared an unquestioned trust with a tight circle bound by their shared lives, not just their common genetics.

When he didn't respond right away, Dot reframed her question.

"What I mean is...has your experience of the silence changed since you've committed to developing your meditation practice?"

"More than I could have expected," he responded. "The first week, before my retreat, I thought my head was going to explode! I never realized how busy my mind was until I had to stand in that circle and try to stay quiet for a few minutes. My mind was going crazy with thoughts of things I needed to do, people I wanted to see, work that was waiting on my desktop, and crazy things, like pieces of dreams or old memories."

"Now, I find relief in the quiet. My mind is still busy when we open and close, but I'm able to step back from all the mental gymnastics and breathe. Maybe it's just me, but it seems like we spend a lot more time in our circle than we did when I first came to the Cave."

"So, you've noticed, have you? Chris was wondering aloud with me the other day as to whether or not you were aware how much he has expanded the opening and closing time."

When Slink looked at her as if to ask, "Why?" she continued.

"Chris is an extraordinarily sensitive man. He can stand in a group and within a couple of minutes detect and locate any discomfort coming from persons in that group. The quiet he initiates as you open the Cave is meant to give each of you the opportunity to focus your mind on the task that awaits and open yourself to any awareness that might come as you build upon the work of your fellows. When you close, he leads you back into the quiet so you have a chance to let go of your work and enter into our collective life on Home. He supports the silence with his own extraordinary inner quietude. He holds the silence until he feels the discomfort of persons in the circle rising to levels beyond which the group can overcome with a collective sense of calm."

"He told me your discomfort during that first week was palpable to everyone in the circle. They'd been holding the silence for about fifteen minutes on average before you joined their circle. After you joined them, they couldn't sustain the quiet for more than five minutes, although I'm sure it felt like it was much longer to you!"

Slink looked at her with obvious embarrassment over the negative effect he had on the Cave circle.

"Understand, Slink, before anyone is invited to join the work of the Cave, besides being identified as someone with an aptitude for analysis, he or she would be taught to enter the quiet. Different people would call this practice prayer, meditation, mindfulness, or spiritual awareness. We don't get caught up on semantics. We simply see to it that any new recruit knows how to let go of all thought or feeling they might have carried into or out of the Cave. We've trained every one of your colleagues to focus on the collective work of the Cave to the exclusion of all distractions that arise from within their minds."

Now his look was one of puzzlement.

"Why throw me in there without any of that training, then?" he asked.

"Gen told me about your extraordinary capacity to learn new things and make connections between them. I knew you were going to help us make progress toward bringing the Supernet down. I wanted to see if you could figure out for yourself the purpose to which the Cave was dedicated. I wanted to know if you could learn to do something you'd never done or if your abilities were limited to assimilating information. I wanted to see if you could make a connection between a practice you'd never experienced, namely entering the quiet, and one that you knew well, like gathering and making connections with data."

"So I was your guinea pig?"

"A guinea pig is used to determine whether something will work on a larger population. I wasn't interested in what anyone else could do. I was interested only in learning more about you. Your intellectual capacity is beyond anything I've ever seen in another person or experienced myself. And don't forget--that's saying something, my parents were both geniuses! I'm not interested in studying you to learn more about others—you're not like anybody I've ever met. Oh, and by the way, since you returned to the

187

Cave after your retreat, you might be interested to know that your circle has held silence together for periods longer than they've ever known before! Your mind is now one of the hubs that binds the others together and directs the focus of your collective work."

Slink sat quietly trying to take in Dot's words. He knew they were true. In the nurseries, he'd learned early on to refrain from revealing how much he knew about any subject they covered in class. His peers felt threatened by his mastery of subjects. His teachers resented the ease with which he absorbed even the most challenging material they could throw at him. In the tunnels, he saw the way his fellow Tunnel Rats looked at him when they passed by the little makeshift library. He caught enough of their whispered commentary as he passed by their tables in the dining room. They weren't unkind to him, but they couldn't begin to understand how he could absorb gigabits of information at a single sitting. In casual conversation he often made references to the Supernet and Grid that were revelations to the most learned of the Tunnel Rats. He grew accustomed to their shocked looks of dawning awareness.

Sometimes, he didn't care for the feeling of being an oddity among his peers. Most of the time, he was too absorbed in the learning process to care much about what anybody else thought. On those rare occasions when he grew weary of sitting in the library or working in the kitchen, he'd sit in the Kansas dining room and engage members of the surface excursions to hear about their experiences and learn vicariously of experiences from which he was excluded. Though he longed to explore the surface with one of the excursions, any suggestion he made to that effect was rebuffed with a gentle laugh or a quick turn of phrase like, "you can't be serious."

He had little clear memory of his experiences aboard Home before his retreat, but the ones since his return were so vivid he felt like they were etched into his brain. His awareness seldom drifted to the past or the future now. Most of the time, he was completely focused on the present moment. His focus was especially profound when they opened and closed the Cave. As they stood in a circle and entered the quiet together, he felt their minds touch, then connect to each other as if across a giant web. He didn't focus on any one connection point, any one mind, but he held the network they formed in his consciousness. He was held by its interwoven connections and he held them, reinforced them, and absorbed the information passed amongst them as intuitive insights that seemed to spring from his own mind though they had never been there before. He felt the same type of intense connection when he shared time with Jenna. He felt at times as if they were not two individuals but two bodies that shared one mind.

So it was that he still longed for adventure every day, but since his retreat, he found that life on Home provided enough adventure that he almost forgot the surface. He said as much to Dot.

"Don't say that," she snapped.

The violence just beneath her words shocked him.

"This," she motioned around her to the ship, "isn't where we belong. We will return to the surface one day, and I sense that day is coming sooner than we think. We aren't meant to live like rats or moles!"

Her voice rose now as she was carried away by her thoughts. Her eyes glistened as if fueled by a distant fire that filled her vision. As she spoke the fire spread from her eyes and filled her countenance until her cheeks were crimson, and Slink realized the fire he'd seen in her eyes came not from some distant dream but from within the woman whom everyone called "commander." He knew no one saw this fire without recognizing the command of the ship rested where it must.

"We'll bring down the Supernet, and when we do we'll return to the surface to show our people how to live. They've lost their way in the darkness of visored eyes, but one day we'll teach them to walk in the light again. The light of the too distant sun may not fill our days because we've removed ourselves from its reach. But the light of human consciousness, fully awake to the freedom for which it never stops yearning, will dawn again upon our people and we'll guide them through this blinding fury until they've learned to walk in its light again."

"Don't ever forget or release your longing for the surface. Let it burn within you and stand in your vision as the destination we'll reach together. Our ultimate goal lies in the hearts and minds of those who now despise us, but we must reach the surface before we can reach them. When we finally climb through a vent shaft and emerge unvisored to walk amongst our fellows openly again, I'll take you to meet your family--our family. I've painstakingly searched through every communication and every Tunnel Rat surface excursion until I've found them all…all except my parents."

She paused and lowered her head. Then she jerked her head back up and the fire burned in her eyes brighter than ever, even as tears streamed down her cheeks.

"I will not concede their deaths until I've searched every detention center myself! If they had died I'd have felt their passing as it happened. Chris thinks I may have blocked that experience because it's too painful for me to receive. He may be right, but I don't think so. I haven't learned how to filter the awareness that comes to me in the inner stillness. Perhaps I have filters I haven't discovered, layers of protection beyond my awareness. The possibility leads me to acknowledge that they may be dead, but I won't accept that possibility as fact until I have no other choice. And now that we've found each other, I hope all the more that we'll find them and they'll embrace the great-grandson who helped bring their reunion into reality."

She fell quiet then, and Slink didn't dare break the silence that fell around them. He noticed in time they were the only ones left in the officers' Mess. He hadn't been aware of any mass exodus, so he assumed that they'd outlasted everyone else in the officer's Mess. Only later, as he met Jenna in the main Mess did he realize the officers had quietly emptied the room to honor their commander. They'd recognized the personal nature of her exchange and had given them the privacy they deserved. The sensitivity and respect the crew members and officers showed each other never ceased to amaze Slink. These were people to whom he was proud to be bound. Their cause was just, their hearts were good, and they counted amongst their members three of the four people he'd ever loved, one of whom was teaching him the heights to which his heart could soar.

Chapter 8

When the settlers began spending their working hours on the surface, life improved almost immediately. Most felt their mood brighten significantly with exposure to a more open environment. Nearly everyone welcomed the broadening of their work to include the construction of surface structures.

They hung powerful lumatorches in the domes, built thermostats to regulate surface temperatures, and developed a computer network to regulate their new power grid. They created a series of vents from the tunnels underneath the dome that equalized the pressure between the tunnels and the surface. The hydrogen generators that heated the tunnels and enriched the tunnel air with oxygen had been designed to supply the same under the domes.

Years earlier, when they began developing the tunnels, Jonathan Lansing had enough foresight to demand that every tunnel project contributed to eventual surface settlements. As the cavern walls were melted and smoothed to create more uniform tunnels, Jonathan saw that the settlers captured the runoff of molten materials in molds that formed two foot square tiles that could be used to create geodesic surface structures.

Jonathan and Adela refused to consider that Garsow might be abandoned before they established surface settlements. They lobbied continually through SASA to keep a steady stream of materials and supplies flowing. They kept their crews motivated to stay on schedule with consistent reminders that their goal was to spend as little time as possible living underground.

The infrastructure that supplied drinking water, electricity, and sewer treatment in the tunnels was built to serve five times the numbers of people who lived underground. While enthusiasm for the Solar-edge settlement was at its height, the Lansings made sure they built the most extensive, least glamorous infrastructure. By the time the fickle public had an opportunity to question the Garsow investment, the Lansings were feeding Dr. Henry White one glamorous development after another. Their director, ever the publicity hound, touted Garsow as the greatest accomplishment humanity had ever seen, and reminded Earth dwellers that Garsow would one day open the Galaxy to interstellar travel. The public swallowed three general tax increases to fund the expedition while visions of grand adventure danced in their heads.

Slink had not been aboard Home long enough to under-stand the meaning of the alarm that crashed through the quiet of the closing circle about six months into his tenure in the Cave. Be-fore he could even withdraw his awareness from their circle and opened his eyes, he felt someone clasp his arm just above the el-bow and turn him away from the circle.

"We gotta go...NOW!"

He was already moving down the top deck corridor, pushed insistently from behind before he realized it was Gen's voice he'd heard, Gen's hand that had grasped his arm, Gen who now pushed him in the back and pleaded with him to move still faster. As they reached the stairway he usually took to descend to the sleeping quarters or further to the Mess, Gen grabbed his arm again and barked, "Up!"

He'd almost forgotten the stairs spiraled upward as well as down. He'd never ascended the stairs he now climbed as rapidly as he was able. Someone thrust a cloak and a visor into his hands. He had only touched items such as these once before and then he'd lost the visor less than an hour after receiving it. The past swept over him and carried him back to the nursery pantry, to Neoko, to that first glimpse of a visor pulled from her cloak and extended to him in her hand.

"We've gotta move! Slink...come on!"

Gen had moved past him on the platform and now pulled him through an open hatch and outside into the tunnel. Then he pushed Slink down the stairs that had extended from the side of the sweeper drone leading to the floor of the tunnel. When they reached the tunnel floor, Gen grabbed Slink by the arm and shoved him in the direction everyone around him was now run-ning.

"Run for the abandoned tunnel! It's straight ahead, at the furthest reach of your vision, at the bend in the main tunnel. We'll pass into the old tunnel through a narrow passage, then another short run to a vent shaft. Put your visor on when you reach the base of the ladder. Climb to the surface. I'll be right behind you.

We'll have friends waiting for us as we reach the surface. Do what they tell you to do!"

Slink had no way of knowing the bridge had detected a DAN patrol streaming into the tunnel through one of the vent shafts just ahead of their current position. The patrol was likely headed toward a Tunnel Rat enclave near the point where they entered, but Home would pass directly across their path and there was a good chance the DAN patrol would stop the drone. Dot could not alter their course without being detected, and she dared not override any Grid command to stop. So she gave the command for companies Alpha and Beta to evacuate. Fully two thirds of the crew responded as they'd drilled again and again in anticipation of such an event. Five minutes later they were all off the drone and headed for the abandoned tunnel, while the drone resumed its previous heading having kept its pause brief enough to avoid any automatic alarm.

When they reached the bend in the tunnel, it looked to Slink like they were all just bunching up against the wall. He could see no opening in the wall, and certainly no entrance to an abandoned tunnel. Then he remembered his arrival at the Tunnel Rat enclave called Kansas. On that occasion, Neoko walked into a shallow hollow and began to trace the broad outline of a shape in mid-air while she was standing facing the back wall of the hollow. He remembered his surprise when a doorway appeared in what he'd taken to be a solid wall.

As he stood near the back of the group gathered at the wall, he lowered his gaze to try to peer through the bodies. Just as he did so, he saw an opening appear in the wall just to the right of where he'd been looking. Within minutes the Technoids had formed a single-file formation from their combined companies and began to walk through the opening as quickly as the narrowness of the passageway would allow. Once he was inside the passageway and had passed far enough inside to allow the few people behind him to get through the opening, as abruptly as it had opened it closed. The darkness that enveloped them was impenetrable. He stood still, suddenly struggling to maintain a sense of balance without the visual confirmation his brain relied on to keep him upright. Then he heard a voice behind him.

"Help me bring this group into the quiet. I'm going to lead them in a simple breathing exercise, and I need you to anchor the quiet so they may enter it without fear."

Chris then gave some simple instruction in a low voice directing everyone to relax, close his or her eyes, and count their breaths without altering the natural rhythm of their breathing. He guided them beyond their fears and anxieties and into the quiet. He helped them slow their breathing until they were taking longer and deeper breaths that became the foundation for a deep sense of calm. Slink felt them one-by-one join the mental web he'd woven. He reached out to their minds reinforcing the calm into which Chris had invited them. It wasn't difficult. His Cave colleagues were in the dark passageway, and as they entered the silence they reinforced Slink's efforts. Within a remarkably short time, everyone in the passageway was breathing deep, long, quiet breaths while standing shoulder-to-shoulder in the impenetrable black.

A few seconds later Slink heard a low, soft grinding noise and the passageway was awash in the soft, blue ambient light of the tunnels. The light, however, was coming from the end of the passage furthest away. Someone in the tunnel they were trying to reach had opened the entry to the passageway from her side. Slink "saw" all this without having yet opened his eyes. As he released the collapsing strands of the mental web he'd woven in the quiet and opened his eyes, he joined his fellows filing out of the passageway. As he reached the doorway, a young woman not of their company held a finger over her mouth to ask for continued quiet. As he looked at her, his inner sense of calm shattered, replaced with an urgent question.

"Where's Jenna?"

He practically jumped through the opening into the old tunnel. It had no lighting affixed to its walls. The light flooding the passageway was coming from lumawands in the hands of the three or four people who greeted them as they passed into the old tunnel. The people with the wands were near the passageway entrance, so the majority of people standing in the old tunnel were well beyond the reach of the light. Still, somehow he knew--she wasn't here!

As the last of the Technoids passed from the passageway into the tunnel, Slink heard Gen's voice commanding everyone to fall into formation. The Tunnel Rats with the lumawands assumed positions at the corners of the formation and a quick but thorough look around bore out Slink's intuition. Jenna had remained behind on Home.

He should've known. Alpha and Gamma companies had day shift and Beta Company worked nights. Most of the officers were split between the two dayshift companies, Alpha company and Gamma company. Only a skeleton bridge crew of officers was assigned to Beta company. Slink was one of the crew members assigned to Alpha company. Jenna, it was becoming quite apparent, was assigned to Gamma company and remained on the sweeper drone with Dot.

Slink felt fairly confident Jenna would be fine. He was at greater risk than she. They were about to make a daylight surface excursion. What bothered him wasn't concern for Jenna's safety but that he had marched off the drone and into this tunnel before he even gave a thought to her. Over the past several weeks, unless he was sequestered in the Cave, she was foremost in his thoughts. And now, when the first crisis swept across their paths, he didn't give any thought to her at all. How could that be? Did he really love her? He'd told himself he did, but how did someone walk away from the one he loved not knowing if he'd ever see her again without so much as saying goodbye?

"Slink...Slink, are you OK?"

It was Chris.

"Yeah...yeah, I'm fine," he mumbled.

"Are you sure? You look like you saw a ghost."

"No...really," his voice trailed off. Then he caught ahold of himself, cleared his throat, and looked at Chris.

"I'm fine, Chris. I just realized that I left something behind."

197

"She'll be fine," said Chris. "There's no time for goodbyes when these things happen. Don't be guilt trippin' yourself, little man. Just make sure you say 'hello' with the proper enthusiasm when you see her again!"

Chris was smiling reassuringly, and Slink returned his smile. It was kind of scary the way Chris got inside his head, but he didn't have any time to worry about that now. They'd reached the vent shaft and it was time to put his visor on and climb the ladder. For the first time in six years, he was going back to the surface!

Even through the tinted lenses of the visor, the brightly lit surface nearly blinded Slink as he emerged from the vent shaft and was lifted clear of the opening. Someone guided him by the shoulders a few steps to his left before another person put an arm through his and began to guide him down the pedway.

"We're going to split up so we don't attract any more attention than we have to," she said.

Slink didn't recognize her voice. The fact that she seemed to know more about what was going on than he did raised no alarms. After all, he knew almost nothing about their plan. He had little choice but to trust her.

She turned to their right down the first alleyway they saw, then back to their left at the next intersection of a pedway. She didn't say a word, and Slink was still occupied with thoughts of Jenna, so he wasn't about to initiate any small talk. Their pace was brisk, though not uncomfortable. They probably looked like two people with a clear purpose in mind, and Slink supposed that was a good thing. He thought they probably didn't want to look lost or uncertain about their destination.

They walked for two or three minutes before they ducked to their left again into another alleyway. A few seconds later they stopped abruptly in front of a doorway. It looked liked a service entrance for a building too large to be a private residence. Slink's mind flashed back on the pantry exit of the nursery through which he'd first seen a wider view of the surface. A moment of alarm sounded as he imagined being at the entrance of another nursery where DAN agents waited to receive unsuspecting Technoids too naive to distrust their guides.

The door opened from the inside and his guide nudged him forward. He stepped through the door and she stepped in right behind him. The door shut behind them even as Slink stepped through a short entranceway and into a larger room. He saw many of Home's crew waiting to receive them. A number waved at him or at the woman who had deftly guided them here. No one spoke and Slink knew instinctively to honor the silence.

He moved around the room to where he was facing the doorway they'd entered. He saw the door open several more times. Each time, their number increased by two, three, or four. The room was probably intended to serve as the center of a business operation, and as such, probably would have comfortably held 30 people. Slink sensed they numbered three times that. They stood shoulder-to-shoulder by the time Gen spoke.

"We're going to be on the surface for about six hours," he started. "This is not a furlow. You have six hours to reach the other side of the Sector, descend the vent shaft and re-board Home. If you walked directly to the rendezvous point, you could reach it in a half hour. That means you have five and a half hours to collect as much information as you can without raising suspicion and endangering our operation. We're especially interested in recordings of visor data transmissions from surface dwellers engaged in conversation. That means...we want you to talk to people."

The room started buzzing as if an electrical current was passing through the floor and into every person there. Slink didn't need anyone to tell him that this was not standard operating procedure for a surface excursion.

"The Tunnel Rats can't get this information--they don't have the equipment we're going to give you. As you pass from this room, you're going to receive a transmitter that connects with

199

your visor. It's capable of receiving data from the Supernet like any commlink would. It won't display all the data on your visor since you'd just be overwhelmed by it. Instead it'll record most of the data it receives for later interpretation. You'll see the signals indicating the state of mind of your conversant. It'll also broadcast data to mimic the broadcasts of a commlink without giving away any change in your emotional state."

"Too cool!" came an unsolicited reply from the back of the room. Gen ignored the comment.

"We need you to engage people in simple conversations. We've preprogrammed the transmitters with prompts to help you direct a conversation around current events on the surface. The people to whom you speak will, undoubtedly, be aware of the events to which the prompts refer. The prompts are phrased as questions. Answer any of their questions with another question. Get them to talk. Your transmitter will record their voice along with any data their commlink sends or receives. We're interested in analyzing the relationship between the commlink data and the conversation."

"A few last tips. Engage people where you can cut the conversation short abruptly and move on with a simple excuse. In most instances, the prompts will let you know when it's time to end a conversation. If you get uncomfortable, don't take any chances. Just give an excuse and move on. We don't need a lot of data from any one person. In fact, we'll benefit more if you have several relatively meaningless conversations with a number of people. You'll travel in pairs. When you reach a point where you can interact with other people, you'll split up from each other and engage people separately. Check back in with your partner every ten minutes. The visor will give you a signal when it's time to check in again. Its lenses will assume a light blue tint. When everything suddenly looks blue, cut off any conversation and find your partner. If the tint of the lenses turns red, head for the vent shaft as fast as you can. A red tint is a signal that either your partner has been detained or our entire operation has been compromised."

"Listen, people. Those of you who've been on surface excursions will have a tendency to be evasive. Those of you who have little or no recent experience on the surface may be a little nervous. Everyone just needs to relax and remember--these are people like you and me. They're going to be moving from one work task to another or from work to home. Just show an interest in their lives, and let them do the rest. Trust the prompts on your visor. The subjects it suggests will be of interest to nearly anyone you meet. Raise the subject, then sit back and listen. I can assure you--this will not be boring!"

No one looked bored--or even slightly disinterested. Slink thought virtually everyone of them looked like he felt--terrified!

His first encounter didn't do anything to set him at ease. He and his partner, Remmi, reached a corner in front of a syncaff shop where a small group of people had congregated. They broke off from each other; Remmi headed toward the counter to order for both of them and Slink sat down at a small table near the center of the outdoor tables. As soon as he sat down, he turned to the tall, sharp-dressed blond sitting to his right and said hello.

She stared at him over the pink-tinted lenses of her visor for a moment before grimacing and turning away. He was duly abashed, but his sense of duty drove him to take another stab at connecting with her. His visor flashed a question,

"Are you going to the mixer tonight?"

She didn't even glance toward him this time. She simply turned a bit in her seat so her back was turned. His visor flashed a follow-up comment to the question he'd asked,

"They're going to feature Vertigo--both vid and audio!"

She snapped around in her chair. Slink was glad he couldn't see her eyes, because he thought they probably would've cut right through him.

"I guess you're too young, too stupid, or both to take a hint, huh kid? If I was going to a mixer tonight that'd mean I was part of your pathetic peer group. I'm not--I'm old enough to be your mother. More significantly, I come here every afternoon for ten minutes of peace and quiet, which any moron would know from their first scan in my direction. Next time you scan a "do not disturb," leave her alone!"

She got up abruptly and walked down the pedway in the direction he and Remmi had come. He watched her go alarmed at how poorly he'd faired in his attempt to strike up a conversation. When Remmi returned with their drinks, Slink related his experience to him. Remmi gave him a quick tutorial on reading the signals on a commlink visor. As they conversed, Remmi drew Slink's attention to the feedback Slink was receiving on the lenses of his visor, indicating Remmi's receptivity to their exchange.

"You would've seen a red circle with a line through it in the rectangle at the upper right corner of your vision when you were talking to that woman. See how the rectangle is tinted blue now? That means I'm calm and receptive to our conversation."

He ran through the other common indicators that could appear in that field. Some appeared as different color tints in the rectangular box, others appeared as symbols or words. Slink couldn't have repeated Remmi's words back to him, but he was confident that he'd be able to interpret the indicators Remmi had identified.

Feeling a renewed sense of confidence, Slink set out for the other side of the patio. He sat down near the area where the pedway flowed into the patio from the opposite direction he and Remmi had come. Before long a threesome of young women about his age walked into the patio and chose a table next to the one where Slink sat. One of the three left to order drinks. Slink was hopeful that trying to strike up a conversation with two young women would be easier than trying to initiate a one-on-one conversation.

He checked his visor as he looked toward the two women sitting to his right. The little box stayed blue. So far so good.

He waited until one of them glanced in his direction.

"Hi," he said with a quick little half wave.

The young woman who caught his attention imitated his wave with a giggle and repeated his greeting.

"Hi."

Both of the young women were now looking at him, and the little indicator box in his visor now tinted green--an open invitation! Slink picked up his drink and walked over to their table. The girls made room for him between them.

"This is going well, very well!" thought Slink.

"I'm Slink," he said as he made his way between them.

"Dora," said the shorter of the two, as she reached behind her head and pulled her long hair over her shoulder so it fell across her chest.

"Jan," said the other, all the while fixing Slink in her visored gaze. Had he been paying attention, he would've noticed the little indicator box of his visor change to a red tint as he returned her gaze.

As Slink set his drink down and sat between the girls, their friend returned with drinks and shot the other two girls a sly smile. She was very slender, as tall as the taller of her friends, and her eyebrows were painted a bright blue to set her visor off from her extremely dark complexion.

"Hi, name's Slink." He offered his hand.

"Hi--Shenti," said the newcomer, raising her eyebrows to reveal a thin line of bright white beneath the edge of the blue outliner. It gave her the appearance of having huge, dark eyes. She could have sworn she saw her visor indicate a flash of red for just a second before returning to a steady blue. He might think he was a pretty cool customer, she thought, but she was getting to him--whether his visor indicated it or not.

"Are you going to the mixer tonight?" Slink asked. He saw no purpose in deviating from the script his visor offered.

"Well, that all depends, doesn't it girls?" The painted lady leaned across the table from where she sat after delivering the drinks. She gave him an exaggerated once-over, sweeping her head down, then up to match the height of her visor to his, then cocked her head to one side. She smiled again, and Slink finally recognized that he was no longer the one doing the hunting.

"They're going to feature Vertigo--both vid and audio!"

He couldn't think of anything better to do than follow the script. Fortunately, one of the girls at his side took the bait and broke the hold Shenti had over the group.

"You true?" she asked. "I love Vertigo, and I'd give up sex for a month to hear their new disc. Are they goin' to give any music away at the mixer?"

Slink recognized the peril of replying to the girl's comment or question. He wanted nothing to do with a conversation that had the slightest reference to sex. He followed the instruction Gen had given all of them: answer a question with another question. His visor supplied the raw material.

"Who's your favorite band member, Jan?" Slink asked, spinning to face his questioner. He was already reading the prompts on his visor and verbalizing them pretty naturally. Out of the corner of his eye, he saw Shenti settle back into her seat.

"She's just waiting for another opportunity to pounce," thought Slink. He knew he had to stay in control of this exchange if he wanted to escape the painted lady's web.

"Derrick, of course," said Jan.

"Of course," mimicked Dora.

Jan stuck her tongue out at Dora and giggled.

"Have you seen any of their other vids?" Slink asked them.

"Any of them?" Dora asked incredulously. "Obviously you don't get Jan. She is wild over Vertigo. If they've recorded it, she's bought it!"

"It's true," said Jan.

"Yeah, yeah, yeah. Some of us just can't get enough of images and sound as long as...we...never...touch, eh Slink?"

Shenti grabbed the table at its edges and leaned up on her extended arms until she was side-by-side with Slink. Before he realized what she was doing, Slink felt something trace the protruding tendon along the side of his neck. He pulled back and turned to see Shenti's outstretched tongue and the long, shiny metal bolt that pierced it protruding downward from her open mouth. She snapped the bolt back and forth through her tongue, making an audible "click" each time she flicked it, then slowly withdrew her tongue and closed her mouth until her lips formed an exaggerated pucker.

"You're as scared of the real thing as sweet girl Jan, aren't you little boy?"

Shenti pronounced the last two words as "yit-toe buoy."

"Hey, hey, honey, why don't you lick on someone your own size?"

Remmi couldn't have picked a better moment to come to the rescue. Slink had been ready to try matching wits with Shenti. He had no idea how overmatched he really was. Remmi had seen the tattooed women of Alpha Sector before and he knew that none of the crew, let alone the kid, should be trying to converse with one of these women.

A moment earlier, he'd finished a short exchange with a young man on a break from his engineering job, and Remmi had almost started in with another young woman who was sitting alone at the counter. Something in the back of his mind told him to go over and check on the kid. When he saw how Slink was surrounded and who was the ringmaster of the circus that had encompassed him, Remmi cussed under his breath. He was amazed the kid hadn't betrayed himself yet. He was in Shenti's face before he quite realized just how far he'd jumped into the fire Slink had ignited.

"You want to play?" purred Shenti.

"I don't play nice," replied Remmi. "It's time for the kid and me to go. Sometime when we have the time and credits to waste, we'll look you up, then you and I can go a couple rounds."

Shenti gave them the flying one-finger salute as they turned to walk away. Remmi opened his mouth to offer a witty reply before he thought better of it and pushed Slink through the gate, leaving the little patio and walking out onto the pedway. After they were far enough away to avoid a scan, Remmi muttered just loud enough for Slink to hear,

"Oldest profession in the world!"

They meandered down one pedway and another, stopping every so often to engage someone briefly. Remmi insisted they work together most of the time, and Slink took no offense at Remmi's obvious attempt to protect him. As far as he was concerned, he could use a big brother to keep an eye on him, and that's just how he felt about Remmi.

A few hours after they'd set out together and still a couple hours before they needed to rendezvous with Home, they found a small restaurant with a pedway courtyard. It seemed like a good opportunity to engage a few more people and get a bite to eat. Remmi had promised Slink they'd use a few of Remmi's credits to get a meal before they left the surface. Remmi said he wanted to treat Slink to some Thai food, and though Slink had no idea what that was, he was happy at the prospect of eating a meal. When they found the little restaurant, Remmi exclaimed,

"This'll do just fine!"

When they sat down, a young man with a face being reshaped by a horrendous case of acne and spiked blond hair that stood like toothpicks driven into his skull came to their table and offered to get them something to drink. Remmi ordered for them both. Their waiter wasn't prepared to take a food order and had to return a minute later to receive the order a second time and tap it into his handheld. Several minutes later, he returned a third time with their drinks and placed them awkwardly on the table, spilling a good part of Slink's water. He apologized, left the table again, then returned a moment later with a towel and swiped at the water quickly leaving half of it behind. When he finally left them alone, Remmi exclaimed,

"It's so hard to get good service anywhere these days," drawling his words with an exaggerated self-importance. His attempt at humor wasn't lost on Slink, and they had a good laugh at their waiter's expense...until Remmi suddenly drew a long, sharp breath across his teeth and lowered his head. He motioned for Slink to bring his head down next to him.

"DAN agents."

Slink started to turn, and Remmi caught his chin before he'd moved an inch.

"They aren't paying any attention to us...yet. They haven't scanned us either--I would've noticed it. We just need to keep a low profile and we'll be fine."

"Remmi--maybe we should just get the hell out of here," Slink whispered.

"No way, little man. I'm eatin' some Thai food, and if I'm eatin', you're eatin'. Besides, we blow outta here now, and we'll attract a lot more attention than we ever would sittin' here."

Slink didn't care for putting his life on the line for a little Thai food however good it turned out to be, but the second part of Remmi's explanation made a lot of sense. He relaxed and sat back at the table.

"Hey pal, you gonna catch Vertigo tonight, or you still gonna be workin'?"

Remmi'd caught sight of their waiter headed by them to check on the DAN agents. The waiter stopped cold and gestured, pointing both index fingers straight down to say, "I'll be right here."

"Too bad, dude, it's gonna be awesome. Maybe you can get a pass from your boss for late admission, huh? It'd be worth a try. They'll let you in late if you got a pass, you know."

"Thanks, man!" exclaimed their waiter. "I wouldn't of thought of that. I'm goin' to go ask her right now."

He turned on his heals and shuffled off in the direction he'd come, forgetting all about the DAN agents he was going to check on. They noticed his sudden retreat and held up a hand to get his attention, but they were too late. He'd already disappeared into the kitchen, no doubt bursting in on his unsuspecting boss to ask a favor. Remmi chuckled to himself.

"No reason we shouldn't have a little fun at their expense too, huh?" he whispered to Slink, gesturing toward the agents.

Slink didn't care for Remmi's little game. He didn't think it made any sense to antagonize DAN agents. Remmi was a tough one to figure out, thought Slink. On the one hand he was very protective over his young partner after Slink got himself in a fix with the painted lady. On the other hand he was clearly in his element taunting the shameless Shenti, teasing their young waiter, or short-circuiting the table service of a couple DAN agents. Slink couldn't figure him out, and right now he didn't care to try. Over the last couple hours, he was finding it increasingly difficult to think about anything other than his anticipated reunion with his sweetheart.

"I'm sure Home is OK," he said aloud, voicing his concern like someone voices a song lyric stuck in his head, unaware he's even talking out loud.

"They're fine," snapped Remmi, resenting the intrusion of Slink's concern upon his little game.

"The kid needs to loosen up," thought Remmi. "He hasn't been on the surface for six years, probably won't be back again for God knows how long, and he's all anxious to get back on board a cramped sweeper drone. Not me--I'm suckin' up every minute, and every bean sprout, for that matter."

He chuckled out loud at his ruminations.

"Relax, little man. We're goin' to be fine. It might be a while before we get back here again, and if we have our way, everyone's goin' to be runnin' around like a chicken with its head cut off when we do get back, so loosen up. I'll take care of you!"

Slink couldn't take or refute Remmi's advice; he was too busy imagining a chicken running around without a head. He assumed it was just another of those phrases that'd passed down through generations until its original meaning was lost, but the headless chicken formed an image in his mind he couldn't shake.

It was too much like another image that had haunted him--that of a giant hand chasing him through an endless dreamscape.

Remmi, for his part, was beginning to regret his promise to Gen. When he'd offered to keep an eye on the kid, he had no idea Slink was so damn helpless. The kid was worse than a fish out of water--at least the fish knew it was in trouble if it landed on dry land. Slink was afraid of some innocuous teasing, but didn't know a pedway-walking whore when he saw one. Well, he was going to enjoy a good meal and a good joke while he had the chance, and the kid could just deal with it!

A few minutes later, while the two of them sat and stared through their pseudo visors at nothing in particular, a young woman with bright blue eyebrows walked up to their waiter as he emerged from the kitchen. They did't see the encounter of the painted lady and their waiter; they did't see the painted lady point in their direction, nor did they see the way their waiter nodded at her words, clenching and unclenching his fists. While they missed all of this, the DAN officers caught the entire exchange.

His boss's flat refusal to help him gain admission to the mixer later that evening had driven their young waiter into a rage. As fate would have it, the painted lady had seen his fury in her visor when his path intercepted hers. She saw in him the perfect instrument for her vengeance without consequence. She used her generous charms to gain his attention, then she drew out the reason for his anger, fed his fury until he burned with rage, carefully refocusing it on the two men sitting at the nearby table. And then she complimented his rage with a good dose of passion. He was young and his passions were easy to ignite. A thrust of her tongue, a squeeze of her hand, and a caress of her cheek and he was ready to do her bidding.

He couldn't see straight when he turned from her and back toward the kitchen. A few minutes later he emerged from the kitchen headed for the table where his customers waited. They thought they were better than people like her, she'd said. They knew they were better than people like him, she'd said. They needed to be taught a lesson, and if he was man enough to teach it to them, she was woman enough to give him the reward a man deserved. She gave him a taste of the reward and he thought it more than fair compensation for doing something he might have done anyway had he thought of it himself. Now that she'd opened his eyes, he could see the arrogance pouring from the one who did most the talking.

"Yeah," he thought, "they definitely need to be taught a lesson, and I'm the man to do the teachin'."

The bigger, louder guy might be more than his match in a fair fight, but this was not going to be a fight, let alone a fair one. This would be a one-sided affair, with the first blow being struck before anyone ever saw it coming. He'd take the skillet of simmering vegetables in his right hand and whack that big-mouthed asshole up side the head so hard he wouldn't wake up for a month of Sundays. By the time the skinny guy, realized what was goin' on, he'd be down for the count too.

The waiter was so intent on his target, he never saw the DAN officer step out of the shadows to his right. He had no idea she'd fallen in behind him. As he arrived at their table, he was delighted and infuriated to see they hardly noticed him. He took the skillet in his hand and brought it back over his head. He was vaguely aware of a sharp metallic squeeze around his wrist accompanied by the sound of rapid, low clicks before he felt his arm being snapped back behind his back and his shoulder being dislocated from its socket. His face hit the floor about the same time the skillet did, with searing hot vegetables landing across the side of his face and the back of his neck.

"OK boys, why don't you tell us why ol' blue eyes was gunnin' for ya', and why your waiter nearly cracked your skull with a skillet."

The DAN agents had already escorted the waiter and the painted lady into the back of the restaurant and out of sight. Slink and Remmi could still hear the whimpers of their waiter as he begged for some medical attention for his right arm and shoulder. They'd thought about bolting when the DAN agents left them briefly. They reconsidered and stayed seated while the restaurant manager came out to offer her apologies and assured them they wouldn't have to pay for their meals. She had one of the other employees assume the responsibility for serving them and made sure the little mess their waiter left was cleaned up.

A moment later, the DAN agents returned. They straddled a couple of swing out chairs from an adjoining table so they could face Remmi and Slink.

"Honestly--I don't have any idea. The whore," he thought better of his choice of words and corrected himself, "escort took a liking to my friend. I told her to buzz off. Evidently, she didn't like getting 'no' for an answer. She's a crafty one--that's for sure. Probably talked the kid into doing her dirty work for a," he paused again, then ended his sentence with a less inflammatory word than the one that had first come to his mind, "favor."

"Good enough. Where do you fellas work?"

Remmi didn't miss a beat.

"We're both engineers in Station 3. Took an early out to talk over a personal problem. Didn't mean to offend the, um, lady--we just wanted to be left alone."

"What ya doin' down here, if you work at Station 3?"

"Ever had their seared veggies?"

Remmi smacked his lips and shook his head with his eyes half closed.

"Yeah, know what ya mean. Tough to beat. OK guys, have a good night. Sorry 'bout the disturbance."

"No problem. Thanks for saving my skull."

"Just doin' my job."

The agent tipped her cap and motioned to her partner and they got up from their chairs, swung a leg over the back of the chair and sat back down facing the table to which their chairs were attached. The one who'd been interrogating them waved her hand at a waiter and a moment later she and the hulk of a man who was her partner were ordering a meal. Slink and Remmi ate theirs as fast as they could and left.

Slink was prepared to beg Remmi if he needed to. He didn't want to spend another minute on the surface. He'd rather take his chances with sweeper drones in the tunnels.

As it turned out, he didn't even need to present his case for heading directly to the rendezvous point. Remmi was a risk taker, but he was no fool. He couldn't calculate the odds they'd run into a vindictive prostitute, a psycho waiter, and two DAN agents, let alone find themselves at the center of a convergence between four such people. He was starting to feel like someone or something had it in for them, and Remmi never went against those feelings.

"I'm no intuitive like that creepy dude who supervises the Cave and goes 'round reading people's minds," he thought. "But, you'd have to have shit for brains to keep stickin' your neck out right after you almost got your head knocked off."

"We're headin' out kid. Stick close cuz I'm gonna keep a pretty quick pace."

Slink breathed a sigh of relief.

"Right behind you," he said.

They stayed off the central pedways. Remmi had made any number of excursions through Alpha sector, so he knew how to keep a low profile. They didn't talk to another person in the half hour it took for them to reach the alleyway they sought. The vent shaft looked like it'd been sealed, and when Slink saw it, he let loose with a groan.

"Don't worry kid." Remmi slapped Slink on the back. "It's fine. We rigged it to look like that to avoid suspicion."

Remmi approached the vent shaft and bent over the hatch that appeared to be bolted closed. After looking at it for a while, he crouched right in front of the hinges, reached under the lip of the hatch with his hands, and pulled upward with all the strength he could muster. A few seconds later, his hands slipped out from under the hatch and he went sprawling backwards.

"Shit!" he exclaimed when he sat upright again staring at the hatch. "I'm gonna need your help Slink. I should be able to crack this thing loose on my own, but I guess I'm gettin' old. It's sealed to stand a quick pull from an inquisitive passerby or DAN agent, but it's supposed to break loose with some elbow grease."

Remmi positioned Slink to one side of the hinges and he stood just to the other. He showed Slink where he wanted him to grab the hatch and motioned up and across the face of the hatch to show him what direction to pull.

"On the count of three," he said. "One...two...three!"

Slink gathered his legs underneath him, threw his shoulders back, and straightened his spine. He'd never received training for lifting heavy objects, but he didn't need it.

"It's just geometry and physics," he thought. "Make sure you establish the right angle between your body and the hatch, then use the most powerful muscles in your body. Simple enough!"

He pulled upward, using his legs to provide the power. At first nothing seemed to happen. A moment later, the hatch snapped loose from its moorings and flew open. Slink tumbled into the open space of the vent shaft (he forgot to calculate that possibility) and barely managed to catch the lip of the shaft with his hands before his chin would have cracked the rim. His knees crashed into one of the ladder rungs along the inside of the shaft. The pain shot through his legs, forcing him to hang by his hands for a minute before he could bend his aching knees enough to find a rung with his toes and gain a foothold.

Remmi tried to jump over the shaft when the hatch broke loose and caught his foot on the edge as he sailed over the shaft. He landed hard, face down on the other side of the opening.

Slink saw Remmi sail by just as he fell into the shaft. At first, Slink was a little preoccupied trying to make sure he didn't fall the 30 feet or so to the tunnel floor. When he gained a foothold and steadied himself, he turned his face up to look out the opening but he still couldn't see Remmi.

He prepared himself to step up with his feet and brace his hands on each side of the open shaft so he could climb out of it. Before he could move his feet, though, he saw Remmi. He reappeared in Slink's line of sight as a silhouette against the bright background of the Alpha Sector sky cover. It took Slink a second to realize something wasn't quite right. Remmi's neck was too thick, and he was standing awkwardly in front of the shaft, almost leaning backward, rather than leaning forward to make eye contact as Slink might have expected.

A moment later, Slink understood. The distortion around Remmi's throat came into focus at the same time the silhouette of the DAN agent appeared next to Remmi. The agent tightened his grip around Remmi's throat, eliciting a choking sound as he screamed down at Slink.

"Climb out nice and slow kid and maybe your friend'll be able to breath on his own when I finally turn loose of his worthless neck. Any fast moves, and I crush his wind pipe before I reach down and pull your sorry ass outta that shaft."

Slink didn't move. He felt oddly calm at this turn of events. He wasn't really scared of the DAN agent or his threats. He wasn't worried about what might happen next. He was just numb.

"You got no place to go, kid. We're goin' to get your sorry ass one way or the other. The harder you make it on us, the harder we're gonna make it on your friend. My partner is gonna join us in a few seconds, and when she does, you better have your little butt outta that shaft or your buddy's lookin' at some long-term therapy to learn how to talk again."

The agent glanced at Remmi, then back to Slink.

"I like squeezin' the breath out of liars. I wanted to believe this one, like I said, but somethin' just wouldn't let me. I left a steamin' hot bowl of rice noodles to track you bastards down, so I don't need much of a reason to snap his neck."

Remmi jerked a fist toward the agent's face. It was meant only as a distraction, and it worked. A second later, Remmi's knee

214

caught the agent square in the groin as he ducked Remmi's swing. The huge hand around Remmi's neck tightened reflexively for just a second before it relaxed and Remmi tore free.

"Get...out," Remmi croaked as he fell to his knees in front of Slink.

"No--wait!" cried Slink.

"No time. Go. Now."

The words sounded like they were being scraped over broken glass as they came from Remmi's mangled throat. Slink tried to protest again, but Remmi wasn't going to give him a chance. He reached back and grabbed the hatch. He pulled it over and held it balanced directly above the hinges.

"Find Home. Tell Dot."

He pulled his head back and punched with his free hand at Slink's hands, still clinging to the rim of the vent shaft. Slink pulled his hands down one at a time and grabbed the first rung of the vent shaft ladder. He looked up to plead with Remmi one last time.

"Bye, little man!"

Slink saw the hatch coming at his head and crouched down in time to keep from getting his skull cracked. The hatch slammed shut with a sharp, "Clang!" The sound echoed in the vent shaft for several seconds, but the echoes continued in Slink's head for days afterward. The sudden darkness entombed him and he wanted to huddle there on the ladder and disappear into the darkness. His sense of duty wouldn't allow it. Every other Technoid on the surface depended on Slink reaching Home without delay. If he failed, the other members of the surface excursion would likely be met by a company of DAN agents.

Chapter 9

The pressure to develop breakthroughs that would open the galaxy to exploration came to bear on Jonathan Lansing and his team even before they had outfitted their surface labs and offices. When he left Earth, Jonathan had been sure they were no more than ten years from developing the means to propel ships into space near the speed of light. He'd sold his certainty at every SASA conference he could attend.

When the research he'd thought most promising yielded nothing, he and his team had no choice but to redirect the research into areas where little or no work had been done. They managed to conceal their setbacks with small breakthroughs made over the first few years on the surface. Dr. White needed little prompting to overstate the significance of the rather modest progress the Lansing team was making.

When SASA celebrated the tenth anniversary of the first Garsow landing, Jonathan and Adela were at the center of every observance. Dignitaries from the Solar Council poured praise on the pioneers for their fortitude and commitment. In the eyes of the public, the Lansings were the darlings of politicians on the left and the right. They could do no wrong.

Behind the scenes inter-solar communiques transmitted a different message. Jonathan and Adela knew they were running out of time. The members of the Council had played every angle to sustain support for the Garson colony, and like most politicians, when the pressure to show results started mounting, the Council started looking for scapegoats.

Just as the Lansings grew certain the Council would call for their return to Earth and replace them with a new team of scientists, everything changed. A communique arrived in their inbox one morning, and when they opened it, they were greeted by Henry White's smiling face. He told them the Council had come to recognize the intrinsic value of a Solar-edge outpost, and felt confident they could turn the public focus from promised breakthroughs in near light-speed travel to the many other benefits of the remote settlement. He spoke of advances in science and technology that had already come from the Solar Council's commitment to develop Garsow and thanked the doctors Lansing for their invaluable contributions to that end.

Dr. White assured them they could work as long as they needed to reach the breakthroughs they sought in propulsion. He even relayed to the Lansings the decision of the Council to increase funding of their research and promote Garsow as the premier research colony in the Solar system. To that end, the Council had decided to expand the focus of scientific research conducted on Garsow, said Henry with a grin so wide the Lansings could count all his teeth.

He asked Jonathan if he could assemble a team to build another facility so scientific teams already dispatched from Earth could go to work on their research the moment they arrived. He

217

assured the Lansings their work would not be adversely affected by the Solar Council's decision to broaden the scope of research conducted on Garsow.

"Oh, before I forget," cooed the SASA director, "the first of the new research teams will arrive on Garsow in three months. They'll need housing for 16 men and 22 women and lab space for the full team. I'm confident you can see they are accommodated when they arrive. Thank you again for all you've given to SASA and the Solar Alliance. The Council is forever in your debt!"

"Sweeper drones move pretty slowly, and they follow set patterns in moving through the tunnels."

Slink reassured himself as he ran. He hoped and prayed Dot had allowed Home to stay on its normal course after getting past the DAN agents. As he reached back in his mind for the memory of the tunnel map image he'd seen on Home's main screen a few weeks before, he was fairly certain the normal pattern of the drone would bring Home to the rendezvous point as quickly as any alternative route Dot could choose. So he trusted her to stay on course. He'd never had the need or the ability to run anywhere, having spent all but about 48 hours of his life living in confined spaces. He'd followed a fairly strenuous exercise regimen every morning, but he still couldn't keep a running pace for long. He alternated between walking as fast as he could and running down the tunnel.

He'd been in the tunnels almost half an hour by his estimate when he began to doubt he was going to cross Home's path. The thought, when it came, nearly undid him. If he didn't reach Home soon, the rest of the crew still on the surface was almost surely doomed. They wouldn't have any way of knowing DAN had discovered their exit. He had to reach Home and have Dot send them a message. He wasn't even certain she had any way of doing that, but he didn't have time to worry about it. Still, his doubts combined with the insistent side ache he'd developed to slow his pace even more.

Just as the sense of panic had risen from his stomach to his throat, he remembered his training. He stopped walking, closed his eyes, and breathed. He reminded himself he could only control his own choices. He needed to trust everyone else would be doing the best they could. He inhaled and exhaled. His heart rate slowed and his head cleared. He opened his eyes and started jogging again.

Then he heard it. Still a way off, but he was certain he heard the sound of an approaching sweeper. He ignored the knot in his side and broke into a hard run again. A minute later he could see the dancing lights on the sides of the tunnel at the furthest reaches of his vision. A couple minutes after that, he saw the drone's sweeper arms retract and Home came to a halt about fifty feet in front of him. It settled to the floor of the tunnel and a few seconds later the hatch opened. He didn't need to wait until he could make out the features of the person who popped out of the hatch. He recognized Dot's silhouette as she turned on the deck.

He never broke stride even as he hit the bottom of the stairs jutting from the side of the drone. She met him midway up the stairs. She embraced him and held him even after he tried to back away and tell her why he was running down the tunnel to meet them. When he tried to speak, she pulled back from him and cut him off.

"It's OK. We got word about the ambush at the vent shaft."

He cocked his head to ask, "How?"

"One of the other excursion pairs saw a female DAN agent running toward the alleyway. They followed her at a safe distance and a minute later watched her help a big male agent drag Remmi out of the alley and onto the adjoining pedway where they were met by a third agent driving a little flatbed cart. They loaded him on the back of the cart, she joined the driver in the cab, and they drove off with Remmi laying on the back of the cart. The big guy went back to the alleyway and is standing guard out of sight at the vent shaft."

"How?" Slink was still out of breath. "How did you hear all this?"

"We use Garson's voicemail system. We have 10 different accounts set up. We trade-off between them. Before you left, we designated one of them for urgent messages to be relayed between the team leaders on the surface. We monitored that voicemail account continuously, so when the report was made, we knew about it. We also knew Gen picked it up a few minutes later and went to work preventing everyone in the excursion from entering the alleyway. Meanwhile, we're working on a solution to get everyone past that agent and down the vent shaft. We determined we can't risk leaving anyone on the surface long enough to set up another rendezvous somewhere else in the sector."

She reached out and grabbed Slink by the shoulders. Her eyes filled with tears and her voice cracked.

"I was so worried about you. I didn't know if they hauled you away before anyone saw anything or if you were wandering around by yourself, or...worse. I'm so glad you're OK!"

She embraced him again, nearly crushing the life out of him. When she pulled back again, her cheeks were streaked with tears as she motioned for him to follow her up the stairs.

"We've got to get moving again, and we could use your help developing a strategy to get the others off the surface. Besides, I'm not the only one who's a little anxious to see you!"

She was waiting for him on the landing as he stepped off the hatch ladder. Her tears prompted his. They stood on the landing in each other's arms and cried. Slink hadn't allowed himself to

220

feel any relief until that moment. He was Home; he was in the arms of the woman he loved; he was safe. The tears flowed and he saw no need to try to stop them. He just caressed the shoulders of his sweet Jenna, felt her hands gently running over his back, and did his best to breathe. She was the one who eventually pulled away from him and looked up into his face.

"Get rid of that visor. I won't kiss you while you're wearing that thing!"

He couldn't believe he still had it on. He tore it off his face and disconnected the lead wires from the little box in the fanny pack strapped around his waist. He unsnapped the fanny pack and held everything out to her.

"I don't want it."

She pushed past his outstretched hand and the visor dangling from it, rose to her tiptoes and threw her arms around his neck. Her lips met his with a ferocity Slink had never felt coming from her. They'd never shared a truly passionate kiss in the weeks they'd spent together. This was different--very different. They didn't kiss each other at all--she kissed him. He had no opportunity to return her affection, she gave him no room for response. He could only hold on and receive her. She consumed him, and he was hers for the taking. It lasted for ten, twelve seconds, maybe fifteen at the most. When she pulled back, he did well to start breathing again.

"I love you."

There was a force behind her words--a power Slink didn't know language could hold. He felt devoured by her words the way he had been by her kiss. Her eyes filled with tears.

"I've spent the last six hours feeling like I was being chewed up from the inside. I haven't been able to eat; I haven't been able to drink; hell, most of the time, I haven't even been able to talk. And before you say anything, I know we've only known each other a few weeks, we're young, and we're infatuated. I know all the analytical stuff. And knowing all that, I choose to love you."

"I'm sorry, Jenna, really..."

She waved him off.

"You're going to do this over and over again. It's who you are—you're going to be at the center of every risky, dangerous thing we do. If I'm going to love you, I have to live with the reality."

She paused for several long seconds, "and I wouldn't have it any other way. I love you; do you hear what I'm saying? I love you!"

The force behind her words made them feel like an accusation. He half expected her to slap him or start yelling at him. But she did neither. She just stared into his eyes. Her eyes did accuse him, and they pleaded with him and made demands of him all at the same time.

"I just thought before you have to answer the next alarm and run off again without saying goodbye, you should know that I'm bound to you, I'm bound to your fate, and if this ends badly for you, it'll end badly for me. It can't be any other way unless we part ways right now, and I'm not going anywhere. I choose to love you!"

She was almost yelling at him now. It broke his heart and it made his heart soar. He'd abandoned her and here she was proclaiming her love--no, staking her claim! He belonged to her, belonged here, belonged at Home.

He whispered, "I'm not even sure I know what love is, Jenna. I'm probably too young and too inexperienced to have any idea. I probably shouldn't be with anybody so soon after my retreat. I know all this as well as you do...and I don't care! I love you, too, Jenna, and I'm more than willing to learn as we go."

He pulled her into his arms and kissed her tenderly, even gingerly. Then they turned and walked hand in hand down the spiral stairs to the command deck and the work awaiting them.

"You need to have everyone poised and ready to go. You can't expect to hold the vent shaft open for more than a few minutes. Once that agent goes down, they'll send a whole company to find out what happened to him. He'll probably be checking in verbally, so if you can get close enough to hear his voice without giving yourself away, you'll be able to time your assault better. Take him out right after he checks in. We have to hope it will take DAN a few minutes to get more agents to the shaft after his commlink relays his distress. We'll pass under the vent shaft at 16:00 standard. Have everyone in the tunnel just ahead of us. Out."

When Dot finished her message and sent it, she turned to face the command crew. Slink took a seat next to the communications officer.

"Slink, I want you to join the group in the Cave. They need any information you can give them about the DAN agent laying in wait at the vent shaft. You can also relay anything else you can think of that might help us get everyone off the surface."

He got up and made his way to the Cave doorway. He paused there to hear the rest of her instruction. She turned to the rest of the crew.

"I'm going back into the Cave. Keep us on automatic until we are 10 minutes from the vent shaft. Then come and get me. We'll gradually slow as we approach the vent shaft unless we see the rest of our crew coming toward us in the tunnel. In that case, we'll come to a full stop and take everyone back on board as quickly as possible. Keep a sharp eye out for anything unusual. DAN is probably operating on the assumption that Slink and Remmi were alone or part of a small surface excursion. We can only hope they'd never guess we'd send so many people up to the surface all at once. If they have any reason to suspect the truth, we're going to find this tunnel crawling with agents and we'll be facing the showdown we've hoped to avoid."

She turned and signaled to one of the other officers. He walked over to her, listened as she gave him some private instruction, then nodded and sat in the command chair. Dot then walked

223

over to Slink, with her right hand tussled his hair playfully in defiance of the mood that hung over the bridge and with her left, motioned for him to lead the way into the Cave.

The Cave's seats were filled with the bridge officers who served with Dot in Gamma Company. It seemed odd to Slink to have anyone other than his colleagues sitting in their chairs. Had it not been a crisis of the utmost urgency, it might have even seemed irreverent.

Slink pushed aside his discomfort at seeing the room filled with unfamiliar faces. As soon as Dot sat down, people began offering their assessments of the situation. One reported no sign of DAN activity in the tunnels. Another reported the other sweeper drones were continuing to move according to their normal patterns. Still another reported they had begun masking their own movements, causing Home to appear on the tunnel map as being substantially behind the point where they actually were. No one was likely to suspect the Technoids were entering the tunnel to rendezvous with the sweeper drone.

They knew Gen had received Dot's message. He was evidently having someone monitor the voicemail account continuously. He indicated that everything was going according to plan. They were using another safe house to keep the Technoids out of sight as they arrived at the rendezvous point. A party of three had been chosen to take the guard out at the appointed time. They hadn't been able to get close enough to the guard to monitor his communications, but they were confident they'd be able to do so, and they would time their attack on him accordingly. Gen fully expected to have everyone in the tunnel and moving toward Home well in advance of 16:00 standard.

Slink took in each report and felt growing confidence their shipmates would be home soon. Despite the easing of his fears, though, something kept gnawing at the back of his mind. He couldn't put his finger on it, but he had the uneasy sensation they were overlooking something.

Dot asked the officers if they saw any reason to abort their planned rendezvous. They offered none, so she ordered them to continue as planned. She then turned to Slink and asked if he had any questions or observations to add to their discussion.

He decided he was going to try to articulate his discomfort, even though he couldn't formulate it in his mind.

"I keep feeling like we're overlooking something. I can't see any logical reason for my discomfort, but I felt the same way and ignored it when Remmi and I were in the restaurant with those two DAN agents. Now, I wish I'd payed a little closer attention and told Remmi how I was feeling. So I guess I'm asking you to indulge me while I try to untangle this."

"By all means, go ahead," said Dot in reply to Slink's furtive glance in her direction.

"These agents are slick," said Slink. "The one who interrogated us seemed almost disinterested in Remmi's answers, but I noticed she was focused pretty intensely on him even as she seemed to pass over his answers. It seems to me she was getting a lot more information from him than he offered in words. It was almost like she was asking questions without listening to the answers. It was like," and then it hit him. "It was like she was reading off her visor the same way I was when I was trying to strike up conversations with people on the surface!"

Slink quickly related to the group how they were outfitted with visors with full commlink functionality and recording capabilities. Some of the officers nodded to themselves as he spoke. Slink could see they clearly knew about their mission and made a mental note to ask Dot just how far in advance this mission had been planned.

"When I was reading the questions off the visor, I learned real fast to pay at least as much attention to the indicators on my visor as I did to any verbal response. More often than not, the visor told me more about how to proceed than the words of the person with whom I engaged. That DAN officer was doing the same thing, and I think something she picked up from Remmi tipped her off there was more to our story than Remmi was telling. She probably knew he was lying before he even finished giving her some bogus story about where we worked. I guess that leaves me wondering--how much more do they know about our operation than we think they know?"

"So you're saying the DAN agents suspected you and followed you to the vent shaft. I don't mean to be rude, kid, but we already know that. It makes sense she could see Remmi was lying. I don't see how she might then suspect you were part of a large Technoid surface excursion. She probably wasn't even sure you weren't surface dwellers. That's why they followed you to the vent shaft. It seems likely to me it was only when the big guy saw you two open the hatch he knew you were headed for the tunnels."

Slink recognized the officer speaking as the communications officer. He probably knew a lot more about commlink communication than Slink knew.

"You're probably right," said Slink. "I'm sorry to hold you all up."

"Just a minute," broke in Dot. "Now you've got me asking questions, Slink. I want you to think this through out loud with us for another second."

"My only thought is this," started Slink. "Remmi and I overlooked something that seems obvious to this circle in retrospect. What might we be overlooking now that is going to seem real obvious when its consequences catch up with us?"

"The recorders--what happened to Remmi's recorder?"

The young woman who had blurted out the question flushed when everyone turned in her direction.

"I'm sorry, it just hit me like a ton of bricks. I'm sure you've all taken into account the agents getting the recorder when they captured Remmi."

"If one of us did, he or she forgot to tell anyone," Dot cracked.

She turned to her chief operations officer, a tall, wiry man with a pale complexion and a graying goatee.

"Jakov, find out exactly what information would be recorded on Remmi's belt recorder. Specifically, look for anything that might give away that he and Slink were part of a larger group."

Dot turned again and faced Slink. "Did the recognition of that oversight clear your unease or do you still feel like we're missing something?"

"That definitely made me feel better, but I think there's something else, and I think I may know what it is. In my mind's eye, I keep seeing Remmi in the clutches of that agent. Something about the way he looked struck me as strange even at the moment I was clinging to the lip of the vent shaft and Remmi first came into my field of vision, but I couldn't figure out why. Now, when I look back, I realize Remmi looked like he was floating on air, and he's a big man--he doesn't exactly float anywhere! The DAN agent was practically holding him off the ground--with one arm extended straight out from his body! No ordinary man could have held Remmi up at arm's length and dangled him off the ground so his toes barely touched."

"What I'm trying to say is...I don't think that guy is normal. I think that agent is much, much stronger than an ordinary man. He's got to be enhanced somehow, although I'm certain he's human. I had a pretty good look at his features in the restaurant, and he wasn't a machine. Still, I think whoever Gen sends to take him down better be prepared for a much bigger fight than they would ordinarily expect. They need to be prepared to exert a lot more force than they would normally employ against a single man."

"OK...so let's say for argument's sake you're right and this guy is some kind of cyborg."

Jakov had stayed to listen to Slink after delegating the responsibility Dot had given him a minute before. He knew Dot well enough to know she'd have expected him to hand off the research on the belt recorder. She needed him to be here for this entire discussion. Now he made sure he earned his keep.

"How do we even know he can be taken out? What if they engage him, deal him a series of what would ordinarily be death blows, and he just stands there and grins? A few minutes later, there'll be enough agents in that alley to take down both companies of our people. If you're right--we better give them something on this guy ahead of time, or we're asking them to take too big a risk trying to take him down."

"His balls."

Slink looked up, saw everyone staring at him, and blushed.

"Remmi kneed him in the balls and brought him to his knees. At least we know he's vulnerable there."

"Was he wearing a visor?" asked a smaller, red-haired woman at Dot's side.

"Yea, of course."

"Then covering the visor with some kind of cloth or spraying it with some opaque liquid should blind him. If he's blind he won't see the blow to his--privates--coming."

"Good thinking, Sara," said Dot. "If they've blinded him and disabled him with a blow to his groin, they should be able to keep him out of circulation long enough to let everyone get down the shaft."

"So let's see where we're at. We'll check on the information the belt recorder was designed to collect. Assuming it doesn't give away our entire surface excursion, we go forward with this operation. We relay the information we've gathered and our recommendations in reference to the agent standing guard at the vent shaft. Gen will make sure the advance party knows what they have to do to get the agent out of the picture. Anything else?"

Everyone turned from Dot and looked around the room. No one else raised a hand to speak.

"Then let's get to work. We have less than an hour to rendezvous with the rest of our crew. I want an immediate report of any suspicious activity anywhere in the tunnels, and especially anywhere near that vent shaft. Let's go!"

Gen was relieved when he heard of Slink's safe arrival. He'd feared the worst when he saw the agents drag Remmi out of the alley. If Remmi wasn't dead when they pulled him out of the tunnel, Gen thought he was probably close. When he zoomed his visor in on Remmi, Gen could see Remmi had no color in his disfigured face and was bleeding from his ears. His thoughts turned to Slink almost immediately. Had these two agents hauled him out of the alley before Gen or the other Technoids had arrived? Had Slink escaped into the vent shaft before Remmi got beaten to a pulp? Gen could only hope for the latter.

Gen ordered Senti to continuously monitor the voicemail account that Home would use to relay information to the surface excursion. He also had her make regular reports of their circumstances as they unfolded so the officers on Home could help them determine the best course of action. They needed to get back in the tunnels as quickly as possible. If Remmi was alive, those agents would manage to get information from him sooner or later and they would know there were still a lot of Technoids trapped on the surface.

Gen considered having the companies break into patrols and head for the various vent shafts scattered around Alpha Sector. If they were spread out at least some of them would surely get back to Home before they could be discovered and arrested, he thought. He gave the order for the companies to separate into patrols, but his intuition prevented him giving the order for the patrols to disperse. He couldn't help but think they would only have one good opportunity to get everyone back in the tunnels and that opportunity was right in front of them.

He sent one of the patrols to check out the safe house nearest the vent shaft. They returned reporting it was clear. He sent most of the patrols into the safe house because they were far less likely to attract attention if they weren't congregated on the pedways in a section of Alpha Sector that ordinarily saw very little foot traffic. This was the warehouse quadrant and most of the operations here were automated and required intense activity only on those occasions when transports arrived from Earth or Mars.

He sent another patrol to scout the alleyway and the vent shaft. They returned to report that the big male agent was standing guard over the vent shaft, tucked out of sight between two of the large dome buildings that bordered the alley. He was positioned to surprise anyone who tried to open the hatch to the vent shaft, but he wasn't even armed heavily enough to contend with a couple patrols, let alone two Technoid companies. It appeared he was hoping to surprise one, two, or at most, a handful of Tunnel Rats. The patrol wanted to return and take the guard out immediately, but by that time, Gen had received the communique that summarized the meeting on Home where they'd discussed the strategy for dealing with the DAN agent, and he ordered them to stand down. He thought the assessment the officers on Home had made was probably correct in its essentials. They needed to exercise extreme caution taking the agent out, and they needed to be prepared to move everyone into the alley and down the vent shaft as quickly as possible as soon as the agent was neutralized.

Gen briefed the scouting patrol on the insights of the Home officers with regard to the DAN agent in the alleyway. They came up with a plan to have one of their members, a sharpshooter, pummel him with several paint balls from atop one of the buildings across the alley from where he stood. The object was to obliterate his sight by completely obscuring the lenses of his visor.

Ordinarily, the paint guns were used to mark routes for Technoid or Tunnel Rat excursions through the surface Sectors. Young vandals were the first to initiate the colorless landscape of the Garson surface with the paint balls in a harmless rebellion against the homogenous domed buildings raised from the surface of the planetoid like blisters on its otherwise smooth, glassy surface. Later, Garsow organized paint ball tournaments and cordoned off a quadrant of Alpha Sector for the competition. The paint sprayed over the pedways and buildings significantly brightened the bland landscape and provided an outlet for youthful aggression.

The Tunnel Rat and Technoid excursions simply picked one or more colors, filled paint balls, and shot them in a prearranged pattern to mark a route. Over time, they became very good at placing the paint balls in precise patterns so they could be distinguished from the random spray of paint that covered a good part of Alpha Sector.

The paint balls had never been used as weapons in anything but mock battles fought in tournaments by exuberant Garson youth. They wore helmets with face shields to protect themselves and prevent anyone damaging his or her visor. Now, one marksman prepared to fire several paint balls with the express purpose of destroying another man's vision.

Gen had been alarmed by the escalation of violence that marked recent DAN encounters with Technoids and Tunnel Rats. Now here they were escalating that violence further in an encounter with a DAN agent. He feared they were today taking steps down a most regrettable path. Unfortunately, he could see no viable option, and he gave the order for the marksman to take his position and fire his shots at precisely 15:30 standard.

He also ordered four other Technoids, all experts in martial arts, to prepare for an attack on the DAN agent. They were to be in position just ahead of 15:30 on each side of the narrow gap where the agent waited in ambush. When they heard the shots from the paint gun, they were to hit the agent with lethal force, understanding that the threshold of lethal force could be substantially higher in this encounter than they would ordinarily expect. Consequently, he instructed them to maximize the force of their blows and be prepared to deliver them in unrelenting succession. They saluted in somber acknowledgment of their orders, turned, and left to take their positions.

It was 15:20 when Gen parted company with the attack patrol. At 15:25, he motioned to a sentry at the other end of the pedway. The figure waved back, then approached the safe house directly behind him, knocked three times on the door, and returned to his position. The safe house door opened and the Technoids began emptying onto the pedway in patrols of four or five, taking up positions in the narrow openings between the domed buildings lining the pedway. They did their best to stay out of sight, although anyone who happened down the pedway would surely have become suspicious in short order. They could only

231

hope no such pedestrian appeared over the next five minutes.

Jerry Bueller loved karate. It kept him in great shape and it gave him an outlet for his competitiveness. He'd always wanted to be an athlete but he was too short and slender for the sports he loved. Then he discovered Karate. It had taken him eight years, but he was the reigning champion on Home. The first time he'd ever used his skills to defend himself, he was fleeing Home thinking DAN was likely to dismantle the sweeper drone when it reached the maintenance yard. He'd hooked up with one of the Tunnel Rat enclaves while he was waiting to hear if and when they could return to the drone.

He tried to make himself useful, and about the only skill he had that translated to life with the Tunnel Rats was his karate. They assigned him to one of the surface patrols where he served as a point man. The patrol had no visors, fake or otherwise. They stole onto the surface during the night hours, scavenged what they could, and returned before the dome's daylight generators kicked in.

On the fateful occasion when he was called on to use his skills, their patrol was making their way back to the vent shaft when he ran into a walker. No one should have been out on the pedways at that time, but here was this guy strolling along when Jerry turned the corner and ran the poor guy over. Jerry's unvisored face further alarmed the shocked man sprawled on the pedway, and he started stuttering and pointing as soon as he gathered himself enough to sit up. Jerry had to make a split-second decision.

Jerry chopped the guy across the side of the head before the guy's stuttering could escalate into screams for help. He didn't hit the guy hard enough to seriously hurt him; he just knocked him out. The guy would wake up a couple minutes later with a throbbing headache and a broken visor.

"This is nothing like that time," Jerry thought to himself. "We're goin' into this alley to kill a man. Oh sure, it helps to think that this is one bad dude who could kill us all if he got the chance, but it doesn't change the fact that we're goin' in there to kill him. I've never delivered a lethal blow to anything but a punching bag. Now I'm goin' to deliver them as fast as I can until this guy stops moving. If he's still alive when he stops moving, that's cool, but it ain't likely. I'm goin' in there to kill him!"

Jerry felt some small consolation in knowing that he wouldn't be the only one throwing blows. He'd probably never know whether he actually killed the man or not.

"But suppose I feel his neck snap under my foot? Is that something I'm goin' to hear in my sleep weeks and months from now? Am I the kind of person who can live with that?"

15:25 - he turned and looked at the other three Technoids assigned this duty. They looked just as uneasy as he felt. They stared at the ground as they walked, looking up only to assure themselves they were on course for the alley. One of them, the little guy, Jerry thought his name was Mel or Mal or something like that, caught Jerry's eye. His dark expression never changed. His lips were drawn tight over his teeth and his jaw was clenched so tight it drew dimples in his cheeks. He just held Jerry's glance for a minute, then looked back at the ground. This wasn't easy for any of them, but they'd do what had to be done or they'd die trying.

As the other four members of his patrol set out, Sung Do, the tall, slender marksman with the paint gun, reached the crest of the building across the alley. He laid flat on his chest and inched his way atop the building to get a clear view of his target. He identified the agent's outline effortlessly against the multi-colored paint splattered on the walls behind him. He slowly raised himself up on his elbows and raised his binoculars to his eyes.

"God, he's big!" thought Sung Do. "All the bigger target," he tried to reassure himself.

In reality, he knew that the size of the guy's body really didn't make much difference as far as his job was concerned. He had to hit him right in the visor with the first shot or he wasn't going to do his colleagues much good. If the guy was a giant, even superhuman, but he couldn't see, they had a pretty good chance. If he saw them coming and he was biomechanically engineered to be stronger and faster than any ordinary human being, they'd be lucky if they took him out before he killed all four of them. Sung Do didn't relish sitting on his perch above the alley and watching four of his friends get taken apart. They trusted him to succeed, even bet their lives on his success, and he was probably lucky he didn't have time to lay there much longer thinking about it.

When the four unlikely champions reached the alleyway, Jerry ordered the little guy to stay with him and sent the other two off at a quick jog around the two large domed buildings that framed one side of the alley. When Jerry could see them at the far end of the alley, he glanced at his watch.

15:28 - they had two minutes to get as close as possible to the crevice between the two buildings on his left and the agent who crouched in the shadows there. They needed to be quick and they needed to be silent. It would have been much easier to choose between the two, but the choice was not theirs. If this guy was some kind of superman, they sure as hell didn't want to give him any warning they were coming. The distance they needed to cover was no more than 40 meters--very doable.

Sung Do saw his colleagues enter the alley and start moving toward their target. He rolled to one side and propped himself on his shoulder. He pulled the paint gun from his backpack, unsnapped its tripod, and set it up in front of him. He snapped on the scope, rolled back to his stomach, and looked through it.

15:29 - He focused on his target--the guy seemed to look right at him. Sung Do resisted an instinctive desire to duck down. If the agent really was looking in his direction, as unlikely as that was, he'd pick up the movement atop the building. On the other hand, if Sung Do was still, the chances were pretty slim the agent could pick him up, even with the help of his visor. Sung Do reached slowly for the zippered pocket of his backpack and pulled out five paint balls. If the first one missed, the other four were unlikely to do much good, but if the first one was true, the other four would help to keep his target off-balance until Sung Do's friends reached him. He loaded his gun, then settled in to do his job.

15:29:30 - Jerry took two deep breaths before he signaled his comrades at the far end of the alley with one hand and motioned to the little guy behind him with the other. Jerry moved out setting the pace and choosing the path and the little guy followed right in his footsteps.

Breathe, step, step, step, step, breathe. Instinctively, Jerry moved up onto the balls of his feet, bent deeply at his knees, and leaned forward. He stayed as close as possible to the domed building on his left, even reaching out with his left hand and steadying himself each time he paused to breath. 30 meters away--so far, so good. He kept his eyes focused ahead, looking for any sign of the DAN agent.

15:29:45 - Breathe, step, step, step, step, breathe--20 meters away. Now, Jerry realized they were going to have a problem. They were at the point where the building reached furthest into the alley. From here, the building curved away from the alley and inward toward the adjacent building. If they walked any further, they'd come into the agent's view and he'd have plenty of warning before they could reach him. They could only wait now and hope the paint balls found their mark.

15:30--Sung Do saw with his free eye that his friends had moved in as close as they dared. He closed that eye and looked through the scope with the other, He aimed just above the agent's forehead and a couple of inches to the left to compensate for the slight angle at which he was positioned relative to his target. He breathed in a deep breath, then released it--steady and slow. As his lungs emptied he began to squeeze the trigger--steady and slow. He felt the tension against his finger hit the critical point before it set in motion the chain reaction that would send the paint ball sailing toward its target, and though he did not pause, the split second expanded in his mind with the critical import of the outcome resting on his actions. Then, before he could finish exhaling, he'd squeezed the trigger five times. For better or worse, his job was done!

Jerry didn't see the paint balls sail between him and his two colleagues who stood against the adjacent building. He heard the first of the loud "pops" from across the alley a split second before the splattering sounds that came from just beyond his sight in the crevice between the buildings. With the first of the sounds, he sprinted to cover the last twenty meters, then he heard the agent scream in rage and caught sight of the man fighting to his feet. The agent's head and left shoulder were pretty well covered in paint, but Jerry had no time to determine whether or not he could see.

He jumped toward the man and cocked his right leg in the air with his foot aimed squarely at the man's throat. In mid-flight he realized, too late to do anything about it, he may have made a costly mistake. He'd instinctively aimed to strike a fatal blow before he remembered he was supposed to be aiming at the man's groin. His foot reached the intended mark at the exact same moment Timo, leading the charge from the opposite direction, struck the agent in the agreed upon target area. The man, or cyborg, or whatever he was, slammed into the walls of the two adjoining buildings, turning awkwardly as his right shoulder made impact an instant before the rest of his body. Jerry went down right next to his victim, landing awkwardly on his back and knocking his wind from his lungs. Timo tripped over the falling agent and fell alongside Jerry. The little guy running behind Jerry had been unable to keep the same pace in the final 20 meters. He'd watched Jerry fly through the air, slam his foot into the agent's throat, then crash to the ground. Now, he jumped over Jerry and planted his feet in the center of the agent's chest with the full force of his weight. The fourth man who'd been following Timo grabbed the little guy before he went down on top of one of the first two men. He jerked the smaller man backward and over their fallen comrades. The two of them stepped backward simultaneously, turned sideways, and raised their arms, prepared to strike their adversary again. There was no need.

The DAN agent was a very big, muscular man, but outside of the tremendous strength his muscles afforded, he was in every other respect an ordinary man. Sung Do's first paint ball had obliterated his vision, but had it missed its mark, he still would've had little chance against four martial artists who engaged him with the intent to kill. Jerry's kick had ended his life before he even hit the ground, though Jerry had been spared any telltale snapping of bones beneath his feet. The two men left standing, once certain the agent no longer posed a threat, helped their comrades to their feet. It took a few seconds for Jerry to regain his breath.

"Go back and tell Gen it's over," he said to the little man. "Tell him to get everyone in here. We're going," he paused for breath, "Home."

The man turned, ran a few steps, then jumped and thrust his fist in the air wildly, before landing in stride and running the rest of the way out of the alley. Jerry looked at his other two comrades. They both were grinning ear-to-ear.

"Come on," he said. "We've got to pop that hatch before everyone starts streaming in here."

The three of them had to work together, but they popped the hatch and descended the vent shaft to make sure the tunnel was clear. Sung Do joined them in the tunnel and after they secured the area, the four men took the opportunity to embrace each other and exchange a word of congratulations to each other. A moment later, the little man rejoined them. Their relief exploded into the celebration of warriors who have walked in the shadow of death and emerged alive. Each had done his job and fulfilled his responsibility.

Minutes later, their comrades poured into the tunnel from the vent shaft. Each one who stepped off the vent shaft ladder shook the hands of the men who had cleared the way and celebrated with them. The five celebrated many sweet moments with their comrades, but none sweeter than the first few the five warriors shared together.

Chapter 10

When the new science team arrived, their representative sought out Jonathan and Adela Lansing and thanked them profusely for the construction and furnishing of their lab. Sarai said their team was prepared to work in a much more austere setting, and they were delighted to find a lab that surpassed their wildest expectations. She asked the Lansings to allow her team to return the favor should the propulsion team need anything the commtech team could provide.

That was the high point in cooperation between the two teams. The commtech team shut themselves away from everyone else on Garsow shortly after they arrived. They insisted they weren't trying to be secretive, only protective of the pristine environment their work required. When Adela pointed out they were protecting against contaminants that did not exist on Garsow, she was told the team needed to follow all the protocols established on earth to assure they could duplicate the success earlier teams had experienced in the labs there.

Adela was incensed at the uncooperative, even condescending attitude she endured at the hands of the commtech team leader, Sarai. Though Adela was 20 years the woman's senior, Sarai treated her like a pesky child who could not possibly understand the work the commtech team was doing.

Jonathan did his best to convince Adela they were plenty busy without devoting any attention to the commtech team. She would have none of it. Adela said the colony was their responsibility and she didn't like the way this commtech team was forced down their throat. She was deeply suspicious of the team's purpose which had only been described to them as "improving communication throughout the colony."

Jonathan shared some of Adela's misgivings, but he was more inclined to give SASA, the governing council, and the Commtech Team the benefit of the doubt. It did not take long before his passive approach to the commtech team's arrival became the deepest regret he had ever known.

The voices in Jenna's head rehashed the argument she'd had with herself numerous times before.

"I'm going to stick with this relationship no matter how much I'm afraid of being hurt," she insisted to herself.

Three months? Could it be? Jenna knew it could and it was--three months since Slink had evacuated Home, left her to wonder if she'd ever see him again, and returned a few hours later with no more warning than when he'd left. She tried not to think about it.

Every day that passed brought the eventuality of another separation that much closer. She'd been terrified when they'd been separated for a few hours; what was she going to do if the next time he was gone for weeks...or months?

Her friends gave voice to the admonitions rolling around in her head.

"You're falling too fast and too hard, girl!"

"Use your head, not your heart!"

"Don't let your guard down--once you start thinking you can rely on him, he'll be too busy to give you the time of day!"

She wondered if maybe, just maybe, she never allowed herself to hope she and Slink could stay together, maybe then their inevitable separation would never come--but that didn't make any sense at all. Besides, she'd already allowed her hopes to sink deep roots, already allowed her dreams to flourish.

"Please. Please. Please."

As Jenna closed her quivering lips over her monosyllabic plea, she received her answer. Little by little the quiet drew her away from fears of what might be and drew her into the present moment. She might not know what tomorrow would bring, but she knew what she had today: pure, unadulterated joy! Her joy filled the stillness, overpowered the silence.

She'd never known such happiness! She never tired of his company and he seemed just as happy with her.

She could let her fear of the future drive her to plead for assurances or she could live into each magical moment. She chose, at least in that instant, to embrace the joy!

"It's only infatuation!" logical Jenna interjected.

That voice might have been her mother's if she'd ever known her mother. Jenna had nurtured that maternal, protective voice in her mother's absence. The logical voice questioned her emotions, stood apart from her feelings, and demanded introspection. Now she wished she could tune it out. Instead she engaged the voice in debate.

"Maybe," she replied, trying to sound confident, maybe even philosophical. "Every life-long relationship started this way, though. And besides," she continued, gathering momentum, "if it weren't for infatuation, the human race would have died out a long time ago. All I know is I'm going to enjoy every moment of this...infatuation...or love...or whatever is happening to us."

Her "mother" fell silent. Jenna smiled to herself but before she had time to bask in her newfound confidence, a shiver ran down her spine, and her smile parted to make way for a gasp. The fear rose so quickly she almost choked out loud.

"Please, please, please!"

Her desperate plea was simple—that she might never have to say goodbye, or worse, find out he was gone without ever giving her a chance to say the dreaded word. She knew such a prayer was probably counter to the best interests of their mission, but she didn't care.

She needed to bare her soul to someone, to plead, to ask for the one and only thing she really wanted, and since she didn't know anyone who could receive her plea, she offered it to the void, the great mystery, the "One." She didn't think much or really care whether the someone or some thing to whom she offered her pleading listened--she just needed to give it voice. She wasn't even sure of the existence of the One. She wanted to believe, but this was not the night for puzzling theology. This was a night for pleading.

"Please let this last. Please. Please. Please."

It was a one-word prayer to which an affirmative answer would have been worth any price she could imagine. What could possibly be more valuable than the assurance they could watch each other grow old? They understood each other, accepted each other, encouraged each other, and supported each other.

"It's still just infatuation," offered the maternal inner critic.

"Time will tell," thought Jenna. "Time will tell, and time is all I'm asking for."

The last three months had been amazing! Their mutual fascination had matured quickly under the pressure of their subterranean existence, and had grown into an unvoiced commitment to listen without judgment, support without question. They repeatedly chose to stand with each other, revealing dark memories to each other, sharing emerging fears and frustrations, and receiving each other with tenderness and compassion.

"I'm so fortunate to have had the last three months, even if it's too early to know if it will last," spoke her inner voice of reason.

That voice would have been her big sister, if she'd had a big sister. It was the voice that listened to her inner critic, took in her adolescent rebuttals of the critic, and offered a calmer assessment of her internal struggle.

"No matter where this eventually goes, it's awesome today!"

Her big sister voice became her voice, strong and confident. Jenna didn't need to criticize or defend herself anymore. She wanted to trust Slink's and her love had staying power, but she'd not be sitting in a candlelit room pleading with a higher power of dubious existence if she already had that confidence.

"Too few ever walk this path," thought Jenna. "I won't run in fear because Slink and I may not share this path forever. I couldn't turn back if I wanted to anyway! For better or worse, I hope, I dream, I love."

Jenna looked around the ambassador's office. All the luma-torches were turned off. The candles threw shadows around the cramped little room. She sighed to herself.

Still...it couldn't hurt to ask...

"Please. Please. Please."

Gen had known Dot expected him to assume a leadership role when he accepted her invitation to come Home. He had no way of knowing the role she asked him to fill would suit him so well. Serving as an ambassador to the Tunnel Rat enclaves allowed him to maintain the connections that had sustained him over the better part of his life. Had he been assigned a role that did not involve contact with the enclaves, he would have had to take regular leave from Home, so the arrangement benefitted Dot as well.

The crisis of the DAN intervention in the tunnels and the ensuing evacuation of Home thrust Gen into a new role. Long before the crisis, Dot had spoken to him of her desire to send Technoids on surface excursions to better understand the Supernet. She'd asked if he would lead some, if not all, of those excursions, and he'd assented. Neither of them had expected a single excursion to include two thirds of Home's crew or to come as a result of crisis. They had planned for a series of small excursions spread over enough time to allow Gen to fulfill his commitments to the Tunnel Rat enclaves.

When the alarm sounded, Dot reached him by intercom in his quarters and asked him to lead the evacuees to the surface. She was afraid DAN would systematically sweep all the tunnels beneath Alpha Sector. Gen was the one who suggested they take advantage of the crisis and get some research done while they were on the surface. Dot saw immediately how his suggestion would help her protect her crew. Two-thirds of them would be out of harm's way and would be occupied and as a result, less prone to panic. In addition, the research on the Supernet would be accelerated bringing closer the day they could all return to the surface.

Gen's leadership during the excursion was extraordinary! The crew never balked at taking orders from him. He knew the surface and he already had the respect of half the excursion members, who had known him in the tunnels. When all but one returned safely to Home, Gen was the number two officer in the hearts and minds of the crew, whether or not he held title to such a distinction. He knew it and so did Jakov, the designated second-in-command and chief operations officer. Jakov approached Dot first.

It made no sense, Jakov had said, for the COO to continue to be second-in-command. They were moving into the next stage of their operation, and they would be spending more and more time on the surface preparing for the day when they returned to the surface permanently. Someone with knowledge of the surface and experience leading excursions would be leading the crew as often as anyone aboard Home. He was happy to continue to oversee operations on board Home, but the second-in-command needed to be someone who could make the transition to the surface better than he.

Jakov had not been to the surface since he was fourteen, and at 44, he tried not to think about the eventuality of their return. He loved Home. The sweeper drone was the closest thing to a wife he'd ever known. He knew her every creak and groan, every bolt and nut. He could read every console on the bridge and repair any moving part in the ship's drive. Aboard Home, he was an unquestioned expert. When the day of their victory came, though, and they abandoned the sweeper drone to realize their dream, Jakov would be at a loss to find his own way, let alone lead anyone else's. He said as much to Dot. She, in turn, put her arm around him, squeezed his shoulder, and said something about that day being a long way off yet. Neither her words nor her obvious appreciation for her chief operations officer changed anything, and they both knew it.

Immediately after the evacuation excursion, Gen returned to his duties as ambassador largely because they included the most pressing matter facing the resistance. He reviewed all the messages they'd received from the Tunnel Rat excursions through memory coin drops and voicemail. As he expected, DAN had destroyed only one enclave in the raid that had precipitated Home's evacuation, but the people there had received warning and escaped. The other enclaves had absorbed the displaced, though every enclave was nearing a breaking point. DAN had destroyed four enclaves over the previous six months, each in raids much like the last. They obviously knew where to look in each instance, and Gen had helped the Tunnel Rats perform investigations after each raid to try to determine the source of DAN's information. At the conclusion of each investigation, Gen was confident they'd tightened operations and communications enough to stop the leaks. Each time, that raid was followed a few weeks or a couple months later with another.

He felt desperate to figure out how DAN was locating the enclaves. Either they'd always known of the enclaves' existence and only now were taking measures to eliminate them or they'd developed some new source of information to help them locate the enclaves. In the first case, assuming DAN had always known where to find the enclaves, the question before Gen was "why?" Why was DAN now clearing out the Tunnel Rats when they'd left them alone for decades? Were they afraid the Tunnel Rats posed a threat they'd never before posed? If that was the case, they were almost certain to step up the attacks on the enclaves after Gen's orchestrated hit on the DAN agent.

On the other hand, if DAN was getting new information, where was it coming from? Were they using some new tools to scan the tunnels or monitor activity in and around them? Or had they gained the cooperation of one of the Tunnel Rats? Gen thought it most unlikely that DAN had a spy within the Tunnel Rats. The enclaves were too small, too intimate, and too isolated for effective spying. Still, he had to overturn every stone, so to speak.

Gen was already monitoring every communication that came from the enclaves. The enclaves could not access the Super-net or the Grid directly, so they had to record messages on memory coins and leave them at designated drop sites or leave voice-mail using the surface terminals when they were on excursions. Gen had ordered all Tunnel Rats outside the walls of the enclaves to work in pairs or small groups. Those pairings and groupings were to be reassigned weekly. No one was, under any circumstance, to leave one of the enclaves alone. It was easy to justify this order for the purposes of safety and security. Consequently, he was confident no one was leaving messages that escaped his awareness.

None of the messages he scanned upon returning to Home raised any concerns. Most were the usual communiques relaying supply needs and surpluses to facilitate the barter economy of the tunnels. Each enclave scavenged what it could from the surface and shared surpluses it gathered of one staple to meet shortages in other staples from the surpluses of the other enclaves.

Gen had grown increasingly concerned DAN was tracking seismic activity or some other indicator to locate enclaves and destroy them. They'd never seemed too concerned with the location of the Tunnel Rats before. In earlier years, the raids always coincided with the occasional political grandstanding of the governing council. It was relatively easy to keep close enough track of political events to predict those excursions and take evasive action. Now, though, there was no such connection between the political rumblings on the surface and the DAN raids. DAN agents came streaming into the tunnels as if a dam had broken, and only the close cooperation of the Technoids saved the Tunnel Rats from being caught unaware. The Technoids monitored all activity in the tunnels through their hacks into the Grid and they saw the DAN raids as they began. In each of the most recent cases, a Technoid sweeper drone had been close enough to the threatened enclaves to dispatch runners to warn the enclaves before the agents could seal them off.

Fortunately, the raiders hadn't discovered the secrets of the locks the enclaves used to seal their entrances, so they still had to rely on getting cumbersome drilling equipment into the tunnels and slowly drilling through tunnel walls adjacent to the enclaves. Their operations usually took several hours, and as such, they were not very effective in snaring the outcasts they targeted, but they succeeded in assuring those same outcasts had no place to return once they fled.

For five weeks after the evacuation excursion, Gen worked day and night to tighten security within and around the remaining enclaves. He consulted the Cave the day after the crisis and the Cave dwellers spent a week scouring every record related to the tunnels before they reported they could find no evidence that

DAN was collecting any information on the tunnels or activity within them that it had not previously collected. Finally Gen had to admit he'd done everything he could, although he was not at all certain he'd managed to alter anything that could enhance the security of the remaining enclaves.

In the sixth week after the evacuation, Dot asked Gen to have dinner with her. He hardly had time to sit down across from her, before Dot launched into her thoughts on promoting Gen to second it command.

"Gen, I want to hear how you're doing and catch up on anything more personal you want to share, but that can wait. We both know why I asked you here, and I'd like to get right to it, if you don't mind."

Gen smiled.

"Please do," he replied. "I'd like to get through this too."

"I know you're uncomfortable holding command over a crew whose collective intelligence rivals any group on Garsow, and I get that. I don't consider myself a slouch by any means, but most of the people on Home are considerably more intelligent and better educated than I could ever hope to be."

"Gen, just because they're intelligent doesn't mean they don't need leadership. Half of the people on this ship wouldn't last an hour on the surface unless someone was giving them orders every step of the way and you know that as well as anyone. The other half are plenty street smart and could go back to living in the tunnels if they had to, but they don't want to go back and they'll follow any leader they trust to make sure they never have to."

"This crew doesn't need leaders who are smarter than them or even as smart as they are. They need leaders who have a vision for a better world, leaders who design missions to bring that vision into reality, and leaders who can execute those missions effectively. I'm not going to promote you to second in command because I think you're one of those leaders."

"You're not?" asked Gen.

He looked thoroughly confused, squinting at Dot from under his furrowed brow.

"No, I'm not," she replied. "I'm going to promote you to second in command because the crew has already decided you're one of those leaders."

"It's not about whether I think you're ready or you think you are," she continued. "It's about the crew of this ship following you without question when you lead them all on a surface excursion or direct a small group of them to carry out a specific task. They know you are someone they can trust to lead them, and they've granted you that trust whether you want it or not."

"If I don't promote you now," Dot said with a sigh, "I'll have one group of leaders on paper and another on the ground. That's a recipe for failure. The designated leaders have got to be the actual leaders. You are the second in command; all I'm doing is formally acknowledging the reality."

"What about Jakov?" Gen asked.

"No one is more in tune with this than Jakov," Dot replied. "He came to me after you'd been on board for a few weeks and suggested I promote you to his position and let him focus on running the ship. He can see how much things are changing, how quickly we're moving toward the day we'll abandon this drone altogether. He knows better than anyone when that happens he'll be a fish out of water. You can count on his full support."

The two sat quietly for a few minutes before Gen finally sighed deeply and spoke up.

"Well, I had a series of objections prepared, but your argument pretty much trumps all of them. I realize now my concerns are just my own insecurities dressed up to look more acceptable. I guess I'm just going to have to find ways of dealing with those on my own."

"No, you'll always have someone who'll listen to you air those out without thinking any less of you," replied Dot. "You know I have my insecurities. You can't serve in leadership effectively unless you're acutely aware of both your limitations and your insecurities. Your awareness is one of the reasons you're such a strong leader."

Gen lowered his head and sighed again. Then he raised up and looked Dot in the eye.

"I'm honored to serve as your second, Dot. I may never feel truly worthy of the honor, but I'll give you my best everyday."

"I have no doubt," replied Dot. "Now, let's relax and enjoy dinner together!"

The two of them fell easily into conversation about their experiences over the past few days, mutual friends, and the quality of the food they were eating. All in all, it was a pleasant evening they both needed desperately.

Gen elevated Jenna to assistant ambassador, and took her with him on three separate occasions to meet the leaders of the enclaves. She was amazed with the people Gen brought into her life.

On their way back from their third and final visit, Gen asked Jenna how she felt about her new role.

"Well, I'm still a little overwhelmed," she said. "I feel a lot better than I did the first time we left Home. I'm actually a little surprised how much I've enjoyed getting away and spending time in the enclaves. I was afraid I'd feel so unsafe in the tunnels I'd have a hard time filling my role. I'm already pretty comfortable traveling the tunnels and visiting the enclaves."

"So why are you feeling overwhelmed?" asked Gen.

"I didn't expect the enclave leaders or the work they oversee to be so sophisticated."

Gen gave a little half smile and raised his eyebrows.

"I know that sounds terrible," Jenna said in reply. "I was only with the Tunnel Rats for six months before they passed me on to the Technoids. The brief time I spent with them I had simple jobs to keep the enclave going but I wasn't close enough to any decision makers to appreciate everything they do. I thought being an ambassador to the Tunnel Rats was going to be all about giving them information and support. I had no idea how much they support us, and now I realize before I can be a good ambassador I've got a lot to learn about their operations."

Gen's smile widened into an affectionate grin.

"Your humility is one of the attributes that will make you a very good ambassador!" Gen exclaimed.

"They really are amazing, Gen," said Jenna. "Their commitment to their enclaves more than makes up for any lack of formal education. They are extremely sophisticated in their understanding of Garson society and their parasitic relationship to that society. They know how to take from the surface those things they need to survive without raising alarm to the point the politicians feel compelled to call for action against them. They know how to collect information on nearly any aspect of surface society without making their presence or activity known. They take great pride in their contribution to our resistance, as well they should!"

Gen just nodded in appreciation of Jenna's astute analysis.

"We're almost Home," he said. "It's been a good trip, and I'm confident you're ready to take the next one without me."

Jenna appreciated the irony of her situation, too. She'd been so worried about Slink leaving the safety of Home and her enduring his absence. Now it was she who left him behind.

She missed Slink when she left Home on her excursions, but she never had to leave without plenty of time to say goodbye. She also loved her new responsibilities, and the pride she felt in her contribution to the Technoid cause.

While she was gone on her first excursion, Slink got a taste of the worry Jenna had felt when he was evacuated. By the time she returned after four days away, his imagination had worn him out with thoughts of the dangers she might be facing. He decided he'd ask her to resign from her new position.

Nonetheless, when she returned and Slink saw how animated Jenna was and heard the passion in her voice as she told of her experiences, he couldn't bring himself to broach the subject with her. Jenna had found her place, discovered her purpose, and Slink couldn't ask her to lay that down. He knew how good it felt to be significant, to be seen by others as significant, to do significant work. He loved her and wouldn't deny her, so he fussed over her, and she loved his every gesture of concern and appreciation.

"Well look who finally found her way Home," Slink exclaimed as Jenna approached their customary table upon her return from her third excursion.

"That's right, let's hear your complaints about the fact that I'm Home two days ahead of schedule," Jenna chided.

Slink jumped up from the table and met Jenna with a warm embrace and light kiss on the lips. He held her close for a few seconds, rubbing his fingers up and down her spine before turning her loose.

They went through the mess line together without saying a word to each other, quickly filled their trays, and returned to their table.

"So, how was this trip?" Slink asked. "You don't look upset, so I'm assuming you're not Home early because something went wrong."

"No, everything went exceptionally well," Jenna replied. "We thought we'd need to be there three or four days to catch all the leaders of the enclave in-between excursions, but DAN had stepped up patrols on the surface, so we sat down with all the leaders individually and together the day of our arrival. We spent the night, toured the enclave early this morning to thank everyone for all their hard work, and headed out a few hours later."

"Their loss, my gain," quipped Slink.

"I'm happy to see you, too," Jenna said, as she reached across the table and squeezed Slink's forearm. "How'd things go here?"

"As far as I know, everything went smoothly. We feel like we're making progress in the Cave. We conducted a few more tests this morning and we learned a few more things."

Jenna grinned and shook her head.

"What?" asked Slink.

"I know you can't say much about what you're doing in the Cave, but repeating the line about conducting tests and learning things is getting comical. If I had a credit for every time you said that, I'd be a rich girl!"

Slink tried to glare at Jenna, but he couldn't keep from smiling.

"What else am I supposed to say?" he asked. "Like you said, I can't say very much, but I don't want to be antisocial."

"I know," soothed Jenna. "It's just funny."

She stared into Slink's eyes for a minute, pursed her lips in a kiss, then smiled.

"So how is your practice going?" she asked.

Slink knew Jenna was asking about the time he committed to sitting in silence. He'd taken to referring to the time he spent in silence as his practice because no other words Dot used quite fit, as far as he was concerned. Sometimes what he experienced fit the ancient description of mindfulness meditation, other times it was more like Zen sitting, and still other times it was most like Hindu Chakra cleansing. He supposed some might call what he did "prayer."

His time in silence had come to be like nothing he'd found described in the ancient texts. Most often when he sat in silence he came to a point where his mind grew so still he could only think of the experience as "nothingness." It was more than that, though.

Within the experience of utter stillness, he felt an intense connection to everyone and everything; not just the people on Home and the things surrounding him, but everyone and everything. It was as if his individual awareness expanded to become an infinite, universal awareness. He experienced the great "nothing" and the great "everything" simultaneously.

As he breathed out he released all thought, all feeling, all experience into the primordial silence and as he breathed in he embraced his connection and the interconnection of all matter, all energy, all reality.

He didn't think he could adequately convey what this felt like, so he just called it his practice. When he'd explained this to Dot, she'd just smiled and said,

"It's a good word."

Slink realized Jenna was waiting for his answer and said,
"My practice is good."

She frowned and tilted her head to the side.

"Really good," Slink added tentatively.

"Come on, Slink, that doesn't tell me anything." Jenna exclaimed. "I really want to hear more about it."

"OK, I'll try," replied Slink. "I'm not trying to be evasive; I'm just not sure I have the words to describe what I experience as I sit in silence."

"There's nothing more interesting, in my humble opinion, than listening to someone try to describe the indescribable," teased Jenna as she winked at Slink. "Use whatever words come to mind, and I'll ask questions if I can't follow you."

Slink trusted Jenna. He also realized she might have some worthwhile insight into his experience. They'd poured out their lives to each other, and Slink knew Jenna had practiced Zen meditation for several years. She was more than a little familiar with sitting in silence.

He took a breath and dove in.

"When I sit now, most of the time at least, I quickly reach a point where my mind grows really still. Dot taught me mindfulness practice, and that helped me pay attention to my thoughts and feelings without judging them. As I practiced mindfulness, though, my mind just naturally started slowing. Maybe I was just relaxing more."

"I get that," affirmed Jenna. "I think most people who stick with a mindfulness practice for a while find their thoughts become less chaotic. But I get the impression you've gone way past that point."

"Yeah, that's right!" replied Slink. "My mind becomes almost silent."

He paused with his mouth half open for a few seconds before he shook his head and said,

"That's not right. My mind isn't silent, it's attentive. Only I'm not watching my thoughts and feelings anymore, I'm watching the silence...the nothingness. I know that sounds strange, but it's like I can see, or even feel, the empty space between everything, feel the…oh…the only phrase I've found that begins to describe it is…primordial nothingness. Does that make any sense?"

Jenna nodded.

"Yes, it makes sense. I can't say I've ever experienced what your describing, but I think I understand what you're saying. That sounds pretty amazing!"

Slink smiled.

"It is pretty amazing, actually," he said. "But then it gets even more amazing. It's not long before I begin to sense the connections between things - between people, objects, everything. I can feel the way everything is connected, the way every little thing is part of one big thing. As I pay attention to the connectedness, it's like the edges of all these individual people and objects go from being solid and definable to becoming more liquid and indistinct. Pretty soon, I just feel a deep connection to it all. I think of it as…the 'everything'."

Slink drew a deep breath.

"So my practice has become this experience of the 'nothing' and the 'everything'," he continued. With each breath I take in, I accept and welcome the nothing, the emptiness, the silence. And with each exhale, I feel the connections that bind us all together until those connections draw us into the everything. I literally find myself breathing to the twin notions of 'nothing' and 'everything', and in some inexplicable way they become like two sides of the same coin. When I'm immersed in that experience, the sense of quiet, of peacefulness, of rightness is almost overwhelming."

He sighed and sat in the silence, head bowed and eyes closed. Jenna shared the silence with him for a long time before she stood and walked around the table until she stood next to him. Then she dropped to her knees leaned into him, wrapped her arms around him, and whispered in his ear,

"You are truly amazing, Slink. I don't know what's happening to you, but I think it's important—for you and maybe for all of us."

Jenna kissed his cheek, and squeezed him. Slink turned and kissed her lips. Then he whispered in her ear,

"Thank you for listening; I mean, really listening. I feel so much more grounded and I can't tell you how important that is to me."

"You're welcome," replied Jenna. "Someday you're going to realize I actually like listening to you!"

Slink kissed her again, then Jenna got up and started rubbing her knees. Without even looking up, she asked,

"Let's see if we can jump in on the card game. I could stand a little boisterous fun tonight. You game?"

Slink suddenly became aware of the noise coming from the other side of the mess. The weekly card game was already in full swing.

"Sounds great," he said. "As long as you won't cry if I kick your butt tonight."

She shot up and lunged for him, but Slink was out of his chair and jumping away before she came close. Jenna laughed out loud and exclaimed,

"You better jump away. I'm not the one who's going to get his butt kicked tonight."

He laughed as she playfully punched his arm, then coaxed her closer. Jenna nuzzled into his side as he wrapped his arm around her, and they made their way to the game.

Gen had expected Jenna's orientation and training to take months. He didn't anticipate that after only a few weeks she would begin working independently, visiting tunnel enclaves and working closely with the Tunnel Rat leaders, but that's how it turned out. Four weeks after he'd made her Assistant Ambassador, he found a message on his desk one morning indicating she'd left Home earlier to address a concern with a face-to-face meeting with one of the enclave leaders. She knew she was ready just as he did and stepped into her role without needing him to hold the door open for her.

Later that morning, he reported to Dot that he was ready to assume any additional duties as second-in-command. Dot was pleased; she was very pleased--with her second-in-command, with her assistant ambassador, and with her sweet nephew who'd begun confiding his deepest concerns with the only family member he'd ever known.

Slink immersed himself in his relationship with Jenna, deepening friendships with Dot and Gen, and his work in the Cave. He and Jenna spent five nights a week in each other's company. Two nights a week, they went their separate ways--Jenna to her circle of girl friends who'd made up her social circle for the years before Slink came on board. She'd endured some gentle ribbing from them when she first started setting aside time for them after neglecting their friendships for the first couple of months she and Slink were together. Their circle had been formed in love over a number of years, and her friends were happy to include Jenna again when her obsession with Slink gave way to more balance.

During his months on Home, Slink discovered the value of friendship. One of his free nights each week was spent with Dot. She was the first person to offer both the time and the effort to form a deeper connection with Slink that wasn't a romantic interest. So Slink had the advantage of forming his first steadfast friendship with the only member of his family he'd ever met. He and Dot were both intelligent, inquisitive, and driven by a desire to understand their world and remedy its ills.

Dot nurtured in Slink a sense of connection with the rest of their family. She shared the family stories that had been passed to her and many others she'd not remembered for years. The tears that often filled her eyes when she told her stories were mirrored in his. Over time, he developed a profound empathy for his family's plight in the nurseries and detainment centers of Garsow. His generalized desire to contribute to a better society became a more personal desire to liberate his family.

Dot also continued to share time with Slink as he developed his practice. Her support had helped Slink dramatically deepen the awareness he'd first developed in opening and closing the Cave. He was gifted with intuition, and Dot showed him how to nurture that gift. He came to appreciate the way his intuition complimented his extraordinary ability to process and compile data.

Slink became much more insightful as he deepened his practice and developed his natural intuition. He still made valuable connections between reported events on the surface and data he'd reviewed in the Cave. He now also saw admirable qualities he'd never before noticed in colleagues and friends whose presence he'd hardly noticed. He saw and appreciated the many kindnesses and supportive gestures others directed his way. He saw and released mistakes--his and his colleagues. Life came into balance, and he saw his role in contributing to and maintaining that balance.

Dot, too, found that her meditation calmed her concerns and cleared her mind so much faster when Slink was present and engaged in his own practice. They reinforced each other's mindfulness and the insights that flowed from it.

When he wasn't with Jenna or Dot, Slink was usually with Gen. As Home's Second, Gen needed someone who could handle him just being Gen - call him by name, take a joke or make one, and treat him like another one of the guys.

Slink needed a big brother who knew how to tease him, make him laugh, and take the lead in social circles. Gen was second to Dot in another circle--he was the second best card player on Home, so he and Slink played almost every time they got together, hoping one of them could eventually best the Commander.

The rest of the time they lounged in Gen's quarters and talked. They sometimes talked about more serious subjects, but more often than not, they just hung out with each other, arguing about who had better taste in women, or wagering on which crew members would become couples, or naming the first place on the surface where they'd have dinner after their triumphal return. The subject was secondary to the release each found in the other's company.

Over time, Slink discovered something else with regard to his closest relationships--thanks to Dot's initiative. On one occasion, Gen was sitting with Dot discussing a couple of staff concerns at her table when Slink and Jenna walked in. Dot invited Gen to remain and join the three of them for dinner.

"Commander, I don't want to intrude on your time with your nephew," Gen protested.

"Nonsense, Gen!" Dot replied. "And you can drop the formalities," she added. "Whenever I meet with any one of you, we spend a good part of our time talking about the other two. It's high time we sat down together...as friends."

"As you wish, uh, Dot," Gen stuttered, trying to loosen up without much success.

"Good to see you, Slink," Dot exclaimed as she stood, rounded the table, and embraced her nephew. "It's great to have you here, too," Dot continued as she moved from Slink to Jenna, wrapping an arm around the younger woman.

"I am just Dot for these weekly dinners Slink and I share," Dot exclaimed. "He got used to it quickly enough and you will too. Our personal lives are intertwined, and I think we can keep our professional roles straight outside the times we gather as friends. If I'm wrong this may be a one time affair, but I think it'll be otherwise."

"Well, I'm glad we're all here together," replied Slink. "I can't think of three people I'd rather be with!"

"If we're going to be doing this regularly," said Gen, "at least I'll be able to see my assistant in person instead of leaving messages for her and listening to the messages she leaves me."

"And whose fault is that?" asked Jenna.

"You can see her, Gen," interrupted Dot, " but you can't talk shop with her--that's a rule Slink and I agreed on when we first started meeting."

"I guess you'll just have to go on listening to my messages," Jenna teased.

"I never knew there was a limit to the length of message the system would record until you came to work with me," Gen countered. "You are the only person I've ever known who can leave three messages in a row and still not get to the point you were making."

Jenna reached across the table and slapped at Gen who moved back to avoid her.

"From formal to feisty--I'm not sure I like this," teased Gen.

"Jenna, I've received a few of your messages, and although I treasure your every word, there is some truth to Gen's observation," Slink injected.

"So the guys have to stick together, huh?" Jenna asked, struggling to keep a smile off her face. "We'll see how long you two stand against the stronger sex."

"Wait a minute," Slink protested.

"You made your bed, and now you don't want to sleep in it nephew?" Dot inquired. "You're smarter than I thought!"

Jenna broke into a broad smile and winked at Dot. Dot winked back.

Two hours later, as they were the last to leave the officer's Mess, their conversation was as free as any circle of friends. After that first serendipitous night, Dot asked Slink how he would feel if once a month their weekly dinner were opened to the other two. Slink tried not to sound overly enthusiastic about Dot's suggestion, but he was truly delighted. He'd wanted to find some way of drawing Jenna into his time with Dot, but he didn't want to ask that she be invited. Gen's addition was an added bonus since it assured no one would have to endure the awkwardness of feeling like the "third" tagging along on a date.

When he was not with Jenna, Dot, or Gen, Slink was in the Cave. Slink's extraordinary intellectual gifts put him at the center of the Cave's efforts. As the Doorkeeper of the Cave, Chris still convened and concluded every shift in the circle of silence. No one remembered exactly how they came to refer to the Cave leader as the Doorkeeper. Several suggested it had started in jest. Nonetheless, the title fit the function and was just eccentric enough to refer only to a leader of the Cave. Outside of opening and closing their sessions, though, Chris was not the source of leadership in the Cave. Slink led by force of presence and power of intellect.

A few months after Slink joined the Cave, the Cave dwellers were having lunch one day and someone suggested they needed a title for Slink. She argued that he was the one at the center of their work, and he deserved a title to acknowledge his place amongst them. She was joking about the need for a title but absolutely serious in her desire to acknowledge their real leader, and in this spirit, another of the consultants suggested Slink should be the Keymaster.

They all liked the name, though none of them appreciated the reference to an old vid that had prompted their colleague to suggest it in the first place. Everyone at lunch thought it had a nice ring to it, was non-conformist enough for the Cave, and somehow fit Slink. So he became the Keymaster.

A few nights later, the vid buff dropped a memory coin off for Slink. He and Gen spent one of their guy nights watching the classic vid the two had copied on the memory coin. Ghostbusters became an instant favorite for Slink.

Regardless of any silly title they gave him, Slink loved working with the Cave dwellers and he loved their work. He believed the day was coming very soon when they would bring the Supernet down. Their success with the belt pack commlink transmitters had shown they could code data well enough for it to be accepted and transmitted across the Supernet and decode Supernet transmissions accurately for display on a commlink. Before Slink joined them, they had tried and failed to master the Supernet coding too many times to count. Now, they were also collecting information about the servers that formed the Supernet backbone and the encryption that protected them. When Slink started working to write destructive code that could get past the firewall protecting the Supernet, his passion for his work rose to a level that rivaled his dedication to Jenna.

Any attempt to send destructive code was inherently dangerous, not only because the Supernet firewall program flagged and attempted to trace all destructive transmissions. More fundamentally, any transmission that looked like a deliberate attempt at sabotage would alert DAN and trigger an investigation, heightened security, and more tunnel raids. The data had to look like it had been inadvertently corrupted at the point of transmission. Slink was the first to mimic the Supernet code with any success. Nonetheless, he found it daunting to write destructive code that could pass for harmless, inadvertent corruption and simultaneously carry executable instructions to the Supernet servers.

He and his fellow Cave dwellers constructed the best firewall they could. They used it to protect Home, and to test Slink's attempts to breach the Supernet firewall. They tested every packet of code Slink wrote. Eventually, he developed code that Home's firewall would interpret as harmless corruption and bounce back to its sender even while it executed the hidden instructions embedded beneath the corrupted message. Still, he worked to refine the data packet further to assure the Supernet would not recognize the executable instructions embedded beneath the corrupted message. When his packet performed as expected in every test he and his colleagues could develop, he petitioned Dot to approve sending his intentionally corrupted packet of data across the Supernet with instructions for Home to reverse its course.

The first morning after Dot had given the go ahead, the Cave dwellers maintained their circle of silence a little longer than usual. There was nothing to set up, so when they broke from their circle, Slink had only to awaken his display, link his station to the other monitors in the Cave, bring up the data packet he had written and tested, and touch the "send" command on his screen.

"Here goes nothing," he said as his hand floated above the screen. They all knew he might just as well have said, "here goes everything," everything they had worked for, everything they wanted to protect, everything they wanted to destroy.

Everyone in the Cave held his or her breath waiting. The first indication of success was the less significant one, but it still elicited a collective sigh from the Cave dwellers when it came a split second after Slink's finger made contact with his screen. The return message read:

Please drop by the Alpha Sector service center this evening between 1800 and 1900 hours. Your commlink is transmitting corrupted data and needs service. The problem will not affect your experience today, but it needs attention, so an appointment has been made on your behalf. See you tonight!
D.A.N.

Because Slink had linked his station to every monitor in the Cave, the message appeared simultaneously on every monitor. The collective sigh was followed by tightening facial expressions and furtive glances around the room. A second passed, then five, then ten. It seemed an unbearable wait. Twenty seconds, then thirty passed.

"Oh shit!" an exasperated colleague voiced the rising fears of the Cave dwellers. Then, a wild cheer went up on the bridge and they knew! A second later, everyone on board Home felt her slowing as their weight shifted in response to the change in the momentum of the sweeper drone. The Bridge broadcast a message to all stations that Home was reversing course and apologized for the failure to warn the crew in advance. When the jubilant cries died down in the Cave, the singular applause coming from the door of the Cave could finally be heard. Everyone looked up to see Dot standing in the entryway, grinning from ear to ear.

"I never had any doubts we would see this day," she said. "I just never dreamed we would see it so soon! Congratulations to all of you. Will you please accept the thanks of the entire crew?

One day, we will look back and remember this day, and count it amongst the more significant days we saw before we returned to the surface. And yet, we have a good piece of work yet to do before our return. Some of that work will be every bit as difficult as the piece you have just accomplished. Don't let yourself get complacent. The closer we get to our goal, the more devastating the consequences of any mistake. We are quickly getting to the point, if we have not already reached it, where any mistake will be disastrous. So let's celebrate our successes and do everything we can to prevent any failure. The future of Garson society depends on us!"

"Three cheers for Slink!"

Dot knew her nephew did not want to be singled out for praise, but she had no power over the spontaneous call that emerged from the circle of his colleagues. They answered the call immediately.

"Hip, hip, hooray!"

"Hip, hip, hooray!"

"Hip, hip, hooray!"

He was just glad they didn't lift him on their shoulders. He tried to deflect their praise as he gestured broadly around to his colleagues, but they'd have none of it. He was forced to receive their praise, their gratitude, and their admiration. In the end, it really wasn't so bad.

"No," he thought, "It really wasn't bad at all!"

Slink bolted upright in his bunk and smacked his head on the underside of the bunk above him. To add insult to injury, Franco, his bunkmate cussed him out for waking him up. If Slink could read minds or see through solid structures like the upper bunk, he might have realized that Franco had been so startled by Slink's head impacting the small of his back that he'd bolted upright and hit his own head on the bulwark. At first, Franco felt foolish, but his embarrassment quickly gave way to anger he projected on his bunkmate.

Slink didn't really care what was happening with Franco. He hadn't heard a word Franco said. He'd barely registered Franco's unhappiness.

His heart was pounding and he was fighting to awaken from his nightmare. He'd dreamed he was having the breath choked out of him, and indeed, he could hardly get a breath down his aching throat. He'd dreamed he was burning alive after some kind of industrial accident in the factory where he was being forced to work under the watchful eyes of a DAN agent with an automatic weapon strapped across his bare chest. In his dream, he was chained at the ankles and joined by that chain with a string of other unfortunate slave laborers. He awoke to discover he really was on fire, but the fire was within. He'd evidently been tossing and turning for a while, because he was completely uncovered and had entangled his feet in the footbars of the bunk.

He couldn't seem to untangle himself from the bed frame even though he felt desperate to get off the bunk and stand. It seemed so clear to him that if he could only stand, his breath would come more easily. As he struggled, he groaned, then let loose with a long, deep grunt as he thrust himself upward only to have the bed frame's hold on his ankle bring him crashing to the floor next to the bunk.

"Damn, Slink, what the hell is the matter with you?"

Franco was standing over him. Slink couldn't focus on his bunkmate. He wondered if he'd smacked his head when he fell to the floor. The room seemed to be spinning around him, and Franco was at the center of the vortex, first looking like he was going to burst a blood vessel in his neck, then looking confused, then looking panicked as he started screaming again.

Then everything went black.

"Two weeks?"

Slink couldn't believe his ears. Jenna, looking like she was the one who should have been laying in bed, eyes bloodshot, worry lines etched in her forehead, tears streaming down her face, nodded. She tried to continue her explanation but she'd lost command of her voice. She just laid her head on his shoulder and cried.

"Two weeks?" he thought. "How could I have been here two weeks?"

He struggled to recall anything of the last two weeks. Jenna told him his fall from his bunk was now ancient history--14 days, three hours, and 42 minutes, to be exact. She couldn't help him with any of the details of events on Home or in the tunnels. She was reluctant to admit it at first, but she finally confessed to him that she hadn't left his bedside for more than a half hour at a time since Franco and a couple of other guys had brought him into the sickbay.

"Two weeks? How could he have lost two weeks?"

He caressed her head, running his fingers across her thick braids and down the lines of her scalp between the braids. She just rubbed her face into his shoulder and kept whispering the same thing over and over again.

"Thank you. Thank you. Thank you."

Her voice trailed off. Slink wanted to interrupt her reverie and quiz her further about his condition, but he thought better of it. He began to wonder if she'd fallen asleep on his shoulder and as she rested there, Slink thought of her keeping vigil at his bedside not knowing if he'd ever wake up, and it brought tears to his eyes.

"What have I ever done to have someone love me like this?" he wondered.

He doubted he'd ever find a satisfactory answer to that question. He knew he couldn't do anything to deserve such love. As its recipient, he could only receive it graciously and marvel at his good fortune. He smiled. He marveled. He fell back asleep.

When he awoke the next time, Jenna was gone. He tried to sit up and look around. He discovered just how much muscle tone he'd lost laying in bed without moving for two weeks. The medtechs had done everything they could to preserve his conditioning, but in the nearly two weeks before his fever broke, they were reluctant to stress his body in any way, so they refrained from using electrical muscle stimulation or passive motion appliances. They'd started those and other interventions over the last forty-eight hours after they were confident the fever had run its course. They weren't sure he'd live at that point, but they were confident that the stimulation could do no harm.

When he tried to sit up, he felt as if a heavy weight shifted inside his skull and crashed against his forehead. He only managed to raise the back of his head about six inches off the pillow before he crashed back.

"Easy, little man. She's OK."

It was Gen. He sat up from where he'd been resting on the cot next to Slink.

"Welcome back amongst the living."

Gen stretched and yawned. When Slink started looking around again, he moved to reassure him.

"When the medtechs saw that she'd finally fallen asleep, they laid her down on a cot in the cubicle right next door. She's only been asleep for about six hours, and you don't want to wake her yet. I'll keep you company for a while."

Gen told Slink what they knew about Slink's condition. Slink had contracted an exceedingly rare and usually fatal viral infection. It had travelled to his bloodstream and in the four hours he slept fitfully on his bunk it had become life-threatening. Had he not awakened and enraged Franco, he would probably be dead.

Franco had enlisted the help of the man in the bunk next to him, and they had carried Slink to sickbay. By the time Jenna, Gen and Dot arrived there, Slink was in a deep coma. The medtechs had resigned themselves to his seeming inevitable death when Dot stepped in.

266

"He's not going to die, do you hear me?" she had demanded. "What do we need to save him?"

Chapter 11

When Dot entered the sickbay, Jerome, the lead medtech, explained their predicament to her.

"The virus is indigenous to the planetoid's surface, and every Garson is vaccinated against it shortly after birth. In addition every citizen is given a booster vaccination at the age of transition. Slink left the nursery before gettin' the booster. We can hold the virus at bay for twenty-four hours usin' standard issue antiviral inoculations, but after that the virus will resume its assault on his system, shuttin' down his kidneys, then his liver, and finally, his heart."

"You're not answering my question," she snapped. "I don't have the patience to listen to someone tell me why we can't do what we are going to do. We are going to save his life--do you understand? So take a deep breath, gather your thoughts, and tell me what we are going to do to save Slink's life."

"There is a medical station in Beta Sector that is said to hold reserves of every medication ever developed for use here. If that's the case," Jerome glanced up to see Dot glaring at him and quickly added, "and there's no reason to believe that it's not," he drew in a deep breath and continued, "they'll have samples of the drug developed to treat the first settlers of Garsow. I haven't heard of it bein' used in over sixty years, but if it still exists, it's in that station."

"Then we need to find that station, retrieve this medication, and get it back here in the next twenty-four hours."

Before he could say anything, Dot answered Jerome's unspoken objection.

"Under the best of conditions, making a surface excursion deep into Beta Sector and returning in less than twenty-four hours would be one hell of a challenge. Given the fact that we're going in while DAN is still on heightened alert, this will be even more difficult. I don't suppose this medical station will be unguarded, huh Gen?"

"It probably won't be fortified with any unusual security, but it's located very near the DAN station. Since we are talking about how we're going to do this thing, I want to point out that it's also very near the crossing between Alpha and Beta Sectors."

Dot's eyes flashed anger. She didn't have time for Gen's seemingly irrelevant observations.

"It matters," he said, meeting her gaze. "I think the proximity to the crossing works to our advantage. Hear me out on this! We hit the medical station just before shift change. The guards going off duty will be distracted, and the guards coming on won't be there yet."

"I see where you're goin' with this," interrupted Jerome. "When you enter the Station DAN'll know—the stations are wired and monitored, so you create a distraction at the crossing."

"Right," said Gen. "Then someone hits all the surveillance cameras with paint balls. If DAN's going to be alerted the minute we step into the Station, we might as well not give them any close ups to identify us later."

"What do you mean, 'we'?" Dot asked. "I need you here, Gen."

"You need me leading this excursion more than you need me here," said Gen. "We need to save Slink because of what he means to all of us, not just because a few of us have grown to love him."

269

"We can't afford to lose both of you," snapped Dot.

"Then we can't lose either of us," replied Gen. "You said we're going to save him, and I'm going to make sure that's what we do. I am going to lead the successful excursion to get the meds, and I will be back here in less than 24 hours."

Dot saw how determined Gen was and realized she needed to hear him out. She knew Gen needed to stay on Home, but she hadn't quite figured out how to make that happen.

Dot sighed heavily. She shifted gears.

"As much urgency as we feel, we need to take the time to plan this out so we can execute the plan."

"We'll need to be bold," exclaimed Gen.

"We time our strike so shift change hits while we're in the station, and when we come out, we make a break for the pedway heading away from the crossing. If we take a small excursion team, get in and out of the station in a minute or less, and head in the opposite direction of the crossing, we'll probably draw most of the DAN agents away from the crossing. They'll be coming our way from the moment we enter the station, and they'll take up the pursuit the moment they see us. Then we double back and blow through the crossing gate."

Dot's mouth dropped open.

"You'll have every agent running for that gate from both sides. You might as well just paint red targets on your backs!"

"Yeah, they'll be running for the gate, but they'll have to run back through crowds on either side of the gate to get to us. We drop smoke bombs when we reach the crowd to add to the chaos. We'll have DAN trying to get to us no matter where we go, but I think we are more likely to evade them in the heavy traffic of people waiting at the gate during a shift change than running from them through Beta Sector. If we get through the crowds at the gate, we won't have far to go to drop through the vent shaft just inside Alpha Sector."

"What? In the middle of a shift change, you're going to push your way through a crowded gate, through the crowd on the other side of that gate, run around the corner, pop open a vent shaft, and just disappear into the tunnels? Are you out of your fricking' mind?"

"I don't know--maybe I am," was all that Gen offered in response to Dot's scathing review.

Jenna, who'd been listening passively off to the side, stepped forward and spoke up.

"I don't think he's crazy," she interjected.

Dot looked at her for a minute, then she just lowered her eyes and shook her head.

"OK, let's hear it," she said.

"Well, I'm just thinkin' out loud now," said Jenna, "but what does the average Garson think about Tunnel Rats and Technoids? They treat us like we have a disease and we're contagious. A few might have some empathy for people who live underground and scavenge to get by, but even those few don't want to get too close to any of us. They wouldn't want our lives rubbing off on them--infecting them so to speak."

Gen smiled in approval.

Encouraged, Jenna continued.

"I think they're going to be scrambling to get away from an unvisored bunch of Technoids who look armed and dangerous. They'll be pushing and shoving to get away and blocking the pursuit of the DAN officers. I think the minute you pull a grate back and jump into a vent shaft, they're going to give you all the room you want. I think you can get a three-person team down a vent shaft fast enough to seal the grate from below and be well down the tunnels before any DAN agents can figure out how to get that grate back open and come after you. At the very least," Jenna lowered her voice and leaned closer to Dot, "Gen can get down that vent shaft with the medicine while the other two draw agents away from the shaft."

"First," replied Dot, "Jerome's knowledge of the stations has a chance of providing the medicine that can save Slink's life. Secondly," and now she turned and faced Gen, "don't think for a second that you're going on this excursion."

She held her hand up in front of Gen's face before he could even start to protest.

"I need you here to keep everything going. Jakov will take command of Home and see that he gets her underneath that vent shaft before we come racing down it. I need you to keep the crew focused on the task at hand. When word gets out that I'm leading the excursion, some of the crew are going to tend toward panic."

"YOU, leading the excursion? That's crazy!" Gen exclaimed.

"You can't be serious! If we lose Slink, we're going to have a hard time finishing what we've started. If we lose both of you, we won't have a chance!"

"You're not going to lose either one of us! I'm going to lead Jerome and our best tracker on this excursion, and we are going to be back with medicine for Slink before you even have a chance to lose a night's sleep worrying about us."

"Dot, please! You're not thinking straight. You can't leave the command of Home to Jakov and me for the sake of one person."

"I'm not going to argue with you, Gen! What do you want to hear me say--that this is personal--it is! I have one family member left, and I'm not going to put his life in anyone else's hands. It's personal!"

She was almost screaming as she made her admission. Then, she drew a deep, slow breath and exhaled in a prolonged sigh. She lowered her voice.

"If this can be done--if he can be saved, we need to save him, and if we can save him, I will risk my life trying, not because he's my nephew, but because he's our best hope. We can't get where we're going without his help. We've made more progress in the months since you and he joined us than we'd made in the years before that. I must choose the more essential work, and I am. Jakov can handle Home and you can handle the crew. I need to lead a surface excursion to save him."

She gestured toward Slink and her eyes filled with tears.

"We will each do what we can, and I pray it will be enough."

Dot worked with Jakov to coordinate the timing of her excursion with Home's course in the tunnels to give her surface party the best chance of dropping back into the tunnels just behind Home so they could run to catch the drone without Jakov bringing it to a complete stop. She then laid out for Gen the goals of each research team so he could oversee their work. Finally, she went by sickbay to say her goodbyes to Slink and Jenna and to demand of Slink that he hold on until she returned with the medication he needed. Slink offered no response, but Jenna appreciated Dot's way of bantering with him even as he remained motionless. It lifted her spirits.

"After all," she thought, " you don't kid around with someone who is going to die. You only do that if you think he's going to pull through."

And Dot had assured Jenna she was coming back with the medicine to save him.

"I need my nephew as much as you need your lover," she'd said as Jenna rested her head on Dot's shoulder and tears streamed down her cheeks. Dot held her for several minutes and let her cry. She was losing precious moments, but she thought Jenna was going to need every ounce of strength she could muster if she was going to keep vigil with Slink. So she held the young woman for several long moments. Then she was gone.

She'd assumed Jerome knew the area where they were headed. His plan was too clear, too precise to have been formulated by someone who'd only seen maps or had a distant, vague memory of a place. Her intuition, as usual, had hit the mark. Jerome had spent two years with a Tunnel Rat enclave not far from the vent shaft where they planned to re-enter the tunnels.

Though they never used that shaft because it was so exposed, he'd made a note of it and remembered thinking, "someday, in a pinch, we may need to remember that shaft!"

Now, here he was, in the tightest pinch he'd ever known. He began to wonder if he wasn't completely out of his mind. He felt like the expedition rested on his shoulders. They were following his plan, and he was either going to be a hero or a goat when this was all over. He suddenly realized his life-long desire to be known as a hero may have betrayed him. Only time would tell.

Joining Dot and him was a woman whose age was a mystery. She moved like she was no older than he, perhaps even his junior, but her face was etched with the lines of someone who'd seen twice the years Jerome had seen. Her olive complexion, dark, deep-set eyes, and wisp of a mouth gave her a secretive, mysterious countenance. The fact that she almost never spoke unless she was spoken to, and then with the fewest words that would get the job done, only added to the mystery. Jerome had managed to get her name--Naomi. Outside of that, he knew she was a tracker and tunnel guide, she lived aboard Home (Jerome did not remember ever seeing her before), and she tired of questions easily. Her patience had extended for all of about 30 seconds in their first encounter, before she looked at him following a question about where she learned her skills, shook her head, spat at his feet, and walked away.

"Oh, now this is really goin' to be fun!" thought Jerome. "If it wasn't enough that I'm riskin' my life tryin' to be a hero, I've got to put up with some nic-spittin', antisocial trail runner. I hope she's better at runnin' trails than she is at makin' a first impression."

Dot had briefed each of her traveling companions separately, so when they stepped off the last stair jutting from the side of the drone and onto the tunnel floor, she motioned for Naomi to lead the way. Jerome fell in behind Naomi, knowing Dot would want to bring up the rear. Naomi led them off down the tunnel toward an elusive doorway they hoped would bring them through an abandoned Tunnel Rat enclave. From there, they intended to enter one of the undeveloped caverns through an escape door one of the enclave's previous residents had described, and if his memory was at all trustworthy, back into the tunnel they were in now at a point just beneath a vent shaft. The shaft they hoped to ascend was only a couple minutes from the gate where they would cross into Beta Sector and search for the medical station Jerome had identified as storing archived pharmaceuticals. Like most of the shafts, though, it was secluded in an alley they expected to find deserted when they pushed up the grate and entered the surface.

Jerome kept his eye peeled for one of the Tunnel Rat doors. They were almost impossible to see even if the seeker knew where he might expect it to be found. At several points, Jerome thought he had spotted a seam in the tunnel wall only to have Naomi walk past the point he suspected without so much as a glance. Almost directly under one of the wall-mounted ambient lights, where they could see the smooth walls of the tunnel with their appearance of interspersed burnt orange and brown glass, Naomi suddenly stopped. Jerome thought maybe she had seen footprints in the dust on the floor of the tunnel. When she turned toward the tunnel wall, raised her arms over her head and brought them down slowly, palms out, in the wide, circular motion that initiated the opening sequence he had seen done before enclave doors, he couldn't believe it! He could see no seams, and he could not imagine the Tunnel Rats would put a door so close to one of the tunnel lights. She had to be wrong.

A moment later, the seams appeared.

"Holy shit!" Jerome exclaimed. He'd meant his words for his ears alone, but even as he uttered them, he felt Dot's arm on his shoulders.

"She's good! That's why I asked her to join us." Then she lowered her voice. "I'm sure you've figured out by now it wasn't her social graces."

Jerome smiled to himself as Dot moved ahead of him and expressed her gratitude to Naomi even as the door opened before them. He loved the way Dot loosened things up. Here they were, racing to save her nephew's life following an uncharted course and she was cracking jokes.

"That's why we call her 'Commander,'" he thought to himself.

They passed through the enclave without incident. They even found the escape door without too much trouble, thanks again to Naomi's uncanny skills. It should have been the easiest part of their trip. It should have been marked by relief, maybe even celebration.

Instead it was a somber passage. The evidence of DAN's destructive capabilities was everywhere. They had smashed any furnishings and equipment the Tunnel Rats had been unable to evacuate. Then they had brought out the construction torches. The planetoid's makeup was such that the materials near the surface melted when subjected to extreme heat. The early settlers had been amazed at the smooth, glassy surface. They had determined they could smooth the walls of the caverns and create nearly circular tunnels with flat floors by melting the cavern walls with high-powered construction torches.

DAN used the torches to etch irregular indentations into the ceilings and walls of the enclaves and create corresponding ridges and raised bumps in the floors beneath the places where the torches were fired indiscriminately. They made sure that no one could easily use these old underground settlements again. They had served as home for the early settlers who had formed them out of the natural caverns, and later for the Tunnel Rats. Now there was no even surface anywhere in the enclave. Anyplace DAN had found abandoned furnishings or equipment they had burned them and melted their remains into the floors of the enclave hallways and hollows.

Without bringing the torches back in a third time and smoothing everything out, no one was ever going to live here again. It felt like a graveyard, even without any bodies. Then they found them.

They noticed the smell first. The occupants of this enclave had not had warning, or at least not enough warning. As near as Dot could tell, those who did not escape had been herded together and forced into one of the larger hollows, maybe the dining area. It was clear from the way the bodies were contorted and burned, visible through or protruding from the amber hue of the hardened material, they'd been alive when the torches were unleashed on the ceiling. The scene was horrific, and Jerome lost the contents of his stomach before he even took in its full impact. These people didn't die in an instant, but over several long, tortuous minutes, burned to death by the melted material falling from above them or by the torches themselves if they tried to escape the room. The DAN agents had tried to entomb them in the room and seal their bodies within the materials they melted from the ceiling, but they'd been forced away from the scene as the melted ceiling material poured out into the hallway where they'd been standing. They'd left their victims looking as though their bodies had been partially exhumed from a mass grave and left in a pile of burial material. Arms and legs protruded in all directions, and even an occasional hairless, charred head could be seen sticking out from the amber flow.

"This is the model society at work! I'll take our very flawed one any day," thought Dot.

"I'd love to turn those torches on the animals who did this!" thought Jerome.

Naomi spat at her feet in disgust. But when she turned to leave, the incongruence of her tears dripping from the sharp line of her clenched jaw said enough for all three of them.

When they passed through the escape door at the back of the enclave and into the undeveloped cavern behind it, they suddenly felt like trespassers in a foreign land. Most of the Garsow they knew was a world of artificial constructs designed to sustain human life. The cavern stood in stark contrast to the domed surface colonies and their bubble-shaped structures. The cavern did bear some signs of human imposition, though they were minimal in comparison to the tunnels. The walls and ceilings of the cavern had not been reshaped by white-hot torches. They felt smooth like the water-worn walls of an earthen cavern, but they were uneven and jagged in composition. There were formations like stalactites hanging from the ceilings and corresponding stalagmite-like formations jutting up from the ground. The walls were dirty brown curtains hanging unevenly at the borders of the cavern. The only indication of any previous human presence was the trail that had been melted along the floor of the cavern. It began or ended, depending on one's perspective, at the door from which they had just come and it wove its way through the cavern as far as the three sojourners could see. It meandered through the cavern following the path of least resistance.

Naomi resumed her place at the forefront of their expedition, stopping every so often to examine one of the unusual formations close to the path or looking overhead at the many protruding shapes. Jerome knew enough geology to be dangerous, and as he looked around he realized one of the reasons Garsow had puzzled its first settlers. The formations in the cavern could only exist in an environment that included water--liquid water.

The only water the settlers had ever found was always frozen--ice trapped in other caverns, like this one in size and proximity to the surface, but entirely unlike it in structure. Those ice-filled cavern were formed when layers of ice were trapped in the formation of the planetoid. The material on the walls of those caverns had not been impacted by any erosive process since they were formed. This cavern had been effected by erosion for centuries. Something in or near this cavern melted ice and kept the water warm enough to prevent it freezing again. It could be that molten material at the center of the planetoid rose in a chimney that brought it closer to the surface than usual and just beneath this cavern. It could be some radioactive process that generated enough heat to change the environment in or near this cavern.

When the network of caverns was first discovered by the Lansings and their crew, the discovery of ice was the coup de gras for the Lansing Plan. Before the first manned mission to Garsow was ever completed, the Lansings had shown the planetoid had an atmosphere, though thinner than Earth's and insufficient for sustaining human life. They knew it had gravity, though less than Earth's, and they knew it had a liquid core and solid rock mass that made up most of its solid material. They suspected that the planetoid had once contained water, but they dare not argue that an expedition could rely on a reliable water source. Instead, they argued their expedition could bring all their water with them and recycle it efficiently enough to sustain a colony for up to three years. The discovery of abundant ice freed them from the challenges of relying on their limited water supplies.

When they had stumbled on the first of the caverns like the one Dot, Jerome, and Naomi now explored, Dr. Adela Lansing, who headed the exploration team on that fateful day, was concerned that the cavern might be less stable given the geological differences that had to underlay its existence. They performed every test they could devise to assure that its atmosphere was not toxic, that its floor was stable, and that it was no more prone to cave-in than any of the other caverns they had found. In fact it was every bit as stable as any of the others, and it had a denser atmosphere than any other cavern they had ever entered. In their first ten years on Garsow, the colonists discovered three caverns like the one Dot and her company now traversed.

Dot was repeatedly tempted to call for them to pick up the pace, but she resisted this impulse. They were moving fast enough to complete their mission. The path through the center of the cavern meandered back and forth to avoid large obstacles. The real factor that slowed their progress was the shear beauty of the place.

Everywhere they turned, they saw natural beauty that stood in stark contrast to the monotony of anything else they knew. Whether his or her mind registered the beauty of the cavern in contrast to Home, the tunnels, or the surface of Garsow, every sweep of a lumawand revealed another spectacle to the one wielding the light. The early settlers had installed light fixtures sufficient to allow safe passage through the cavern, but their limited coverage left most of the cavern hidden in shadow.

Dot felt an innate longing being filled for the first time, a desire satiated after a lifetime of neglect. She would not deny herself these few extra minutes. Even if she had been willing to neglect her own need, she could not have demanded the same from her fellows. So they walked, they "oohed and awed," they sighed, they even wept at the sights that assaulted their eyes.

In her mind's eye, Dot saw cavern walls crumple like an accordion when the cavern ran headlong into some imaginary, unmovable obstacle. Jerome imagined water dripping from ceiling to floor and carrying with it the mineral deposits that formed stalactites and stalagmites. He could only guess the distance from the floor of the cavern to the ceiling, barely illuminated by their wands. Naomi surmised that at some points the cavern had to reach within a few feet of the surface. She saw pillars rising from the floor of the cavern to reach out toward the limits of her vision.

They all saw formations of mineral deposits that called forth all sorts of imagined or freshly recalled creatures completely foreign to Garsow. More than once, one of them started or jumped as the shadows played tricks on their eyes.

Dot recalled vids that featured cloud formations on earth and a little girl laying on a hillside pointing out shapes that she saw in the clouds. These were her clouds, her canvas upon which her imagination drew all sorts of fantastic scenes.

For the first time since they had made the decision to embark on this excursion, Dot found time moving too fast for her comfort. All the time they were preparing, moving from the ship into the tunnel, walking to the Tunnel Rat enclave, even surveying the sickening remains of the enclave, they seemed to move too slowly. Everything took too long to accomplish, to traverse, to open or close. Now she wished that she could slow time and stay in this cavern for hours while only giving up the minutes actually required to travel the course of the path that provided their passage. She felt sadness at reaching the doorway that would lead them back into the tunnel and from there up to the surface and a short distance from their goal.

If Naomi felt any of these things, she said nothing to betray her feelings. She simply stepped forward reassuming the place she had relinquished to Dot midway through the cavern. She raised her arms, palms open and facing each other, then brought her hands slowly to her sides. After a couple of other hand motions in close to her body, the outline of the door appeared and the door broke free of its seal. None of them looked back. They passed into the sterile monotony of the tunnel and the quest that propelled them forward.

They waited outside the medical station, tucked back into an alleyway across the pedway from the station. Despite their leisurely pace through the cavern, they had still arrived at their destination well in advance of the shift change. They wanted to exit the medical station at the height of the chaos of shift change, so they had no choice but to wait until primary shift was about to end before they entered the station. Dot reviewed with Jerome the likeliest locations of the medication they sought. He'd managed to bring up a floor plan of the medical station aboard Home and reiterated his opinion the medication would be preserved in a liquid nitrogen deep freeze in the rear of the complex. The manager of the station was probably the only person who could operate the freezer and retrieve the sought-after medication, so they had to hope the manager worked primary shift. Jerome reminded his colleagues the manager would likely be in the office at the rear of the complex as primary shift drew to a close.

"Naomi and I will enter first, shoot the cameras with paint, and instruct any customers to," (he placed his hand over his mouth and mimicked a voice coming over an intercom), "remain calm and exit in an orderly manner." He lowered his hand and re-assumed a monotone recital of the steps he'd memorized. "Then we lock the place down and round the other employees up in the front of the station."

They'd gone over the plan before they left Home, but Dot insisted Jerome run through it again.

"While we're taking care of our business, you jump the counter," he said to Dot, "and meet the manager who'll probably be rushing up front in response to the alarm set off by the employees. You impress on the manager in your inimitable style our need for his cooperation, after which he opens the deep freeze for you and retrieves the medication. You will then check the reference data on the vial to make sure you have the right medication. We'll keep everyone calm up front until you get back. When you call to us, we jump the counter and the three of us exit the back door, avoiding the crowd that likely has formed in front of the station. We move out to our right, away from the crossing. We double time it until we hit the second alley. From there, we slow to a normal pace, turn down the alley to the parallel pedway, head back to the crossing and, hopefully reach the checkpoint without raising any alarms. If there is a guard at the checkpoint, we wait to be asked for scan access, then we blow through the crossing and break for the vent shaft on the other side. Naomi leads the way, you follow, and I bring up the rear. When we reach the vent shaft, we crack the hatch, you descend first, then Naomi, then me. If one of us is apprehended, the others go on!"

It was this last part of the plan, as essential as any other, that went against every impulse in Dot's being. She was "Commander." Though she knew she dared not turn and intervene if either of her crew were caught by DAN agents, she shuddered to think of the prospect. She silently prayed she would be spared that decision. She swallowed hard, then nodded in assent to their plan.

They waited for a half hour that seemed to stretch on for days. Jerome stood against one of the curved walls of the buildings until his back started to bother him. Then he sat cross-legged in the alley until his foot fell asleep. He stood again, and when his foot stopped tingling, he paced back and forth until Dot's arm came flying out from where she sat and caught his leg as he passed next to her. She raised her head to look at him, jaw clenched and head tilted to the side. He certainly didn't need a visor warning to know she didn't approve, so he went back to leaning against another of the curved walls.

Dot sat, closed her eyes and tried to still her mind. She visualized every step they'd take, every encounter they'd have, and tried to imagine everything going exactly as they'd planned. It wasn't that she really thought her imaginings could shape the circumstances; her visualizing was simply a relaxation technique designed to help her release her fears. It worked until Jerome started pacing. His incessant, purposeless movement and the anxiety behind it infected her calm, burning its way into her awareness, demanding a response in kind. The transmitted anxiety rushed from her brain in a neural impulse expressed through the muscles of her arm and her hand as she grabbed his leg, then through neck muscles that pulled her head up and to the side as if she was staring through him. She never opened her eyes, but Jerome could not see beyond the tinted lenses of her visor, and her message was clear without needing to employ her eyes.

Naomi stood in the center of the alley, legs spread at about shoulder width, and stared out at the pedway that intersected the alley. The foot traffic was light, and the associated white noise of commerce was barely audible. It was another form of the quiet that always came just before the storm. She sensed the tsunami of human activity rising within the buildings around them. She could feel the energy of human consciousness turn from countless, largely unrelated tasks and unite in a common desire for liberty, for ambulation, for interaction. Naomi snapped her fingers: it was time to move!

When Dot called to her compatriots and they came bounding over the counter and into the stock room of the medical center, she couldn't believe the good fortune they'd encountered. Everything had gone according to the detailed plans they'd made, with one glaring exception. That exception aside, they couldn't have hoped for the mission to go so smoothly! When they entered the station, there were no customers inside. None of the employees had offered any resistance. They seemed unable to comprehend what was happening. None of them had ever heard of a takeover robbery, let alone experienced it first hand. They complied with every request the three intruders made.

The manager, an elderly man of considerable girth and balding pate, complied with Dot's instructions to open the medication vault. He only inquired of Dot why she wanted a medication that treated an illness that no longer existed. Dot offered no response and simply repeated her request for the obscure anti-viral serum, at which point the manager entered a combination on a keypad, spun a dial, then another, and opened a compartment. As Dot reached for the vial inside the compartment, the manager grasped her arm and stopped her.

"Touch that without gloves, and you'll lose any part of your hand that makes contact."

Then he reached above his head to a shelf over the freezer and retrieved two bulky gloves. He placed them on his hands and retrieved the vile. He held it out to Dot in his gloved hand and turned the vial to expose its label asking her to make sure it was what she wanted. She looked it over and reassured him it was the right vial. He shook his head in obvious puzzlement and withdrew the vial, placed it in an insulated container, sealed the container, and handed it to Dot.

"We have more in other stations. Stealin' this won't allow you to threaten us."

His words took her back. Why would he assume she meant to threaten others by stealing this vile?

"You're the Lansing girl. I remember seein' your face on the vid. You're the one who got away. I don't know where you been hidin', and I don't care, but this isn't goin' to get you anywhere. Every Garson carries an immunity to the virus this medication treats. The virus is indigenous to this rock. We're breathin' it in right now! Releasin' more of it in the domes won't hurt a soul, so you see, confiscatin' this drug won't do you any good."

"You've been listening to too much propaganda," replied Dot. "We're not here to hurt anyone. Look at the way we've treated all of you working this Med Station. Do you hear anyone begging for mercy? We haven't touched one of your people, and we're not going to!"

"Every Garson carries an immunity to this virus, do they? Well, it just so happens that there's at least one Garson who's not immune, and I need this medication to save his life. I'm not trying to hurt anybody, I'm trying to save someone's life, so take your petty little fears and move up front with your employees. I don't have time to set you straight on this!"

Dot turned from the frumpy old man to call her comrades from the front.

"I knew your father, girl!"

If he'd stuck a gun in her back, it wouldn't have been any more effective at freezing Dot in her tracks. A part of her, the daughter forcibly parted from the father she loved, waited to hear the old man insult her father's memory, prepared to take his head off when he did. Another part of her, the commander practiced in listening beneath the words for intent and implication, registered the tone of his voice. His words rolled off his lips not with disdain or disgust, but with the odd combination of anguish and admiration. Dot turned slowly to face the heavy-set man again. He smiled.

"I lied when I said I saw you on the vid. Well, I didn't really lie, I did see you there. But I also saw you in person," he paused, then finished, "many times. Your Dad and I worked together for many years, and stayed in touch for many years after our work took us in different directions. He was more than a strong leader, a good engineer, or a famous pioneer. He was a good man. He was a good father to you kids, a good husband to your Mom, and a good friend to a great circle of us. And any of us who saw you two together couldn't help but notice how much he loved you, Dorothea!"

She nearly lost her composure at the sound of her full name and the reference to her father's love. From the time she was very young everyone called her "Dot," even her Mom. The only exception came from her father. He used her full name the way most kids' parents might use their favorite term of endearment.

Dot's mind raced. "What were the chances this man really knew her father? He could've just watched one of the family's many appearances on the vid and committed to memory the Lansing kids' names; maybe just her name? Had he actually worked with her father--he looked like he could be old enough to have been a member of the first expedition, that was for sure! Did he just happen to fall into the address he used with her or did he realize that her father used her full name as a sort of pet name?"

"Of all you kids, he felt certain you'd be the one to fill your Mom's and his shoes. He loved all of ya' of course, but he waited and watched for one of you to express a deeper sense of vision for Garsow. He was best known and celebrated for his accomplishments as an engineer, but he was consumed with being a visionary leader. He'd tell us all that one day you'd follow in his footsteps!"

He couldn't tell if he was getting through to Dot, so the old man started talking a little faster.

"Your father oversaw the building of the tunnels and then, when most of us were perfectly happy to stay there, he brought us to the surface because he saw that we could never build a better society underground. 'People need to be out under the sky,' he always said, even if the sky is black or artificially illuminated. He and your mother designed our surface structures to create a sense of belonging and interdependence. Alpha Sector looked just like the layout of an ancient Earthside Polynesian village of grass huts. They were built to provide safety and comfort to be sure, but they were also built to create a sense of community. They're large enough to meet the needs of the inhabitants but there's no wasted space. Every person on Garsow had the same amount of space--singles were paired up, couples had their own dwellings, and families moved to family quarters, slightly larger with common areas for raising the children together. He wanted so badly for this to be a place where humanity could build on the best of its values and leave behind the worst of its faults and failures. He hand-picked the first crew and even sent a few of us back when they proved to be incompatible for the society we were building."

Dot fought to stay in command, but little Dorothea, Jonathan Lansing's eldest daughter, rose from the shadows to occupy her consciousness, and Commander Dot knew she had to push the anguished daughter aside...again. She fought down the crying need within her to hear out the old man and the threads of his story that now wove their way into Dorothy's memories and through those memories to her aching heart.

"This is all very fascinating," said Dot as she put her hand up to silence the old man and cleared her throat while she fought to clear her head. Daughter Dorothea receded, as she had done so obediently every time her alter-ego demanded it. Once again, Commander Dot resumed control. She took a deep breath and laid her plan before the station manager."

"I'm here on a mission that depends on some rather exact timing and some extraordinary luck for its success. We came from the tunnels and we need to get back into them, preferably without 20 or 30 DAN agents hot on our tails. We've planned our departure to coincide with the shift change so we'll have some hope of blending into the crowds of pedestrians crossing back into Alpha Sector. Then, if we make it to the Alpha Sector gate, we're going to blow through the checkpoint while it's jammed with people and attempt to get back underground while people are too shocked to stop us. If I don't get out of here with my crew in the next five minutes or so, we're going to miss the shift change. Besides that, DAN is probably running for this station right now. They have to know we're here. I'm sure your crew tripped an alarm when we came through the door and started obliterating the security cameras."

She paused for emphasis, then looked up into the manager's visored face, "even with all of that--if one of my most important crew members' life didn't depend on me returning with this medication, I'd stay to listen to your story. His life does depend on me, though, and I can't let him down."

"Now," continued Dot after taking another deep breath, "I've got one minute for you to get to the point, if you have one, and show me the best way for my crew and I to get out of here."

Again, the old man smiled.

"Well, you've made my point for me. You are certainly everything your father might've hoped you'd be! I don't know who you're leading or the purpose of your mission, but I have to believe it's for the good of our society."

Now the station manager did something Dot could never have predicted. He reached up, disconnected his visor and removed it from his face, revealing his eyes. They were wide open, despite their sudden exposure to the light, and they burned with the passion of a man who's seen something he's waited a very long time to see. He looked through her as much as at her.

"Your Dad was right about these damn things!" he said as he waved his visor in his right hand. "Every day I have to wear it is another day in prison, as far as I'm concerned. I was too frightened to stand with you and your family, so I've got no one to blame but myself for the wires comin' out of my skull and the chips in my head. Still, if I thought I could help a cause that'd let me take this off and restore my humanity, I'd do whatever was asked of me. Somethin' tells me you're going to help us get rid of them, and if that somethin' inside me is right, I'm just glad I was still alive to see this day!"

He held his hands up to ask for Dot's patience.

"I know you have to hurry, but you may be in better shape than you think. What if I told you I might be able to help you get back to the tunnels without blowing through any checkpoints? If I can do that, would you tell me what you're doin' and, if I'm right about your purpose, give me some way to help your cause?"

"Show me how you can get us back to the tunnels and I'll do what I can to answer your need," replied Dot.

Once more, he flashed that disarming smile, made all the more endearing now that Dot could see his eyes. He motioned for her to follow him.

He led her behind the vault that held all the medications and pointed to the floor. She recognized it immediately--the sealed hatch of a tunnel vent shaft!

"Every medical station has one!" said the station manager. "It gives the service techs access to all the equipment that maintains the medication vault--the liquid nitrogen canisters and other stuff I've never cared about enough to understand. You'd know better than I whether or not you could get to where you need to be from beneath this station. I don't know the tunnels at all--in that regard, I won't be any help to you."

Dot turned from the station manager to find Jerome and ask if he knew whether they could get back to the Alpha Sector tunnels from beneath the Beta Sector medical station. They had to know for certain whether or not the tunnels were interconnected. They couldn't afford to wander in the tunnels looking for some way back to Alpha Sector. Even if they eventually managed to find their way back, Slink would die while they bounced around in Beta Sector passages looking for one that would get them back to Alpha Sector and Home.

When she rounded the vault, Dot was surprised to find Jerome and Naomi had already jumped the counter and found their way to the back of the station.

"What the hell is going on?" asked Jerome. "We should've been out of here ten minutes ago. Are you all right?"

"I'm fine. I'll catch you up after we get back into the tunnels, but right now I just need to know one thing," said Dot. "Do you know whether we can cross from Beta Sector tunnels into Alpha Sector without losing too much time? We might be able to take a shortcut from here back into the tunnels if you can get us from a tunnel right under this station to the rendezvous point in Alpha Sector."

"Getting from a tunnel underneath this station to one in Alpha Sector is no problem," said Jerome. "The problem is getting into the tunnels from the Beta Sector surface. There are no vent shafts in this sector. Remember, no one ever intended to live in the tunnels underneath this Sector. It was built long after all the settlers had moved to the surface. I hate to be the bearer of bad news, but unless they've got industrial cutting torches stored in this back room, we've got no way into the tunnels from this sector."

"Are the station employees OK?" asked Dot, wanting to tie up this loose end.

"They're fine," said Naomi, glancing at Jerome.

"They weren't interested in offering any resistance," said Jerome. "We bound them loosely--they could escape their bindings if they really wanted to. Naomi wanted to tie them more tightly and gag them, but I insisted we leave things as they are. I don't really know why, and if I should have done as Naomi wanted, I'll go back up front and take care of it."

"I think Naomi's initial response to my question was right on--they're fine. Come back here, Jerome, I need to show you something," Dot said as she turned back toward the space between the vault and the back of the room.

Jerome followed her.

A moment later Naomi heard Jerome exclaim, "Well, I'll be damned!"

A second later, Dot came back around the vault and into Naomi's line of sight. She waved Naomi forward.

"We're going out this way," said Dot.

As usual Naomi said nothing, just shrugged her shoulders and followed Dot back to the now crowded area behind the vault. The station manager was squeezed as far back against the wall as he could get. Jerome was crouched over what Naomi recognized immediately as a vent shaft hatch. The manager threw him a key, he unlatched the locking mechanism, and with a loud "swoosh" of air, popped it open and flipped it back. He tossed the key back to the manager.

Dot turned her head away from her comrades and spoke to the manager.

"I need to talk to you, and to hear the rest of your story. I want to sit down opposite each other, share a meal, and get to know one another. That's all going to have to wait, but I at least need to know your name!" Dot said as she stepped forward.

"It's Gregorio," he said. "And I'd love to share a good meal and a story, especially if you'd be willing to tell me one in return. I understand your need for haste; we'll have to trust we'll see each other again."

"I'll leave in a minute, Gregorio, but I have to take enough time to keep my part of our bargain."

She took a deep breath and then spoke in hurried tones.

"I am the commander of the underground resistance known to most people as the Technoids. We are not blindly opposed to technology as your news media would have you think. We make great use of technology. We are opposed to dehumanizing applications of technology like the commlink. Our opposition to the commlink has led us to set as our highest priority bringing down the Supernet."

Gregorio drew a deep breath across his clenched teeth, making a loud whistling noise. He looked as though he wanted to speak, then thought better of it and made small circles with his right hand to signal Dot to continue.

"Doing so is the only way to break the hold of the commlink over our society. We know our success will bring chaos to all of you. If we could find another way, we'd pursue it. There is no other way--the commlink is too deeply embedded into Garson culture. We're past the point of convincing people to reject it. We must now disable it and force people to live without it. When we've accomplished our mission, we'll return to the surface to help rebuild a society without the commlink. Some will undoubtedly want to arrest us and perhaps even kill us. We'll take that risk to offer our help. I think calmer heads will prevail and those prevailing voices will belong to people who recognize that we who have lived our lives without the commlink are better suited than anyone else to aid in rebuilding a healthy society."

"As to how you might help us. Your help today is more than we could ever ask. We've never before received aid from a surface-dweller, so your aid means more than you can ever know. Nonetheless, I think we could both benefit by ongoing contact. If you'll give me your messaging address, I'll send you correspondence as soon as I'm able. If you choose to respond, I'd be grateful. I'd especially be interested in any information you might gather as to the condition and whereabouts of my family. The last I heard, they were being detained in correctional centers or nurseries. Any specifics you might discover would be most welcome information, indeed!"

"Gregorio, I thank you for giving us safe passage. I wish you well and hope we'll see each other again. Will you be all right when DAN reaches this station and discovers we're gone?"

"My crew and I will be fine," said Gregorio. "They share my, shall we say, 'odd perspective?' We have access to classified Garson medical reports and studies, so we know more about the effects of the commlink than our fellow citizens. Those in our position fall into one of two extremes. Either they are zealous in their support of the commlink or they are zealous in their opposition. None are ambivalent after they understand the full effect of the implants. Those of us who oppose the commlink have learned how to recognize each other and have banded together, though we dare not offer any public opposition. With your permission, I'll spread the news of your mission with those I know to be trustworthy, and we'll discuss how we might be of greatest support to you. I'll give you my messaging address and when I receive your initial message, I'll offer whatever help we've determined is within our abilities."

"As to your family, I know very little, but I will seek information on each of them. I do know this--your parents are still alive..."

Dot leaned in toward the man and Gregorio attempted a weak smile.

"I should qualify my statement by saying I received a report indicating your parents were alive a few days ago. That same report suggested your father is in poor health. We have reason to believe they're being held in isolation from other detainees, though still somewhere within the confines of the central Beta Sector Correctional Center."

"Now you've aided my spirits as well as my cause!" exclaimed Dot. "Thank you, Gregorio. I'll message you as soon as we're safe and I've delivered this medication to the one whose desperate need brought us here."

"Go!" said Gregorio. "I'll be able to deflect DAN after you're gone, but we dare not allow them to find you here. I count myself blessed to have seen this day. Let it end well--go!"

Naomi was the first to descend the shaft ladder and she gave the all clear a few seconds after she dropped to the floor of the tunnel. Gregorio closed the hatch as soon as Dot followed Jerome into the shaft. They dropped beside Naomi and found they were in a small alcove off the tunnel. Tanks and other unrecognizable equipment filled all but a small area of the alcove. They walked through an unobstructed arched opening into the tunnel. The Beta Sector tunnels were narrower than in Alpha Sector, but otherwise much the same.

Naomi pulled out her locator and double checked their heading. A few seconds later, she pointed in one direction down the tunnel and waited for Dot to assume point or direct her to do so. Dot motioned for Naomi to lead the way.

They'd only walked a few hundred meters before they saw another open archway in the tunnel wall much like the one they'd just vacated. Naomi motioned for her companions to hang back while she poked her head into the opening and looked around. It opened onto another tunnel obstructed by a door about four meters beyond the arched opening in the main tunnel wall. Naomi motioned for her companions to join her.

When her companions advanced toward the opening, she turned and surveyed the door. It was molded from indigenous materials and looked like any of the doors along the tunnels.

When the construction crews molded the natural caverns into uniform service tunnels or used torches to cut tunnels, they would create small hollows every few hundred meters and seal those hollows with airtight doors. Most of the hollows contained service equipment for installing or modifying electrical wiring or conduit. A few contained specialized equipment like the one they entered beneath the medical station. Naomi was fairly confident this door did not lead into one of these small hollows but into a linking tunnel between Alpha and Beta Sector. The doors were almost never locked. Naomi placed both hands under the lever that protruded half way up the door on the right side and pulled upward. The latch moved smoothly at first, caught, then with a loud, metallic grinding noise moved slowly upward again until the door swung outward with a loud gushing sound as air burst through the opening, equalizing the pressure between the two chambers. Naomi walked around the edge of the open door and leaned into it, pushing it the rest of the way open.

The passageway on the other side of the door was less than seven feet around and the floor was narrow enough to limit passage to one person at a time. Naomi shined the beam from her lumawand into the passage and she could see at the far end another door identical to the one she'd just opened. Dot and Jerome came up behind her and Naomi related her findings.

"You lead the way, Jerome will follow, and I'll bring up the rear. I'll close this door once we're all inside the passageway. I think the doors are designed to compress the air inside the passage to aid in opening the doors outward into the tunnels they link. When you reach the other door, it should open outward into the Alpha Sector tunnel without too much effort. We don't have any way of knowing what we're going to find on the other side of that door, so use caution."

Naomi acknowledged Dot's words with a nod, though her slight smirk suggested Dot's warning amused her or irritated her-- it was hard to tell which. Jerome didn't waste time trying to figure out what Naomi was feeling; he just prepared himself to cover her when she popped the door open and stepped into the tunnel.

The door at the far end of the passage popped open with the expected burst of air and Naomi placed her shoulder against the door and began to push it open. The door moved on its hinges ever so slowly. Naomi leaned into the door and grunted as she pushed against it to create an opening she and her comrades could pass through. Just as the door opened enough to allow her to pass through the doorway, a hand came from around the back side of the opening door, grabbed a handful of Naomi's jump suit and yanked her out into the tunnel. Jerome leaped forward instinctively to try and grab her. He missed. A moment later, someone grabbed him and pulled him clear of the doorway. At the same time, another person shoved passed him and yelled into the passageway.

"Get down on the ground and stay there if you want to live!"

Under his breath, Jerome cursed their luck at stumbling into a DAN patrol, then cursed out loud; then his mind registered the words tumbling from the the man who'd forced his way past him as he was being yanked from the passageway.

"Sorry, Commander, we didn't know what to expect when that door suddenly broke open toward us. We had strict orders to intercept anyone who came through the door. We never expected you'd be coming from that direction. Are you OK?"

Jerome was only marginally aware of Dot's response. His attention was on the full head of red hair framing the bright blue eyes of one of the Technoid rendezvous party. He'd been jerked from the passageway by a brawny man who'd thrown him clear of the doorway before rushing through it to back up the man who'd barked the order to get down a moment before. Now the young owner of long red locks pulled him to his feet and chided him for cursing his rescue party.

"That's no way to speak to your friends," she said. "I'd hate to hear how you'd greet your enemies!"

"Sorry about that," Jerome stammered. "I thought you were DAN agents."

"Do we look like fearsome DAN agents?" she asked, knowing her gentle ribbing was flustering the pretentious young medtech and enjoying every minute of it. She'd also started to attract an audience from the other members of the rendezvous party, and they roared with laughter at her jibe about their appearance. Jerome had no way of knowing the young woman had an ulterior motive for teasing him. He'd been too preoccupied to notice Anntherese the many times she'd concocted some excuse to stop by sick bay. He didn't even realize the young woman teasing him was the same one who'd interrupted his work in the sick bay half a dozen times over the last few weeks. Now she enjoyed his complete attention, in addition to the attention of an appreciative audience, and she wasn't going to relinquish it easily.

"And here I always thought they'd be wearing visors and packing weapons--in other words, I thought they'd look more like...you!"

Jerome had completely forgotten he still had his fake visor on, and he reached up and pulled it from his face as Anntherese and the other Technoids burst into laughter a second time. By this time, Jerome felt relief wash over him and his sense of humor returned. He decided to turn the tables on the young woman and see how she handled the heat.

"OK, just because you're cute doesn't give you license to be a smart ass," he said.

"I suppose you'd correctly identify the person whose arm reached around a door and yanked your comrade through a doorway. And I guess you'd recognize your friends when one of them grabbed you and threw you to the ground. I envy your extraordinary perceptions. I don't have your quick wits, so I just had to rely on my instincts. Unfortunately, my instincts saw a threat instead of your pretty red hair and deep blue eyes. Now that I have my wits about me, I can see you're a friend with whom I would be well served to be especially friendly. If you want to accompany me, I know a nice place where we can get a drink, and I can treat you with the deference you deserve."

The cat calls went up from their audience as soon as Jerome finished speaking and everyone turned to Anntherese to hear her response. The color rose in her cheeks and she looked down at the ground, momentarily rendered speechless. Dot rescued her from the need to respond.

"OK, OK, we'll have time for all manner of touching homecomings, but now we need to tend to duty," she said. Turning to the man who'd rushed into the tunnel and barked the order to get down, she continued, "Captain, lead the way. We're ready to go Home!"

Chapter 12

"Providence wants you alive, the way I see it," said Gen.

Slink was shaking his head in disbelief over the story of Dot's quest to obtain the medication that had saved his life.

"I mean, think about it, little man," Gen continued. "If you were not the Commander's nephew, she might've dispatched a surface excursion to try to retrieve the medication, but she certainly wouldn't have led that excursion. And if she wasn't leading the excursion, who knows whether or not the excursion could've ever blown through the checkpoint and escaped the surface with the medication. One thing for sure, we wouldn't have made contact with the surface opposition through the station manager. He only revealed himself because he recognized Dot."

"By the way, that connection has proved more helpful than any of us could've ever imagined. Dot is anxious to have your help to analyze and interpret the data Gregorio's group is sending us. Even without your extraordinary mind, we're moving ever closer to our goal. When you're up to it, we're ready to move into the final phase of preparations for our attack on the Supernet."

I'm ready now--let's go," said Slink as he sat up and started to slide off the side of the bed.

Gen reached for Slink to prevent him from sliding off the bed. Before he could even reach him, Slink fell back on the bed awkwardly, overcome by sudden vertigo. He started to retch as his stomach revolted in response to the dizziness.

"Easy, little man! You aren't going anywhere for a while. Your system's been messed up pretty bad, but the good news is you should recover completely--with enough time and rest. Our research indicates your remaining symptoms should dissipate over the next two or three days. After that, you'll probably need two or three more days of electrical stimulation and physical therapy to regain enough strength to start back to work--part time, of course," he added quickly.

Gen helped Slink stretch back out on his cot as his dizziness passed and the nausea eased. He tussled Slink's hair playfully and shook his head as Slink rolled his eyes in protest.

"Very part time," offered another voice from behind the curtain that was drawn across the adjacent cubicle. "And even that is a ways off yet, young man."

Jenna pulled the curtain back and peaked out from the cubicle. She caught Slink's eyes through the transparent panels that separated them before winking at him and stepping into the hallway and around into his cubicle. She leaned over one end of his cot and kissed him, lingering for a moment before withdrawing and taking a seat next to him.

"You two ought to have some time alone," said Gen. "Besides, playing the storyteller has worn me out. I think I'm going to head to the Mess and see if I can find something to eat. Want anything?"

"I think a big plate of gorp would do nicely," said Slink. "And maybe a banana split for desert."

"I'll take that as a 'no thank you,'" replied Gen. The chef's concoction of leftovers they called "gorp" was the subject of universal derision amongst the crew. Slink had always replied to any inquiry about dessert with a request for a banana split--it was a delicacy whose ingredients were too exotic on Garsow for any but the most privileged.

"Actually," said Slink, "I think I could tolerate a little soup."

"Soup it is," said Gen. "How about you, Jenna?"

"I'll take some soup, too, if you don't mind," she replied.

"Two bowls of soup. I think I can handle that. See you two love birds in half an hour or so."

Gen turned and disappeared through the open sick bay doors. The doors swished closed behind him.

Slink reached up and ran his fingers over Jenna's braids. He wrapped his hand around the back of her head and pulled her face down toward his. They kissed again, this time lingering a little longer. A few moments and several long kisses later, Jenna pulled her head back and stared into Slink's eyes. Her dark brown eyes filled with tears and rolled onto her high cheekbones, then dripped off her face and onto the blanket Slink had pulled up over his chest.

"Hey now, you're going to soil the sickbay blankets," Slink joked. He reached up and with his thumbs gently wiped the tears from her face. "What's wrong, J?" he asked.

"Nothing." She lowered her eyes and stared at the spots on the blanket where her tears had landed. A moment later she looked back up at him again. "Nothing's wrong, Slink, really," she said to reassure him.

"I was just so afraid I was going to lose you. Now, every time I look at you I have a hard time not breaking into tears."

Her eyes filled with tears again. Slink reached up to her and pulled her down for another long, gentle kiss.

"I don't deserve your devotion," he said. Now his eyes filled with tears. "But I'm so grateful to have it. You mean so much to me, J, more than I ever thought possible!"

He pulled her into him. She climbed up next to him on the cot and he wrapped his arms around her. They held each other until they heard the doors of the sickbay open followed by Gen gently clearing his throat.

Slink's recovery progressed more rapidly than anyone could have expected, with the notable exception of Slink himself. He'd insisted he'd be back at his station much sooner than the week to ten days the medtechs had suggested. In fact, he was insisting he felt no dizziness or nausea a couple days after he awakened from his coma and demanded they start his rehabilitation. Against their better judgment, the medical staff complied, releasing him at night to sleep in the men's barracks. After three days of rehabilitation, Slink convinced everyone involved to allow him to return to his work in the Cave. He was to start slowly, two hours each of the first couple days, a half shift the remainder of the first week with a re-evaluation to follow his first week back at his work station. He worked a half shift the first couple days and dove into full-time work after that, pushing aside any concern.

"It's going to overtax my system and the systems of anyone around me if I have to go back to wandering around with nothing to do!" Slink insisted. He was sitting in the sickbay late one evening, debating the merits of his decisions with Jerome at his overdue one-week check up. "I sit and stare at a monitor all day. How taxing can that be?"

"We don't know if the virus affected your brain in any way," said Jerome, frustrated with the head-strong Slink. "We performed a body scan and discovered the inflammation of your major organs, but the plate in your skull prevented us from determining if the brain was involved. We're just trying..."

"What plate in my skull?" interrupted Slink. "I don't have a plate in my skull."

"Technically, I suppose you're right," replied Jerome. "You have six of them! It looks like your skull may have been underdeveloped when you were born or you suffered some head trauma later in childhood, and the doctors decided to encase your brain

301

with a series of plates. I'm amazed you don't have any memory of surgeries. Some of those surgeries had to be done well after your fifth birthday to allow for your growing brain. You don't recall having any surgery on your head?"

"I don't remember having any surgery anywhere!" said Slink.

"You don't remember ever wearing any protective head gear?" asked Jerome?

"You mean like some kind of helmet? No, I never wore anything! Like I said, I never had any surgery."

"Well Slink, how much do you remember from your child-hood before, say, age six?"

"Not much--but who does?" asked Slink.

"Do you remember anything at all?" Jerome persisted.

"I don't know--what does this have to do with anything?" growled Slink. "I thought we were arguing about whether or not I should return to work full time. If I was born with some kind of birth defect and they put a plate in my head, I really don't care. I just want to get back to work!"

"Yeah, sure Slink," replied Jerome. "It's no big deal. I was just saying that we couldn't get any reliable images of your brain, so I just wanted to error on the side of caution. The fact of the mat-ter is—you're showing no ill effects from your brush with death. Like you say, it'll probably be good for you to get back to work. Just do me one favor."

"What?" asked Slink.

"Come and see me if you start to get headaches, feel dizzy, or experience blurred vision, OK?"

"Whatever you say--you're the medtech," said Slink.

He turned and walked out of the sickbay without so much as saying goodbye.

Jerome, for his part, was more than a little puzzled by their exchange.

"How could Slink have undergone childhood surgeries on his skull without any memory of the surgeries or the follow-up care that would surely have included his wearing protective head gear around the clock?" thought Jerome. "Maybe it was so traumatic he blocked the whole experience out," he reasoned.

Now and again, over the subsequent weeks, Jerome returned to the films they'd taken of Slink's head. He'd never seen anything like Slink's cranial plates. It was almost as if his skull had been replaced with metal plates. They covered almost his entire cranium. They couldn't have been implanted all at once, and the more Jerome looked at his films, the more he was convinced they'd have been implanted later in Slink's childhood, certainly after his fifth birthday, probably even later than that. And Slink had no memory of any surgeries! He searched his own mind and his research texts repeatedly, but he couldn't find an explanation for the surgeries, the lack of any noticeable scars, and Slink's blank memory. He couldn't help but wonder if Slink had been subjected to his surgeries for some more sinister reason than remedying a birth defect or head injury. Finally, after another late night looking over the films and pondering their meaning, Jerome decided to let it go.

"Pushing the issue with Slink isn't going to help him," thought Jerome. "If Slink was traumatized as a child and forgot the events of his trauma, he's not the first, and sadly, he's not going to be the last, either. Someday, if nightmarish memories suddenly arise in his mind or someone reveals a more diabolical reason for his cranial plates, he'll be older and wiser and better prepared to deal with any trauma it brings up." Jerome assured himself, "Best to leave a sleeping dog lie."

Jerome went around the sickbay and shut down for the night. He chuckled to himself at the odd colloquialism that had just arisen in his mind as he reached his conclusion. It was yet another of those phrases that surely referred to once common experiences but meant nothing to anyone who spent his life on an outpost without a single dog, let alone a slumbering one. He assumed that dogs must have been somewhat dangerous when they first awoke.

"Why the hell would you keep something like that around anyway?" he wondered.

Slink suffered no setbacks as a result of his decision to push himself beyond the recommendations of the medical staff. He thrived. The Cave was alive with energy, and Slink both fed on it and added to it. Everyone sensed they'd soon discover the Achilles' heal of the Supernet, and when they did, they were confident Dot would order them to bring the network down.

They discovered a number of vulnerabilities in the network hardware that would have allowed them to scramble transmissions and create instantaneous and universal chaos. It was not enough. They discovered "back doors" in the network software and quickly figured out how they could paralyze the Supernet for days or even weeks while the technicians scrambled to restore servers from back up files. It was not enough.

At one of their weekly briefings Dot laid out what they needed, "When we strike, we must strike a fatal blow! If we succeed only in interrupting the status quo for a few days or even weeks we will, in the end, have only strengthened the Ideal Society. If they can fix the damage we've inflicted, they'll bolster their defenses and seek and destroy any opposition. They'll have the full support of the public, and our opportunity will be forever lost. If we have to work longer, harder, and smarter, that's what we'll do."

Slink and Chris quickly voiced their agreement. They knew they'd have only one opportunity. They embraced the substantial challenge of making sure an attack would destroy the Supernet before it was deployed. To do so, they set about building the most substantial database network they could conceive, replete with the strongest encryption and firewall Slink could develop. The network servers took over three months to build and required four of the Cave consultants give up their work stations to house the servers. The Technoids undertook numerous surface excursions to acquire the hardware piece by painstaking piece.

Fortunately, Gen's efforts to tighten security within the Tunnel Rat enclaves bore fruit, reducing the risk of the excursions. One night, when most of the members of a large Tunnel Rat enclave called Georgia were either asleep or out on excursion, a slender athletic young woman stole out from the enclave and into the tunnels. She made her way to a sealed hollow bearing the mark of Garson Tunnel Maintenance. She bent and pulled a memory coin from her cloak. As she squatted to place the coin under the door, she was apprehended by two Tunnel Rats who had followed her undetected. She struggled only briefly.

They escorted her back to the enclave and determined the coin contained information on the location of the enclave, scheduled excursions, and targets of those excursions. She was convicted of treason by the enclave governing council, bound, and carried to the surface, where she was placed along a busy pedway a half hour before the morning chime sounded.

The excursions to acquire parts for the new network were always carried out to look like industrial vandalism. Jenna oversaw the coordination of the excursions. The Tunnel Rats led the excursions, taking the greatest risks to reach and return from the targets and suffering nearly all the casualties. The Technoids contributed only two members to each of these excursions, and those two knew only what components they were to acquire without reference to their ultimate application. Dot, Gen, Chris, and Slink had conferred on this matter as well, and decided no one with substantial knowledge of their project or its goals could be put at risk. No one could endure prolonged interrogation, and they dared not tip off DAN to the extent of their preparations and progress. They never stole an entire server or station. Instead, they would dismantle larger pieces of equipment, leaving most of their component parts strewn about the office where they'd been housed and taking one or two components for their use. Then they'd fire paint balls randomly throughout the room to further conceal their purpose.

Their activities raised the ire of surface dwellers and turned public opinion against them even amongst those Garsons who had previously been apathetic or ambivalent toward the tunnel dwellers. Most surface dwellers made no distinction between Tunnel Rats and Technoids. They were all Tunnel Rats in their minds. As long as the Tunnel Rats limited their thefts to castoffs and refuse, the surface dwellers were willing to tolerate the Tunnel Rats' existence. Many surface dwellers even expressed pity for the poor unfortunates or castoffs. Their pity and tolerance turned quickly to condemnation and vilification, as more and more surface dwellers entered workplaces violated by a break-in.

Dot had hoped such a turn of events could be avoided. She didn't want to antagonize the surface dwellers if it could be avoided. Unfortunately, it could not. She knew the actions they now took to build a test network would make reunification with the surface far more difficult. She could see two compelling reasons for continuing on their current course despite the damage it was doing to their relationship with the surface dwellers. The more compelling of these reasons came in their need for a much more complex network against which they might test any weapon they developed to bring down the Supernet. Secondarily, she was confident the surface dwellers' desperate need after the collapse would lead them to welcome the assistance of the Technoids, however reluctant that welcome might be. She ordered the excursions to continue until Chris and Slink indicated their needs had been met.

Twice a week at odd intervals excursion parties of eight people, six Tunnel Rats and two Technoids, stole into the laboratories and office buildings of Beta Sector and harvested parts for what Slink affectionately called "Son of Supernet."

DAN agents identified and sealed every vent shaft hatch they could identify in Alpha Sector. They tripled the night shift guard at all three crossings between Alpha and Beta Sectors. Still the reports of break-ins with their attendant vandalism poured in. For a presumably unsophisticated band of outcasts, the Tunnel Rats were proving to be a formidable foe. The public frustration with DAN rose to a fever pitch. The long-standing director of DAN and most senior commanders were released or demoted. Still the reports came.

Speculation grew rampant on the surface that the tunnel dwellers had found some way to infiltrate and assimilate into surface society. Security was increased in all sectors and liberties were curtailed.

Amongst those liberties temporarily suspended was the freedom to move about outside one's dwelling after the evening chimes. Social mixers were suspended, and anyone found on the pedways after evening chimes had to carry an authorization from their workplace detailing work-related reasons they were required to be about. Those found outside their dwellings without authorization were cited upon the first offense, escorted to their dwelling where their identity was further confirmed, and placed under even more restrictive curfew. Notation of their citation and consequent curfew restriction was placed on file so any subsequent offense would result in their arrest and detainment.

In addition, passage through the Sector crossings was monitored far more closely, with each Garson enduring a deep scan before being allowed to cross. The short walk across the crossing went from taking an average of five minutes to commonly requiring 30 minutes or more. Frustration mounted in all circles of society. At first, the frustration was focused on the governing council, but public service announcements interspersed with all vid programming shifted the blame to the Tunnel Rats and encouraged citizens to report any suspicious behavior of neighbors, acquaintances, and even friends or family. An air of suspicion replaced the extraordinary atmosphere of trust that had been touted as one of the greatest benefits to living in commlinked society.

With the advent of the commlink, Garsons had grown unaccustomed to questioning appearances or detecting duplicity. They trusted the feedback on their commlinks to relay correct information, including the identity of others and the veracity of their words. The idea that someone could masquerade as a trustworthy member of society and all the while be a member of an underground organization would have been extremely disturbing to most Garsons if that organization was harmless.

The daily reports of break-ins, plots, and even assaults by the underground opposition quickly took Garsons from disturbed to terrified. The fear that this new enemy could be living amongst them, unknown and nearly undetectable, shook the foundation of their society.

All the while, the excursion parties ventured from their safe havens in the tunnels or aboard converted sweeper drones to the surface of Beta Sector through the access hatches built into the medical stations. The providential meeting with Gregorio had proved most profitable for their cause. With his help, the Technoids were able to enter Beta Sector through any of three different stations, slip into surrounding buildings and make their acquisitions, and return to the tunnels by the same route without ever being detected. With most of the security being focused in Alpha Sector, around the now sealed hatches known to be used by the Technoids, and at the crossings into Beta Sector, the excursions found less opposition than would ordinarily have been the case.

If they were stopped while they were out on the pedways traveling from one of the medical stations or returning to it, they had forged medical authorization for being out after curfew. Since the work of building the test network went in fits and starts, Slink had also worked with a small team of Cave consultants to refine the visors and transmitters worn by the members of surface excursions so they could withstand a deeper scan by a DAN agent without raising suspicion. Unless one of the excursion party broke down and blurted out their true identity or the party was subjected to a physical search while they were carrying components they'd just acquired from a nearby lab or office, the chances of their apprehension was virtually nil.

So the excursions sought out components for the network and other supplies for daily living with relative impunity. The anxiety of the surface dwellers increased on a daily basis. And the inevitable clash between surface ideals and tunnel vision grew ever closer.

Slink's illness didn't dull his affinity for his work. He needed a couple of days to absorb the developments that had occurred while he was away, but that was to be expected. Once he was up to speed, the connections between various bits of information jumped out at him like route lines on a map. As he recognized the connections and brought disparate pieces of data together, they seemed to fit like puzzle pieces to form a picture of the Supernet and the members of Garson society networked together through their commlinks. The more he learned, the more disturbed he became at the implications of the picture that emerged as the pieces came together. He might have spent every waking minute trying to coax from the data a complete image of linked society, but the three people closest to him would not allow that to happen.

Jenna went so far as to meet surreptitiously with Chris, the Cave convener, and extract assurances from him that Slink would not be allowed to remain in the Cave after they closed it each evening. By that time, Slink had already prevailed in his request to extend the hours of Cave sessions by an hour each day. Jenna knew Slink was determined to fulfill his responsibilities to their quest, but she feared that he would be consumed by that determination unless he was forced to focus some of his attention elsewhere. Of course, she had a vested interest in seeing that Slink reserve some energy for other concerns.

Jenna became more valuable each day in her role as ambassador to the Tunnel Rats as she oversaw the detailed preparations for surface excursions and coordinated the various cooperative efforts of the Tunnel Rats and Technoids. Even Gen felt that she was quickly becoming a better ambassador than he had ever been. She, too, could have been completely absorbed in her work, but unlike Slink, her makeup would no sooner allow such self-absorption than it would allow her to cut off one of her limbs. She was a gregarious, extroverted, intelligent woman, but she was nothing if not fiercely loyal to her relationships, beginning with those closest to her and working outward in ever widening circles.

She was never confused as to her most important commitment: maintaining and strengthening her relationship with Slink. Left to his own devices, he might have lost himself in his work, but Jenna would never make such a mistake, and knowing him better than anyone else, she would not allow him to be destroyed by his own obsessions.

She recruited and trained a capable assistant and accelerated his training with regard to face-to-face interactions with the Tunnel Rats. Then she talked with Gen and Dot about her need for her travel to be kept to a minimum so she could be available to support Slink. She requested that her new assistant be elevated to Assistant Ambassador well in advance of the established timeline for such a promotion. Gen and Dot saw the wisdom of her request and were more than happy to grant it.

She then asked for assurance that the four of them would continue to maintain their close personal ties. She was very open with regard to her desire for closer friendships with both Dot and Gen and less forthright about her concerns for Slink. Dot and Gen recognized and appreciated both of her motives. They, too, had concerns that Slink was driving himself too hard, and they'd determined, apart from Jenna, to do everything they could to help Slink maintain some balance in his life.

Dot felt especially responsible for Slink since she'd solicited his help with the many projects that now centered around him. She knew how important he was to their success, but after his brush with death, she was more aware than ever of his importance to her personally. She saw how his gifts for data processing and analysis were both boon and bane for him. His mind seemed to shift into another gear when he sat at his station and in some ways he seemed to be most alive at those times. His eyes widened, as if to take in everything he saw all at once. He sat erect, his head hardly moving, while his hands became a blur above the interactive screen and his voice uttered a steady stream of commands turning the screen into a blur of changing images.

However, there was a trade off for his extraordinary concentration. He was so thoroughly disconnected from everything and everyone around him he might as well have been in an isolation chamber. The longer he remained at his station, the more resistant he was to leaving it, even to eat or take care of his personal needs. He'd unknowingly soaked himself in his own urine on more than one occasion, and was only aware of his embarrassing circumstances after Chris drew him away from his work.

Even before Jenna had approached him, Chris established a regimented schedule for the entire Cave in order to create a structure of mandatory breaks every two to two-and-a-half hours. This way, he could assure that Slink didn't surrender himself completely to the demands of his work. Jenna had drawn Chris' attention to the fact that Slink was re-entering the Cave after Slink had dinner with her and working late into or even through the night. Chris confronted Slink, who reluctantly acknowledged his violation even as he tried to justify his actions. In the presence of all his colleagues, Slink apologized for his conduct and agreed to be bound by the same boundaries that applied to all Cave consultants.

Chris had called upon Dot and expressed his concern for Slink. He told her he was convinced Slink would literally work himself to death unless someone placed limits on his work hours. He shared how he'd seen the young man with Jenna or even with Dot or Gen, and he knew Slink's value to the resistance went far beyond his analytical skills. Dot listened and thanked Chris for his insights and concern. Chris had told her nothing about Slink that she didn't already know, but he'd relayed the depth of his concern for her nephew, and she was gratified to hear it.

Dot thanked Chris for his attentiveness and intervention to protect her nephew. She shuddered to think of Slink reduced to the same end from which they were trying to deliver their surface counterparts. She would not allow that to happen to a human being under her command--whether through the implantation of a commlink or the exploitation of that person's innate character. She could see that Chris shared her determination in that respect.

That night, she thought of Chris, Gen, Jenna, and her amazing nephew Slink, and she slipped off to sleep with the awareness of her good fortune at being surrounded by such good people. They were each extraordinary individuals whose profound skills had drawn them to her attention. She had always recognized talent when it revealed itself to her. She had always surrounded herself with talented people, as had her parents. Her inner circle was filled with extraordinary people, but that night she was especially aware those same people were more than talented, they were good people, and that knowledge gave her peace of mind and restful sleep.

At first, Slink was only mildly aware of his double nature. When he wasn't sitting in front of his work station, he had little awareness of the effect his work had on him. When he was in the company of friends, he almost lost sight of his work altogether and he reveled in the waves of pleasant emotion that washed over him. When he was with Jenna, and to a lesser extent when he was with Gen or Dot, he felt a heightened awareness of each moment-- a conscious appreciation of all the little things, like Jenna's animated facial expressions when she spoke, like her sweet, musky smell when she drew close to him, like Gen's extraordinary listening skills, and like Dot's openness to his every expression. Occasionally, he also felt a wave of fear sweep over him when he recognized the depth of his feeling for others. He'd known loss, and he knew the pain of past losses would pale in comparison to the pain he'd feel if he lost Jenna or Dot or Gen. Nonetheless, he gave himself over to the joys of life and to the love he shared with his inner circle.

Even after he left Jenna or the others, he'd sometimes carry into his solitary moments the contentment he felt in their company. He'd prepare for sleep or attend to other personal matters content in the knowledge his life was good. His contentment also made it a little easier to bear the absence of Neoko. He'd vowed he'd never forget her, though the vow was unnecessary. He couldn't have forgotten the woman who'd led him to freedom if he'd tried. He'd never stop hoping for the day of her rescue.

If he stopped to think about it, though, he could see how over the past few weeks his attention would shift to his work the moment he left his friends. He'd no sooner reach the men's quarters then he'd start seeing his station and the endless data that waited there and he'd drop into a near trance. He could sit motionless for hours at a time on his bunk or stand unmoving before a mirror in the men's showers until someone interrupted his reverie and called him back to the present moment. He sometimes found it odd to recognize how much time had passed after one of these periods, but he never carried enough awareness from his ruminations to be concerned with their power over him. It was as if he'd been dreaming and could only grasp small fragments of those dreams after awakening. It never dawned on him that most people didn't get lost in daydreams lasting more than a few minutes, let alone an hour or even several hours.

The first time he caught an objective glimpse of the power his work held over him, he was with Dot in her quarters to practice meditation. They'd both settled into their respective postures, Slink in what he'd come to know as a half-lotus, sitting on a pillow, legs crossed in front of him one over the other, and Dot in a kind of kneeling position with a miniature little bench Slink had learned to call a prayer bench placed behind her just above her ankles to bear her weight. Slink entered the silence after taking a few deep, cleansing breaths and sought a connection with what he'd come to call "the nothingness."

He'd learned he felt most peaceful and serene when his center seemed to be just below his solar plexus, in his lower abdomen. He relaxed and watched his breath to see where it seemed to stop. If it filled his upper chest and puffed him up like a rooster, his center was too high, and he'd learned these were the times when he tended to be uneasy, impatient, and irritable. If he entered the silence and found himself taking shallow breaths and holding his center too high, he'd learned to deepen his breaths, hold his shoulders steady, and let his breath seem to pass right through his lungs and into his lower abdomen. In this manner, he could bring his center down, and as it came down, his mind slowed and the uneasiness gave way to serenity, the impatience gave way to mindfulness, and the irritability gave way to acceptance.

Slink first began to notice something was amiss as he and Dot sat across from each other and he tried to enter the silence only to find his center felt like it was up near his throat. He slowed and deepened his breath trying to gently lower his center and felt his mind erupt with energy. It was as if someone had thrown a switch and his mind had instantly been engulfed in a storm. The more he tried to relax and quiet his mind, the more the storm threatened to overwhelm him.

After several minutes of trying to slow down and make a connection to the nothingness without success, he decided to do something completely out of character. He asked for help.

"Dot...I'm sorry to interrupt the silence," he said hesitantly.

Dot opened her eyes, smiled, and nodded at him.

"I can't quiet my mind," said Slink. "No, it's worse than that. If I was just having trouble embracing silence, that wouldn't be so bad. There's something else going on."

Dot waited, but Slink didn't say anything else. He just unfolded his legs in front of him, then raised his knees and wrapped his arms around his legs, resting his chin on his knees.

"What's it feel like, Slink?" Dot asked.

Slink raised his head just enough to speak.

"It starts out like it usually does--like taking a slow walk through a busy neighborhood pedway and pausing to appreciate every beautiful thing I see, but instead of slowing down and quieting my mind, all hell breaks loose and before I know it I'm drowning in chaos. Every time I close my eyes and slow by breath, it's like a storm erupts in my mind. Ordinarily, I'd let go and fall

314

into a quiet expansiveness; now before I can even let go, streams of thought come crashing down all around me. It's like..."

Slink paused for several breaths and Dot waited patiently for him to continue.

"It's like everything I've been working on in the cave is waiting just on the edge of my consciousness, and the moment I relax all those problems simultaneously demand a resolution. I've never had a problem keeping those ideas at bay before; I don't understand why they're wreaking havoc now."

"You taught me the best way to resist the mind is not to resist at all but to acknowledge it, attend to it for a moment, then gently reassert my desire for quiet. I'm not sure how to go about that process now. Usually, if my mind bothers me during meditation, it's a specific task, a problem, or a specific person, like Jenna. Now, though, my mind just seems to hum with energy drawing my consciousness in."

He sighed and shook his head.

"I try to acknowledge my thoughts of work and promise myself I'll attend to those thoughts later. I gently reassure myself there's plenty of time for work when we've finished our practice. The moment I open myself to the quiet, though, I'm overwhelmed. It's like a storm sweeps over me and I'm engulfed in wave after wave of data and an irrepressible urge to make connections between floating bits of information. My mind compels me to draw the connections, put the puzzle together. I'm literally breaking into a sweat with the effort to resist being sucked into the chaos!"

He looked up and caught Dot staring through him, her forehead creased with worry. She swept the room with her eyes as if looking for a solution for him. She then closed her eyes and lowered her head. Slink was beginning to think she'd decided to resume meditating when she finally raised her head and opened her eyes.

Slink regained his half-lotus position atop his pillow and lowered his head.

Dot spoke so softly she was almost whispering.

315

"Wait."

Slink looked up and saw Dot's peaceful countenance and noticed she even had a hint of a smile on her lips. She raised herself up onto her knees and placed a hand on Slink's shoulder.

"Others have described similar challenges as they moved deeper into a meditation practice, Slink, but I think your experience has a unique quality to it as well. I'm only guessing, but I think your extraordinary intellect not only allows you to master meditation techniques much faster than we more ordinary folks might; it also creates challenges we don't experience—at least not with the intensity you describe."

Slink started to protest Dot's suggestion his intellect was superior to hers, but stopped himself when he realized he'd only distract from Dot's point.

"So what would you suggest?" he asked.

"There are long-established techniques for cutting through annoying or resistant thoughts or emotions, and though your experience may be somewhat unique, I think those techniques may still help you. Will you let me guide you through one?"

"Of course," replied Slink. "I trust your intuition."

Dot's smile widened until it reached her eyes. She'd once thought Slink might never trust her or anyone else. Now, after just a few months, he was a very different person from the isolated, fearful young man she'd first met.

Dot caught Slink's eye and gave a quick bow in appreciation.

"Then I want you to find an object you can focus on within easy view from where you're sitting," said Dot in reply. "We're going to follow the same process we usually follow to enter the quiet, but I want you to keep your eyes open throughout our meditation. Anytime your mind starts to gear up, I want you to focus on the object you have chosen. What object are you going to focus on?"

"I've always been fascinated by the beautiful slender-necked vase amidst the books on the shelf behind you," answered

Slink. "It looks like an artifact from Earth, but it's coloring suggests it was made from materials found here."

Dot smiled and nodded.

"One of the engineers on board Home has been experimenting with using ancient glass-blowing techniques to shape Garson materials into works of art. He asked me if he could make me something, and I showed him a picture of a vase my mother brought with her from Earth. The vase you're looking at is nearly identical except for its coloration."

"It's beautiful," said Slink.

"So focus on the vase as we move into meditation."

Dot settled herself back on her prayer bench, arched her back for a moment, then lowered her head to face Slink and placed her hands, palms up, on top of each other in her lap. Dot held Slink softly with her gaze, not looking directly into his eyes, but seeming to focus just in front of him.

"Notice your breathing," she said. "You don't need to alter it in any way, just notice it as you focus on the vase."

After a few breaths, Dot spoke up again.

"Now let your breaths slowly become deeper and longer. Breathe in and look for some detail in the vase you hadn't noticed before. Breathe out and try to take in the entire vase at once. Each time you inhale, focus on a detail of the vase; then each time you exhale, try to take the entire vase in at a glance."

Dot watched Slink and could see him visibly relax as he focused on the vase and followed her direction. She led him through several different breathing exercises, always pausing a bit longer anytime she saw signs of stress on Slink's face. After about fifteen minutes, Dot watched as Slink closed his eyes, lowered his face and slowed his respiration even further. She kept an eye out for any sign of distress as Slink moved into a deep meditative state. She saw none. After another fifteen minutes passed, she led him out of meditation and invited him to tell her what he experienced.

"It was really pretty incredible," Slink said.

He looked down, took a deep breath, then exhaled slowly and looked back up at Dot.

"When we first started, I could sense all this excess energy just buzzing around me. It didn't quite coalesce into specific ideas or thoughts, it just stayed in the background like a deep feeling of anxiety."

Slink looked down and his eyes nearly closed as his speech picked up pace.

"As you directed me to look for a detail in the vase, the energy receded a little bit, and when you directed me to widen my focus to take in the entire vase, it receded a little further. Then, as I deepened my breath and continued moving my focus from a specific detail in the vase to a wide view of it, it was like someone just threw a switch and the energy was gone. I went from feeling super anxious to feeling completely at peace. It was kind of unnerving."

Slink looked up at Dot and shrugged his shoulders to invite Dot to offer her thoughts. She just nodded for him to continue. Slink took another deep breath and looked back down.

"After I took a few more deep, slow breaths and I was still feeling calm and relaxed, I decided to close my eyes and seek that deep quiet I call the 'nothingness.' I had no problem embracing it. I connected to the primordial silence beneath all sound, the nothingness beneath everything. After a few more breaths, I was alternating between a deep awareness of the nothingness and a deep appreciation for everything that is. I breathed in the nothingness that upholds all that is and I breathed out into the connections that bind us all together. It was as if I had never struggled to reach that deep meditative place. My mind was truly quiet again."

Dot and Slink sat opposite each other for several more minutes before Dot finally responded.

"I have heard people describe the efficacy of this particular practice, but they've usually described a gradual attainment of inner quiet, just as they initially described any intruding thoughts or feelings as overtaking the quiet rather gradually, even insidiously. Your experience seems quite different. You described the

318

intrusion of thoughts as coming on suddenly, even explosively and their cessation as coming just as suddenly. Is this truly how it felt to you?"

"Yes; like I said, it was as if someone had thrown a switch. First I experienced an explosion of energetic thought, then I experienced an equally dramatic quietness. It was like one part of my brain went nuts for a while, then it suddenly stopped. It kind of freaks me out because I have no idea what brought it on, so I can't help but be afraid it will come on again, just as suddenly."

"I understand your fear," assured Dot. "Have you ever felt this sudden explosion of energetic thought before, Slink?"

"No, this is the first time it's ever bothered my meditation," Slink replied.

"What about outside of your meditation?" asked Dot. "Have you ever felt this in another context where it might not have seemed so…unnerving?"

Slink squinted at Dot for a second, then his gaze roamed around the room like he was looking for an answer. Suddenly, his eyes widened, and he smiled sheepishly.

"I see what you're getting at," he said quietly.

Dot didn't say a word or change expression. She waited for Slink to finish his thought.

"Every time I sit in front of a monitor, and many other times when I just get lost in my thoughts that's exactly how it feels, but I'm used to that so I don't think anything of it. Sometimes the energy is so all-encompassing I lose track of everything around me. I've gotten better about that, but Chris tells me there are still times when someone in the Cave has to literally shake me to get me to look away from the monitor and interact with them. I guess ideas have always had an ability to captivate me."

Slink shook his head and sighed.

I've told you about my experiences in the nursery when I'd suddenly become aware of Mrs. Cuff smacking me around for being in the Citizen's study late at night. I never once had any memory of leaving my bed at night to sneak into the study. I really am different, aren't I?"

Dot rose from her kneeling bench and pivoted on her knees to sit next to Slink and take him in her arms. He leaned against her without a moment's hesitation.

"Yes, you are different, Nephew," Dot answered. "You are wonderfully, amazingly, and sometimes frighteningly different. And I am determined to help you safely develop your extraordinary abilities without losing yourself. I understand your abilities frighten you at times. They frighten me occasionally, too. Today proved, though, that your remarkable mastery of meditation practices is a big key to helping you find your way. If you can develop an ability to throw that switch you described earlier so you can choose to immerse yourself in thought and choose to extract yourself and rest in the quiet, there's no limit to what you might accomplish."

Dot pulled Slink in close and rubbed his scalp through his short-cropped hair.

"Thank you, Dot," Slink whispered.

Thank you, Slink," Dot whispered back.

After his session with Dot, Slink's time in the Cave was less and less an alternative reality where Jenna, Dot, and Gen, might as well not even exist. Previous to working with Dot, when he was in the Cave, he was only aware of his Cave colleagues and even then his awareness of them focused on their contributions to his work.

Over the days immediately following Slink's session with Dot, whenever Slink sat in silence for his practice, he placed an image of Jenna, Dot, or Gen in front of him. He then repeated the meditation exercise he had done in Dot's cabin using the image in the same way he had used the vase. He then started meditating with his eyes closed for several minutes after which he would open his eyes and immediately seek out a detail in the image before him. He conditioned himself to seek a detail in the image each time it appeared before him.

After about a week of this practice, when Slink went to the Cave one morning, he set up his computer to superimpose over his work an image of Jenna, Dot, or Gen every half hour. When the image appeared, he immediately sought a detail in the image, breathed in slowly and deeply, then tried to take in the whole image in at a glance as he breathed out.

When Slink was engrossed in his work, he saw everything in terms of data streams and connections between those streams. Sometimes he thought he could actually feel his brain buzzing with energy when he was engrossed in his work.

Now, when the images appeared on his screen, the buzzing stopped. He'd found a way to throw the switch! He continued to find that sitting at his station in the Cave or even just daydreaming about his work threw the switch on, but now he had a way to throw it off. It was an indirect path, to be sure, but Slink felt he was on his way to developing a way to engage and disengage his extraordinary intellect at will.

For several weeks after he'd emerged from his illness, Slink had deepened his connections to others, and now those connections helped him balance his mind and his life. Immediately after his illness, he spent many long hours listening intently to Dot's stories of her early days on the surface, Gen's stories of building the Tunnel Rat enclave of Kansas, and any story Jenna would tell him about any part of her life. He loved listening to Jenna talk about her role as ambassador, the challenges of working with the Tunnel Rat enclaves, the joy of successfully bringing Tunnel Rats and Technoids together to meet a common goal. He was falling deeply in love with Jenna and she with him.

"How was work today?" Jenna asked after she greeted Slink with a kiss and sat across from him in the mess.

Slink smiled broadly and said, "It was great. We're making remarkable progress!"

"How was the executive life?" Slink asked in return.

"Oh, just amazing," replied Jenna. "I spent the day combing through old records tracing the movements of one of our Tunnel Rats who suddenly disappeared last week. Given that our enclaves aren't very good about keeping records in the first place and many of their records have been lost or destroyed, it was pretty much an exercise in futility."

"So you're saying being an executive isn't all it's cracked up to be?" Slink jibed.

"The only people who think I'm an executive are the ones who don't know anything about me or my work," Jenna retorted.

"Don't get all serious on me, now, Sweetie" said Slink. "I know you spend most of your time trudging through dark tunnels or sitting at a terminal tending to mind-numbing tasks. I know you've got a tough job, which is why I was teasing about you having it easy."

"Lately I've spent too much of my time sitting at a terminal as far as I'm concerned," Jenna grumped. "But at least that means we get to see more of each other!"

She grinned at Slink and he reached across the table to take her hand in his.

"I'm really grateful for that," he said as he kissed her hand.
Slink shifted subjects abruptly.

"You know how absorbed I can get in my work, right? How I can lose track of everything around me when I'm focused on a problem I'm trying to solve?"

"Yeah, we've talked about it several times and I've been with you when you just seem to disappear into your thoughts. It used to freak me out, but it seems like it's been happening less and less," Jenna replied.

"It has!" Slink exclaimed. "I think I'm finally learning how to shift my focus from inside my head to outside it and back again. Most importantly, I'm learning how to pull my focus away from work without someone having to jar me from my thoughts."

"That's great, Slink," Jenna said as she brought her free hand up and cupped Slink's hand in both of hers.

"I think it's huge," said Slink. "It was getting so bad it started interfering with my practice. When I met with Dot a while back, I couldn't quiet my mind at all and I asked for her help. Dot helped me learn some new meditation techniques that have really helped. I think I'm finally getting a handle on this!"

"I'm really happy for you," Jenna replied as she caressed Slink's hand.

Slink appreciated Jenna's enthusiastic support. She was so good about celebrating his successes, whether they were personal or professional. He hoped he was as helpful to her when she shared her many successes.

"Let's get out of here and find a quiet corner somewhere," Jenna said.

"Aren't you hungry?" asked Slink. "I've got to get something in my stomach really quick, and then I'd love that."

Jenna smiled and lifted her eyebrows.

"Really quick, I promise," replied Slink. "Are you sure you don't want something?"

"I've got a trail ration in my pack," said Jenna. "That should be plenty for me. If I take my time, it might last three or four minutes, and then I'll have to find someone who can give me his undivided attention."

"Three or four minutes will be more than enough time," Slink quipped. "I can't have someone else taking my place!"

Jenna leaned in and whispered in his ear,

"No one could take your place, Baby!"

Slink blushed and pulled back from Jenna. Then he gave her a quick peck on the lips and bolted from the table to keep his end of the bargain. They walked out of the mess hand-in-hand a few minutes later.

The next morning, as Slink opened the Cave with the other consultants, he felt as good as he'd ever felt. He held a deep connection to the silence and an equally deep connection to everyone around him. His life seemed just about perfect. Then, out of the blue, the switch he'd thought he could control clicked on without warning and his mind flooded with thousands of data points that eclipsed all other awareness.

He did feel some mild embarrassment when he wet his pants at his station. He couldn't really comprehend that he'd been so absorbed in his work he wasn't even aware of the growing pressure from his bladder or its eventual release. It troubled him, for the few minutes it took for him to get cleaned up, but his concerns evaporated the moment he re-entered the Cave having donned a clean jumpsuit. The third time Chris pulled him away from his station and pointed out his soiled condition, he promised Chris he'd go to sickbay and have them check him out to see if he had a bladder infection or some other reason for his lack of control. Of course, he set aside that promise as soon as he returned to the Cave and dove back into his work.

Chris had seen other consultants become so fixated on their work they needed help to disengage. Slink's case was extreme, but it was not completely unique. Chris reasoned that Slink's abilities were extreme as well, and extreme gifts were certain to carry with them extreme liabilities. He saw no reason for alarm, even as Slink had a harder and harder time disconnecting from his station. He simply instituted new rules to enforce healthier boundaries for Slink and hoped they'd benefit all the consultants.

Slink's colleagues and friends thought he was nothing more than an eccentric genius. None of them had ever known someone with his extraordinary cognitive gifts. They had no way of comparing his behavior to other super geniuses in the midst of their greatest work. It was easy to assume Slink was as normal as Slink could be.

Slink knew he wasn't normal. He'd always known he wasn't normal.

When he joined Dot for spiritual practice, she couldn't even comprehend what she was witnessing. Slink didn't even close his eyes before he went into a catatonic state, remaining un-responsive until Dot grabbed him by the shoulders and shook him. When she expressed her concern, Slink listened intently to her concerns and promised to have Chris give him a complete physical exam as soon as Chris had an opening.

For his part, Slink knew his work in the Cave wasn't just getting more intense--he knew he was getting sucked into the overpowering cloud of energy; he just couldn't do anything to stop it.

He remembered being swallowed up each time Chris drew him back out, even though he could never remember much about the work he'd done and had little or no sense of how much time had passed.

Worse yet, with each passing day he felt like the cloud crept closer until it was just behind the veil of his awareness, lurk-ing in the background as he ate, as he shared time with friends, and as he connected with Jenna. It couldn't overtake him, but its very presence robbed him of the joy that the moment might oth-erwise have held. He was terrified it would one day swallow him for good, and no one, not Chris, or Dot, or Gen, or even Jenna would be able to bring him back.

He hated the nights worst of all. As he laid down on his bunk, he could feel the cloud creeping up on him like a fog bank rolling in off the ocean. Like a man standing on the shore watch-ing the giant waves of fog roll in, he felt too insubstantial to do anything about it. When he laid down and closed his eyes it came, and his mind shifted into high gear until he was exhausted. Then sleep came, but the cloud infected his dreams preventing any real rest. He could awaken on his own, but he awoke in a fog that only receded far enough to allow him to function, to be "half there," never so far as to allow him to hope he could spend a day outside its reach. He knew each day he'd either need to enter the cloud to fulfill his role in the Cave or it would come unbidden as his friends said their "good nights" or "goodbyes."

He wanted to cry out, to let Dot know why he could not bear to enter the quiet with her, to let Jenna know why he was slipping away even as she worked so hard to keep him close. He could not. He had always known he wasn't normal. He'd sensed it from the time he was a little boy in the nurseries. He'd known it while he lived in the tunnels and saw the way the other Tunnel Rats would steal glances at him as he worked in the kitchen or studied in the library. He felt it aboard Home in the way everyone treated him like he was fragile and breakable. His latest struggles only confirmed something he'd known his whole life. There was no point in asking for help or reaching out to anyone--he was not normal, and there was nothing anyone could do about it. Slink just hoped he could crack the Supernet and help his comrades bring it down before he disappeared into the fog for good.

Chapter 13

"That's it!"

"Are you sure?" asked Chris.

"I'm sure," replied Slink. "I'm sure Son of Supernet is as close to the real thing as we need it to be. If we can bring this down with a software virus, we can bring the Supernet down. You can tell Dot we don't have another list for her. The surface excursions can go back to scavenging for food and supplies."

The network didn't look anything like Chris had imagined. He thought anything designed to mimic the Supernet would be more, how could you say it...more...threatening. This looked like any network backbone consisting of servers strung together with connecting cables and two shelves of routers and modems. The components looked the same as the ones that made up Home's server. "Son of Supernet" just looked like five or six of Home's servers placed side by side.

Slink powered up "S.O.S." as they had taken to calling it, and tested the network software they'd built to resemble the Supernet. It could handle a steady stream of 300 wireless feeds-- about a tenth of the Supernet. They'd built all of S.O.S. to one-tenth scale of the Supernet. Slink loaded it down with the full capacity they expected it to handle. It never even hiccuped.

They'd figured out pretty quickly that they needed to and could do the research they needed with a much smaller server than the Supernet. They needed to do it on a smaller scale because acquiring the equipment to build a duplicate of the Supernet would cripple the surface networks from which they acquired their components. They could do it on a smaller scale because they were less concerned with issues of capacity and more concerned with defeating security. Slink secured S.O.S. to match the Supernet. He assured his colleagues if they could hack S.O.S. without detection, they could hack the Supernet. He also insisted their virus would not be adversely affected by the Supernet's larger scale.

He shut S.O.S. down and started loading the security software on the drives. He then loaded the virus detection software he'd built from the ground up based on their models of the same from the Supernet. He routed the traffic cables through the hardware firewall. He set up both software firewalls. He activated the "spiders," software that detected any unusual increase in network traffic and tracked its source. Now their network was as secure as the Supernet itself. He was sure of it.

What he was not so sure of was whether or not they'd figured out how to get past all the security, plant a virus, and get out without being detected. He wasn't sure the virus they'd nearly finished developing could disable the network hardware so thoroughly the network would have to be re-constructed from the ground up. He was even less sure the virus would travel through the network as intended and short-circuit the commlinks worn by the surface dwellers. If it didn't, all their efforts would fail. It would take time, but the Supernet could and would be rebuilt-- unless the clients it was intended to serve had also been disabled.

He reminded himself they'd built this network just so they could test these things. They expected to fail several times before they succeeded, so they'd divided their effort into several components. First they'd work to get past the security and leave a harmless virus on S.O.S. Once they succeeded in doing that, they'd try to repeat their first stage with the added intention of getting S.O.S.

to transmit the harmless virus to the two dozen working comm-links they had on board. Stage three would be the deployment of the virus they intended to use on the Supernet. First they'd intro-duce it directly to three of the commlinks and analyze the damage it caused. It needed to destroy the transmitter and receiver on the commlink without damaging the processor chips. They couldn't risk causing brain damage to all of the surface dwellers by de-stroying the chips imbedded in their heads.

Once they succeeded with the commlinks, then they'd have one shot to test their killer virus along its intended course. They would introduce it into S.O.S., get it past the network's built-in security, get S.O.S. to transmit it to three networked commlinks, and have the virus do its destructive work throughout S.O.S. and within the commlinks. If it worked, none of the tested components would be in working or repairable condition when they were done. If it didn't, some of the components would survive but they would not have enough working equipment left to test it again. Consequently, it had to work the first time for them to be reason-ably certain they could succeed against the Supernet.

Slink went back to analyzing the Supernet structure to map a path for introducing the virus. As soon as he sat at his sta-tion and turned his attention to his colleague's collected data on the Supernet, he felt the window to the outside world close. He was almost happy. It took way too much energy to do any serious thinking and communicate with his colleagues. It was much easier to disappear into data analysis.

A few minutes or a few hours later, Slink didn't know which and didn't really care, he felt Chris's hands gently massag-ing his shoulders and heard him whispering to him.

"Time to wrap it up, little man."

He snapped a mental picture of where he was in the sea of data. He saved his work on the desktop and withdrew his aching arms from above the monitor. His shoulders throbbed. He had ad-justed, for the most part, to the unusual demands of working at his station 10 hours a day, with the notable exception of the shoul-der strain. When he worked, his hands were outstretched above the interactive screen, moving data packets into various alignments even as his voice called for specific information to be added to the screen. His hands were a perpetual blur above the screen the entire time he sat at his station. He never felt the strain on his shoulders until he finished his day and dropped his arms to his side. Then the pain ripped through his shoulders and down his sides.

Tonight, the pain seemed particularly ferocious. He knew it was time for another stop by sickbay for a "lube job," as Jerome referred to it. He'd put the trip off as long as possible, not wanting to engage Jerome again. Now, he knew there was no more putting it off. He'd never be able to lift a utensil to his lips without an injection. He leaned forward and grimaced.

"You OK, little man?"

"Yea, Chris, I'm fine," Slink replied. "My shoulders are just real bad. I've been putting off going by sickbay. I'll make sure I stop by before I go to dinner. Don't worry about me--I'm fine."

Chris wanted more reassurance from Slink that he'd go by sickbay. He knew better. Slink never responded well to prodding. He could tell Slink was in a lot of pain. He could only hope the pain was enough to get the kid to follow through.

Slink did go by sickbay. He really didn't have much choice. He felt like the tendons in his shoulders were going to snap. He couldn't move his arms at all without having pain shoot through his shoulders.

Jerome gave him an injection in each arm. The pain receded immediately. Slink sighed in relief.

"I don't suppose you'll listen to me if I tell you to take a day off and let those shoulders rest, will you?" Jerome asked.

Slink shook his head.

"We're close Jerome. I'll have all the rest I want soon enough. Thanks for fixing me up. I've gotta run. Jenna's waiting on me."

He jumped off the examination table and gave Jerome a little wave as he passed through the entryway and into the passageway. He was almost giddy with relief that he had avoided any cross examination from Jerome with regard to his health. He'd thought sure Jerome would've heard something about his mental struggles and would at least try to get Slink to submit to more tests. He'd steeled himself to repel Jerome's queries. When they didn't come as a prerequisite to receiving pain relief, Slink wasn't about to wait around and give Jerome another chance. He practically sprinted out of sickbay and down the passageway to the Mess.

It was Jerome's turn to shake his head. He couldn't tell what was going on in Slink's head, and he wasn't sure he really wanted to know. Even if he was sure he wanted to know, he wasn't sure how he would go about diagnosing the kid. The plates in his head repelled any scan Jerome could perform and Jerome certainly didn't feel confident enough to remove one or more of the plates just to take a look around in Slink's head.

Dot had sought him out several weeks earlier for his medical advice with regard to Slink. She told him about some of her experiences with Slink, both in her quarters and in the Cave. Jerome told her he'd seen some pretty severe compulsive-obsessives. From what she told him, her nephew seemed at one and the same time to have the worst case ever and a remarkable ability to compensate for his condition. Nonetheless, his mind showed signs of cracking under the stress. At the same time, his body was losing its ability to keep up with the demands he made on it. It frightened Jerome to think where it would end--especially for Slink.

"What's your excuse this time?"

Jenna looked like she was more put out with him than usual. He was used to her being a little unhappy with him if he didn't get to Mess in time to share dinner with her.

"In fact, that's probably what's getting me in trouble," thought Slink. "I don't think it's a good thing for me to be getting used to her being upset."

"I'm sorry, J, really," he pleaded. "At least this time, you'll be happy to hear why I was late...wanna hear?"

"This better be good. Unless you were in sickbay, I can't think of anything that's going to make me happy about you being late again."

"We have a winner!" exclaimed Slink.

"Really?"

Jenna slid to the edge of her chair and up against Slink's right shoulder. She slipped an arm around him and kissed him on the cheek.

"You were really in sickbay? Did you get checked out? You let Jerome know what's been going on with you and he ran some tests? What did you find out?"

Slink had a bad feeling that pain injections in his arms was not going to measure up to the expectations Jenna had for his visit to sickbay. He was right.

"We didn't have time to get into that," he said.

She pulled away from him, turned him in his chair and glared at him.

"So what did you go to sickbay for? Don't tell me you just had some more pain killers shot into your shoulders! That is not what we've been talking about almost every night."

He lowered his eyes.

"Shit, Slink!"

She punched him in his sore shoulder. He yelped.

"You deserve it!" she said. "I'm done begging you, Slink. Something's not right with you and you wanna stick your head in the sand. Why can't you apply that oversized brain of yours to this problem? Last night you blanked out on me mid-sentence and stared into space for two and half hours! It was like something just snapped in your head. I could tell you were breathing, so I just left you to see how long it would last. After two hours, they kicked us outta the Mess, or you might still be sitting at the same table staring into space. That's not just a sign of being overworked, Slink. Something's wrong! Please go back to sickbay and ask Jerome to check it out. Please!"

She was crying again. Slink hated it when she cried. He wanted to give her what she asked for--just make her happy, make her stop crying.

"I'll go!" he blurted.

"Really?" she asked.

"Really. I'll go by sickbay Thursday."

Jenna jumped back out of her chair and screamed, "No! That's too long. It's Monday, Slink! You need to go tonight. I can't sleep. I'm worried sick. Please go with me right now, Slink--get this thing checked out--please--go with me right now!'

She was sobbing now, her words coming in short bursts. Slink stood and took her into his arms.

"Hey...hey, Jenna! Come on now! I can get my part of our research on the Supernet back doors done by Thursday. I'll take Friday off and spend the weekend in sickbay. Jerome can run all the tests he wants and we'll know for sure what's going on. Come on, J. I'm scared too, but I need these three days. Please--I need you to hang with me for three more days. Please don't shut me out now--I need you too much!'

His eyes were filling with tears now. He hadn't even admitted to himself the fear he now confessed. As the words came from his mouth, he shivered. He knew he wasn't normal, and he'd feared hearing Jerome confirm his intuition. But what if it was worse than that? What if something was really wrong with him? What if this wasn't just the progression of his abnormal existence? What if he was dying...or worse? He really was scared!

"I'm not going away, Slink. You're the one who's slipping away. I'd love to have you cry in my arms all night. At least I'd know you were really with me the whole time. But if this night is like any other, as soon as we get past the emotion of this moment and we check in with each other, at the first lull in the conversation, you'll be gone. I'll nudge you back and you'll stay with me for a few more minutes, but then you'll be gone again. It'll keep on like that until we leave each other and go to bed. Then I'll lay awake and worry about you, and you'll do God knows what because when you wake up you won't have any reliable memory of your night. Maybe somebody will tell you later that you sat on the edge of your bunk all night. Maybe you'll lay in your bunk with your eyes open until someone shakes you and tells you it's time to get up. Then you'll crawl out of bed exhausted and head to the Cave to start the whole thing over again. It has got to stop, Slink. You've got to make it stop, or it'll kill us both!"

He didn't look up at her. He only held her a little closer and pleaded with her.

"Thursday. Please. Thursday," he whispered.

Jenna didn't respond. After several minutes passed, she felt Slink stop shaking in her arms and under her breath she whispered, "I hope you last three more days."

She felt his breathing deepen as he became dead weight in her arms. He was gone again. She started to cry...again. She could only hope the next three days passed quickly.

Jerome saw Slink walking toward him in the passage the next morning. Slink looked like he'd endured another tough night. Jerome took a mental inventory of the young man. He wore the same jumper he'd worn the previous day--Jerome could identify it by the blood stains on the neck line. Slink had been wearing it when he became ill, lost consciousness, and took a header in the men's quarters. Slink kept his hair cropped close to his head, but Jerome could still see that it was matted to his head on the right side. His eyes were glazed and bloodshot. The coloring had left his face so his complexion looked almost gray. He hadn't shaved for several days and the stubble was peppered with flakes of dry skin.

"God, he looks bad," thought Jerome. Had he overlooked Slink's appearance the previous evening or had Slink's condition deteriorated that much in one night? He figured it was probably a little of both.

"Hey, Slink," Jerome called out after Slink had passed him in the passage.

Slink whirled around.

"Oh...hello," said Slink.

His response was muted as though Slink didn't recognize Jerome. Jerome pretended not to notice.

"I understand you're coming in on Thursday," said Jerome. He knew his revelation of Slink's intention would come as a surprise to Slink.

"Jenna tells me you're finally ready to let me help you. I'm glad to hear it, Slink. You look like shit!"

Jerome paused for effect. He got no reaction from Slink. He continued.

"I hope you're going to take it easy between now and then. Otherwise, your colleagues are going to be dragging you in here unconscious long before Thursday rolls around. I'd rather have you come in on your feet, Slink. Take it easy for the next couple of days and when you get here, I'll be ready to run the tests we need without keeping you here any longer than absolutely necessary. I know you've already had enough of this place to last a lifetime, and I can't say I blame you!"

"I appreciate your concern, Jerome," replied Slink.

Jerome couldn't tell whether Slink was being serious or sarcastic. He suspected the latter, but Slink looked so worn out he might have been sincere.

"I am concerned Slink, and I'm really glad to hear that you're coming in. See you Thursday," said Jerome.

"OK," said Slink.

He shuffled down the passage and ascended the ladder to the Bridge.

"The vultures are circling," thought Slink as he walked across the Bridge to the Cave. "I better make these three days count--who knows what'll be left when Jerome's done with me."

Slink joined the circle of opening, bowed his head, and closed his eyes. A moment later, the energy surge came and he entered the cloud. Fatigue meant nothing in the cloud. He was a disembodied data processor, and that morning, it felt...so...right.

An hour later it happened--the pieces fell into place and Slink knew he'd found the way in--all the way in! He ran the simulation and saw the virus pass through the back door, by the firewall, past all the security and into memory. A few seconds later it was transmitted out onto the network, and a few seconds after that it was executed across the network. Every alarm remained silent, every hitch disappeared, and every command was executed. For the first time since they started, the simulation program detected no errors! Slink sent the results across the Cave network. He was barely conscious of the cheer that went up across the room as the results hit the screens of his colleagues. A moment later they pulled him away from his station, pulled him back from the cloud and nudged him back into reality. He struggled to breath and open his eyes. Chris was struggling to get through the crowd of people surrounding Slink.

"Hold on, hold on!" cried Chris over the cheers. The room slowly grew quieter, though far from silent.

"This is a big step, and I don't want to throw cold water on the celebration, but the real test is still before us. We need to compile the harmless virus and try to get it into Son of Supernet. We have an hour before lunch to set everything up and run the test. If it works with real hardware as well as it did on the simulation, I'll lead the celebration! For now, let's keep it low key, stay focused on the task in front of us and get through this next step. Maybe we'll have something worth sharing with the whole crew by lunch time."

The thought of running a real world test on the network they'd all worked to construct energized the entire Cave...except Slink. He sat at his station and stared off into space. For the first time in weeks, his work was done, at least for the moment. He'd compiled the test virus and mapped the way into the network. Now it was his colleagues' turn to test his work. They'd decided beforehand that upon reaching this point, he'd stay out of the work to make sure the test was conducted independently. For the first time in a week, he slept, head resting on his station console. Chris threw a blanket over him and ushered his colleagues away from him.

They woke Slink up just as they were ready to run the test. It took a minute for him to shake the effects of sleep. When he gave them a "thumbs up," Chris touched the screen at his console and the test began. They all held their breath. Several seconds later and no alarm--the virus had passed into the network undetected. They waited. A minute later, the receptor lights on the three test commlinks flashed red--they were receiving data from the network! Two minutes after that, the commlinks and Son of Supernet all shut down on cue--the test was a complete success!

This time when the cheers went up, Chris was at the forefront of the celebration, as he'd promised. They threw the doors of the Cave open, and Chris raised his fists and pumped them in the air as the crew turned to see what the commotion from the Cave was all about. Instantly the crew joined the cheer. Dot came up to Chris and embraced him.

"We're not there yet," he cautioned. "But today is big--really big! We got the test virus all the way through the network, onto the commlinks, and executed. When the work on the killer virus is done, we'll be ready."

Chris released Dot and stood next to her, facing the Cave and all of his consultants. Dot leaned next to him and whispered in his ear.

"How long?"

Chris whispered back to her.

"I can't be sure, but I think we're really close. Slink tells me he thinks we only need one more breakthrough. It could come anytime. For his sake, I hope it comes soon!"

Dot caught sight of her nephew at the back of the consultants who'd crowded in the doorway of the Cave. The sight of him made her draw an involuntary breath.

"Oh, God," she hissed.

"I know," whispered Chris. "I'm doing everything I can to take care of him, but there isn't much I can do. I don't think he's sleeping, and I know he isn't eating much. This stretch has really taken a toll on him. I'm sorry!"

"You have no reason to apologize. I know you're doing everything you can. We all are. He's the only one who can change the course he's on. Jerome tells me he'll report to sickbay on Thursday. I aim to see that he does!"

Dot moved away from Chris and started shaking hands with all the other consultants. She thanked each of them for their hard work and dedication. They beamed with pride over passing such a significant milestone. When she reached Slink, she put her arm around him, pulled him in close and whispered,

"Well done, nephew, well done!"

"We're not done yet," he replied.

"I know, but it is time to rest a while. I've asked Chris to see that the Cave is closed for the rest of the day. Would you dine with me in the officer's Mess today? We can find Jenna and invite her to join us. Gen will be there already--we can ask him to join our table. Won't you please have lunch with me--it would mean a lot to me!"

"Sure, Dot, you know I can't refuse you. I just need to go by the head and clean up. I rolled out of the sack this morning without so much as throwing some cold water on my face. I can't let Jenna see me this way."

"OK, Slink. I'll find Jenna and have her join us. See you in a few."

A half-hour later, Jenna knew Slink wasn't coming. She knew he could get ready for any occasion in fifteen minutes. He wasn't a big groomer. She excused herself and went to find him. It wasn't difficult. She headed for the men's quarters. The bunks were full of men from the night crew, most of them sound asleep. She found Slink tucked beneath his bed covering, sleeping like a baby. She looked at him laying peacefully on his right side, head nestled deeply into a puffy pillow. The anger that was bubbling just beneath the surface when she left the Mess evaporated. She sat on the floor next to his cot and laid her head next to his face so she could feel his breath across her forehead. She rested her right hand gently on his left shoulder.

She was startled awake when one of the men coming off shift gently shook her shoulder. She snapped her head up and saw Slink's bunkmate looking down on her. She raised her finger to her lips. He nodded and smiled at her. He offered her a hand. She took it and stood. He walked her out to the landing between the men's and women's quarters.

"Please let him sleep," Jenna started.

Franco nodded. "Of course. We all know he's had a tough one. He don't share his bunk, so he can stay there as long as he needs to. You ought to get some dinner before they shut the Mess down for the night."

"Dinner?" Jenna asked. "What time is it?"

"Almost twenty-one hundred," he answered.

"You're kidding," she exclaimed. "I've been sitting next to him on the floor for eight hours? I'm surprised no one came looking for me. I better let Gen know I'm OK."

Franco smiled. He couldn't follow all her references, but he knew she didn't expect him to. He nodded to her.

"Good night," he said.

"Good night," said Jenna.

She looked over Franco's shoulder in the direction she'd come.

"We'll keep on eye on 'im, don't you worry," said Franco. "He hasn't been hisself since he got sick. I hope whatever's ailin' 'im has finally run its course."

"Me too, Franco," replied Jenna. "Me too!"

Slink awoke the next morning before the other men started stirring. He had a vague memory of leaving the Bridge and coming into the men's quarters to clean up. After that, there was nothing.

"Everyone's gonna want a piece of me now," he thought, remembering his agreement to meet Dot, Gen and Jenna for lunch in the officer's Mess.

He assumed someone had found him asleep.

"Probably slumped over at one of the sinks," thought Slink. "Oh man, I hope it wasn't Jenna. She's going to want to tow me right into sickbay if she found me collapsed somewhere."

He couldn't do anything about that now. He took a shower, shaved three, or was it four days' growth off his face. He felt good; no, he felt great! At least all that sleep had done him some good. It was a little easier to think of facing the others feeling so much better. He moved to his bunk, put his razor away, pulled out a brush for his hair, then caught himself and laughed. It had been months since his hair was long enough for a brush to do any good. He got dressed and headed for the Mess.

Then, it hit him. The fog was gone! Not just receded a little further than usual--it was gone. He wanted to stop and call his work to mind--see if the wave would rise to engulf him. Then he thought better of it.

"If there was ever a time to leave a sleeping dog lie, whatever the hell that means, this is it," he thought. He took a deep breath and looked around. "Home never looked better," he decided.

When he got to the Mess, he was surprised to find the door slid closed. He approached it and it opened, so it wasn't still closed for shift change. The day shift cooking crew were in the kitchen at work, but the Mess wasn't open to anyone else yet.

"Hey, lover boy, what's the occasion?" asked one of the crew as he carried a tray by Slink.

"What do you mean?" Slink asked in return.

"You're all spit-polished--it must be some anniversary for you and Jenna, huh?"

"Not that I know of--I just woke up early," said Slink.

"Yeah, right, whatever you say, little man," said the tall, scruffy looking man. "Well, she just happened to wake up early too, imagine that!"

"Really? Where?" Slink's voice drifted off. He was hoping he would have a few minutes to figure out what to say when he saw Jenna.

The man laughed a hearty laugh. "Over there," he said pointing to the other side of the Mess, just out of sight behind the serving line. He shook his head and headed back for the kitchen and another tray.

Slink walked slowly in the direction he'd been pointed. He wondered if he should blurt out an apology the moment he saw her.

"Or maybe I should wait to let her blow off some steam first," he thought.

He looked up just in time to see Jenna racing toward him. She threw her arms around him and almost knocked him down.

"I'm sorry," he started, unable to contain himself.

"It's OK, Baby, it's OK," she said. "God, you look good," she stuttered. "I mean, you really look good...like before," her voice trailed off.

"I know," he said, then "I mean..."

She laughed and he laughed with her.

They walked back to the table where she'd been sitting.

"I mean, I feel good...like before," he said to try to cover her obvious discomfort over making the reference herself. "And Jenna, you look great! You look as fresh as I feel, and I slept almost 16 hours!"

"I did, too," she said.

341

He looked at her, tilting his head sideways, and raising his eyebrows.

"I came down to check on you and found you all tucked into your bunk, sound asleep. You looked so peaceful, and I knew you hadn't slept--really slept--for a long time, so I just sat down next to you to keep you company for a few minutes. The next think I knew, Franco was waking me up--almost eight hours later! I was going to go down and get something to eat, but I felt so tired, I just went across the landing, and crawled into my own bunk. I was out again in no time. Then I woke up about an hour ago, cleaned up, and decided to come down here and beg the crew for a cup of syncaff."

She leaned across the table and kissed him.

"You look so good, Baby," she said to Slink, as she leaned back in her chair and took him in.

Slink felt stirrings he hadn't felt for a while. He was happy to feel them and he leaned toward her. She met him over the table and they kissed again, this time longer and deeper.

"I missed that," he said, falling back into his chair.

"I'm glad to hear that," she said staying perched above him. "I thought maybe you'd given up kissing for good."

"OK, I deserved that," replied Slink, "but I'm going to make up for my wayward ways, I promise."

He leaned forward again. They held a long, passionate kiss. He pulled away from her, then leaned in again and rested his forehead against hers.

"I don't deserve your love, J, but I sure as hell appreciate it. Thanks for not giving up on me!"

"Well, I didn't have much choice," she teased. "There aren't many options available for lovelorn women aboard Home."

"Choice or not, I know you, J. You would have stuck by me even if you had men knocking each other over to get to you. It's who you are, and I love you for it," said Slink.

"Maybe you're right," she said. "But I know a good thing when I see it. You've been through a rough stretch, but at your worst, you're still the best catch on the ship!"

342

She initiated the kiss this time, and he reached around her with his right hand and caressed the back of her neck as they kissed.

"Enough already!"

The voice belonged to Etta, the head chef.

"People gotta eat in here," she joked.

"OK, Etta, we'll stop," said Jenna. "Besides," she continued looking over Slink's shoulder at the entire kitchen crew staring in their direction, "if we're going to put on a show, we should charge for it!"

The crew laughed and Etta barked at them to get back to work. She was a big woman and she lumbered over to their table. When she got there, she rubbed Slink's bristled head.

"You look a helluva lot better!" she exclaimed. "Bout time you woke up. We was all startin' to worry about cha!"

"What, did everyone but me realize how bad things were getting?" Slink asked.

"Is that a rhetorical question?" Jenna quipped. "Most days, you looked like you spent half the night poppin' and the other half sleepin' in your clothes. It was kind of tough for people not to notice."

"Yeah, and if they didn't notice the way you looked, they sure as hell noticed they way you smelled," said Etta.

"OK, that hurts," said Slink, and it did.

Had he really been walking around looking and smelling like a zombie? He knew he'd been a little obsessed with his work, but the picture he was getting was of a man completely off the deep end.

"We're scaring him, Etta; we better back off," said Jenna.

But Etta didn't back off.

"Good!" replied Etta. "You need to be scared. You don't wanna go back there, little man. Next time people tell you you're lookin' bad again, you know what we're sayin' to ya! This is a small ship, Slink. We know what you mean to us, even if we don't know or understand everythin' you and your Cave buddies are up

343

to. We care 'bout cha. You be takin' better care of yourself now, ya hear?"

Before he could even reply, Etta slapped him on the back hard enough to knock his wind out and turned away. She shuffled back into the kitchen and started hollering orders to her crew.

"She means well, but she can be so harsh," Jenna said, trying to dismiss the comment she could tell had stung Slink pretty badly.

"I knew I was pretty wrapped up in myself, but I had no idea I was walking around like that. I'm sorry--it had to be tough to watch."

Slink hung his head and shook it side to side in disbelief.

"Hey!" Jenna exclaimed.

Slink looked up to see her staring intently at him.

"That was yesterday. It wasn't easy, but I don't care. I'm glad we have today, and I'm glad it doesn't look at all like yesterday. Let's not waste any time on regret. OK?"

"OK," said Slink. "But what happens..." he trailed off.

"What happens when you go into the Cave," Jenna finished for him. "Maybe you shouldn't go back."

She knew how he'd respond to that suggestion, but she had to say it anyway.

"Jenna," he pleaded. "You know I have to go. I'm sure you heard what happened yesterday. We're really close now. I have one piece of work left. I think I'm really close to having that finished too. When I'm done there, I'm done--at least for now."

"I know," she said. "I just wish it wasn't true. I want so bad to wake up and have every day start like this one. Do you have any sense whether or not you'll be OK when you go back into the Cave?"

"It's different today--I don't feel my work hovering just behind me like a hungry fog waiting to swallow me up. It's the first day I haven't felt that since," he paused, " since, I went back to work after I got sick, I guess. I'm kinda afraid to even think about it until I have to. I don't want to miss any of the time we have this morning."

"Then don't think about it," she said.

She'd never heard him speak of how the past weeks had felt for him. She shuddered to think he'd felt so haunted, so hunted by his work.

"I feel so bad for you," she said. "I didn't know."

"You couldn't know," he told her.

He reached across the table for her hands. He took them in his and rubbed the back of her small knuckles softly with his thumbs as he spoke.

"I thought I was getting a handle on it. I spoke to you about my practice and the advances I'd made in gaining control over my obsessive thought patterns. I really thought I'd figured out how to shut out my work and refocus on my immediate surroundings."

"I remember," said Jenna softly.

Slink smiled, then shook his head slowly and grimaced.

"It all changed in a flash one morning when I was entering the Cave. I felt my mind switch on right in the middle of our opening meditation, and there wasn't anything I could do about it. I worked until I was exhausted, then when I was too tired to think straight, my mind switched off. The moment some thought of work crossed my mind, though, I'd feel the switch get thrown in my brain and I'd be gone.

I'd start thinking about some small problem I was working on while I was washing my face or shaving and after a while I'd realize I hadn't moved for what seemed like several minutes. I was shocked to find out that sometimes I'd been standing there two or three hours. I talked to you about that--you told me it wasn't normal. I just thought I was over-stressed with work and I just kept telling myself that it'd be over soon enough.

"It even affected me when I met with Dot in her quarters for meditation. I couldn't even begin to use the techniques she'd taught me that had been helping so much. It was like my mind was electrified. It felt overwhelming.

"After that, I couldn't shut it off, I could only hold it off. It felt like a charged particle cloud that followed me around and swallowed me up the moment I turned my mind to anything I was working on. It got harder and harder to hold it off, and so it got harder and harder to pay attention to others or even take care of myself.

"When I'm in that cloud, as near as I can remember, which isn't very well, it's not painful or even uncomfortable. In fact, I think it is amazingly peaceful. Everything in there is data and potential connections between related data. Anything else disappears, which would be horrible if I couldn't get out, but as long as I am in there everything seems...right."

Slink had been staring down at their hands while he talked. When he looked up, he could see Jenna looked alarmed.

"Am I scaring you?" he asked.

"Not really," she said. "You're not telling me anything I didn't already know on some level. It's just hard to hear you talk so comfortably about an existence where there's no room for me and it was all..right."

"I understand, J. It bothers me now to know that's how it feels when I'm there. But you know, I don't think it's going to haunt me the way it did before. Even sitting here and talking about it, I don't feel the electrified cloud threatening to engulf me. Even yesterday, if I tried to talk to you about any of this, I would've been..."

"Gone." she finished the sentence for him. "I know. I hope you're right. I wish you never had to go back there again."

"Two more days--I promise. Maybe even less. As soon as I finish this last piece of work, I'll come find you and we'll go to sickbay together. Are you scheduled to leave the ship?"

"No, and if I was, I'd cancel my trip."

"Good. I need you here with me. I'm more scared of what Jerome might find than I am of the cloud."

"I'll be there--I promise."

She withdrew her hands from his and leaned over the table. They kissed again. She pulled back from their kiss, then leaned forward until her lips were next to his ears.

"If you thought we had an audience before, you better not turn around," she whispered.

Before he could even finish turning, the applause started. As he turned to face the full Mess, the cheers rose higher and higher. He could do nothing but take it in. His eyes filled and the tears started to flow down his cheeks as the cheers joined in a unison cheer.

"Bravo, Slink, Bravo," the people cheered. Slink saw most of his colleagues interspersed in the crowd and leading the cheers. He was overwhelmed. He leaned and sat awkwardly on the back of his swivel chair. He lifted his hands, palms out asking them to stop.

As the cheers started to die down, and before he could say anything to acknowledge their praise, a voice rose above the rest. Dot stepped forward as she spoke.

"We took the cloak of secrecy from the work you've been doing in the Cave, briefed the crew on the breakthrough we made yesterday, and thanked your colleagues, but we all felt a little cheated that we didn't get to thank you at the same time. Stanis Web Macdonald, on behalf of the officers and crew of Home, on behalf of the resistance, on behalf of all those who hope for a better future for our world, I say 'thank you!'"

She stepped forward and embraced her nephew as the cheers rose again. She stood next to him with her arm around him while they waited for the cheers to die down again. He leaned into Dot, raised his lips to her ear, made one statement and asked permission to share that statement with the gathering. She pulled back for a minute, then leaned in and asked him one question.

"Are you sure?"

He made eye contact with her and nodded once.

She nodded her assent. When the crowd grew quiet, he cleared his throat and spoke.

"If you now know our aims then I'm sure you were told we're not finished yet. We have more work to do, but let me be the first to tell you that we will finish that work."

The cheers burst forth from the crowd again. He motioned for quiet, and before it grew completely quiet he spoke again, ever louder with each word.

"We will finish that work--this week--and we will free our brothers and sisters--across Garsow--once and for all. This week--we will see--the collapse of the Supernet!"

The cheers rose again, this time to almost ear-splitting levels. Slink raised a fist in the air and pumped it each time he looked at another of his mates. He'd never felt so certain of anything as he was of the statement he'd just made. Now all he had to do was go back into the Cave and back up his talk with action. He was ready.

Chapter 14

Slink entered the Circle of Opening with his colleagues expecting to feel his mind erupt with energy, expecting to be overwhelmed by that energy, sucked into the cloud. It did not come. He entered the quiet, found his center deep in his abdomen, breathed into the silence and felt...peace. His mind was still, leaving him to find the "nothing"- the spaciousness surrounding and upholding all that is. He'd most often been able to reach that awareness when he and Dot were sitting back-to-back in her quarters. Dot said it was easier to reach such depths in the company of another seeker.

Now Slink and his colleagues sought the quiet together, and the calm was truly amazing. Slink rested in the stillness, in the assurance that he was...right, that everything was right. The circle was strong that morning; Chris detected no restlessness from the circle until they'd been standing for over a half-hour. Finally, one person adjusted his stance another stretched her spine, and Chris broke the silence.

"May we carry the stillness within us as we seek understanding."

He always broke the silence of the circle of opening with the same words. This morning, they seemed to take on additional

349

meaning. Would they reach the understanding their task required? He did not share Slink's certainty, but that was no surprise. Slink had worked on developing the virus in near isolation. He was the only one who could know whether they were close or not, whether they would reach their goal or not. Chris wanted to trust Slink's judgment. The problem was, the kid had demonstrated some pretty poor judgment along with his genius's insight. He hoped his judgment flowed from his extraordinary insight in this particular case, otherwise the kid's brash prediction was going to end up biting them all in the ass.

Slink walked to his station, bent over his chair and powered up the console and brought the virus data up on his screen. The screen filled with images of folders, different symbols on each one. Only then did he pull the chair out on its swivel and sit down. He looked at the screen and felt a momentary panic. What if his mind couldn't engage the data as before? As much as that highly energized concentration had caused trouble for him outside the Cave, he needed to reach that state here or he couldn't possibly work with the complex information before him.

He closed his eyes and raised his hands to the screen. He could see in his minds eye each of the folders and he understood the symbols on each folder, understood the nature of each folder's contents. He breathed. He felt it then. It was little more than a tingling at the base of his neck at first, then it became a buzzing all across the back of his head. His hands moved, the folders began to open, data packets sprung to life under his guidance and connecting lines appeared between the packets, drawing their complex mosaic on his screen. The cloud was upon him now, wrapping him in its foggy tentacles, and he welcomed it.

His eyes were open now, but he was looking beyond his screen to see those pieces of data that were yet to be drawn into the pattern forming on his screen. He could see them now, see the places where each belonged, see the missing connections that must be drawn to pull each into its place. He drew with his mind, and his hands followed. The pattern on his screen grew in size and complexity. Still he found more pieces, drew them in, and fixed them in place. He was missing key components, but he knew where to find them. He reached out across the network, acquired a protocol from one colleague, acquired code from another. It was coming together--he could see it.

Then the gentle voice came. He wanted to turn it away, insist on finishing.

"No need. There is time."

The message came from another place in his consciousness, allowing him to disconnect from the mosaic, release his work, and emerge from the cloud.

"You still need to eat," Chris was saying. "Do you have everything you need? Tell me how we can help you over lunch, and I will see that we have at your fingertips anything you require."

"Thanks, Chris," Slink replied.

Chris stepped back and looked at him, a half-smile painting his puzzled face.

"What, I never thanked you before?" Slink asked.

He could tell Chris was taken back by his simple expression of gratitude.

"I'm sorry, Chris, you deserve better. You've saved my life with your gentle but firm insistence that I step away from my station. You deserve my profound gratitude, and I'm embarrassed I didn't offer it everyday. Please forgive me."

"Forget it, Slink. I'm just glad to see the change in you. I could go without hearing a 'thank you,' but I was really starting to worry we were losing you. You seem changed--for the better. Maybe you just got a good night's sleep for once, but it seems like more than that. Let's have lunch and you can tell me what it feels like to you. Come on."

The Circle of Closing served to renew Slink and reorient him to the present moment. After a few minutes, Chris broke the silence and they dispersed for lunch. For the first time in a month or more, Chris didn't have to escort Slink to the Mess to make sure

351

he didn't return to his station in the Cave.

Chris hardly said a word while Slink did his best to tell Chris how it felt to enter the cloud and work with the data. Chris didn't seem bored; to the contrary, he seemed fascinated by Slink's description. When Slink told him about the difference in the way he had felt earlier that morning as he sat down at his station, Chris just said, "I'm glad, Slink."

Each time he described it to another person, Slink was getting a little better grasp on the way his perceptions changed when he was working. It was all fine and good to talk about clouds of energy and overwhelming fog, but those images were only metaphors for internal experiences. Slink was beginning to realize what he was really experiencing were periods of intense concentration that both enhanced his awareness and dramatically narrowed it.

It felt like disappearing because his concentration was so intense it left little room for reflection upon the experience, either as it happened or in retrospect. He hoped he was again gaining some modicum of control over the experience. Was it slowly becoming something he could do rather than something that happened to him? He realized how fortunate he was to be surrounded by so many good people who'd recognized his limitations and intervened on his behalf. He shuddered to think what might have happened if that weren't the case.

When they returned to the Cave, and joined in the afternoon Circle of Opening, Slink reached out to his fellows. He'd often done so before he got sick, using the time to call each person in the circle to the forefront of his consciousness and passing along his desire for their well-being. Since returning to the Cave, he now realized, he'd never thought of anyone or anything other than his work and the cloud of energy that alternately sustained and threatened him. It felt good to turn his thoughts outside himself again.

After Chris closed the circle, Slink again stood in front of his station, awakened his screen and took stock of the image floating there. It was hard to believe he was building something so destructive. It looked so beautiful, so perfect in its exquisite lines, its countless facets, like a diamond of incomparable complexity. He pulled out his chair and sat. He took a deep breath, closed his eyes and reached out for his creation. Within a few seconds, he was turning it, studying it, marking imperfections and seeking their perfection.

His colleagues sat at their stations and made sure all their resources were ready and available if Slink should call for any of them. They occasionally glanced in his direction, watching the blur of motion that was his hands above his screen, growing in confidence and anticipation.

Some time later, Slink was down to the last puzzle piece. He had no awareness if hours or only minutes had passed since he sat down. His mind was bent entirely on finding the last piece of data and fitting it into its place. He reached out to his colleagues. One of them recognized the request and knew she had the requested communication protocol. She brought it up and before she could even call to Slink, he retrieved it from her station. A moment later he stood up and turned toward the center of the room, an expression of sheer exultation across his face.

"We're finished," he said softly. "We're finished," he repeated.

There were no cheers this time. There were only restrained smiles and nods from his colleagues.

Chris interrupted their reverie.

"How do we test it, Slink? Do you have some simulation to run, some verification program?"

"It has been verified every step of the way," said Slink. "The only thing left is to run the test on S.O.S. I'm not being impulsive, Chris, it's the only step left that can offer any further assurance."

"Then we'll run it first thing tomorrow morning," Chris declared.

A chorus of groans went up across the room.

"I know what you're thinking," said Chris. "You don't want to have this test hanging over us all night long. But consider the alternative. If we run the test and succeed, as I expect we will, then we'll have the deployment hanging over us all night. Better to spend the night anticipating the test, I think."

As usual, Chris commanded compliance, not by virtue of status but by virtue of stature. Everyone in the Cave had seen Chris's judgment proven again and again. They gathered in the Circle of Closing. Slink entered the silence feeling an odd heaviness. The exultation he'd felt when he completed his masterwork had evaporated.

He'd never doubted the efficacy of their goal. The Supernet needed to be brought down. Now though, having nearly reached that goal, the weight of their impending success nearly crushed the breath out of him. Tomorrow, if all went well, the foundation of a society would be destroyed. The fundamental assumptions upon which an entire civilization had come to rely would be undermined. What would happen when the commlinks stopped working? Most productive work would cease. Relationships would be strained. Suspicions, only recently waning with the end to the Technoid surface excursions, would flare into open conflict. What they were doing was surely right, but it just as surely was not going to be easy--on anyone. When life deteriorated on the surface, it was sure to become more difficult beneath the surface too. Tomorrow would be a great day, and a terrible one.

When Chris broke the silence and closed the circle, Slink could tell the same realizations were hitting his colleagues. Everyone left in silence.

"This would not be a good night to be alone," thought Slink.

He headed for the Mess and Jenna. If he ever needed to look into her loving eyes, he needed it now.

The next morning, Slink awoke with a different sort of cloud hanging over him. Like the inventors of great destructive weapons before him, he carried a burden no one could lift from him. Jenna had tried the previous evening. She'd asked Slink pointed questions to try to ease his burden. Had the tunnel dwellers not endured enough difficulty, even persecution? Wouldn't the surface dwellers come to appreciate their freedom once they got past the initial shock? In the short run, their actions would bring pain, but ought not humanity always act based on long-term consequences?

None of her questions eased his pain. He awoke feeling no relief from the burden he'd felt when he laid down. People he'd never known, most of whom he would never meet, were about to have their world torn apart by something he created. The Technoids, led by Slink, were going to force Technoid ideology onto a surface society whose members had voluntarily chosen an opposing ideology. How could he be sure they were justified in taking such radical action?

Slink could barely go through the rituals of starting his day. He didn't go to the Mess; he had no appetite. Even still, he was almost late for the Circle of Opening on the day toward which all their efforts had been aimed.

There was no consolation in the circle. There was calm but no peace. He'd done his part, and he could not withdraw the product of his efforts. He didn't really want to. He was still convinced they were doing the right thing. That fact could not hide from him the full reality of what they were about to do. That fact could not console him, because he knew it would not console anyone living on the surface and those people were his kin as much as anyone on board Home.

The test was straightforward. The network was booted up and linked to three of the on-board commlinks. Once it was up and all the security was operational, Slink sent the virus to Chris's station. Chris placed it in queue.

"Here we go," Chris said. "Have the extinguishers ready. If this does what we want it to do, it will overwrite the drives, infect the memory, shut down the cooling fans, and send the hard disks into overdrive. Everything will overheat pretty fast. Be ready to blast it at the first sign of fire.

"I'm going to count down from five. OK."

He took a deep breath and started counting.

"Five, four, three, two, one. Virus deployed."

Several seconds later and no alarm--the virus had passed into the network undetected. They waited. A minute later, the receptor lights on the three test commlinks flashed red--they were receiving data from the network! Two minutes after that, the commlinks flashed warnings on their visors:

"Connection to server severed. Attempting to reconnect."

A few seconds later, another warning flashed across the visor screens:

"Attempt to reconnect failed. Server not responding."

The commlinks could not receive or send data.

About the same time, S.O.S. began to show visible signs of distress. First the hum of its fans stopped. Then the whine of the drives picked up dramatically. A few seconds later, the smell of an electrical fire reached those closest to the test network. There were no visible flames, but one of the consultants closest to the hardware yelled out.

"That's enough--I smell burning. Blast it."

Three of the other consultants brought extinguishers to bear on the servers and released a shower of suffocating coolant. Two others turned the overhead fans on "high" to keep the contents of the extinguishers from fanning out through the compartment.

Slink was not surprised at all by the complete success of the test. He knew they'd succeed. Of course, they'd have to physically confirm their success by tearing down the servers and examining the damage to the memory, drives, and processors. He knew they'd find everything so thoroughly infected with destructive data that even those components that could be salvaged would be useless. He'd seen enough. Chris was sitting right next to him. He leaned over to speak to him in a barely audible voice.

"I'll be in sickbay if you need me. You can carry out the rest of the mission without me here. My work is done."

"You OK?" Chris whispered in return.

"I have to keep a promise," Slink replied. "I'll be fine. Just thought I better get down there and let Jerome get started before...before whatever happens happens," he finished.

Chris nodded to Slink. He got up quietly. The other consultants were so busy with the test and its aftermath, they never noticed him leaving. He made his way across the bridge, down the double deck of stairs and down the short passageway. The door of sickbay slid aside and Slink walked in. Jenna sat waiting for him. His eyes filled with tears. Jerome came around a partition.

"Let's get this over with," Slink said.

"Let's," said Jerome.

Jenna took Slinks hand, locking her fingers with his. They walked behind the partition, where Slink laid down on the examination table and Jenna sat next to him.

Slink turned his head to the side and locked eyes with Jenna. Tears leaked from his eyes and rolled over his nose, down his cheek, and onto the paper sheet.

"Don't let go," he said.

"I won't," she replied. "Not today, not tomorrow, not ever."

———————

Slink was having a hard time following Jerome's explanation of the procedures he intended to perform to try to get some idea what was going on in Slink's head. It wasn't because Jerome was using medical terminology Slink didn't understand. The vocabulary was well within Slink's reach. As Slink recognized he had stopped listening to Jerome yet again, he smiled.

"What is it, Slink?" Jerome asked. "It really won't hurt, I promise."

"No it's not that. If you assure me something's not going to hurt, I trust you. I was just having a tough time paying attention, and then I realized the irony of my problem. I mean, if I wasn't so damn good at concentrating, we wouldn't be here at all! Here I am--someone who can concentrate on tedious technical information for hours at a time, even when I should be sleeping or relaxing, and when you try to talk to me for five minutes, I can't stay focused. It just struck me as funny. I guess you have to be me to see the humor in it. I'm sorry. Go ahead."

Jerome wanted to acknowledge the humor in the situation, but he didn't appreciate it enough to bother. He raced ahead with his explanations.

"First, we'll take some more blood and run all the routine tests to see if you have any recurrence of infection. That's highly unlikely, but we have to rule it out completely. Then, I'm going to take a biopsy of the plate in your head, well not really a biopsy, since it isn't living tissue, but a sample--you know what I mean. I want to analyze the plate and see what kind of metal they used so I can devise some plan for seeing through it. Assuming I figure out a way to do that--see through the plate that is, then we'll do a brain scan and see what shows up. If we can't see past the plate, then it will be time for Plan B which I think we'll leave for later. OK? Any questions?"

"How long is this going to take?" Slink asked.

"Ladies first," Jerome chided.

"I'll leave the questions to Slink," said Jenna.

"I knew I would have to answer that one," Jerome said, turning back to Slink. "If I find a way to get past that plate, I've got everything set and ready to go, so you'll be out of here tonight. If I can't get past the plate with a scan, then we need to talk about a longer stay, but let's hope for the best and deal with the worst only if we have to, OK?"

"That second part sounds rather ominous, but I'll play along for now," said Slink. "So I guess you'll want an arm for the blood sample, huh?"

Jerome took the blood and set up the lab tests on it before he returned with a tray bearing an array of instruments. Slink saw a syringe, a scalpel and a few other tools that looked like they belonged in a repairman's toolbox. He raised an eyebrow toward Jerome.

"Don't worry Slink, I won't leave a scar you can find a month from now, and I won't hurt you."

Jerome had Slink lay on his stomach and turn his head to the side. Jenna released one hand long enough to let him turn over and took the other hand as soon as it was within reach. Jerome immobilized Slink's head and shaved a small area of Slink's scalp above and behind his left ear. He then injected the area with an anesthetic. A minute later, Slink felt warmth on his neck and twitched.

"Don't worry, Slink, I'll make sure it doesn't stain your jumper," Jerome said. "Just another minute, and I'll be ready to collect the sample. Then a little surgical glue and you'll be as good as new."

Slink waited to feel pain. It never came. A minute later, Jerome warned him.

"You're going to hear this more than you'll feel it. You may feel some slight pressure, but you're going to hear a scraping sound that's going to sound a lot louder to you than it really is. Remember, I'm working right behind your ear."

The scraping came and went, and Slink felt no noticeable pressure.

"Sit still for a minute," Jerome commanded. "I'm going to put this under a scope to make sure I got a sample before I close you up. I think we lucked out. That material is a lot softer than I expected, and I think I scraped enough to suit our purposes with one pass."

Slink squeezed Jenna's hand.

"You OK?" he asked.

"Me?" she responded. "I'm not the one laying on the table."

"Sometimes, it's harder to watch, or so I hear," said Slink.

"I'm fine," Jenna reassured him. "I just hope Jerome can identify that stuff and figure out a way to take a picture of your brain."

"Me too," mumbled Slink.

They fell silent. Jerome was back a couple minutes later.

"Well, I think I know what to do from here," he said.

"That's good news," said Jenna.

"That material isn't metal at all," said Jerome. "It's mostly silicon, with a reflective coating applied to the side next to your scalp to reflect ordinary scans. I can work around that. I just need to make a few quick calibrations on the equipment, and we should get some pictures we can use. But first, how about we close that gash in your scalp and let you sit up?"

"Sounds good to me," replied Slink.

It took a few minutes for Jerome to close the incision and stop the bleeding. Then he and Jenna helped Slink turn over on his back. After that, Jerome elevated the back of the exam table so Slink was in a reclined sitting position.

"Stay put for a minute," he said to them both. "I'm going to make a few adjustments to the scanner and then I'll come back and position the camera to take a few shots of your head."

He didn't wait for a reply. He was out of the cubicle before either of them could acknowledge what he said.

"Well that wasn't so bad, huh?" Jenna asked.

"You weren't the one getting your head cut open," whined Slink in mock reproach.

Jenna laughed at his weak attempt at humor and leaned over to kiss him. After a short, tender kiss, Jenna sat back down in the chair next to the examination table.

"Sounds like good news--with the sample Jerome took," Jenna said.

"We'll see," said Slink.

"What--it didn't sound good to you? It sounds like you're going to get out of here tonight--that's good news, isn't it?"

"It'll be nice to get out of here, that's for sure."

"Then what is it?" Jenna asked.

"Jenna..." Slink paused.

"What, Slink. What is it?"

"If this turns out to be...something bad, something...well...frightening, I want you to know that I would understand if you...."

"Stop it, Slink!" Jenna interjected. "This is not going to be anything bad, and even if it was, I'm not going anywhere."

She lifted up their clasped hands and shook them at him.

"I'm not going to let go--ever!"

Jerome walked in with a device that looked like the shower cap Jenna wore most mornings to avoid having to redo her hair. He saw the intensity in Jenna's face, the tears in Slink's eyes, and he instinctively moved to reassure patient and loved one.

"Look, you two, whatever we find, the chances are extremely high that we can deal with it. We've got excellent equipment on board--you're not the only one who benefits from surface excursions, you know! Now, let's get this over with and deal with the reality, OK. The fear of the unknown is always worse than the reality."

"We're fine, Jerome, just getting a little sentimental, that's all," said Jenna. "Slink's ready--what do you need from me?"

"You can stay right there, said Jerome. "I'm just going to slip this hood over Slink's head and the camera will take an image of his entire skull. Before I do that, I need to immobilize your head again, though. OK, Slink?"

"You're the medtech; I'm just the guinea pig," said Slink.

"What's a guinea pig?" asked Jenna.

"Hell if I know," replied Slink. "Just another thing I picked up in the nursery. I think it meant the object of an experiment."

Jerome put his hands under Slink's cheekbones and moved his head until his chin was almost touching his chest. He then swung the supports around from the rails on the sides of the exam table and positioned them to hold Slink's head still.

"You OK, Slink?" he asked.

"Just great, Jerome," Slink said through clenched teeth.

Jerome slipped the hood-like covering over Slink's head and taped the edges around the edges of his scalp. When he was done, he stood back and looked over his work.

"Looks good to me. Now hold still," he said.

Slink chuckled to himself. He didn't have much choice in the matter.

A minute later Jerome came back in and took the covering off Slink's head. He loosened the braces on the sides of Slink's head and raised the back of the exam table a bit more. Then he lowered the rail on one side of the table and put a hand out for Slink.

"You can get down now," he said. "Let me help you though. You might still feel a little woozy."

"I feel fine," said Slink as he released Jenna's hand and slid off the table.

Jenna walked around the foot of the exam table and took Slink's hand again. Jerome led them out and around the partition to another cubicle that had three comfortable chairs facing each other.

"Have a seat, and I'll be right back as soon as I have the images ready. I'll tell you what I see and give you my opinion of where we go from there. It'll be just a minute."

He was gone again before either of them could interject a word. Not that either of them wanted to. They sat down in two of the chairs still holding hands and Jenna rubbed the knuckles of Slink's hand with her free hand. They glanced at each other and forced a smile from time to time, but neither could find words to fill the silence.

When Jerome returned, Slink knew it wasn't good. Jerome couldn't look Slink or Jenna in the eyes. Instead he busied himself pulling a table monitor from another cubicle into the space be-

362

tween the chairs. He reached under the table and threw a switch illuminating the translucent surface of the table. A few seconds later three distinct images came into focus on the table top. Jerome cleared his throat three times before he spoke.

"It isn't at all what I expected. The images are not images of your brain. They are images of the plate that pretty much replaces your skull. I took a variety of images, and the ones taken of the brain itself look fine."

"That's great news," Jenna interjected.

"Yes, it is," said Jerome. "You won't need any surgery to resolve any further problems you might have, Slink. It seems to me your brain is fine. The problem, if you even want to look at it that way, is with the plate that surrounds your brain.

"I took these three images with the intent of looking at the cortex or surface of your brain. If you look closely, you can see a shadowy image of the cortex, but you can more easily make out the under-surface of the plate, the side closest to your brain. It has a very distinct appearance. I can only speculate as to what it's appearance might indicate, but I would like you to take a look at it first and give me your impression."

Jerome's approach might have seemed odd in another circumstance, but Slink had a pretty good idea of what Jerome was trying to accomplish. He looked closely at the images on the table. They looked like maps of a sort. Straight lines ran parallel and at right angles to each other across the entire surface of the plate. The only places that weren't covered with the closely spaced lines seemed to mark some kind of structures. Most were rectangular, but a few were circular. When he looked more closely, Slink could see the lines connected these various structures to each other.

"Does it remind you of anything in particular?" asked Jerome.

"It's obvious, isn't it?" replied Slink. "I'd started to suspect it was something like this. I thought the plate was probably just a means of keeping the secret, not the secret itself. I wonder what they intended to do with me."

"Wait a second," said Jenna. "I don't know what you're talking about. It looks like the plate has markings etched all over it, but if those markings have some kind of meaning, I don't know what it is. If you two recognize them, tell me what they mean."

"They're not markings," replied Slink, "they're pathways. Electrical pathways."

Jenna squinted at Slink and tilted her head to the side, still not comprehending the implications of his words.

"The plate in my head is a giant circuit board."

"No!" she thought. "That's just not possible."

"But...why? Who would do this?" she ended up asking.

"That's the big question isn't it?" replied Slink. "When most kids turned ten, they got three chips implanted in their brain as part of their commlink. I got a lot more than that. It seems to me, I was or I am some kind of grand experiment. Maybe I carry in my head the next generation of commlink, without a visor across the eyes or a crystal in the ear. Maybe I'm something else entirely, but whatever I am, I'm one hell of a poster boy for everything we're fighting against!"

Slink bolted up from his chair, turned away from the table, and raised his fists into the air. He looked like he wanted to scream, but he made no sound. Then he put his hands to his head, bent over, fell to his knees, and moaned. It was a deep, agonizing sound; something you might hear from a man absorbing a mortal wound. Jenna sprang up from her chair and rushed to his side. She put an arm around him and leaned down next to him, the left side of her face against the right side of his.

"How can you even stand to be next to me?" he wailed. "I am the cyborg. Here we're opposing something we claim is the first step in turning people into machines and all the time, I'm light years further down that road than any of the visored people we're trying to 'save.'"

Slink spit this last word out with thick sarcasm. He shot to his feet, tearing away from Jenna in the process.

"Behold your savior, Garsow! The one who delivered you from beneath the shadow of darkness is the offspring of the very darkness itself. Just as you learn to love the light, you will grow to fear the one who brought you into it."

"Stop it!" yelled Jenna.

She rose to her feet, came around in front of Slink, cupped his face in her hands and kissed him—hard. Then she pulled back and stared intently into his eyes for several long seconds before speaking.

"Stop it," she said with tenderness seldom associated with those words. "You can play the victim for a little while if you need to, but then what? You'll still have a plate in your head, and we'll still be on the edge of the biggest changes our society has ever known, and I'll still love you. When you're done feeling sorry for yourself, we'll still need to stop the sick animals who did that to you."

Slink shrunk back ever so slightly and put his hand to his lips.

"That damn plate almost killed you, Slink. It would have driven you to exhaustion and then squeezed the last little bit of life out of you---if it defined you. Instead the people around you wouldn't let that happen--people like Dot and Gen and Chris and me. If the bastards who did this had their way, maybe you'd be a robot somewhere hooked up to intravenous feeding tubes and crunching data faster than any supercomputer ever could, but you're not a robot. You're the man I love, the nephew Dot loves, the friend Gen loves, the colleague Chris loves. We define you, not that stupid plate! All that's left is for you to choose how you'll define yourself. Are you the poor bastard who had his skull replaced with a circuit board or are you the man we love? We've made our decision, now it's time for you to make yours!"

Jenna pulled Slink's face down to hers and kissed him again. After a few seconds, Slink pulled back from her, stared into her eyes for a few seconds, then squeezed her in an embrace.

"Thanks, J," he whispered. "I'm not sure I deserve your love and your trust. I...."

Just then, Dot's voice came pouring from the intercom, detailing the evacuation protocol and ordering everyone on board to make preparations in compliance with that protocol.

Slink pulled back from Jenna and stared off into space.

"Wait a minute," he hissed.

"What? Are you in pain?" Jerome asked as he stepped forward and took Slink's arm.

"No, I'm fine," said Slink. "But I need to take another look at those images!"

"Right now?" asked Jerome. "You heard the Commander. We've got to get a move on!"

"Yes, right now!" Slink asserted. "This can't wait."

Slink kissed Jenna softly, then turned quickly and bent over the table monitor. He began to pour over the images, magnifying the view several times and tracing the pathways with his index finger. After a few minutes, he froze and nodded to himself. Then he stood and looked up at Jerome.

"You're going to need to do some surgery after all," Slink exclaimed.

"What are you talking about?" asked Jerome.

"You have a laser-equipped robotic surgical station here, don't you?" inquired Slink. "I'm pretty sure I spotted it on one of my previous visits."

"Yeah, we have some of the best equipment available. But Slink, you don't need surgery, and we don't have time to do it even if you did."

Slink ignored Jerome's protests and pressed on.

"If you loaded these images into the surgical station, could it be programmed to make cuts in the plate in my head?" asked Slink.

"Well, yes, it could be programmed to make precise cuts on any surface I've previously scanned. But Slink, I don't know anywhere near enough to begin to remove the plates in your head. I'm not sure that could be done under any circumstances without killing you!"

Jenna stepped in and started to protest.

366

"Just hear me out," Slink pleaded.

"I don't want you to remove anything," Slink assured Jerome. "I just want you to make two tiny cuts in the pathways on the circuit board. I can show you just where those cuts need to be made, and all you need to do is program the robot."

Jerome said, "I need to know what you're asking me to do, Slink. I can't program the robot to make cuts without understanding the intended outcome."

"No problem," said Slink. "It's really pretty simple. See this square near the edge of the plate that covers the left side of my head? That little square is just behind my left ear."

"Yeah, I see the square," answered Jerome.

"That's a transmitter," said Slink. "I can tell by it's shape and the pathways running to and from it. That little chip would allow someone to send instructions to the other components on the circuit board, any of which in turn could send instructions to my brain. That little chip might also transmit to someone any information stored in the memory chips embedded in the circuit board. If I'm going to stop anyone from messing with my brain and prevent those same people from downloading information I've acquired, we need to disconnect that chip."

"Couldn't that cause other problems, maybe even damage your brain?" asked Jenna. She reached out and grasped Slink's hand in hers.

"No, it can't damage my brain," assured Slink. "The circuit board in my head is just a specialized computer. When that computer detects that the transmitter has failed, it'll just send to memory any data it would've transmitted. We're not going to damage any of the data paths. We're just going to sever the low voltage power supply path that feeds the transmitter."

"Wow, Slink, are you sure about this?" Jerome asked. "I don't want to take a chance I'm going to cause permanent brain damage!"

"I'm sure," said Slink. "You're going to have to trust me. I'm a danger to all of us as long as someone out there can access any data I collect. We have to disable that transmitter. They probably can only connect intermittently since wireless transmission is pretty spotty in the tunnels, but we need to cut them off completely. We need to do this right now; there's no telling what's going to happen over the next few hours. It could be a long time before we get another chance to deal with this."

Slink looked at Jerome and Jenna. They both knew enough about the Technoid's objectives to appreciate what Slink was saying. Jenna rested her head on Slink's shoulder and squeezed his hand.

"So that's the first cut I need you to make," continued Slink. "See this round chip at the edge of the plate that covers the right side of my head?"

"Yeah…" repled Jerome hesitantly.

"That's a geolocation chip. We need to disable that one too. They can't be able to trace my movements, or we'll all be sitting ducks."

"Oh man, Slink! This really bothers me," exclaimed Jerome. "I'm just barely getting my head around the discovery we've just made and you're asking me mess with something I couldn't even imagine a few minutes ago. I don't know about this!"

"Jerome, I need you to trust me. This will only take a few minutes, it won't cause any damage to me, and as soon as it's done, Jenna and I will get out of your way. Please, you've got to do this!"

"Oh, man!" exclaimed Jerome.

He blew out two quick breaths in succession.

"OK, OK," he said. "Let's do it."

Slink marked the precise points where the robot needed to make the cuts. Jerome programmed the surgical station. Slink laid down on the table and Jerome fixed his head in place. Jenna leaned over Slink and gave him a kiss.

"Are you sure about this?" she asked.

"I'm sure," he replied. "Everything's going to be fine; I promise."

Jerome double and triple checked his calculations. He made sure the scans of Slink's head were loaded properly. He checked Slink's position on the table for the third time. Then he took a deep breath and ushered Jenna away from the table so the robotic arm could move into position around Slink's head.

Jerome stepped back into the control booth and glanced over his monitor. Everything was ready. He shook his head in disbelief over what he was about to do. He touched his screen. The robot moved into place; a light flashed. The robot moved again; another light flashed. By the time Jerome came around the corner of his booth, Jenna was already at Slink's side. She stood over him, stared down into his face for several seconds, then gently lowered her head onto his chest and cried.

Chapter 15

Chris knew they couldn't fire the virus at the Supernet without making preparations. They had no way of predicting what the reaction would be when the Supernet went down. They needed to be prepared for any and all eventualities. That meant everyone on board Home needed a deadline toward which to prepare. He consulted with Dot, who in turn, consulted with Gen and Jakov before setting 1400 hours as zero hour. That gave everyone on board Home about three hours to prepare.

Dot instructed the crew over the intercom to be ready for a full evacuation. That meant in addition to being prepared to leave Home, each crew member was responsible for making sure his station could be abandoned without dire consequence for the sweeper drone. Three hours was not an abundance of time to carry out the necessary preparations, but Dot didn't want her crew to have an abundance of time of their hands. They needed enough time to prepare and no more.

Dot went to her quarters and chose those things she'd carry off the drone if they were forced to abandon ship. She hoped they'd be able to ride out the initial wave of chaos in the relatively safe confines of their converted sweeper drone, but she knew they might be forced to the surface. If DAN launched an all-out assault on the tunnels, they'd have to act quickly to get everyone off the drone. They couldn't take the chance that anyone would be trapped aboard the drone and associated with the attack on the Supernet.

She hadn't bothered to order Chris to destroy the evidence of their work to bring the Supernet down. She knew that unless they physically destroyed every piece of computer hardware aboard the drone, a good computer programmer could retrieve evidence from the drives of the linked stations in the Cave and figure out pretty quickly that the occupants of the converted drone were at the center of the attack.

If DAN launched an offensive, it was her intent to abandon the drone completely. If, by some incomprehensible stroke of luck, Home was never discovered to be more than a sweeper drone, she and a portion of the crew would return to the drone. Otherwise, they'd be forced to find shelter in remote undeveloped caverns or on the surface, doing their best to blend in under extremely difficult circumstances. Dot knew it wasn't easy to feign the kind of terror most of the surface dwellers would be feeling. She only hoped most of her crew wouldn't have to try.

At 1300 hours, Dot met Chris in the Cave. He went over the sequence he'd follow before deploying the virus. He told her what he expected should follow, assuming the virus worked on the Supernet as it had on Son of Supernet.

At 13:30 hours, Dot checked in via the intercom with her company chiefs. They indicated they'd be ready to evacuate at 1400 hours or anytime thereafter. They awaited her further orders. She commanded that at the first sign DAN agents were entering the tunnels, they were to get off the drone. If there was no such indication, Beta Company was to evacuate at 1400 hours and deploy to the surface, Alpha Company was to evacuate at 14:20 hours and deploy to the undeveloped cavern Jerome, Naomi, and Dot had found. Home would pass very near the abandoned enclave through which the cavern could be accessed at right about the time Alpha Company would disembark. The company chiefs communicated their understanding and Dot signed off.

At 13:45 hours, the Cave consultants and Bridge crew gathered in and around the Cave. Together, they made up most of Gamma Company. They'd witness the deployment together. No one spoke. Some of the Cave consultants sat at their stations. None of the Bridge crew stayed at theirs. Everyone did his or her best to pass the interminable minutes before the deployment. Some prayed, some fumbled with a small object they'd found within reach, others just fidgeted where they sat or stood.

At 13:55 hours, Dot nodded to Chris and he stood before his station. He awoke his display and double checked his preparations. Everything was ready. He had only to touch the icon on his screen and the one minute countdown would begin.

At 13:59 hours, Chris touched his screen. Large numerals filled the screen. 59, 58, 57, 56. The air in the Cave felt too heavy to breath. It did not matter. Most of the occupants were trying not to draw breath. 34, 33, 32, 31. People glanced away from the screen to glimpse the others in the room. Occasionally eyes would meet and, typically, eyebrows would be raised and shoulders would shrug. and furtive, tentative smiles would be exchanged. 15, 14, 13, 12. No one looked away from the screen now. 8, 7, 6, 5.

The screen went dark.

It took a moment for the assembled people in the Cave to realize that the entire room had gone dark. A second later the auxiliary generators kicked in and the safety lights went on. Dot looked at Chris. He shrugged and shook his head.

"The sweeper drones draw power from the grid through an electrical interface near the top of the drone. It's a tension line that maintains contact with the open conduit line running along the ceiling surface of the tunnel. The current passing through the tunnels is regulated from the Grid as is most electrical supply not associated with the Supernet. As near as we can tell all power coming from the Grid has been interrupted. That's why we're running on backup power. We just got word from a surface excursion active on the surface as this went down that all surface power seems to be running from emergency backup generators or battery banks. More importantly, and perhaps more surprisingly, it appears the Supernet is down."

Forest waited for this last statement to sink in. Since becoming chief communications officer he'd never been called upon to make a presentation to the Commander's Cabinet. He wanted to impress, but he also wanted to make sure the import of his words was understood.

"Forest, I don't understand," Gen interjected. "The Supernet is independent of the Grid isn't it? Aren't they totally separate systems, and doesn't the Supernet have its own backup system to prevent any power failure from bringing it down?"

Forest was nodding in the affirmative to each of Gen's questions.

"Then how could one event cause the other? Wouldn't it require two separate events to bring down both the Grid and the Supernet?"

"As far as we know, you are correct," said Forest. "We've been unable to postulate how both networks could come down for the first time since they were brought online and at the exact same moment. Perhaps if we caused the Supernet failure, that somehow led surface engineering to shut down the Grid."

"But we didn't cause the Supernet failure," Dot interjected. "Chris and his colleagues have gone through the memory banks in the Cave and confirmed that the virus was never deployed. Whatever happened to the Supernet, it had nothing to do with us."

"Are we still running blind?" asked Gen.

"No," replied Jakov. "We've brought the Bridge's operations back online, at the risk of alerting DAN to the fact that there is more to this sweeper drone than meets the eye. We felt the risk of detection was outweighed by our need to see what is happening in the tunnels before we stumble upon our ruin."

Dot rose from her chair to command the floor. She motioned for Forest, still standing at the center of the room, to take his seat. Everyone turned in his or her seat to give Dot the attention she deserved.

"So, people, I need to hear your ideas as to how we've come to this point," proclaimed Dot. "If we didn't bring the Supernet down, someone else did. Who might that be, and what would be their purpose in doing so? Given the simultaneous nature of the Grid failure, I would assume the same person or persons brought the Grid down. If you have another theory, I'd be open to hearing it. Assuming the two failures are the work of one person or group, again we need to ask, 'why?' Who stands to gain by such an action?"

Dot paused before asking her more ominous questions.

"Given the fact that both failures occurred within seconds of our intended deployment of a virus we created to destroy the Supernet, we must ask ourselves if, as almost certainly appears to be the case, the person or group behind these failures knew of our intentions and timing. And if we conclude they had such information, we must further ask ourselves how they came about it. Finally, I am most interested in any speculation as to what you might anticipate as the next move of the person or group behind today's events."

Dot sat back down in her chair. No one stood to offer his or her speculation with regard to her questions. She was about to stand and try to coax answers from her gathered leaders when someone spoke up. She hadn't seen Slink come into the room, since he entered the open door just behind her. She was startled by his voice and somewhat dismayed he'd made his way to this gathering. She instantly regretted her decision not to interrupt Jerome's tests in sickbay to invite her nephew to join them. Now she'd have to live with the impression he formed at discovering this gathering to which he'd never been invited.

I will offer my thoughts on your questions Commander," Slink said.

He stepped into the center of the room. He nodded to each of the people there in turn as he surveyed the room.

"I believe I'm responsible for the uncanny timing of today's events," he continued. "Jerome discovered earlier this morning the reason for my extraordinary abilities when it comes to data analysis and programming. It appears I carry within my skull, or more accurately, in place of my skull a circuit board. We must assume the circuit board carries upon it a series of processors wired directly into my brain. I am the solar system's fastest, most complex data processing system."

A hush fell over the room. Everyone struggled to comprehend what they'd just heard.

"It would seem I carry in my head the next generation of commlink, and as such, I must assume the circuit board in my head was designed to communicate continuously with the Supernet or some other receiver in the same manner any visor wearing member of our linked society might. I can only assume someone monitoring the transmissions I was unwittingly making determined our intentions and timing and took the only action available to stop us. I think there is a good chance we're safe from any further monitoring as long as the Supernet is down, but once they bring it back, they will certainly attempt to reestablish contact through me."

Dot interrupted.

"Slink, I don't like where this is going," she said as she stood. "I'll hear you out, but in return, I'm going to ask you put aside any actions you have in mind until we're finished here. Agreed?"

Slink had to think for a minute. He was planning on saying what he felt he needed to say and leaving. It had taken nearly three hours for him to reach his climactic decisions, and he wasn't ready to let go of them so easily.

"I've thought this through..." he started to say.

"I'm sure you have," Dot interrupted once again, "but the rest of us have not, and I believe the decisions we're going to make today are far too important to be made by any one of us in isolation from the rest. Tell us what you think; tell us what you've decided if you must, but withhold taking any action until everyone has the opportunity to reflect on your words and offer their best ideas in response. Only then can we hope to make the best decisions. This is no time for any of us to think in terms of ourself alone. You have no more right to do that than does any other person here. Agreed?"

Dot had taken on the air she assumed when she was giving orders as Commander of Home. Slink knew there was no room for discussion. Dot was demanding he set aside his intended actions for the benefit of them all. He could make only one response.

"Agreed, Commander," he said.

"Then continue, and we'll hear you out without further interruption," Dot said.

She sat down and Slink turned to the gathered contingent once again.

"I was saying I'm not making any unwitting transmissions as long as the Supernet is down, and while I had Jerome cut the two most obvious transmission points on the circuit board in my head, I cannot be certain I won't pose a threat the minute the Supernet is restored. Even though I prevailed upon our Medtech, Jerome, to disable the transmitter and geolocater in my head, I still believe I should leave Home immediately and head for the surface.

"In retrospect, I don't think it was coincidence that Remmi and I were identified by DAN agents the last time I was on the surface. I'm sure every DAN agent now has my description and orders to detain me, and I'm quite certain they'll stop at nothing to carry out those orders. I don't want to put every person I've ever cared about in harm's way, and I also have a burning desire to face the people who did this to me. Since they will likely be determined to bring about that meeting, I think it would be best to expedite it. I came here to state the obvious: it is time to negotiate safe passage for everyone onboard Home in exchange for turning me over to DAN."

Slink turned and sat in the nearest empty chair. As he did so he was shocked and somewhat dismayed to find Jenna sitting in the next chair to his right. She took his right hand, interlocked the fingers of her left hand in his, and leaned over to whisper in his ear.

"Not today, not tomorrow, not ever."

He didn't look at her. He knew her resolve matched his. He might be determined to give himself away, but Jenna was no less determined to hold onto the man she loved.

He'd left her sleeping in the unused officer's quarters where they'd gone together after Jerome had finished his work in the med station. They'd talked for a while. They'd cried. They'd come together in passionate expression of their extraordinary love.

Slink had come here wanting desperately to protect everyone aboard Home; he'd wanted desperately to face the people who'd carried out their hideous experiments on him; and now he wanted just as desperately to stay by Jenna's side. Unfortunately, he couldn't imagine a single course upon which he could fulfill those desperate longings simultaneously.

Looking around the room, Jenna was confident she wasn't the only one determined to keep Slink from acting on his half-baked ideas of heroism. Everyone looked to be poised to pounce. Had Slink bolted for the door, Jenna was convinced he would've been tackled before he got half way there. Then as she surveyed the room, Gen stood to speak. He walked across the small room and stood before Slink's chair. He spoke softly, but Jenna was sure everyone in the room could still hear his every word.

"Slink, you have no idea what you mean to the people in this room do you?"

He paused and motioned for Slink to look around the room. Everywhere he looked, Slink saw people nodding, no, bowing to him.

"Your extraordinary mind is a great treasure for all of humanity regardless of how you came about your gifts. You may've been exploited, even abused, by people who saw you as nothing more than the latest generation of super computer, but you came to us, and we see you as a colleague, a friend, a hero.

"I think because of your unique nature, you've suffered greatly as you've focused your gifts on finding the solutions we sought. I think your resolve to help us has cost you more than you or any of us may ever understand.

"Your most recent discovery about yourself does not release us from obligation toward you, it increases both our gratitude and our determination to stand with you as you stood with us. I, for one, would like nothing more than to turn this forum into a discussion as to how we might best do that. Unfortunately, we cannot make any one person's plight the focus of our attention today.

"I trust we will, one day, turn our efforts to finding and holding accountable the ones who abused you. As of right now, we have no choice but to turn our attention to finding the best course for our entire community. We all must trust everyone is setting aside his or her individual needs for the sake of the whole."

Gen turned from Slink, toward whom he had focused his words up to that moment, and addressed the rest of the room.

"It's time for all of us to turn our minds to seeking a way forward--together. We must better understand how we came to this crossroads before we can hope to find the best path forward. Here are a few of my reflections.

"Even before Slink joined our little meeting, I was convinced that DAN acted with full knowledge of our intentions. The Grid and the Supernet could not go down within five seconds of our planned attack by sheer coincidence. I'm sure most of you'd already reached the same conclusion.

"Slink suggests DAN was receiving information from him. Though this is plausible, I think it's unlikely. First of all, Slink left the Cave three hours or so before the virus was to be deployed. The timetable for its deployment wasn't developed until after he left. The deployment was scheduled on a very short countdown-- one minute to be precise. Had the shutdown come several minutes before we intended to deploy the virus, it might be conceivable that Slink was the source of DAN's information. With it coming five seconds beforehand, it seems highly unlikely DAN could determine the timing of their actions based on information they received from Slink.

"Secondly, none of the commlinks we've developed can transmit from beneath the surface. There's too much interference. If Slink carries a transmitter that can send data from underground, we've heard nothing of it. Furthermore, the people who operated on him couldn't have dreamed he'd need to transmit data from underground. Nonetheless, we can run a couple simple tests to find out whether or not he has an active transmitter embedded in his head. I think we'll find there are no transmissions emanating from him.

"If I'm right, DAN has found some other way to monitor our activities. Since we didn't use a lengthy countdown process to deploy the Supernet virus, it would appear that DAN is monitoring us very closely indeed. Other than setting Slink's mind at ease regarding his complicity in DAN's actions, I don't think we're well served to waste a lot of time trying to figure out where or how DAN is getting information. Instead, I suggest we use their awareness against them. To this end, I've spoken with Chris, the Cave convener, and he had an idea that may accomplish our purpose whether the virus is ever deployed or not. If I may, I would defer the floor to Chris."

Dot signaled for Chris to stand and speak. He stood in front of his chair and without so much as looking around the room, he launched into his discourse.

"When we first started to look for ways to infiltrate the Supernet, we developed a way of piggybacking an executable instruction sequence with an innocuous error message from a visor. We even tested it and got a visor to send, without detection, instructions for Home to reverse course. Many of you remember that event several weeks back."

379

The room erupted with chatter as people shared their experiences of the sudden course change. It took Chris several tries before he had the attention of his audience again and could continue.

"We set aside the idea of transmitting the virus from a commlink when Slink later found back doors right into the Supernet mainframe. If the Supernet comes back up, it is very likely those back doors will have been closed. If DAN knew what we're up to and shut down the Grid and the Supernet because they realized their vulnerability, they'll only bring both networks back on line when they are confident they have protected themselves.

"I propose we piggy-back the virus on an innocuous packet of corrupted data and load it on as many commlinks as we can get our hands on. We set them to transmit as soon as they detect a network connection. Each time we gain access to another commlink, we load the virus on that commlink. I polled the Cave consultants, and we're confident there is no effective way to screen incoming commlink messages for the virus. The Supernet and all of the commlinks would have to be completely reconfigured to block the virus. At best, that would take years. Even if DAN figures out a way to protect the Supernet, they won't be able to block the virus from disabling the transmitters on every commlink on the surface once the network is up and active again. The Supernet is nothing without commlinks!"

Chris sat down while the room spontaneously broke into small groups of two or three to discuss his proposal. Dot let the gathering of her best leaders, her best minds, continue with these informal discussions for several minutes while she walked over to Slink. She gestured to the white-haired man who was sitting on Slink's left, who happened to be one of her Bridge officers, and he nodded to her and vacated his seat so she could sit next to her nephew. She sat down and put her arm around Slink.

"You weren't really going to walk out on us, Slink."

Her words were delivered in the same tone Dot delivered orders; they were a statement not a question. Then she lowered her voice and softened her tone.

"I couldn't possibly know how it feels to make the discovery you made this afternoon, Slink. If I found out someone had done to me what's been done to you, I'm sure I'd want to kill the person or people who did that to me! At the same time, I might think I'd be doing everyone a favor if I just dropped out of sight altogether.

"What I'm trying to say, Slink, is that while I may never fully understand what you're going through, I can certainly understand some of the feelings you've expressed and some of the ideas you're entertaining. But just because I understand doesn't mean I support you doing something that would be stupid or irresponsible."

Her volume remained low but her tone regained the sharp edges of her initial statement as she continued.

"If I have to, I'll have you confined to one of the vacant officer's quarters and have a guard posted outside the door until we make a decision as to our next move. I'm not going to take the risk you'll act on your feelings and place yourself at unnecessary risk. I hope you heard what Gen said and are beginning to realize your concern about transmitting data unwittingly to DAN is probably misplaced. I hope you're beginning to realize you have taken this...this...crime that was committed against you and turned it into an extraordinary blessing. I hope you're beginning to see you have the power to turn their intentions on their ear and use your abilities to subvert those intentions."

Dot couldn't tell if she was getting through to her nephew or not. He stared just over her left shoulder while she spoke. His countenance seemed to soften as she spoke of her hopes for the ways his perspective might change, but she wasn't sure if it really had or if her desire to see it soften was creating the illusion that her words were having their desired affect.

"Slink, at first my parents, your great-grandparents, weren't opposed to commlink technology. They recognized the tremendous benefits of enhancing human awareness and capability with embedded technology. When it appeared the technology would be tested with a group of volunteers and later deployed to a larger segment of the population on a voluntary basis, they supported it! They dreamed of the day we'd develop near light-speed travel, and they could see how the commlink would advance that dream. They sounded the alarm when it became clear the governing council intended to deploy the technology across Garsow, whether or not people volunteered.

They were horrified that something so...experimental, so...untested would be forced on an entire population long before we could possibly understand the full ramifications of such radical interference with natural brain function. They were finally galvanized to take action against commlink deployment when they saw what was happening to our society--people made permanent outcasts if they couldn't or wouldn't accept the commlink; children being removed from their homes and raised in nurseries; social interaction being reduced to a fraction of what had been normal before the commlink; people working 80 to 100 hours a week; most of all, everyone being turned into placid little robots who processed information and did little else.

The advancements that came with the commlink were amazing--breakthroughs came in every area of scientific research. Problems that had baffled our best minds were solved seemingly overnight. It was easy to look past the fact that life-long friends stopped speaking to each other, that people rarely formed new friendships, that the birth rate dropped to a third of what it had been before the commlink. It was easy because open conflict almost disappeared from society. Productivity went through the ceiling and crime almost disappeared. Our family eventually became the sole voice of opposition. It was pretty ironic if you think about it--the two scientists that led the expedition to settle a distant planetoid later become the voice of opposition to the latest technology. My parents were more than scientists, though Slink. They were good people, and they believed that human beings benefitted at least as much from their indomitable spirit as they did from their intellect."

Dot could see she was finally getting through to Slink, although she suspected his reaction wasn't what she'd hoped. Finally, he went from subtle shakes of his head to verbal outburst.

"Damn it, Dot--do you really think I need a history lesson right now? I know all this! What the heck does that have to do with my situation?"

He shot up from his chair, but before he could turn from her, she grabbed his sleeve and pulled him back into his chair.

"It has everything to do with your situation, nephew! Step back from your anger and outrage over your recent discovery and think about it. Have you lost your ability to express yourself with passion and spirit? I think your reaction just now answers that question! Have you lost your ability to love others and let them love you? Shall I ask Jenna for her opinion in that matter? Have you been reduced to a placid little robot? I see fire in your eyes that tells me you most certainly have not! You, nephew, have not lost your spirit--and you have gained intellectual capacity so far beyond anything any human being has ever known.

"I don't know what the perpetrators of the crime committed against you intended, and I don't really care. If I needed an excuse to hate them, I could come up with a half dozen. I'm sure they never intended for you to find the wholeness you've found. I'm sure they intended for that circuit board in your head to dominate you, to even define you. But regardless of what they intended, you've become a great man. You already dwarf me in potential and one day soon, you'll dwarf me in accomplishment as well. One day, you'll dwarf your great-grandparents, the great Drs. Lansing.

"The bastards who put that circuit board in your head might have wanted to make you the final chapter in the domestication of the human spirit. Instead you've become the first chapter in our transcendence. You've found a middle way, crossing boundaries of intellectual development and passionately weaving your life into the fabric of our souls. You've shown us what we can be! Regardless of how angry you might be, how much you might want revenge on the animals who did this to you, how much you might want to sacrifice yourself and avoid fulfilling your destiny, as long as I draw breath, I won't let that happen. If that means you'll project your anger onto the commander who insisted you live up to your potential rather than the surgeons who replaced your skull with a circuit board, so be it! I'm convinced you'll one day soon be the most important person in our society!"

Slink started to protest, but Dot waved his weak attempt away with a firm shake of her head.

"You never asked for your role, and you may always resent it. Be that as it may, you are who you are and nothing will change that now. You're the most brilliant human being who's ever lived, and you are my beloved nephew, Jenna's lover, the brother Gen never had, and your shipmate's shipmate. Ready or not, Slink, your time has come!"

The room had grown so quiet Dot's words echoed in the still air of the chamber like a thunderclap. Everyone looked at Slink. He wanted to bolt from the room more than ever, and at the same time, he knew he had to stay. Though he wanted to protest with primal screams of defiance, he knew Dot spoke truth. He felt Jenna's grip on his right hand grow tighter. He felt her breath upon his ear before he heard her words.

"Not today, not tomorrow, not ever. I'll never leave your side, Slink, and as long as we're together, I'll share this and any other burden you bear."

He leaned against her and closed his eyes. Tears traced their recently-traveled paths down his cheeks once again. She wrapped her right arm around the back of his head and pulled him close. Dot stood as she began to shed her own tears. She prayed Slink's dawning awareness wouldn't come at the price of their relationship. She'd pay the price if it must be paid—she'd made that decision before she approached him. She could only hope the price she paid would fall short of the ultimate price she risked.

—————————

The sound of the alarm didn't register in Slink's mind right away. He was too lost, too overwhelmed by Dot's words. He wanted to melt into Jenna's embrace and escape the obligations implicit in the truths Dot had given voice. Time and circumstance conspired to rob him of any such opportunity.

Jenna withdrew from their embrace and shook him, gently at first, and then more forcefully.

"We have to get up Slink," she pleaded.

Dot's voice boomed through the ship's intercom.

"All stations--abandon ship!"

She turned away from the intercom on the wall and yelled to Gen.

"Get these people out of here. I'm going to make sure the last of our Company is making their way out. I'll see you in the hold."

She was out the doorway and gone before Gen could respond.

Gen turned away from the monitor where he was surveying the report from the Bridge. He raised his voice above the tumult in the little room where the leaders had convened to chart their response to the unexpected shut down of the Grid and the Supernet.

"We have to get off the ship and into the undeveloped caverns. DAN is flooding the tunnels with agents. You'll all be escorted to safety first. The remainder of Gamma company will stand against the agents as long as they can to give you time to escape. There'll most probably be an exchange of weapons fire. Keep your heads low and keep moving. Your evacuation packs have been placed in the rear hold just ahead of the hatch we'll use to evacuate. Grab your pack and a commlink. Once you exit Home, follow the person in front of you until someone directs you to stop. Let's go people, you don't want to end up in the hands of DAN agents!"

It seemed like a dream to Slink at first--like a nightmare where he was desperately trying to wake up but couldn't quite escape the hold of sleep. He wanted to respond, but he just couldn't. When Gen pulled him roughly to his feet, Slink finally came around.

"Don't make us carry you out of here," Gen yelled. Then he turned to the man on the other side of Jenna. He was a tall, muscular man with a bushy mustache and dark complexion. "Gordon, help Jenna get Slink up and out of here. He'll probably be OK once you get him moving, but he's not steady on his feet just yet."

"Yes sir!" responded Gordon.

"I'm OK," Slink wheezed.

"I don't think so," replied Jenna. "You're doing better. Just keep stepping, and we'll keep supporting you for a while. You'll be fine by the time we get to the hold."

She was right. By the time they reached the hold, the adrenaline was flowing and Slink felt a surge of energy. The sound of the alarms and the frenetic activity took his attention away from his own circumstances. He gathered his pack and grabbed a commlink. Someone pushed him toward the hatch.

"Jenna!" he yelled.

He was not going to leave Home this time without making sure she was at his side.

Jenna popped up a few meters away with her pack hoisted on her back, grabbed a commlink, and lunged by two other crew members to reach Slink. He reached for her and they grasped hands. He stepped out onto the stairs that jutted from the side of the sweeper drone and started his descent, pulling her behind him. They crouched low to avoid the overhanging arms of the drone.

Just as Slink reached the last step, he heard a thunderous clap next to him that set his ears ringing and rendered him momentarily deaf. He looked up and saw one of the Gamma company men pointing something he'd only seen in vids before that moment. As he watched, the shiny black hand gun recoiled in the man's hands as another thunderclap echoed through the tunnels. Jenna pushed him forward, to the right of the man with the gun. He looked past the gunman and saw his intended target. The DAN agents were streaming toward them on foot. Even as he watched, he saw a flash emanate from the midst of the onrushing agents, and a split second later, the man who had fired his gun at the onrushing agents fell backward and crashed into the side of Home.

Jenna thrust past Slink and yanked him forward. They broke into a run together. They were only a few meters behind the ones who'd evacuated ahead of them. They saw Gamma company men and women lining the sides of the tunnels, down on one knee, pointing hand guns at the onrushing agents. Slink couldn't hear the guns fire. His ears couldn't register any sound. The concussions of the gunfire in the tunnels rocked him and he found himself losing his sense of balance. Jenna, too, found it hard to keep her feet, even though they were running on a flat surface. One of the people in front of them fell, and they nearly went sprawling as they darted to avoid the sprawling figure. They knew instinctively to keep running and hope their fallen comrade could regain her feet in time to escape.

Twice more before they reached the doorway to the Tunnel Rat enclave connecting the undeveloped cavern with the finished tunnels they saw people fall and lurched to avoid the fallen figure. Somehow, they managed to keep their feet and reached the enclave. Dot stood at the doorway and ushered them in. She was waving past them to all of their comrades. The agents would be upon them in a few more seconds. She needed to get everyone into the enclave and close the door before the agents could reach them. The agents couldn't open the door; they'd have to drill through it, and that would take time. If she could get everyone inside and shut the door, they could make their way through the hidden door at the back of the enclave and into the undeveloped caverns before DAN could breach the door and discover the passage into the caverns.

Dot shuddered at the sight of her fallen crew members. They'd suffered far higher casualties than she could ever have imagined. Still, all the losses could be justified if she could protect Slink. What she hadn't spelled out in her little speech to her nephew was the one question that had yet to be answered with regard to his role in society: would he lead the resistance to the repressive regime that had deployed the commlink or would he be the most powerful weapon that regime had ever had at their disposal? That was the question whose answer laid in the outcome of this conflict, and Dot was determined to see it answered in favor of the resistance.

As the last of her remaining crew ran for the door, she could feel the disturbance of the air around her as bullets whistled by her on both sides. She reached for the young woman running toward her. Dot recognized the terror on Shema's grimacing face as the young woman ran. She'd stood her ground until the last possible moment, biting back her fear and firing at the oncoming DAN agents until she was almost overrun. A bullet shattered Shema's left femer when she was only two meter's from Dot's outstretched arm. Dot lunged and caught her. They dropped together to the ground under a hail of bullets. Dot pulled Shema up, and secured her arms around Shema's chest. She dragged her backwards toward the door. As she reached the threshold, Gen and Jakov reached out and grabbed Shema, pulling her into the enclave. Dot tumbled backwards and sprawled onto the floor. She looked up and saw two other crew members pull the door closed and secure it. They'd made it!

Jakov and Gen were crouched on their knees over Shema. Jakov yelled for Jerome. Jerome called up to them.

"I'm coming! Hold on!"

He was there a few seconds later looking over Shema and her shattered leg. He called over his shoulder to one of the other medtechs for a tourniquet and a splint. A few seconds later, both requested items were handed forward. Jerome grabbed them, tore open the packaging and applied the tourniquet. Shema screamed in pain.

"Easy," said Jerome. "It's the only way. We have to stop the bleeding."

He called back for pain medication. A moment later, he had it in his hands, drew a syringe full of milky liquid from a vile and administered the injection into Shema's undamaged hip. A minute later, she was unconscious. Jerome then quickly set her leg as best he could and splinted the leg.

It was only then that Jerome looked up from Shema and saw that hers was not the only injury.

Gen was still slumped over on one knee next to Shema. He coughed and spat a mouthful of blood on the ground before he rolled over on his side. When he rolled, Jerome saw the circle of red that already covered half of Gen's chest. Even as he watched, blood spurted rhythmically from the hole torn in Gen's chest. Jerome knew the bullet had pierced a major artery. There was nothing he could do. He yelled.

"Dot!"

"Here!" she said, raising herself to her knees and scooting up alongside Jerome and in front of Gen.

Jerome pointed down at Gen and fell backward into a sitting position, hands grasping his calves, rocking in horror. Dot saw her wounded friend and looked back to Jerome, searching for reassurance. Jerome shook his head and lowered his gaze.

"Oh shit, Gen!" she exclaimed.

She scooted forward and pulled Gen's torso up and into her lap. She felt the warmth of his blood soaking through her clothes almost immediately. Heedless, Dot cradled Gen's head in the crook of her elbow and leaned in close to him.

"Hold on, Gen, we'll find a way to get you through this," she lied.

Gen coughed, turned his head, and spat. He turned, looked up at Dot and smiled ruefully. He rasped,

"Dot."

Her ears were just beginning to recover. She could barely hear Gen's voice. Dot leaned close to him to catch Gen's precious last words as they fell from his blood-stained lips.

"Take care of Slink," he croaked.

He coughed violently then, spraying blood over the side of Dot's face. She didn't even flinch. Gen groaned. Dot clutched him tighter as if somehow she could delay the inevitable if only she could clutch him closely enough. He motioned for Dot to give him her ear.

"You're the best friend I've ever had," he managed.

Tears ran down Dot's cheeks, but she paid them no mind. She tried to smile, and barely managed to pull some air by the rock-hard lump in the back of her throat.

Gen gasped twice, then leaned forward and struggled to speak one last time.

"Tell..." he coughed, spat more blood in the direction of the ground, spraying most of it across his jumper, and forced himself to draw one last breath as he turned back to Dot.

"Tell Neoko I never stopped loving her."

His eyes glassed over and his last words came as a whisper as his final breath escaped his lungs.

"Find her...and..tell her."

Then he was gone.

Dot's emotions exploded like fireworks, giving rise to a half dozen simulltaneous impulses. She wanted to cry out in pain and disbelief. She wanted to issue a command and see Gen standing unscathed before her. She wanted to hold her dear friend and weep until she could no longer summon tears. She wanted to escape the chaos and grieve with colleagues and friends over a great life cut short. She got to do none of those things.

"Commander!"

It was Jakov.

"Commander, they're already drilling with torches. We have no more than a minute to reach the caverns or all is lost."

Jakov motioned for a couple of his men to relieve Dot of Gen's body, but she would have none of it. He then leaned down, wrapped an arm around Dot, and lowered his voice as he leaned into her ear.

"Dot, either we leave him now, or we die here with him."

Dot took a deep breath. She lifted Gen's lifeless head, kissed his forehead once, and set him gently down on the ground. She stood, wiped her eyes, set her jaw, turned, and still covered in blood, gave the order,

"Company--fall back. Double time. We need to vacate this area now!"

Her command was relayed by officers down the line, and in no time the company was moving quickly, but orderly toward the back of the abandoned enclave.

Slink had been spared the sight of his friend's final moments. His back was turned from the scene, head buried in Jenna's neck, ears still ringing from the assault they'd suffered. He held his beloved Jenna and wept with gratitude for their safe passage.

Jenna couldn't avoid the dreadful sight of Gen's final moments. She'd seen, had wanted to cry out, had wanted to scream, and in the end, had only drawn Slink's head into her chest, stroked his bristled scalp, and wept in silence. She would not, could not, draw Slink into that pain. She bore it in silence, weeping in grief, knowing Slink would think she, too, was overcome with gratitude.

Gamma company parted to allow their commander to pass and lead the way. They walked through the abandoned enclave and into the cavern without further incident. When the hidden doorway closed behind them, their grief threatened to sweep over them and bury them there. Everyone had lost friends, coworkers, colleagues. They needed to stop, to weep, to grieve.

The one whose grief ran deepest would not allow it. Dot ordered them through the cavern. They made their way in silence, the cloud of grief bearing down on them more heavily with each step.

Most of the members of the traveling party had never seen a cloud in the blue skies of earth. If they had, they might have known one cloud in an unblemished sky is often a portent of bigger things to come. Sometimes the singular cloud is a precursor to a fearsome storm, a warning to take cover. Other times it portends a season of renewal bringing life to a parched land and a thirsty people. Their cloud of grief served as a bit of both, raising fears of a coming storm and binding them together, renewing their strength and solidarity.

In the process of walking through the cavern, shedding tears in the tomb-like catacombs, offering a word of encouragement or a quick squeeze of a shoulder, their grief birthed resolve and the company emerged in the back room of the Beta Sector Med Station more determined than ever to unify their society. They were determined to see people were never again forced to live as scavengers or outcasts in the tunnels beneath Garsow.

Now began the struggle to reunite a broken surface society. There, too, an era had passed. Whether a future could be forged from a shattered past depended on the as yet untested fortitude of a dispirited society whose guiding light had failed in what would come to be known as the Collapse.

Here ends Tunnel Vision.

www.ingramcontent.com/pod-product-compliance
Lightning Source LLC
Chambersburg PA
CBHW051549250626
47157CB00001B/236